A PRIVATE WAR

A

PRIVATE

W A R

Patrick Sheane Duncan

G. P. PUTNAM'S SONS

NEW YORK

G. P. Putnam's Sons
Publishers Since 1838
a member of
Penguin Putnam Inc.
375 Hudson Street
New York, NY 10014

Library of Congress Cataloging-in-Publication Data

Duncan, Patrick Sheane, date.
A private war / written by Patrick Sheane Duncan.
p.   cm.
ISBN 0-399-14885-X
1. Military police—Fiction. 2. Policewomen—Fiction. I. Title.

PS3554.U467 P75 2002   2001059154
813'.54—dc21

Printed in the United States of America
1   3   5   7   9   10   8   6   4   2

FOR TIMOTHY CRAIG DUNCAN—
"THE GOOD SOLDIER"
AND BEST BROTHER

●

A PRIVATE WAR

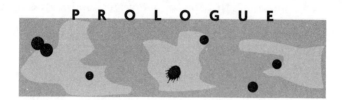

PROLOGUE

Georgia Carnes awoke to see her face reflected in a pool of blood. She was having difficulty coming fully to her senses, so it was a few seconds before she realized that the red puddle on the ground mere inches from her face was her own blood—and it was still dripping from somewhere.

She looked at her reflection. Usually she liked what she saw—a smooth complexion creased by two dimples on each cheek—but cute being a handicap in her profession, she had learned how to use them for a stern glower. Right now there was no cuteness, no glowering, just a haunted stare of pain. Her eyes were wide, her mouth open panting for air, and she didn't know where she was or how she had gotten here.

She tried to move so she could look at her body, locate the source of the blood, but the searing torch of pain that blasted through Georgia made her gasp breathlessly. She almost passed out.

Then, while she waited for the swirling dizziness to subside, she saw the dark stain across the front of her fatigue blouse. And the torturously slow drip of brighter blood falling from her body to the dark puddle that had collected in the dirt beneath her.

Georgia realized with a sudden, frightened start that she was horizontal, suspended about two feet off the ground, facedown, spread-eagled and bound by her hands and feet.

And there was pain, great pain. One huge, overwhelming, all-encompassing fire blossomed in her chest and sent an intense, pulsating wave through her body that rose and fell in sync with what she finally discovered was the beating of her own heart. Even at its lowest ebb the pain was so immense that it flooded her senses making it a struggle for her to focus—a forced, singular effort to clear her head of the agony and accomplish the smallest task.

Like turning her head.

To see that her wrists were indeed bound, tied with olive-drab nylon parachute cord. The cord had bitten so hard into her skin that her flesh had swollen over the bindings and her extremities had turned purple, her fingers puffed and fat with engorged blood.

Her fingertips were the source of ten somewhat smaller aches. And there seemed to be a hundred daggers shoved into Georgia's back and the backs of her arms and legs. The source of this pain was the metal plate to which she had been tied. It looked to be half-inch steel plate maybe ten feet high and twenty feet wide, cut in some configuration that she couldn't recognize from her current position.

There were hundreds, perhaps thousands of holes in the steel, irregular perforations that were big enough to poke a finger through. The holes had been punched with such force that the metal had been extruded on the side to which Georgia was tied, leaving jagged metal ridges along the circumference of each hole. Jagged metal ridges that scraped and stabbed her body in a hundred places. A hundred throbbing hurts.

The sun was up, bouncing off the pool of blood and through the perforations in the metal, creating a pretty mosaic of light and shadow that danced before Georgia's eyes. The air was still and damp with the morning mist. The sun was bright. The weather was going to be hot later today—would she be alive to feel it? she wondered. Probably not.

How did I get here?

No answer came to Georgia's mind. Just the taste of bile in her throat that, gratefully, never rose to the stage of vomiting. She somehow knew that the subsequent convulsions would likely kill her more quickly.

Georgia knew she was dying.

And she didn't know where. Or why.

How did I get here?

Again no answer was provided within the dark, muddy water of her thoughts. She tried to force an answer, focusing with every bit of concentration she could muster.

And in the midst of the search for the answer to how she got here she realized *where* she was.

And then she tried to scream.

Even though the effort brought blinding, thunderous pain to every cell in her body.

She tried to scream.

This is going to be fun, Private First Class Hardy told himself. *This is going to be Big Fun.*

The Range Officer was droning on about Range safety and getting about the same amount of attention from the other soldiers in the bleachers as an airplane flight attendant does reciting the crash procedures.

Personally, Hardy was more interested in the six weapons lined up on the firing mound. Six tripod-mounted fifty-caliber machine guns. Squat black metal insects, their deadly probosci were aimed downrange where battered berms denoted the 300-, 500-, 750-, and 1,000-meter target positions.

The Range Officer segued into the nomenclature of the fifty-caliber machine gun, facts and figures falling off his tongue like widgets along an assembly line. This was reiteration of dull information by a man who had taught it a few thousand too many times and had substituted volume for elucidation.

"The tripod-mounted, recoil-operated, air-cooled M2.50-caliber machine gun can also be used in the bipod, antiaircraft pedestal, or vehicular ring mount. Fired from a closed bolt position, it is belt-fed by disintegrating metallic linked ammunition . . ."

C'mon, c'mon. Hardy's left knee was jumping rapidly up and down in nervous anticipation. *Let's get the gab over with and start shooting something.*

Most of the other guys in the Motor Pool dreaded weapons qualification, but Hardy volunteered for it every chance he got. First off, it was a day out of work. Hardy was an Eighty-eight Mike, his MOS—Military Occupation Speciality—a truck driver. He drove an eight-by-six medium equipment transport truck—an M-920 if you had to fill out the trip log. When Hardy was behind the wheel hauling matériel from post to post or on maneuvers, he was a happy soldier. He liked to drive—that was why he had selected his MOS. But the downtime killed him.

Sitting in the Motor Pool doing his weekly PMCS, Preventative Maintenance Checks and Service, that was okay, but most of the time he was doing the scut work for some asshole mechanic: cleaning the grime and grease off parts so that the wrench monkey could put them back, or scrubbing down batteries and getting acid oxidation in his eyes, or just doing some numbnut's dirty work.

A day off, out in the fresh air blasting away at targets with government ammo, was not only a welcome release, but something Hardy looked forward to eagerly for weeks. And especially the fifty-caliber. Crouching down behind that big, ugly, black gun blowing down target after target—target, hell, he got a kick just blasting divots out of the berm.

Luckily for Hardy, the fifty-caliber was a weapon that the Army sometimes mounted upon the roof of an M-813 five-ton in a combat convoy. That meant he could volunteer to qualify every six months with his current MOS.

Hardy's only regret was that he couldn't qualify with the twenty-millimeter antiaircraft gun. Now, that would bring fun up to a whole new echelon.

Abruptly the Range Officer finished his spiel and grabbed his bullhorn and ordered everyone onto the firing line. Hardy jumped to his feet and rushed past the other soldiers descending the bleachers, plowing his way through the other qualifiers so he could be first in line behind one of the big guns.

For a second he was worried as the Range Officer divided the line of soldiers behind the guns into two sections, gunner and assistant gunner. Assistant gunners were the poor schmucks who monitored the ammo feed and supposedly supervised the firing. Hardy wanted to be the man with his finger on the trigger; everything else was bullshit, and if some fool thought he was going to tell Hardy how and where to shoot, he had another think coming.

Hardy sighed with relief as he was chosen as first gunner and the man behind him, a corporal who still wore Army-issue glasses, as the assistant gunner. Hardy wore the yellow-tinted shooting glasses he had purchased just for these occasions.

"Lock and load!"

Hardy placed an ammo belt the schmuck handed him into the feedway, yanked the bolt back, and let it fly forward, slamming home the first round. He placed his hands on the twin butterfly grips and settled himself behind the weapon.

Big fun.

Big fun with hyperdrive.

The scream never came. All that Georgia Carnes could express was a dry, guttural croak. Even that sound triggered an explosion of pain that burst inside her brain with a brilliant white flash that just as quickly became a black void.

When Georgia returned to consciousness a few moments later, the slow dripping of blood from her chest wound had become a steady stream.

Georgia felt herself weakening as the red pool beneath her body grew larger. She was the top half of an hourglass and her sand was running out.

The sound of the Range Officer's bullhorn-distorted voice carried to her across the firing range. It sounded alien and evil.

"Prepare to fire!"

Gingerly, tentatively, Georgia tried to flex the muscles in her arms and pulled with her legs, testing the nylon cords that bound her. The cords relaxed not at all—she achieved nothing in exchange for the pain the fruitless effort caused her.

"Fire!"

The air was ripped by an erratic cacophony of heavy gunfire.

The 300-meter target line.

Georgia knew that she was on the 1,000-meter range, where steel silhouette targets popped up from the ground to be fired upon. She was tied to what she now decided must be the tank silhouette. As long as the target lay horizontal, she was safe.

No, she wasn't. Pretty soon she was going to bleed to death.

But as soon as the Range Officer gave the order and the switch was thrown for the 1,000-meter line, the six metal silhouette targets would flip up and she would no longer be even relatively safe.

She would be a target.

For six fifty-caliber machine guns.

She had been on the Firing Range with the General once, a demonstration for some dignitaries, months ago. She knew what was coming next.

Six fifty-caliber machine guns.

Firing rounds as thick as her thumb. Fifty-caliber meant half an inch in circumference. The M2.50-caliber recoil-operated, air-cooled, belt-fed machine gun. Maximum range 6,800 meters, maximum effective range, 1,830 meters. Cyclic rate of fire 450 to 550 rounds per minute. She knew the numbers, the stats. She hadn't been nominated for "Soldier of the Month" three times in one year for nothing.

"Five hundred meters!"

The Range Officer's voice, warped by the bullhorn and echoing through the open air, didn't sound human.

"Fire!"

Again the air was destroyed by the thunderous report of the machine guns.

Georgia gathered her strength and renewed her struggle against the nylon cord. It was tough, durable, Army-issue cord. She had used it herself to tie up her sleeping bag and once to make an impromptu leash for her dog. Not even her one-hundred-pound golden retriever named Hunk, slavering after a frightened rabbit on the run, could break parachute cord—if the knots were tied correctly.

These knots *were* tied correctly.

And a 108-pound female human being with a bullet wound in her chest had no chance at all against it. None.

"Seven-hundred fifty meters!"

Oh, God. Oh, shit. Mamma. Daddy. Who's going to feed Hunk? Who . . . ?

How the hell did I get here?!

"Fire!"

She yelled for help, over and over, each scream straining her lungs with such pain it was as if they were being ripped out of her chest.

But she realized the futility of screaming. No one could hear her over the sound of the guns. She stopped, gasping for breath. She forced herself to wait. There must be a way out—if only she could think.

Georgia was overcome suddenly by a fit of coughing. Great gouts of blood flew from her mouth with every spasm. When the coughing finally subsided, she couldn't draw a deep breath. As desperate as she was for air, she could breath only with shallow, feeble panting.

Lung shot.

Pretty soon she would either bleed to death or drown in her own blood. She would die from a lack of blood or too much of it in the wrong place. She almost laughed at the irony of it.

And then Georgia realized how she got here.

This is a shitload of fun. Hardy almost giggled, but he stopped himself in time—giggling would seem unmanly. But this was fun on a bun with all the trimmings.

Hardy watched as the tracers, one glowing red phosphorus-tipped round in every five on the belt, walked up the 750-meter berm and into the paper target. He put five or six rounds into the black center.

"Two- or three-round bursts, soldier!" a range NCO barked at Hardy. "Controlled fire! Controlled fire!"

So Hardy had a heavy trigger finger. So what? He wasn't paying for the ammo, and besides that, he was concentrating. He was putting the face of a certain wiseass Motor Pool mechanic in front of each target.

Take that, Broadax, you little pissant grease monkey sonofabitch.

"Prepare for the thousand-meter target!" the Range Officer called out. "Wait for the 'fire' command before you engage your target!"

C'mon, c'mon, just say it, Hardy silently urged the Range Officer.

"Upon the 'fire' command you will fire a short burst, observe the impact of your rounds, then traverse to correct any errors of range or deflection."

Yeah, yeah, yeah. Hardy wondered what would happen if he just started blasting away on his own. Well, he knew what would happen—they would never let him behind another fifty caliber—and that was the only thing that kept his finger off the trigger.

He waited for the Range Officer to finish, proud of his own patience.

"Wait for the target," the Range Officer cautioned.

C'mon, c'mon, c'mon, c'mon, Hardy chanted in his head.

"Fire at will!"

Fire at will. Hardy smiled to himself. *What a great phrase.* He readied himself, trying not to let his leg jiggle. A bad nervous habit that drove his wife crazy. He tried to control it. He didn't want it to spoil his aim. He didn't want *anything* to spoil his aim.

Hardy waited for the metal silhouettes on the 1,000-meter range to pop up, hoping for a truck.

He got a tank.

Disappointment was overcome quickly by the urge to shoot. And he did.

Two five- or six-round bursts.

"Control, soldier!" The Range Officer walked behind Hardy. "Control! That didn't sound like two- or three-round bursts. Maybe you just can't count."

Fuck you where you breathe, Hardy thought. *This is my last target.* Besides, he had missed.

Both bursts had gone low and to the right. The second was closer, but still Hardy had only blown big puffs of yellow dirt into the air four meters away from the tank silhouette.

Yeah, he had missed.

Fuck.

"Sustained fire!" The Range Officer called.

This was what Hardy had been waiting for all along. He squeezed the trigger without letup, this time marching the rounds up into the tank target. Explosions of dirt stitched a dotted line up into the center of the tank outline, pink tracers painting a pretty streak through the air and into the heart of the fake tank.

This was as good as sex. Better. He had been married for eleven years.

Finally the belts of ammo ran out.

The firing line was quiet.

The cloud of cordite smoke wafted across the firing line.

Hardy reluctantly rose from behind the machine gun and was replaced by the next soldier in line.

He hadn't noticed the puffball of pink mist that had blossomed behind the tank silhouette, then dissipated quickly in the light morning wind.

No one did.

O N E

Meredith Cleon drove with the top down. It was one of those beautiful late-summer days, and it had been a pretty drive. She had taken 65 South from Michigan and then at New Albany caught 64 West through the Cumberlands.

Northern Indiana had been mostly flat, peaceful farm country, cornfield-lined highway skirting the intermittent small town with only the roadside antique/junk stores and fruit stands to break the monotony.

Meredith didn't like taking the highway; she preferred the back roads where she could cruise through the little burgs, stopping occasionally or making small side trips to search out whatever might pique her curiosity. An odd tourist attraction, the Ten Commandments illustrated in sand sculptures, or just to see what Hell (the

Michigan town) looked like. Most of all, Meredith just enjoyed driving anywhere, anytime, especially in a halfway decent automobile—and the classic Mustang she was driving now was a superb machine.

But today she was in a hurry, having delayed her departure from Michigan too long. The funeral had been postponed for two days to wait for a fear-of-flying great-aunt to arrive by train from Idaho.

The southern end of Indiana segued easily into hills and the drive through the Cumberlands was more than pleasant, the highway cutting a swath through long stretches of pine and hardwood forests.

Altogether it would have been an enjoyable drive if it hadn't been for Meredith's mood. She swung from anger to frustration, then to depression that surprised her with its depth. She had thought she was over that.

The sign announcing "Walhalla, Indiana, Population 26,139" made her slow and turn off the highway and onto the business route, which took her into town. There was nothing extraordinary about the town of Walhalla itself. It had the usual mix of business and residential areas, with that Midwest propensity for a big white church every three blocks. There was a college—that was a good sign—surrounded by some impressive old Victorian houses, and a downtown area that seemed to be thriving as a one-way promenade despite the sprawling mall she had seen at the east end of town.

What was surprising, as she neared the fort, was the lack of the usual military base atmosphere. True, there were fast-food joints lining the highway, more Army-surplus stores and Korean restaurants than you might usually have in a town this size, and an overabundance of pawnshops—the poor soldier's answer to payroll shortfalls.

What she didn't see was the standard cluster of strip clubs, ugly buildings with cheap marquees shouting that curious "Live Nude Girls" tease in neon. Meredith did note a few bars that looked like trouble, even from the outside—places where it was evident that blood was one of the fluids that flowed every Friday, Saturday, and payday.

But no topless bars. Odd.

Strip joints were an easy way of making a buck around every military installation. All those single young men boiling over with testosterone were a ripe crop ready to be harvested of their pay.

Four walls, a bar, a rudimentary stage, a stereo system on steroids, and some women who were willing to take off their clothes for many times the money they'd earn at the mall selling corn dogs or Levi's. All it took was some eager entrepreneur who wasn't afraid to go to court every few weeks to protect his First Amendment rights.

Meredith didn't care one way or the other about the clubs, who went there or why, but they were a major problem in executing her mission. Their absence in Walhalla was a good sign, at least as far as the local authorities were concerned. But she did wonder how they had won the war of the titty bars. Maybe it was an approach she could apply in the future.

Driving through the gates of Fort Hazelton, Meredith flashed her military identification at the MPs posted at the guardhouse. It was just a cursory glance. She made a mental note of that and to ask how often they ran spot checks on outgoing vehicles to search for stolen military property.

The fort itself was not impressive. Old, wooden World War II barracks like every other post she had been on. Built during the 1940s wartime expansion as temporary buildings, they had remained through the Cold War, and the Korean and Vietnam booms, only now finally becoming obsolete. There were also some more permanent structures of brick and stone, but all showed a lack of maintenance. Peeling paint, crumbling concrete steps, broken fences, even a cracked window or two. All little cosmetic failings that could have been remedied easily. The blacktop roads were eaten up by potholes and crumbling along the shoulders. One whole section of wooden barracks was caving in, the roofs sagging like sway-backed horses, the windows staring with empty eyes, the walls leaning.

The only saving grace was a new Post Exchange surrounded by a couple of fast-food restaurants, a lemon lot, a miniature golf course, and a convenience store/gas station. The on-post residential area, one-story ranch-style dwellings all exactly alike, block after block of them, were obviously built in the sixties, fairly well-kept, most lawns manicured, houses painted.

But somehow the overall impression of Fort Hazelton was that of a neglected, unkempt, seedy camp in need of attention.

Not at all the sort of post that Schwaner would normally run, least of all tolerate.

Meredith was worried.

The next MP she saw on duty was at a cross street, apparently assigned to monitor traffic where a signal light was not functioning, but he was talking to a pretty, young civilian woman in a Honda Civic.

Meredith buzzed right past him in her Mustang, and he took no notice.

That Meredith was driving a 1968 Shelby Mustang KR500 convertible, cherry from roll bar to custom wheels, black with red racing stripes down the hood and trunk, with a red interior, did not seem to interest the young man with the Military Police armband and helmet.

Maybe he just wasn't into cars.

But Meredith was a more-than-attractive female. Sure, her short brown hair was hidden under a Detroit Lions baseball cap, her brown eyes lost behind her Ray-Ban sunglasses, her more-than-ample chest, one curse of her military career, today draped in an extra-large

T-shirt. But she was still a head turner in civilian clothes, and often enough in military dress.

Apparently not today, though.

Maybe the young MP just wasn't into women over thirty. That thought did nothing to improve her mood.

Fort Hazelton was a large post, the little clusters of buildings, grouped by company, battalion, or service orientation, spread out and separated by expansive green fields and pine woods. It was evident that Meredith was not going to become familiar with it all in one drive, so she headed back toward the Post Exchange. She quickly became lost as she drove near an abandoned airfield. The runway was cracked and sprouting sizable weeds. A movement in the woods caught her eye, and she pulled over. A doe and a fawn walked delicately out of the woods and into a field. She watched them graze until a Humvee roared by and startled the gentle creatures back into the tree line.

Meredith didn't believe in omens, good or bad, but at the same time she was desperate for some kind of sign that Fort Hazelton wasn't the career quagmire she had built it up to be in her mind. She took great satisfaction in her early-morning jog, and at least Fort Hazelton would provide endless possibilities for enjoyable routes. The air was scented with pine, and it was remarkably quiet for a military post. She turned off the car and sat there a moment, relishing the gentle breeze drifting across her face, the Mustang engine ticking as it cooled.

The installation comprised more than 42,000 acres, supporting a military population of nearly 6,000 military service members and their families and employing another 2,800 civilian workers. An additional 4,000 military personnel could be on the post at any given time undergoing training at one of the three schools, and in the summer months another 3,000 to 5,000 U.S. Army Reserve or National Guard might be using Hazelton's facilities for training exercises.

In other words, Meredith's new home was a small city that fluctuated in population between twelve and seventeen thousand and had all the usual facilities. Hospitals, residences, taverns, stores, churches, amusements, and the problems of any American town, plus a few more complications caused by the peculiarities of the military mission.

Meredith's new home. *My new headache. My responsibility and, usually, my pride.* She caught herself at the *usually.* She had a job to do, and it wouldn't be right for her to adopt any kind of negative attitude that could get in the way of the performance of that duty.

Meredith keyed the ignition, the powerful engine rumbled to life, and she pulled back onto the road in the direction the Humvee took, eventually returning to the populated area of the post. She came up behind an MP cruising in a sedan and resisted the urge to blow past him in the Shelby and see if he would ticket her properly. But her test could backfire, and the post rumor mill could take the incident and grind it into something else. She had experience with that type of runaway gossip.

Finally Meredith made her way to the Post Exchange and parked at one of the fast-food restaurants, the Bowser Burger. The sign bore a picture of a big-eyed mutt with its tongue hanging out. Meredith wondered what marketing genius had come up with that one and what recreational drugs they had been using at the time. Inside, the counter was being monitored by a middle-aged woman with hair a shade of red not found in nature. She smiled at Meredith, showing the lipstick on her teeth.

"Help you?"

"Yes, I'd like a salad with chicken on it."

"We don't have nothing like that on the menu." There was a

twang in the woman's voice. Not the northern Indiana accent or Meredith's familiar Michigan cadence, but there was a definite southern lilt to the phrasing.

"All right," she said, reading the menu on the wall behind the counter. "What I would like is one of your ready-made salads, no dressing, and a piece of broiled chicken from one of your sandwiches laid on top," Meredith explained. "I'll pay for the salad and the whole sandwich. And an iced tea, no lemon, small. Thank you."

"Well," the woman drawled the word out for a few seconds. "I 'spose we can do that." And she went into the kitchen.

Meredith found herself a tray, napkins, three nearly useless flimsy plastic utensils, and a post newspaper from a stack by the door.

The woman returned with her salad, but Meredith couldn't even see the lettuce beneath the mountain of croutons and mound of bright orange cheese.

"I put a mess of croutons and cheese on there for you, no extra charge. If you-all want, I can give you the bread from the sammich."

"No, thanks." Meredith smiled and paid her bill, carried her tray over to a vacant table. While picking the cubes of dried bread and shredded orange cheese off her salad and fishing the *two* lemon slices out of her iced tea, Meredith surveyed the interior of the restaurant. There were several other customers in the place: three civilian men, a pair of sergeants in fatigues, and a teenage boy filling out an employment application while he gobbled french fries.

A couple of the civilians gave her the once-over, and one of the sergeants gave her one of those "testing the waters" smiles. Meredith didn't respond.

Picking up the newspaper, the *Hazelton Lanthorn*, a thin, eight-page weekly, she perused the front page for clues about her new post, eating her chicken and lettuce without the benefit of even one of the six packets of French dressing provided by her helpful new friend behind the counter. Meredith was on a diet these days. She had eaten endlessly throughout her nearly twenty-day leave. Various relatives and friends of her father had stopped by the house to drop off every sort of fat and carbohydrate fixed in every tasty form known on the planet, or at least in West Michigan. She was required to partake of each dish, just out of politeness, she told herself. The fact that she ate until every plate, bowl, and Tupperware container was empty Meredith blamed on her depression. True or not, she was now on a diet, and she grazed her way through the lettuce and some tasteless, crunchy red things that at least looked like tomatoes and felt self-righteous with every bite. The chicken was greasy and cold. She should have peeled the skin off, but she couldn't manage that delicate operation with her plastic fork and knife and she had no inclination to touch the poultry with her fingers. Meredith ate it, skin and all, with a thin seasoning of guilt.

Reading the post newspaper, Meredith discovered a big article on the new drawing and painting classes at the Youth Services Center. She was sure the local teenagers would be lining up early for that one. Bingo was expanding to six nights a week. There was an article urging parents to accompany their children to all extracurricular school activities. The fort was joining with the Walhalla City and County local agencies in a tornado-preparedness exercise. A new bulk trash collection schedule had gone into effect. Bowling, karate, and football were in the news, and some forty-six-year-old Quartermaster and Supply Warrant Officer was pursuing his Ph.D. in Romance languages at the local college.

She put the paper down before it made her even more depressed. She felt her career slipping away from her with every article and advertisement she read. This was a backwater post, that was evident, so far removed from any Pentagon or Department of the Army visibility or overview that chances for promotion were slim. And she did want promotion. But in order to be promoted, you had to shine. Fort Hazelton was so far in the dark that her little light was going to be lost.

Trying to focus on something else, Meredith looked out the window for distraction. The PX was doing some light business. A pair of what looked like retirees were taking the miniature golf course far too seriously and arguing over a stroke one of them had taken. The lemon lot, a used-car lot, was kitty-corner to the golf course. She looked at the cars.

Meredith knew cars. You don't grow up in Michigan and not know cars, and in Hamtramck, where everyone worked for one of the auto factories that dominated the town, automobiles were dinner conversation, dating conversation, and career conversation.

There was a nice-looking, rather new Dodge Ram 1500 with overtestosteroned big fat tires and a butt-ugly custom paint job. Some sergeant used his reenlistment bonus for the down payment and now couldn't make the monthlies. That happened a lot. There was also a twenty-year-old 280Z with the rocker panels rusted out. Otherwise it was a bunch of Japanese and American look-alikes. Little cookie-cutter cars that bored the hell out of her.

She got up and dumped her tray, took one last sip of the iced tea, which tasted of coffee—probably brewed in the same pot—and dumped it and the paper and went outside.

Taking her garment bag from the backseat of the Shelby, Meredith returned to the restaurant to use the ladies' room. She changed out of her jeans and T-shirt and into her Class A dress greens, applied makeup and a touch of lipstick. The uniform was a little tight, all that fine Michigan cuisine. The last time Meredith had worn it was at the funeral. Everyone thought it was to honor her father, only she knew it was her final act of defiance. She checked her reflection in the mirror, adjusted her cap with the gold officer's filigree—called "scrambled eggs" by some—then left the ladies' room and walked back through the restaurant. The Sergeant who had smiled at her earlier did a double take, focused on the silver oakleaf clusters signifying her rank of Lieutenant Colonel. His startled reaction tickled her, and she smiled as she got into her car and drove away.

On her way to headquarters Meredith drove past a female MP helping a motorist jump-start a car. She liked to see that, wished she could see the MP's face for future reference, but it was buried under the hood of the car. Headquarters was easy enough to find; she had passed the sign earlier. A cluster of newer buildings, four-story concrete monoliths, surrounded an old red-tile-roofed single-story structure probably built during the World War I era—Fort Hazelton Command Headquarters.

Meredith parked in one of the visitor spaces and walked across the lot. Each of the parking spaces had a neat sign in front of it, following the old Army motto—"If it moves, salute it. If it doesn't move paint it. And whenever possible put a sign in front of it." She had served on posts where every piece of shrubbery on the parade field bore a little plaque that gave the Latin name for that particular bit of foliage. And every tree had been adorned the same way.

There was a sign for the Command Sergeant Major, Staff Duty Officer, Aides de Camp, and then the Commanding General— Brigadier General Thomas H. Schwaner.

In spite of being pissed at the old man, Meredith felt a little rise of empathetic pride on his behalf. He had his command, his post. The *raison d'être* for any Army command officer. The dream of every soldier who aspired to a general's star. A dream that Meredith shared. Schwaner was driving a two-year-old Chrysler Town & Country van. Next to the Commanding General's spot was the Deputy Commander's, a Lexus. The Chief of Staff, General Marvin L. Ringstall, was next; he drove a twenty-year-old diesel Mercedes 300D. Nice car, but an unreliable pig in cold weather.

Then the Garrison Commander. Lincoln Town Car—black, new. Meredith's immediate superior, the person to whom she would report.

Colonel J. Peter Levy.

Meredith froze in midstep.

"Fudge!"

She said it aloud.

A passing Private looked at her curiously. She glared at him, still angry. He saluted to collect himself and moved on quickly.

A great way to create a first impression, Cleon.

Meredith returned the Private's salute and said it again.

"Fudge." But this time she said it to herself.

She was going to hate it here.

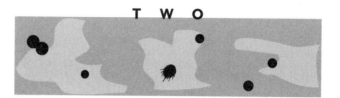

T W O

Meredith walked down the hallway of the headquarters building, her footsteps echoing loudly on the highly buffed linoleum floor. Too loudly. Each step was a reflection of the anger still burning inside her. Levy. She stopped at the drinking fountain, a thirty-year-old porcelain fixture, and took a drink—not because she was thirsty, but to try and get her emotions under control. The water was lukewarm.

The end of the hallway widened into twin offices, that of the Chief of Staff, General Ringstall, on the left, that of the Garrison Commander, Colonel Levy, on the right. There was a large reception area in front of the offices, with room for each respective officer's secretary and Aide de Camp. Both secretaries were busy typing, fingers tripping swiftly across their computer keyboards as if they were in a race. The Aide's desk on the left was vacant, the one on the right occupied by an extremely neat and tidy Second Lieutenant, African-American, male, mid-twenties, looking every inch the perfect soldier.

The secretaries could have been sisters, except for their hair color, one gray, one brunette, both poufed as big as a can of hair spray would support.

Meredith approached the secretary on the right, the brunette, a large, big-boned woman with too much liquid foundation. Meredith could see the demarcation line around the woman's neck where the makeup application had stopped. The name plaque on her desk said she was Kay Higdon. She stopped typing and looked up at Meredith.

"Lieutenant Colonel Meredith Cleon reporting for duty to the Garrison Commander."

"Welcome to Fort Hazelton, ma'am. Just a sec, I'll tell the Colonel you're here."

Kay Higdon got up and went into the Garrison Commander's office, careful to close the big wooden door behind her.

Meredith stood there and waited. Levy's Aide glanced her way, but averted his eyes when Meredith looked back.

There was a sudden commotion in the office behind Meredith.

"Marga! Marga! Any word from Carnes yet? Where the hell is she? Have you called her residence?"

The other office door was opened and Meredith turned and saw a general come out, circle the gray-haired secretary's desk, and walk over to the vacant Aide's desk. He stared down at the chair as if it should answer his questions.

"I called and got no answer, sir." This from Marga, the gray-haired secretary.

"Then maybe you should send—"

"I sent your driver over to her house to see if she's sick or something, or slept in or whatever. She wasn't there. Her neighbor gave him a key, and he checked inside. Sorry, sir."

Marga was way ahead of the General. The secretaries usually were.

"See if you can find the Suicide Prevention Makeup Session attendance records. Carnes was collating them." And the General, obviously peeved, headed back to his office. He glanced at Meredith briefly, just a quick look, but Meredith knew that she had been noted and filed away for later retrieval. Generals noticed everything.

Ringstall was a red-haired man, but the hair was receding, his orange widow's peak being marooned gradually into an island all to itself. His skin was as pale as only a redhead's can be, so his blue eyes burned brightly, angrily right now.

Kay Higdon came out of the Garrison Commander's office.

"The Colonel will see you now."

The secretary's smile was perfunctory, and she held the door open for Meredith to enter, then closed the door on her way out.

It was a large office that easily accommodated the big, old oak desk. There were hardwood paneling and built-in bookshelves from a more prosperous time for the post.

J. Peter Levy, full-bird Colonel, sat behind the big desk. He didn't smile, didn't rise from his chair, just turned his face to stone and waited.

Meredith braced herself, snapped to attention, tucked her chin into her chest, stared off into a horizon that she couldn't see, and spoke in her best command presence voice.

"Lieutenant Colonel Meredith Cleon reporting for duty, sir."

A little too by-the-book, Officers' Candidate School, but Meredith knew she was on shaky ground with Levy as the Garrison Commander.

Levy drew it out, letting her stand there for a three-count.

"At ease, Cleon. Sit."

She sat in the wooden chair on the other side of the desk.

He didn't say a word, just looked at her. Meredith knew better than to try and outstare him. Don't get into a contest you might regret winning, she cautioned herself. And she was far too smart to speak before Levy did, so she let her eyes wander around the office.

There was the usual glory wall. Plaques, trophies, photographs of Levy with Colin Powell, various generals domestic and foreign, the usual combat pose from his days as a major, three swords bedecked with gold and ivory, two pistols—one a beautifully engraved 1911A1 in a glass-front presentation case—and a Viet Cong AK-47.

When Meredith finished her visual tour of the office and Levy still had not spoken, she looked back at him. He was a small man with more forehead now than he'd had the last time she had seen him. He used to comb his hair back, but now he was combing it forward to reclaim as much of that bare skin as he could. It was a battle that he was losing. The pouty lines at each side of his mouth were deeper, the ever-present dark circles under his eyes were mottled with spots and more wrinkles, the weak chin was further softened by a bit of fat. Not a face you'd follow into battle, not a face to command, to bring fear or garner the respect of his troops. He looked like what he really was—a politician.

His eyes saved him from appearing weak. Dark gray, hard eyes that looked angry even at rest, which was rare. Intelligent eyes with what a colleague once called "career radar." Arrogant eyes. She knew that firsthand. All in all, he looked to be the same sonofabitch she had known fifteen years ago.

The sonofabitch put his palms down on his immaculate desktop and looked at her.

"Are we going to have trouble here?"

Meredith looked back at him. She was assessing her first move, and she made him wait this time. *Think about this hard, Mere, look both ways before you step off the curb, like your daddy always said.*

The thought of her father suddenly stabbed Meredith in the heart with a sharp pain that surprised her. She spoke quickly to recover.

"Trouble, sir, is something that I find enough of in the daily performance of my duties. I don't seek it out or bring it with me."

The words sounded a bit mealymouthed to her ears, but they seemed to satisfy Levy. He nodded.

"I didn't want you assigned here, Cleon. But I want you to know that I didn't fight it. The General wanted you. That was good enough for me. I want you to know we are on an even footing here. A clean slate. History is . . . just that, history."

"I . . . appreciate that, sir." Meredith continued to walk softly.

"I do expect of you what I expect of every other soldier under my command—complete loyalty, total diligence to duty, and twenty-four-seven. Do you know what I mean by twenty-four-seven, Cleon?"

"Twenty-four hours a day, seven days a week, yes, sir."

"Now we are in difficult circumstances here at Fort Hazelton. But I don't see this as any reason for excuses and whining. I won't stand for whining. It isn't professional."

"What kind of difficult circumstances, sir?" Meredith was curious anyway, but also felt that she had been prompted by him to ask the question.

"We'll get to that. First I want to discuss our mission here. My mission. And my mission is your mission. My goal is to keep General Schwaner happy. There will never be a briefing where the general asks a question regarding your unit for which I don't already have an answer. I insist on knowing everything that happens in your command." Levy was using his "God speaks" voice.

"Everything," he repeated. "Immediately. And always before the General knows. A problem will never, I say again, *never* be placed before the Commander without a solution well in hand. Do you understand me on this, Lieutenant Colonel?" He fixed her his laser stare.

"Yes, sir," Meredith replied. She wasn't going to give him any room to misinterpret her words and drive a wedge into them. No little opening that Levy could fill with his special blend of acid.

"Completely, Lieutenant Colonel Cleon?"

Meredith wondered if as a child Levy had picked at other kids' scabs.

"Completely, sir."

"I don't want any misunderstanding here, Cleon."

Meredith sat there clenching her jaw, trying to think of a reason not to yank the two gold-plated pens out of the fancy holder and jam them into Levy's eyes.

Levy could see her struggling to control herself. He was waiting for the explosion, looking forward to it.

There was a knock at the door.

Levy's eyes sparked with fury at the interruption.

The door opened and General Schwaner leaned inside.

Levy killed the spark and forced a smile.

"General."

"Pete! Hope you don't mind my interrupting." Schwaner came all the way into the office and noted Meredith's presence.

"Meredith, good to see you again. Welcome, welcome."

"Excuse me, Pete, but I need you to reconcile the OOTW reports. I just received a Priority One from higher and higher. If you can."

"Operations Other Than War reports, sir." Levy looked around his compulsively orderly desk to find the right file, located it.

OOTW covered disaster relief, counterdrug operations, civil disturbance, antinuclear protests, and other scenarios where the military was called in, but not against a foreign hostile force.

"Can do, sir," Levy said.

"That's what I told them." The General smiled, turned to Meredith. "Cleon! Welcome to Fort Hazelton! How long have you been here? You're looking great! Top notch! When did you get in?"

The General spoke with contagious enthusiasm that was very boyish and kind of sexy even for a sixty-year-old man. It was one of the many reasons Meredith had liked Schwaner all these years. As a Major, then a Colonel, one-star General, and now Brigadier. Most generals played stone-face. Levy, for instance, had been practicing since he was a Captain, before that probably. Those men ruled out of fear and revealed nothing—no enthusiasm, no emotion. It left you wondering constantly where you stood. But Schwaner was full of excitement; he let his emotions run full-tilt. His life, his career, his men, his Army, his country, his family, his mission—his feelings about all were apparent.

She realized that both men were waiting for an answer.

"I just reported in, sir."

"Good, good, welcome aboard. We need you here. Now, Peter, there's next month's National Guard exercise over on the North Quadrant. They say our Consolidated Equipment Pool is not sufficient for their vehicles, which I find hard to believe, but . . . They want to use the old airfield, but that means using those old dirt roads, and if it rains, which it does that time of year, I don't have to draw you a map . . . Can you screw the lid on this for me? Thanks."

Before Levy could answer, Schwaner was off in another direction.

"And while you do that, I'll walk Cleon here over to her new posting. What do you say, Pete?"

"Can do, sir."

"Can do, can do. I like a 'can do' man. Meredith, come walk with me."

Schwaner walked toward the door. He was a short man, but wide, with a big barrel chest and thin legs—not fat, but pugnacious-looking.

Meredith looked at Levy for permission, not wanting to appear too eager to grab the life preserver the General offered.

Levy finally nodded, the pouty lines drawn tautly.

Meredith got up and followed the General out the door, almost bumping into Levy's Aide, the Second Lieutenant she had seen in the reception area. The Aide's name tag read "Vernor." Meredith's favorite beverage, Vernor's Diet Ginger Ale, almost impossible to find outside of Michigan. Maybe some of the stores here in Indiana carried it. This was the closest she had ever been stationed to her home state. The ironic fact that there was no longer any reason to go home did not escape her notice.

She followed General Schwaner down the hall, wondering if his interruption had been intentional. Never underestimate a general. He turned to look at her. Maybe there was something in her face, because his expression sobered—he was too damned perceptive.

"I'm so sorry to hear about your father." His concern was sincere.

"Thank you. He had a good life." That was the phrase she had settled on as an appropriate response while she was receiving condolences in Michigan. It revealed little enough.

"And he was proud of his daughter, I'm sure."

"Yes," was all she could manage to say.

They went out through the double doors and down the steps of the headquarters building. Schwaner leaned down and replaced a loose brick in the low wall that enclosed the steps. The mortar around the railing posts was crumbling to dust.

"Look at this. It breaks my heart. I hate to see a noble old place like this go to rot. She must have been a grand sight when she was in her prime." He looked around, taking in the tall pine trees in the distance, the equally tall oaks that had been planted neatly around the parade grounds decades ago. Acres of brilliant green grass spread out in front of the headquarters building like the voluminous skirts of a southern belle.

Meredith looked around, and she, too, could see the grand old dame beneath the tattered, worn dress. It *was* sad. They started walking, skirting a parade field. A sign, of course, this one in brass, declared the parade field to be Robert Allen Quiller Field. The rest of the embossed print on the sign was too small to read from this distance, but Meredith didn't have to read it to know it was named for a soldier who had given his life for his comrades. If you were to be remembered for being a hero, a green field and trees were better than a statue or a building, Meredith thought.

Schwaner looked at her. "Fort Hazelton is on the BRAC list. Base Realignment and Closure. We're shutting her down. She's supposed to be closed by 2005, all units and missions moved to Fort Knox. Every quarter we lose a little more funding and personnel. The trouble is that our mission has not decreased accordingly. Our day-to-day operations continue, but we have to accomplish it with less and less.

"That is our challenge." He stated it simply, clearly.

The General was never a whiner, and he didn't have much use for anyone who complained.

"I am putting you into a very difficult position, Cleon. Do I have you behind me all the way?"

"You do, sir."

"I'm sorry to cut short your leave."

"No problem, sir. After he . . . my father was . . . gone there wasn't much reason to hang around. I'm glad to have something to occupy my time."

He stopped a moment, looked her in the eye.

"You didn't want this assignment, Meredith, and I want you to know I appreciate your accepting it."

"Anything to serve under your command, sir."

"Bullshit." He smiled. "Brightly polished bullshit, but manure all the same." The smile faded. "I know you were looking for a field command."

A field command was a combat arms unit that would have a chance to go to war. This was the sacred heart of the Army, its sole purpose and the focus of almost all promotion boards above captain.

Meredith thought for a moment before answering. "A field command *is* the keystone for advancement, sir." What she wanted was an infantry battalion of her own. No woman had ever commanded an infantry battalion. Only the top five percent of Lieutenant Colonels would make any kind of Battalion Commander—and for a woman, that percentage went south. Meredith knew the rarity of the position she coveted, and she knew exactly what it would take to get her there.

"If you perform up to your usual level of competence, Cleon—no promises, mind you, but your next move will most likely be more in line with your career goals." The General was waffling, knowing he couldn't promise her anything but wanting her to know where his very influential prejudice lay.

"Can I be frank, sir?"

"Of course."

Could she? Meredith suddenly felt she had nothing to lose. Where that feeling of freedom came from she didn't know, but she plunged ahead before she could change her mind.

"I know how evaluations work, sir. You have combat officers here who are looking for their own field command—to move on and up. The Provost Marshal office is not usually a place for any kind of actions that may draw evaluation highlights. I know you have to put your evaluations on a curve. I can't afford to be in the middle of any curve, sir, not if I am to pursue the Army career I see for myself. I don't want to get lost, sir."

"Since when have you been in the middle of any curve, Cleon? You will excel as always. And that excellence will be seen—and rewarded. Here's your new office."

The MP station was a three-story building, World War II vintage. The parking lot was filled with Military Police vehicles, sedans, four-wheel-drives, and a slew of civilian cars. There was a particularly nice '70 El Camino and, next to it, near the front doors, an empty parking space labeled "Provost Marshal."

The General ushered her inside.

As Meredith entered the MP station with Schwaner, she came face-to-face with one of those old-fashioned five-foot-high desks meant to intimidate any alleged miscreants who were brought in. There was a sergeant behind it, a female. The Sergeant shouted "Ten-hut!" and an MP filling out a form at another desk snapped to attention.

"Carry on." The General gave them a friendly nod and started through a door and up a flight of narrow stairs. The door closed automatically behind Meredith and Schwaner and gave them a moment of privacy.

"I need you here, Colonel. I'm not asking you to make this into a silk purse, but a sow's ear will not do. There are good people here, but they're working under difficult circumstances. Motivate them—make them proud again."

"I'll do my best, sir."

"I know that, Colonel. It's pretty routine here at Hazelton. That makes it harder, motivating people through the mundane. This isn't Sin City, it's a quiet post. This is Mayberry. The trouble is that I had Barney Fife in charge and I need Andy."

Meredith smiled. "Andy Griffith? I'm not sure I can live up to that, sir. Mayberry . . . wasn't that where Gomer Pyle got started?"

"True. But Gomer Pyle was a Marine, and deservedly so. C'mon, meet your people."

Schwaner stopped at the top of the stairs and plunged through the door into the squad room.

The usual "Ten-hut!" was cried out by an MP, and the General muttered his usual, "Carry on," as personnel snapped to attention.

The General and Meredith crossed the squad room, a large room dominated by a long, narrow folding table, a refrigerator, and a partitioned coffee corner. At the opposite end of the squad room was a secretary's desk in front of two offices. Behind the desk was a tiny woman who was dwarfed by the piece of office furniture and attached typewriter return.

"Mrs. Kappadonna," the general called out to the secretary, "how are the twins?"

"Football morning, noon, and night. Football and cheerleaders, football and cheerleaders. Better than dope and tattoos I guess, but . . ."

"Wait 'til they bring up body piercing," the General added. "Nothing like the topic of a belly button ring or a nose ring to give a parent's head a spin. Is Mr. Underhill available?"

"I'm sure he is, sir."

Mrs. Kappadonna pressed the intercom button on her desk and announced the General.

Meredith and the secretary looked each other over. Mrs. Kappadonna had the smoothest skin Meredith had ever seen, with a light scattering of freckles. It made you want to touch it, see if it really was as soft as it appeared. Her hair was light brown and worn chin-length with what seemed to be natural waves. She wore no makeup and had been blessed with girlish good looks into what appeared to be her forties. She sipped Dr Pepper from a can with a flexible straw and surveyed Meredith over the top of the can. Finally done with her perusal of Meredith, she put down her soda and stuck out a hand.

"Annika Kappadonna. Call me Ann if your tongue trips over all the rest, or Mrs. Kappadonna if you're ticked at me. Gives me fair warning."

Meredith took the hand and shook it.

"Fair enough," she replied.

The office door on the right opened and a tall African-American man came out. You could have used the alternate, not politically correct, term "black" and been accurate. Black is what he was. Not brown, not chocolate, but black—with a crown of white hair cut close to an impressive skull. He wore a white shirt and a hideous tie that reminded Meredith of slides she had seen in hygiene class that showed the advanced stages of syphilis. His eyes flitted past Meredith and fixed on General Schwaner.

"General." Mark Underhill's voice was a deep basso profundo that seemed to rise from the depths of a cave.

"Mr. Underhill, this is Lieutenant Colonel Cleon, your new PM. Meredith, Mark Underhill, your Director of Community Safety." Underhill looked at Meredith as Schwaner continued. "I'll let you two make your own how-de-dos and head back. I have a budget meeting that's gonna keep Excedrin in business until the end of the millennium. Mr. Underhill."

"General." Underhill nodded to Schwaner but never took his eyes off Meredith.

"I'd wish you luck, Meredith, but we both know that luck has nothing to do with success. It's all perspiration and perspicacity." The General clapped her on the shoulder, then walked back across the squad room and down the stairs.

That left Meredith with Underhill, who was already stepping across the reception area to the office on the left.

"Welcome to Fort Hazelton, Colonel Cleon. Here's your office." There was very little welcome in the voice.

Underhill opened the door and allowed Meredith to precede him inside.

It was a small space, just big enough for the metal desk, a small institutional sofa and chair, a bookcase and coffee table. There was nothing on the walls. The gray Steelcase desk with a side table and an old gray computer screen and keyboard dominated the room. All in all, pretty depressing.

"The SOPs and regs for this station are on your desk. Pleasant reading, every page." Underhill showed her the stack with a wave of his hand. The stack was unpleasantly high.

"Let's sit," Meredith suggested, and took the plastic-cushioned sofa—gray, of course. Underhill took the matching gray chair. He waited impassively for her to speak. This man was going to be hard to read. Meredith began.

"The General waylaid me before I finished all of my introductions. I still haven't been to Housing. Could we set up a department briefing here in, say, an hour or two? All department heads?"

"Can do." Underhill dipped his head once in agreement, an efficient man. "We don't have a CID Chief, and the next higher is out on an investigation, I think, until sixteen hundred."

"Get together whoever you can. I don't want this to be formal, just a familiarization for me. And I need to speak with the Judge Advocate, I guess, touch base there, too."

"Mrs. K. can set that up. Mrs. K.!" Underhill raised his voice. Annika Kappadonna came into the office after a moment.

"Heard it. I'll set a meeting—seventeen-thirty okay, Colonel?" Mrs. Kappadonna put a pager and a walkie-talkie on the coffee table in front of the sofa. "These are yours. Take them at your own risk."

"Is there anything I need to know immediately—high-profile cases, any red flags?" Meredith asked Underhill.

"None." Just a twitch of Underhill's head punctuated the word. "We have a hate crime brewing, maybe. I have some people on it."

"Anybody hurt?"

"No, just literature. Some pamphlets on the PX bulletin board. Appeared over the weekend. Probably kids. As I said, we're on it. I'll have a report ready by our staff meeting. It's a pretty quiet post— Mayberry, R.F.D. We've got more than we need keeping us busy, but as I said, it's pretty quiet."

"So I've been told." Meredith rose and picked up her pager and walkie-talkie. "I'll finish my check-in, come back here, and we can talk through some things."

"I'll be here," Underhill responded. "I'm always here."

"I could hold off my introductions for a while if you think my time would be better spent here." She tried kissing his ass. No tongues, just a little peck to see if that was what Underhill wanted from her.

"Don't rush on our account, Colonel. We're understaffed, overextended, and shortchanged, but we manage. Take your time."

Meredith wondered if that was a "fuck you, stay out of our way and let us do our job." She didn't press it—there would be time enough for her to find out. She headed for the door, then stopped.

"Uh, could somebody give me directions to Housing?"

"I'll show you myself." Underhill got up.

Underhill led Meredith down the stairs and outside. There was no conversation, just the hollow echo of their footsteps in the narrow stairwell.

Once outside, Underhill pointed to a four-story concrete block towering over the headquarters building.

"Housing is on the second floor," he said. "Is the Director of Resource Management on your list of introductions?"

"Not really," Meredith answered. "Not today."

"If you don't mind a recommendation . . ."

"That's what I will depend on you for, Mr. Underhill. I'm new here."

The compliment bounced off Underhill like spit off a hot griddle.

"I don't want to prejudice you, but I would go over to the DRM's office as soon as possible and be prepared to brown-nose to the best of your capability."

"For any particular reason?"

"The last PM pissed him off all to hell. We've suffered ever since, our department."

"Should I know how the previous PM ticked him off?"

"Ran off with the DRM's wife. The PM took early retirement, the DRM's wife, and his motor home. Took a job with some Silicon Valley security company."

Underhill didn't smile, so Meredith contained hers.

"From what I understand," Underhill continued, "The DRM loved that motor home."

He still didn't smile, but Meredith allowed herself one.

"The DRM is on the fourth floor." Underhill pointed at the building again. "So, if you don't mind, Colonel, you could do us some good in there. Do what you do best."

"And what might you think that is, Mr. Underhill?" she asked him with curiosity.

"Charm him, Colonel. A young woman like you can't have made Lieutenant Colonel without a packload of charm. See you at seventeen-thirty."

Underhill turned and went back inside the station house.

Meredith stood on the steps and simmered for a moment before walking toward Housing. She hadn't been in a very good mood when she arrived, and everything since then had only made it worse.

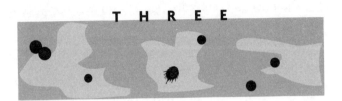

T H R E E

Meredith had taken the big step four months ago. Her twenty-year anniversary in the Army had come up—the big one. Most officers retired at that point, going into civilian life with a somewhat comfortable monthly check from Uncle Sam. Most were able to slide into another career with relative ease, the military résumé of an officer popular among corporate recruiters.

But Meredith saw the twenty-year out as an act of weakness. For her it was thirty years or nothing. She had decided she was going all the way.

She wanted a general's star.

There were a lot of reasons. The personal challenge—the blue-collar kid from Hamtramck, Michigan, trying to overcome the embarrassment of being poor white trash, wearing ill-fitting hand-me-down clothes and shoddy Salvation Army shoes, sneered at by the rich kids in school. Meredith thought at times she was over all of that, but every once in a while the shame of her background tapped her on the shoulder and reminded her that it never really went away, it had just been shoved in a corner.

There were also the gender reasons. Meredith didn't call herself a feminist—for some reason she couldn't get herself to join any group other than the Army—but she had suffered under the burden of being a woman in the most macho of all men's worlds. Very few women ever climbed to the rank of general. There were only ten so far, not counting the Medical Corps. Ten. In the history of the Army. Meredith wanted to be number eleven. Maybe all the snide remarks, the pinched butts, the bitter and lonely times she spent being ignored or abused by her male counterparts, maybe it could all be justified only if she made general. More than one man had stated flatly that she wouldn't make it.

Or maybe it would finally prove something to her father, who was still alive at the time. What, exactly, she didn't know—the relationship had been so complicated and fraught with emotional minefields that she had trouble venturing even a toe into that dark territory.

Meredith knew none of these was a sensible reason to reenlist, but they were all she had and so she signed her name, making her commanding officer and the re-up officer very happy. She didn't understand it when her action put her in a blue funk that lasted over a week.

And then her aunt Leweese called and said, "Come quick, your father is dying."

Meredith had requested a thirty-day leave and flown to Michigan.

Her father, Rudell, was lying in a hospital bed surrounded by his three sisters, Leweese, Lorrayna, and Judi. Meredith had always thought that Judi had escaped a hillbilly name only because her mother was under the influence of drugs for the first time during childbirth and her father was off to war.

Meredith had barely escaped the family naming curse, her mother insisting on Meredith Josephina, which her father immediately turned into Mere-Jo. But only he called her that; anyone else risked a black eye. Of course her cousins, once seeing how angry it made her, used the dreaded nickname to torture her—whenever they had room to run.

The aunts had left Meredith alone with the dying old man. He was small and withered in the bed, which terrified and shocked Meredith. She knew he was a small, thin man, "wiry" was the term, but his presence had always been huge to her. The frightened, intimidated ten-year-old in her wasn't that far away in Meredith's psyche.

But now he had shrunken to a tiny, fragile-looking figure. His hollow-eyed, sunken-cheeked skull prominent beneath the weathered skin of his face, his arms thin sticks that reminded Meredith of the starvation victims she had seen in Somalia.

He opened his eyes and instantly gained a modicum of his former power over her. Pale blue, hard, mean eyes that allowed no mercy. For you, or now, himself. He put a finger over the plastic vent in his throat and croaked at her.

"Get me a cigarette."

He was dying of lung and throat cancer. The first time he had been to a doctor in his life was the day they put him in the hospital, refusing for years to acknowledge all of the warning signs or to succumb to what he considered the betrayal of his body. He had passed out while pumping his own gas, and once at the hospital the inevitable X rays had revealed his future with certainty. He was never leaving the hospital alive.

"No," she replied.

It had taken her over thirty years to be able to say that. Of course, it was hard to be afraid of the frail person in the bed.

"What's it gonna do, kill me?"

"No," she said. "The smoke bothers me."

He laughed. The laugh quickly became a painful cough.

"So much for a dying man's last wish."

"Ask me for something else."

He thought for a while and finally requested a banana malt. Not a milk shake or one of them goddamn yogurt foul pieces of baby vomit or any of that McDonald's crap, but a real banana malt with real bananas, real vanilla ice cream, and malted milk powder.

Meredith left and found an ice cream store that would make what her father wanted, and she brought it back to him. It had been a minor quest, but she had fulfilled his wish.

And that was how it went for two and a half weeks. She booked a room at the nearest hotel; she couldn't spend much more than an hour at one time in the house in which she had grown up. She spent eighteen, twenty hours a day at his bedside in the hospital, running out for whatever he needed. Some of those cherry-flavored money candies, though he had no teeth to chew and only sucked on one of the half-pound she had purchased. Li'l Abner comics. Jimmie Rodgers tapes—the fella they called the Singing Train Man—he'd like to hear that ol' boy once more. It was the Singing Brakeman, but she found a tape and a small boom box to play it on.

For eighteen days, not a day or night going by that he didn't tell her to leave, go back to her "soldier life," let him die in peace.

Other than that short, repeated conversation and the occasional request from him—some of them chocolate things with the little white doohickeys sprinkled on the top, nonparallels or something—they didn't speak. Neither one discussed the past, their lives together. Once tears formed in the corners of his eyes and he whispered.

"I missed your mama's birthday."

So Meredith took flowers to the cemetery and sat and tried to bring her mother up-to-date, as her father had done every year on her birthday for the last thirty-one years.

Other than that, they didn't speak.

She was thankful for that.

The aunts, though, wanted to talk all the time. Rudell just refused to respond. Meredith tried to participate, but after the polite questions about who was doing what among her cousins and inquiries into Meredith's career (Leweese still thought Meredith was a nurse), they found out how little they had in common and settled into a quiet deathwatch.

Meredith finally gave in after seventeen days and snuck the old man a cigarette—unfiltered, of course—and turned off his oxygen tank before she lit it for him. She could see him struggling to inhale the smoke that had killed him, but he sucked the cigarette down to a butt barely large enough to hold and handed that tiny remnant to her with a defiant, triumphant spark in his eyes.

He died the next day.

Nothing spectacular, no last words, though he had attempted to give some sort of advice to everyone on the sixteenth day. He just closed his eyes and his chest stopped moving.

Meredith waited around for the funeral, then left from the cemetery, driving right out of Michigan to Indiana, not wanting to hang around to see her aunts haggle over the meager estate, his depleted savings, the house, not wanting a single item outside of the photograph of her mother that had sat on his bedside table until it was transferred to the hospital room. The car, which he had said in front of all the four women was to be Meredith's, was kept outside the rest of the estate that would be divvied up.

Rudell Cleon left no will, viewing them with the undisguised suspicion of most rural, anti-authoritarian urban transplants. He had lived in Michigan for forty-two years, but he still considered himself a Kentuckian from the "holler." So because Rudell had never put a word in writing, his estate was up for grabs.

Meredith wasn't in the mood for grabbing, so she packed up the car and left. She was crossing the Michigan-Indiana border when she realized that she hadn't transferred the title for the Mustang or arranged for insurance.

At the next stop she opened the glove compartment and pulled out the various legal documents, registration, and so forth—all in a neat plastic bag. The car was in her name, and it had been for the last twelve years.

That was when she cried.

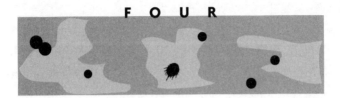

F O U R

Penny O'Leary, a kindly, grandmotherly type who smelled—no, nearly reeked of gardenia perfume, did nothing to improve Meredith's frame of mind. The old, frail-looking woman invited Meredith into her office, welcomed her to Fort Adrian Hazelton, offered jelly beans from a bowl on her desk, and further ruined Meredith's day.

There were no openings in any of the post housing, and the waiting list was eighteen months to two years long. The Bachelor Officers' Quarters was full, the guest quarters in the process of being torn down as it had been recently condemned. The older residences that were in greatest disrepair were being torn down and sold as scrap lumber and brick as they became empty, so the wait would be even longer than usual.

O'Leary apologized for not being more helpful, asked Meredith to call her Penny, gave her a list of hotels and motels in Walhalla recommended for military personnel as temporary living quarters, and apologized again. Meredith knew only one thing—she would now have to go on a hunt for some place to live, a process she hated. And she would have to live off-post. She was of the opinion that the Provost Marshal should live on-post, be part of the community they were sworn to protect. But the worst part was searching for an apartment or a house, for Meredith a bête noire that a person who moved as much as she did from assignment to assignment should have gotten over or accepted a long time ago. But she hadn't, and she dreaded it more with every new move. She wanted to rage at someone, but she couldn't yell at kindly Penny O'Leary, which was probably the reason the old woman had been given the thankless job.

Taking two red jelly beans, Meredith left. The candy was hard and stale. She spit the jelly beans into the first hallway wastebasket and climbed the stairs to the fourth floor. A wrong turn down the hall was corrected by a passing private whom she stopped for directions. She finally found the door marked "Otto Wojahn—Director of Resource Management." Arguably the most powerful person on any military installation these days, the DRM controlled the disbursement of all monies on the post, and with the service-wide downsizing, every commander of every unit was desperate for their share of the shrinking funds. The DRM had become the focus of whining, bitching, intimidation, and all forms of seduction, subtle and otherwise. Meredith had yet to meet a happy DRM.

She opened the door and announced herself to the secretary guarding the inner office, a plump twenty-something with a little face and more big hair. Big hair was as popular here as it was with Meredith's aunts.

"I'd like to see Mr. Wojahn."

"He's very busy," was the curt reply. No jelly beans in the offing here. The desk nameplate designated her as one Jerri Rose Breen.

"I'm the new Provost Marshal." Meredith pronounced it "pro-vo," remembering her instructor at the MP Training Center at Fort McClellan making them repeat the same rhyme before every class: "Those in the know say 'pro-vo.'"

"Provost Marshal." The secretary rhymed it with "post," perhaps out of spite, Meredith couldn't tell. One of the penciled eyebrows below the big hair slid up and hid behind the pinkish platinum bangs.

The woman stood up and went into the inner office behind her. Meredith speculated that the hair was a necessary counterbalance for the butt.

The inner-office door was left open, and Meredith could see Wojahn peer around the skirted beam of his secretary. He grimaced and looked over his reading glasses at Meredith.

Wojahn had a vividly pink face with tufts of white hair poking out of his ears. They looked as if they had been stuffed with wads of lamb's wool.

"All right, all right," he growled to his secretary. "Send her in, dammit."

Happy to meet you, too, Meredith thought. This was going to take more than charm.

She was waiting for the secretary to trot back out and pass on Wojahn's invitation when the hall door opened and a young black female MP entered.

"Sergeant Gorman!" Meredith exclaimed, seeing the familiar, friendly face. The Sergeant's face broke into a big smile that matched Meredith's own.

"Colonel, it's great to see you!" Gorman beamed, then remembered her purpose and put on her professional face. "We've been try-ing to beep you, ma'am. I have a request for your presence."

By now Wojahn's secretary had returned to Meredith. "Mr. Wo-jahn will see you now."

"In a second, ma'am," Meredith said, and she turned back to Gorman. "I haven't turned my beeper on yet. Didn't think there was a need. Can this wait? I'm about to go into a meeting."

"Not really, ma'am," Gorman replied, a bit nervously. "I was told to bring you—ASAP."

The secretary fidgeted. "Colonel . . ."

"Well, Colonel?" Wojahn hollered from his office. "You *did* ask to see me."

Meredith looked into Wojahn's office. He was now standing be-hind his desk. Wojahn was a short man with a big head, and the pink face had deepened to the color of a ripe tomato and was verging on purple.

Gorman leaned closer and whispered into Meredith's ear.

"We have a homicide, Colonel."

Meredith felt the blood drain from her face and a knot form in her stomach. Gorman looked as stunned as Meredith felt.

"Colonel!" Wojahn yelled from behind his desk, his voice going up an octave. There was warning in that yell, maybe a threat.

"Colonel," Gorman prompted. "I have orders to bring you out to the murder scene. ASAP."

"Murder." The word seemed to stay with her even after she ut-tered it. "Let's go."

She called to Wojahn. "I'm sorry, Mr. Wojahn. We'll have to reschedule."

Meredith thought she heard a noise as she shut the door behind her and Gorman, something between a grunt and a curse.

But her mind was already elsewhere.

A homicide. On her first day. First this lame assignment, then Levy, now a homicide.

God.

Sergeant Beth Gorman's sedan, a government-issue Ford Taurus—stripped down to the bare bones, with no accessories, certainly no bells, and absolutely no whistles—was waiting out front.

Gorman opened the rear door, but Meredith made a point of sitting in the front seat with the MP.

"Were you jump-starting someone's car a little while ago, Gorman?" she asked the Sergeant.

"Yes, ma'am. Mrs. Stanhower. Third time in the last two weeks. She replaced the battery, but she's still having problems keeping a charge. Used up all her Triple-A freebies."

"What can you tell me about the homicide?"

"Nada, Colonel. I was just told to bring you out to Pelzer Range."

"Well, it's nice to see you again, Sergeant Gorman. I see you gained a stripe. How long have you been stationed here?"

"Seven months plus." Gorman drove across the post. Meredith tried to pay attention to the streets and landmarks, but she was soon lost. She noticed the decommissioned tanks and helicopters, a few old artillery pieces, all plopped down on the grounds of various units as if they were statuary or lawn ornaments—which, in a way, they were.

"Pretty good duty. Quiet place," Gorman commented. "So far."

They were already driving through a forest, mostly pines with the occasional hardwood. Every few hundred meters the trees were interrupted by a dirt road or a training facility.

Then they approached the firing ranges. Pistol, rifle, machine gun—wide acres of bermed dirt cleared of trees and brush. There were the usual bleachers, an occasional range building, a small shack for the range cadre. None of the firing ranges was currently being used.

Gorman began to slow as they passed the Urban Combat Training Range, a series of raw concrete walls, the mere semblance of buildings with square holes for windows, rectangular openings for doors, walls all of bare cement block without roofs. The structures were used to train soldiers for house-to-house searches, enemy-held-building assault tactics, and other urban combat exercises.

Meredith was familiar with this type of training facility; she had run more than her share of squads and platoons through the training herself. She had also overseen the Special Reaction Team training, the Army MP version of a SWAT team.

But right now the Urban Combat Range was vacant, and it looked like a housing development that had been abandoned in mid-construction. It was ghostly, haunting.

Next door was Pelzer Range, which, on the other hand, was very busy. A half-dozen vehicles, including a pair of MP-marked 4 × 4's, were parked near the bleachers where fifty to sixty troops were hanging around. Some were being interviewed by MPs; the rest were doing what a soldier does most often—waiting.

Gorman called in on the radio and announced the impending arrival of the Provost Marshal. She was instructed by radio to bring the Colonel to the rear of the range and was given further instructions on exactly how to do just that. It was a bumpy ride over roads that obviously didn't get used very often by standard vehicles. The Taurus bottomed out a few times, the gravel scraping across the steel gas tank with a sound like nails across a blackboard; it sent chills up Meredith's spine.

They passed the berms for 250, 500, and 750 meters and, at the 1,000-meters berm, took a left to ride down behind the target ridge.

It wasn't hard to find the crime scene—it had the same air of the firing line. A half-dozen vehicles, including the El Camino Meredith had seen in the MP station lot, and an ambulance. A dozen people were lounging around, waiting. Waiting for one person—Meredith. As Gorman parked, everyone turned to watch Meredith get out of the MP vehicle.

The stares were neutral, but she imagined them judging her. This was the new Provost Marshal. A woman. She had felt it before.

It was slipping into late afternoon. The warmth of the day was beginning to be eroded by a fall chill that was carried on the occasional breeze.

Underhill walked over to her. He wore a blue blazer over the shirt and syphilitic tie.

"Thank you, Sergeant Gorman. This way, Colonel. I hope you have a strong stomach."

Underhill led Meredith over to the berm. The targets were in their upright position, black silhouettes of trucks and tanks, their solidity not lessened by the thousands of fifty-caliber perforations.

"I've seen dead bodies before, Mr. Underhill," Meredith replied. "Saudi, Panama, Somalia . . ."

"There are dead bodies and then there are dead bodies, Colonel." Underhill was right.

The area around one target was cordoned off with yellow crime-scene tape laid out on the dirt and held down with rocks. A slight wind rustled the tape across the ground, making it hiss like a snake. The sound grated on Meredith's nerves—that and the smell, the sweetly sickening odor of blood and bile. The scent of death, once experienced, was never forgotten.

She expected the body to be on the ground within the perimeter of the crime-scene tape. And there *was* blood on the ground, a lot of it, but no body. And flies. Where death walked, flies filled the footprints. Months after Somalia, Meredith couldn't bear to have a fly land on her skin.

It was the flies that took Meredith's attention from the pool of coagulated blood upward to the target.

There was the body.

But not much was left of it.

Just meat. Meat chewed, ripped, torn, and blown apart by fifty-caliber slugs. Meat in the vague form of a human being. Meat and white splintered bone. It was ugly.

There was clothing, scraps of bloody, ragged BDU mixed in with the raw flesh. A boot was still attached to the target with green nylon parachute cord; the other had fallen to the ground below, with part of the leg and foot still inside. Both of the victim's hands were still tied to the steel plate of the target with what appeared to be more parachute cord.

The whole scene froze Meredith. When she finally inhaled, the movement of her own chest surprised her. She had seen bodies before. Incinerated, frozen in blackened contortions, flesh burned to the skull revealing an evil rictus grin. Bodies shot, curled up in fetal balls of peaceful sleep. Bodies swollen from tropical heat, ready to burst with noxious gas, discolored flesh ripe with rot.

But this was as brutal and ugly a sight as she had ever seen.

Meredith was so absorbed in the horrid violence of it all, the vulgar blasphemy of what was once a human being, that Underhill's voice, though soft, startled her.

"The body was found at thirteen hundred hours." His tone was just above a whisper, reverent in tone. "The mechanism that brings up the target was jammed and the range crew came to check it out. Looks like a piece of . . . meat jammed the gears."

Underhill spoke privately to her, close, watching her expression. *To see if I'm going to faint?*

Meredith tried to breathe through her mouth so the stench wouldn't overcome her. Retching her guts out wouldn't help Meredith's standing as the new Provost Marshal.

"Any ID? Do we know who it is?" Meredith asked him, looking at where the victim's face should have been. It was a dark, bloody cavity swarming with more black, shiny flies.

"That's the bad part," Underhill replied.

"The bad part? What could be worse than this?" Meredith asked.

"This is . . . was . . . Second Lieutenant Georgia Carnes." He held up a plastic evidence bag with a bloody dog tag inside.

Meredith's mind raced. The name was familiar. Why? Had she served with Carnes somewhere?

"General Ringstall's Aide," Underhill filled in the blank.

Meredith remembered. An empty parking slot at Headquarters, a name painted on the curb. An empty desk, a nameplate on that desk now taking on the import of a tombstone.

Then the impact of what Underhill just said filtered down to her consciousness. The Chief of Staff's Aide. She would be dealing directly with generals on this one. She took another breath.

"So, what are we doing?"

"We've cordoned off the immediate area. Vehicular tracks are pretty much destroyed on the access road, but there are some clear impressions near the body. They've been roped off. There are also some footprints. We're taking impressions of everything."

"You'll get the range crew's boots for comparison?"

"Yes, ma'am." He seemed irritated by the suggestion.

Careful, Meredith, don't step on any toes.

Underhill continued. "We're waiting for the medical team. Meanwhile, CID is surveying the scene. The SAC will supervise the forensics gathering."

Meredith nodded, looking around for the CID Special Agent in

Charge. She was going to need someone experienced on this—a General's Aide, for God's sake. Her first day, her first case . . .

Underhill turned and called out. "Mr. Tate!"

"Mr. Underhill, on my way!"

Meredith looked for the source of the unfamiliar voice and found a young man bent over a Humvee, vomiting onto the ground. He stood up and walked over to them, forcing his gaze away from the body. "Mister" Tate looked barely old enough to hold the title.

Meredith figured he was in his mid-twenties, but with the kind of looks that would get him carded into his thirties. A wisp of a mustache below his nose didn't help at all; in fact, it exaggerated the impression that this was a mere boy in a man's suit. He was dabbing at his mouth with his tie.

"Jeez, you ever seen anything like this before? Jeez." He was muttering to no one in particular. "Who would . . . Jeez."

"Anything from the private who found the body?" Underhill asked.

"No, sir." Tate's eyes flicked past Meredith's face, took in her rank, then went back to Underhill. "We've got our photos. Can we lower the, uh, target so we can take prints now, sir? If it's okay?"

"Ask the PM." Underhill turned Tate over to Meredith. Tate looked back at her, eyes wide. He self-consciously straightened out his suit, tucked his shirt in, and wiped his mouth again, this time with his sleeve.

"Colonel." He tried to smile, had second thoughts about the appropriateness of that under the circumstances, and got rid of it. "Ma'am, uh, may we . . . ?"

"Do whatever you have to do, Mr. Tate, just do it to the letter." Meredith presented a neutral front so she wouldn't intimidate the young man, but at the same time left no room for any misunderstanding. "Follow procedures. One step at a time. We're going to have a lot of eyes on this. At least one general's."

"Yes, ma'am." Tate nodded seriously. "To the letter, ma'am. I'll do it by the book."

"I'm sure you will, Mr. Tate. Proceed." Meredith said it with as much confidence as she could muster. If Tate was the SAC on this case, he was going to need as much moral and technical support as he could get from everyone involved.

Tate walked over to a couple of people in civilian clothes, a woman and a man. Meredith assumed that these were other CID officers. The Criminal Investigation Division, while members of the military, were allowed and almost required to dress in suits and ties.

By rank they were Warrant Officers, an officer's rank usually reserved for highly trained technicians like helicopter pilots and other specialists—and in this case criminologists. They each had an officer's uniform in their closet somewhere, but since most of their work involved interfacing with civilian law-enforcement authorities and off-post investigative duties, they were usually in civilian attire.

"He's new, but he's thorough." Underhill spoke when Tate was out of earshot.

"How new?" she asked.

"Fourteen months out of school," Underhill replied. "Four of them here. He's your senior CID investigator."

Fourteen months? In her last assignment, Meredith's senior investigator had been at it for eleven years.

"We have no Officer in Charge," Underhill added. "Tate'll do a good job at the crime scene."

Meredith noted the qualification in Underhill's endorsement of Tate: ". . . at the crime scene." A crime scene itself was only one aspect of an investigation. She had a major homicide on her hands, not a quick and dirty domestic dispute gone nuclear with a drunken husband or wife crying on the curb with the murder weapon in their bloody hands.

Gorman came over with a cup of coffee.

"From the medics, ma'am. They always have the best coffee."

Meredith took the proffered cup. Gorman looked at the body.

"Somebody hated her real bad."

Meredith looked at the body of the victim still hanging from the target. Underhill looked, too.

"A mean and ugly way to die," Meredith agreed, then turned to Underhill. "Mr. Underhill, do me a favor? Get on the horn and find out what's taking Meddac so long. If he needs a vehicle, get him one. See if Mr. Tate needs assistance, and have Mrs. Kappadonna—"

"We call her Mrs. K," Underhill said.

"—Mrs. Kappadonna gather everyone else together for that meeting. *Everyone.* And I need you to brief me on exactly how short-handed we are. I have a feeling we're going to need every man and woman we have for this investigation. And get Lieutenant Carnes down from there as soon as you can."

Underhill waited until she was finished.

"The Pathologist is in the middle of something," Underhill began. "There's an MP standing by to rush him out here, lights and sirens. Mr. Tate, despite his inexperience, is competent, and frankly he's the only trained forensics person we have. He and his crew are at work, and adding people to his team would, in my opinion, just get in his way and slow him down. The heads of all departments are standing by in my office."

He paused a moment and turned his attention back to the body.

"Lieutenant Carnes . . . Georgia . . . was a friend of the family. She . . . had been to my home more than once. My wife is . . . particularly fond of her. But right now Lieutenant Carnes is evidence in her own murder, beyond feeling pain, and will hang there as long as it is needed in the investigation."

"Mr. Underhill, that was all a version of 'mind your own business,' wasn't it?"

"To be frank, ma'am, yes."

"Let's walk and talk, Mr. Underhill."

She took his arm and led him away from the others.

"Sometimes when two people dance for the first time they step all over each other's toes. That doesn't mean they shouldn't dance together. They just need to find a common rhythm. Now, I know you've had, let's say, different working relationships with your other PMs. Good and bad. I want us to have a *good* one. So get it off your chest, Mr. Underhill. We have to work together. We can't be at cross-purposes. Spit it out."

"All right, ma'am." Underhill bored into her with his eyes. "Our last PM spent all his time and much of Mrs. K.'s time working on his résumé and looking for a civilian job. For the last three years I have run this Community Safety Office at half-strength with shrinking resources, and no funding, *by myself.* It hasn't been fun, but I've done it."

"Well, Mr. Underhill, you're not by yourself anymore. I'm here to do my share. More if need be. So maybe it's time for you to redefine your areas of responsibility and for me to take on some of that load. If you could bring me up to speed as soon as possible, we can do that."

She looked him in the eyes.

"Now," she continued. "I gather you think we're in good hands here."

"The best we have, unless you have forensics experience." He hadn't let go of the reins yet. "As for a redefinition of our areas of responsibility . . . All you need to do, Colonel, is keep the brass happy.

We'll have our little staff meeting, bring you up to speed. Then, if you would stay out of our way, we will proceed with our usual operations and this investigation. See you at the staff meeting."

And he headed over to the El Camino, pausing to tell Tate to call him if there were any questions or problems.

Meredith watched Underhill drive away. She tabled her response for the moment and walked over to Tate, who was instructing one of his people to take soil samples from the area. These would be needed if a suspect vehicle or footwear were discovered that might have trace evidence—dirt embedded in the tires or soles. Comparison tests of homicide-scene soil had helped lock up more than one murderer. Meredith felt reassured about Tate's abilities.

"Mr. Tate," she said, making her presence known, and he snapped to attention. "At ease. Did you happen to find out who was shooting at this target?"

"Yes, ma'am." Tate nodded seriously. "First thing. There were six of 'em who went through qualification before the target jammed."

Six. Meredith did some mental calculations to try and figure out the number of fifty-caliber rounds that had been fired at Georgia Carnes.

"You have their names?" she asked Tate.

"Yes, ma'am. And we did the preliminary interviews."

"Anything turn up?"

"I wouldn't venture to say, Colonel."

Good answer.

"We can follow up anytime," he added. "Or, ma'am, we can go talk to them again in your presence."

"No, no," Meredith declined. "Your word is good enough for me."

Tate smiled, looking ten years younger, which was probably why he didn't do it very often.

Six shooters. Meredith hoped that Lieutenant Carnes was already dead before the first fifty-caliber round tore into her body. But then what would be the point of the murderer tying her to the target? To destroy the body beyond recognition? Then you wouldn't leave the dog tags around her neck.

No, Carnes had probably been alive.

"Ma'am," Tate interrupted her thoughts. "Anything else?"

"Yes, make sure Meddac gets Carnes's medical and dental files. Have them fingerprint the body and check them against her personnel file. Just because you found Carnes's dog tags on the body, don't assume that it's her," Meredith cautioned, having learned from experience. "Also, get an MP over to Carnes's residence. Lock it up until we can conduct a thorough search."

"Yes, ma'am." Tate was making notes. "You've been through a few of these, huh?"

"A few," Meredith confirmed.

"Routine, huh?" he added.

"The procedures are routine, Mr. Tate," Meredith said. "But when death becomes routine, quit."

"Yes, ma'am. Anything else?"

"No. Carry on." Meredith left Tate and sought out Gorman for a ride back to the MP station, taking one last look at the body as she left.

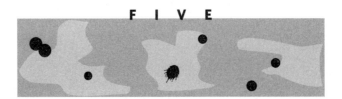

FIVE

The drive back to the MP station was quiet, Meredith with her own thoughts and Gorman knowing better than to disturb her.

The first day on a new post was supposed to be a leisurely introduction, walking from office to office, a series of informal greetings and icebreakers with the various people who populated your new home. You chatted about the universal dislike for the constant packing up and moving, your last assignment, acquaintances in common, war stories, Pentagon jokes, scuttlebutt, and rumor. All very meaningless on the surface, but as important as all good reconnaissance. It was putting your toe in the water before deciding to take the plunge and swim, a way of wading out to check the depth and footing.

But Meredith had just been dumped into the deep end of the pool and the water was a cold shock.

Now she had a homicide investigation, a rarity on a military reservation, and a hot one. A case rife with political pitfalls. She needed to get her people organized and operating at peak efficiency. But she didn't know who her people were and had no idea of the political landscape across which she would be maneuvering, internally or externally. Within her own unit she had Underhill, who was demonstrating some definite attitudinal problems, and Tate, a neophyte who seemed capable but still was without the experience she needed for a case of this enormity.

On the outside she had Levy, who wouldn't give her an inch of slack, she already knew, and Schwaner, who would bend over backward if she asked, but asking would be cashing in a chip she might need later, and it would cost her the respect of many of her peers. Nothing caused you to lose face like asking Daddy to fight your battles for you. That was something she wasn't going to risk unless her back was against the wall.

She was in unknown territory with few friends. She had been there before. She would cope. She would do more than cope.

Meredith found her own way upstairs this time. Gorman was left to resume her usual patrol duties.

The long table in the squad room was surrounded by people, who all stood as Meredith entered. Underhill came out of his office and made the introductions.

Game Warden Carolyn Bosch-Stuckey was a rugged-looking, outdoorsy woman in a green uniform; Provost Sergeant Raul Kahla was a strikingly handsome man whose long eyelashes and soft brown eyes were in contrast to the deep scar that ran along his jawline. Fire Chief George Lindell was a tall, skinny older man with a hangdog expression emphasized by his stoop-shouldered posture—he looked like he was carrying the world on his shoulders and was about to drop it out of despair. His blue uniform was dusted with a fine snow of what looked like cigarette ash, and the first two fingers of his right hand were nicotine-stained. Unfiltered—the old school. Meredith had a flash of her father's yellow-stained fingers. She shoved it aside.

She told them all to take their places, and they sat around the table. Mrs. Kappadonna took a seat, writing tablet and pen at the ready for notes. Underhill took the seat next to Meredith.

Meredith looked everyone over. These were some of the people on whom her career, at least during her stay at Fort Hazelton, would depend. And she as yet knew nothing about them. What motivated them, what made them want to do their best? What were their strengths, their weaknesses? She would have to find these things out—as quickly as possible even under normal circumstances. But especially now.

"Thank you all for coming in at such short notice," she began. "Now, I know you all have problems, big and small, and I am here to address them all. . . . But we have, as I'm sure you all have heard by now, a priority homicide. So we'll make this first meeting short and sweet."

The phone rang. An MP answered it and came over and tapped Mrs. Kappadonna on the shoulder. She took the call. Meredith vamped while she waited for her to return.

"What I'd like to do is go around the table and have each of you bring up anything, *anything* that you think is critical to your individual mission. Then we will break down this homicide investigation, the little we know so far, so that we can all be up to date."

Mrs. Kappadonna walked back to the table and leaned down toward Meredith. "Colonel, I'm sorry, but that was Colonel Levy and he requests your presence immediately at his office."

Meredith struggled to hide her irritation. It wasn't good for her to be seen in conflict with her superiors.

"Mrs. Kappadonna, could you fine-tune the 'request' and 'immediately' parts of that message?"

Mrs. Kappadonna smiled. "By the tone of his voice, I'd say 'request' was more like a commandment from God's own lips and 'immediately' was five minutes ago."

"Did you tell him I was in a meeting?"

"Yes, ma'am, I did."

Meredith looked at Underhill. He seemed to understand and perhaps enjoy her predicament, but that could have been her own private interpretation.

"Go on, ma'am," he urged softly. "We have other business we can tend to." Maybe she was wrong about him.

Meredith rose from the table. "Well, I'd best go and fulfill my job description and keep the brass happy."

She aimed the last at Underhill, but he didn't react, then she chided herself for the dig as she went out the door and down the stairs. Childish. A stupid little comment that would do nothing to help their relationship. Never attack until you have all the available intelligence about your enemy. And the primary piece of intelligence was to confirm the fact that this was indeed the enemy. She didn't even know if Underhill was against her yet. Maybe he was just grouchy.

Meredith was still reprimanding herself when quick footsteps echoed behind her. She turned to see Fire Chief Lindell running down the stairs toward her. And this man wasn't made for running— not anymore, at least.

She stopped and waited for him. He caught up with her, panting to get his breath back, looking a little embarrassed.

"Colonel, I have to talk to you," he gasped. "It is an urgent matter."

"Is it life or death, Chief? By that I mean, will someone die in the next hour or two?"

"No, I suppose not. No. Nothing immediately life-threatening." He was shaking his head with more emphasis than necessary.

"Well, right now I'm up to my behind in alligators, so if whatever it is could wait for an hour I'd be mighty appreciative."

She gave him a moment to think about it. Surprisingly, he took it, finally nodding as vigorously as he had shaken his head earlier. "It can wait that long, Colonel."

"I'm sorry, Chief. But I'll be right back."

She went out the main doors, wondering, *What was that all about?*

Meredith walked down the hall to Levy's office, trying to put aside the irritation she felt toward the Colonel for interrupting her staff meeting. She needed a clear, calm head to face him. Experience had taught her that.

On General Ringstall's side of the hall, his secretary Marga was typing, her eyes rimmed in red from what Meredith assumed was crying. They had most likely already received the news about Carnes's death. Word of mouth on a small post was often faster than any of the high-tech communications equipment.

Levy's secretary, Kay Higdon, was absent from her desk, but his Aide, Vernor, was at his workstation. Meredith planted herself in front of him.

He looked up from the material he was reading.

"Help you, Colonel?"

"Colonel Levy requested my presence."

"He's busy right now, ma'am."

Meredith set her jaw and bit back a hasty response. *Don't take it out on the messenger.*

"He called me out of a meeting."

"The Colonel left strict orders not to be disturbed."

Meredith nodded, trying to control her anger. She looked for something to distract her while she cooled down enough to respond in a calm manner.

"You knew Lieutenant Carnes?"

"A little, ma'am."

"You worked across from her."

"We got to know each other during duty hours, ma'am," he admitted curtly.

"And off duty?"

"No, ma'am."

"She have a boyfriend?"

"I don't know, ma'am."

"C'mon, Lieutenant. I know how the world operates. You work within ten feet of someone you know their menstrual cycle, whether they have a pimple on their behind, or if they ate garlic the night before. Did anybody love or hate Carnes enough to want to kill her?"

"I don't know, ma'am," he reiterated impassively.

"Well, maybe you know this." Meredith leaned across the desk and put her face within inches of his. "A perceptive aide constantly evaluates and reevaluates his orders to serve his commander efficiently. Why don't you get up and go on in there and tell the Colonel that I can talk with him now on whatever urgent matter is on his mind, *or* I can return to the station, where I have many pressing problems of my own, which is only a thirty-second walk away so that when he has the urge to call me over again I will respond immediately. But right now I am too busy, as he should well know, to hang around outside—"

Despite herself, Meredith was building to a major explosion and

Vernor, not blinking or verbally responding, was backing away from her, leaning way back in his chair.

But both were saved by the office door opening and Levy coming out with his secretary. Levy looked at Meredith like people look at the newspaper when it gets drenched in the lawn sprinklers.

"Cleon. Come into my office."

Levy preceded Meredith, sat behind his desk, gestured to the chair in front of it.

Meredith settled herself and realized this time that the chair put her six inches lower than Levy even though she was taller than he. She hadn't noticed it before. She didn't have to waste time wondering if the choice of furniture was mere happenstance.

Levy spoke first. "What do you know about Lieutenant Carnes's death?"

"Probably less than you do, sir, since I'm in your office instead of meeting with my people." It wasn't necessarily true, with Tate probably still at the murder scene and a preliminary report an hour or two away, but Meredith had made her point. Levy was surprised by the obvious reprimand.

"I'll need a report for the General, ASAP," he blustered as he backpedaled.

"You'll have a report when I have something to report, sir." Meredith said it in as neutral a tone as she could manage. It wasn't good enough.

"Are we being hostile, Lieutenant Colonel?"

It was common practice to call a Lieutenant Colonel by "Colonel." The "Lieutenant" was usually dropped except for official document usage or unless someone was trying to make a point. Like a full colonel pulling rank.

"No, Colonel." *Careful, Meredith.* "Factual."

"Do you know there hasn't been a murder at this facility in

twenty-seven years?" Levy picked up a gob of what looked like shiny blue clay and began kneading it with one hand. "Then you arrive, and on your first day . . ."

"I didn't bring it with me, sir." Meredith smiled at the thought that Levy would even try to imply that somehow the homicide was her fault. "Is that why you called me here, sir? To discuss the homicide investigation? Because if that's it, I have little to—"

"No." He cut her short and clenched the blue clay with a death grip. It was some kind of hand exerciser. "The General interrupted us before I could talk to you about this. I consider it a priority for your department."

With his free hand Levy picked a pamphlet off his desk and handed it to Meredith. Meredith looked at it.

It was computer-generated, the pixels evident to the naked eye. The swastika was a bit blurry when viewed closely. There were the usual key words, "Jew," "Nigger," and phrases, "Eliminate the Mud Races," "White Power"—and the authors of this particular piece of filth called themselves "The Guardians Against Babylon."

Meredith had seen this type of hate literature before on other posts and in inter-Army memos. Hate crimes were a sensitive issue lately.

"This hate literature has been showing up around the post," Levy continued. "You do know the Army position on hate literature and hate groups. Of course you do. I want you to know mine. This *will* be stopped. It will be stopped with all dispatch and with all of the resources at your disposal."

"I respect the Colonel's feelings on this matter and I also find this an abhorrent action, but I do have a homicide investigation, sir."

"Your unit works on more than one case at a time, does it not?"

"Yes, sir." Meredith wasn't going to argue about this one. She looked at the pamphlet again, read some of the words and phrases, felt the anger and bile rise in her stomach.

"Stop this," Levy ordered. "I don't know if you're aware of this, Lieutenant Colonel, but I am of Jewish heritage. This filth is particularly offensive to me and my family."

"Sir, this will be met by all the resources I have at my disposal."

She started to rise, assuming the meeting was over.

"That's not all, Cleon. You weren't dismissed."

Meredith let herself fall back into the chair.

"I was looking at your file. You're overdue for pistol qualification. Eleven days overdue."

Meredith was stunned. It took her a second to collect herself and respond.

"I was on leave until today, sir."

"You have five days to correct this. I will not have a senior officer ducking their responsibilities."

"Ducking . . ." Levy was being unreasonable, but Meredith decided not to argue with him. It was an argument she couldn't win, and she had other more important matters in which to invest her energy. "Yes, sir. Is there anything else, sir?"

"No. Dismissed."

Meredith rose and headed for the door.

"One other thing, actually." Levy stopped her again. "The DRM called, quite agitated, and stated that you walked out of his office after demanding a meeting."

"That's not exactly how it occurred, sir."

"No excuses. It does none of us any good in these times of fiscal constraints to piss off the DRM. Mend that fence, Cleon."

"Yes, sir."

She waited to see if he really was done this time. Levy glanced down at the papers on his desk, then back up at her with an irritated, *are you still here?* look.

She turned and made good her escape.

Back out in the hallway, Meredith walked past Levy's secretary and the smug Vernor, oblivious to both of them. Levy was Jewish. It was odd that she had never even thought about his ancestry. He had always been just another petty martinet to her.

Once outside the headquarters building, Meredith tried to dismiss her dislike of Levy for the moment and focus on the homicide and the hate literature. How to proceed? She would have to discuss the assignment of manpower with Underhill. Underhill—there was another problem.

She was so engrossed in those thoughts that Gorman was at her side before Meredith noticed the Sergeant.

"Ma'am, Mr. Underhill said to fetch you," Gorman said. "We have something that requires your attention."

"The homicide?" she asked. "Any developments?" Meredith felt a surge of hope.

"A whole new thing," Gorman replied. "Mr. Underhill called it big trouble."

"Big trouble . . ." Meredith mused. "I can't wait to see what Mr. Underhill calls *big* trouble." She followed quickly to Gorman's car.

"Mrs. K. tried to beep you," Gorman said once they were inside and moving.

"Darn." Meredith opened her briefcase and took out the beeper and turned it on. "I hate these things."

She also dug out her mobile phone.

"What's Mrs. Kappadonna's number?" she asked.

"Seven-two-two-eight," Gorman answered. They were on such a small base that every phone number was a four-digit reference because the prefix was the same for everyone. "But you can use the radio." Gorman indicated the police-band unit hanging below the dash. Meredith had to remember to also get a radio unit put in her Shelby. So many little things to do, but she was going to be occupied, and rightly so, with a lot more important concerns. Like a homicide, a hate crime, and whatever Underhill called "big trouble."

Meredith dialed the number on her phone. There were some things she didn't want everyone within range of a radio to overhear.

Mrs. Kappadonna answered after one ring.

"Community Safety Office."

"Mrs. Kappadonna, this is Colonel Cleon. Could you set up a new appointment for me with the DRM and slide in an abject apology for my walking out on him? An emergency came up, et cetera, et cetera . . ."

"You walked out on Otto?" The tone of disbelief was evident in Mrs. Kappadonna's voice even over the mobile phone.

"Yes, I walked out on him, sort of," Meredith admitted grudgingly.

"He's gonna have a cow."

"The cow's been had. See what you can do to smooth his fur. Make the appointment at his convenience. And as soon as possible."

Mrs. Kappadonna agreed to do her best, and Meredith thanked her and hung up, thinking about how she might patch things up with the man who controlled her unit's purse strings.

"Colonel?" Gorman interrupted her thoughts. "A bit of personal business, if I may?"

Their route took them around the large parade field, where a platform was being built and an honor guard was rehearsing.

"You may."

"I'm thinking of going for Warrant Officer School. CID," Gorman ventured. "You always said if you're going to be a bear, be a grizzly. What do you think, ma'am?"

"If you want it, go for it, Sergeant," Meredith encouraged her. "And if there's anything I can do to help, you let me know."

And Meredith meant it. If it hadn't been for the encouragement of a few of her officers, male and female, General Schwaner primary among them, she would never have gotten past Levy and others of his ilk to the rank she held today.

Gorman cruised across the post, past what looked like a high-tech prison complex. Big block buildings with very few windows, a double fence topped with razor wire and video cameras.

"Chemical Warfare Training," Gorman explained for Meredith's benefit. "They pretty much take care of their own security. We just patrol the perimeter."

They passed the Motor Pool, or as it was newly titled by the Army, the Consolidated Equipment Pool. There were very few vehicles within the fenced compound. Meredith tried to imagine it when it would have been packed with Hummers, Dodge 1008s, HMMETs, and five-ton trucks—the post at one time a busy anthill of people going about their various missions. She loved the vitality of a post like that.

Gorman drove for miles past old barracks, physical training grounds, parade fields, and administrative buildings, all empty and abandoned. There was a certain peaceful quality about it all, a stillness that made Meredith want to start the day over from her arrival, when Fort Hazelton's only threat was boredom and professional stagnation. Now it seemed a dangerous place for a wholly different reason: She had an investigation that could drive a stake through the heart of her career, and Levy poised with a mallet.

They finally arrived at an old warehouse area. Long structures with loading bays every few meters, most also abandoned.

At the end of the row of buildings, across the rusting railroad tracks, there was a cluster of military vehicles gathered around a flatbed truck. A crane towered over the scene like an iron praying mantis, and a line of Conex containers, eight-foot square metal shipping containers, lined the road next to the flatbed truck.

One Conex container was perched on top of the truck's long double trailer. Underhill was standing alongside the truck cab.

Gorman parked. Meredith climbed out and walked over to Underhill.

"What's that Chinese curse, Colonel?" he began. "May you live in interesting times? Any Chinese mad at you, ma'am?"

Meredith smiled, appreciating the joke, but got down to business. "Show me, Mr. Underhill."

He led her around to the other side of the truck.

"They were outloading matériel for shipment to Fort Knox, excess equipment left over from downsizing and closure of various units. The crane operator had a mishap."

A Conex container had burst open like a dropped milk carton. The metal seam had split and spilled the contents of the container across the ground.

Sandbags. Sandbags were a quick and cheap construction material used on military bases all over the world. Retaining walls, bunkers, foxholes—sandbags held down tin roofs in windy locales, reinforced eroding terrain, propped up buildings, and were put to a thousand other uses that only the ingenious GI could think up. Sandbags were everywhere. Every day, every hour, on some military post somewhere on the planet some poor soldier was filling a sandbag.

But no Army ever shipped filled sandbags from post to post. Empty bags, yes, but there was plenty of fill dirt anywhere they landed.

"What did the shipping manifest list, Mr. Underhill?"

"Typewriters, computers, and calculators."

Valuable items, high in demand, easily sold.

"Have you checked any of the other containers?" she asked.

"We're in the process of doing that right now, Colonel. So far two out of fourteen contain sandbags instead of their packing list cargo."

Now she asked the big question.

"Were there any weapons on those packing lists?"

Meredith had seen before what kind of pressure a weapons theft could put on a Provost Marshal and the Community Safety Office.

"Thankfully, no." The relief in Underhill's voice told Meredith that he, too, understood the implications.

"Well, then," Meredith began. "Let me proceed with my recommendations. And so we don't tick each other off, you can tell me where I'm out of line, you're already on it, or I'm totally off the mark."

That actually provoked a smile from Underhill.

"That's one way of doing it," he admitted.

"I assume that you will have the insides and outsides of these bogus containers fingerprinted and that all personnel who had anything to do with the invoicing, loading, and sealing of these containers will be fingerprinted and interrogated."

"You assume correctly, Colonel."

"Were the seals broken?"

"They were intact, ma'am. But it's not hard to counterfeit a new seal."

"Do you have any idea where we will find the manpower for this case, both of us being fully aware of our homicide priorities?"

"I'll grab some MP investigators to assume some of the workload. Officially this isn't proper procedure—this being a felony theft, as you know—but we don't have much choice. Unless higher-and-higher objects."

"I'll take care of that," she assured him. "This shipping process has been going on for how long?"

"Two years plus."

"And at the destination point are the containers opened, unloaded, and inventories checked?"

"I was told that they go right into storage awaiting disposal, ma'am."

"Do you see where I'm going here, Mr. Underhill?"

Underhill nodded. "I'll have Knox check the previously shipped containers on their end. I'll notify the Knox PM and CSO."

"Anything on the Carnes homicide?" Meredith shifted gears.

"We're working on a timeline, tracing her movements for the twenty-four hours before she was found. Meddac has the body. They put a priority on it. Her roommate has been taken to the station for interrogation. She's not a suspect—yet. Who knows?"

"I'd like to be there for some of that."

"I'll save you a seat." Underhill walked Meredith back to her car. "You know we will have to talk to General Ringstall. . . ."

"I'll arrange it. Put Levy's Aide, Vernor, on that list. What else is going on?"

Underhill looked peeved at her question or the order, she couldn't tell which. Meredith waited him out. He finally continued.

"We put an APB on Carnes's POV. It wasn't at her residence." He pulled a small scratch pad from his jacket pocket and checked his notes.

"A 'ninety-four Pontiac Sunbird, green metallic."

Meredith frowned for a moment. The description of Carnes's Personally Owned Vehicle sounded familiar. Then it hit her.

"I saw a 'ninety-four Sunbird in the lemon lot across from the Bowser Burger when I drove in today."

Today? Was it only this morning, a few short hours ago? That didn't seem possible to her.

Underhill didn't hide his surprise at her information. "Are you sure, ma'am?"

"I know cars," Meredith explained. "I'm from Michigan, it's in our DNA. For example, you drive a 1970 El Camino SS, big block with all the bells and whistles. Restore it yourself?"

"No, I bought her like that. I take care of my . . . The lemon lot, huh?"

Underhill left her and walked over to his El Camino, grabbed the radio mike. Meredith looked for Gorman.

Gorman was waiting nearby and telling war stories to three other soldiers and another MP.

" . . . we got three hundred kids in school buses, children of American residents, in convoy heading to the airport for evacuation. Noriega's police, thugs more like it, they stop us. Barricade. Three hundred kids. Six MPs against thirty, maybe forty, Panamanians with full-automatic weapons. The Colonel—she's a Major then—she goes face-to-face with these thugs, gets on the horn, and all of a sudden we got three MP platoons in by Blackhawk.

"I remember what the General said when he gave her the medal. 'Nicely defused. Nicely defused.' I thought we were gonna die. Us *and* the kids."

Meredith got into Gorman's car, slamming the passenger door with more force and noise than necessary, getting the Sergeant's attention without having to embarrass both of them.

Sergeant Gorman took the cue and returned to the car just as Underhill walked back to Meredith.

"The license plate checks," he told Meredith. "Want to go over there with us?"

"Glad to," Meredith replied, and turned to Gorman. "The lemon lot, Sergeant."

"On our way, ma'am." Gorman started the car and took off.

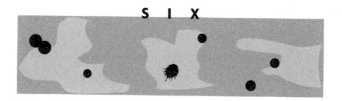

S I X

Some military careers take on the trajectory of a ground-to-air missile, a nice steady climb to a certain apex that finally hits the target—General for officers, Sergeant Major for enlisted personnel.

Meredith's trajectory had been more like a stone skipped across a pond, rising and falling with the whims of her assignment and superiors—and the result of her own personality.

She had entered the Army after Vietnam, just when it was opening up to women and moving toward an all-volunteer, all-professional organization. But just because the politics of the day and latecoming common sense dictated that the Army become a true democratic, equal-opportunity employer didn't mean that it didn't still have the legacy of an all-male tradition. Veteran hard-liners and the well-entrenched sexism of the country made the path a particularly tough one for every woman who was willing to charge ahead. Meredith had hit every barrier they could provide, more than once, and still encountered them and accepted them as part of the life she had chosen.

Meredith had been willing to fight every battle—and won more than she lost. Verbal abuse, physical harassment and intimidation, sexual advances large and small. At Fort Hood, home of the First Cavalry, die-hard old tank drivers who still thought of themselves as horse soldiers refused to let her wear the pants authorized for her dress uniform, insisting she wear the skirt. She had been gigged at Fort Bragg for her lipstick being too red, too much dangle in her earrings.

Once she had been forced to repeat her PT test because the testing officer refused to believe a woman had beaten most of his men in push-ups and running.

She had endured it all with little protest, knowing she had to be better than any man. Sometimes the abrasive side of her personality got out of control and she was constantly pulling herself back, repeating over and over the phrase a kind female major had whispered in her ear one day: "Do you want to make promotion or make a statement?"

Meredith fought every battle, every skirmish, every confrontation to win, sometimes to her detriment. The only problem she never could overcome was a mediocre assignment.

Part of the difficulty came with her specialty, Military Police. All the fast tracks—combat arms specialties, Infantry, Armored, and so on—were unavailable for women since they were forbidden by Congress to be put in harm's way. The only fast track for women had traditionally been the Nursing Corps. Career-wise one could lose their shirt working in the MPs, and especially as Provost Marshal, because your senior officer, the Garrison Commander or Commanding General, was evaluating your performance against that of combat arms officers. Your box check, the little notation on your Army report card, could suffer. More often than not, the evaluating officer would round out your profile with a 2 block because some battalion officers needed a 1 to move on.

The combat officers had more opportunity to prove themselves with combat training exercises providing a more spectacular platform, with the occasional real conflict supplying even better advancement opportunities.

So Meredith had struggled with stagnating assignments outside her specialty, Ordnance Quartermaster Company Executive Officer, Personnel Resource Manager, even clerical positions in which it was impossible to make her mark. But then every once in a while she would get that assignment that made her able to demonstrate her true worth: Fort Bragg, North Carolina, also known as FayetteNam for its neighboring town and its mean reputation; Somalia; and her performance with the Rapid Deployment Force in Panama had been highlights, in addition to her recent short tour in Afghanistan.

Each time she felt like she was treading water, Meredith had found something to test her and she had been able to prove her worth as a soldier and an officer.

And now it had happened again. When she had received the call about her father, Meredith had been stewing in her own juices at Fort Sill, Oklahoma, languishing at a desk in the Doctrine and Training Developments Division.

She thought nothing else could be so paralyzingly dull. So when Schwaner phoned her in Michigan and asked her to come to Fort Hazelton as a favor to him, though she had doubts about the assignment's benefit to her career, the thought of returning to her little rubber-stamp factory was even more dreadful. And she owed the old man.

Fort Hazelton on paper didn't look like it would provide any kind of promotion springboard. Meredith had already put in her time as Provost Marshal on much larger and more visible facilities. For her it seemed like another place to tread water, despite Schwaner's promise that she wouldn't be neglected.

Now her whole world had changed. She had not one big case, but two, and a chance to prove herself worthy of the next advancement. Of course, if she made one mistake procedurally or politically, especially with Levy watching, Meredith could easily crash and burn after twenty years.

It was what she loved, what she lived for, and right now in her life, just what she needed. The death of her father had, she admitted to herself only, shaken her up and she still hadn't resolved everything that had been brought back up during the last three weeks of her life. And she didn't want to. She wanted to push it all back in a corner of her mind, a dark corner, and deal with it some other time. She was looking for something to occupy her time and her thoughts.

Now she had it—in spades.

Two cases to concentrate on. Two potentially very treacherous cases. The Carnes murder and the transport theft.

The first question was, Were the two cases linked? Two extraordinary crimes being discovered on the same day was beyond coincidence, way beyond. Connections had to be sought, connections difficult for Meredith to make with only one day on-post. She would have to lean on her people and her own investigative experience.

Despite the tragic circumstances of the Carnes murder, Meredith felt a small thrill grow in her chest.

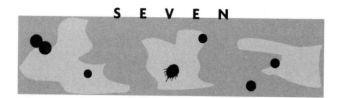

SEVEN

Every post set aside a small parking area where anyone trying to sell their POV could put it on display. It was called the lemon lot for a reason. Most of the cars were towed to the lot and, in the unlikely event they were purchased, towed away by the new owner. To Meredith the lemon lot was just a step above putting the junk heap up on blocks in the yard.

The green Sunbird was the only car without a For Sale sign or price in the window.

When Sergeant Gorman and Meredith pulled into the lot and parked next to a powerboat that someone was willing to let go for "Best Offer," Underhill was waiting. The MP who had been dispatched to check the license plate was laying out crime-scene tape using an industrial stapler to pin it to the tarmac. Great idea.

Meredith made note of it and his name, Meiers, wondering if it was his idea.

Meredith and Underhill walked over to the Sunbird together.

"Good eye, Colonel," Underhill complimented.

Meredith looked through the windows of the Sunbird at the interior, shading her eyes and being careful not to press her nose or hand against the glass. "Like I said—cars. My father worked at Ford for thirty-four years," Meredith told him. "Looks like her purse is on the front seat."

"I'll get Tate and a forensics kit out here." Underhill went back to his car to use the radio.

"I've never run out of fingerprint dust in one day before," Tate later told Meredith, somewhat embarrassed. "After the homicide scene, the matériel theft, and now the car . . ."

His young face looked surprised, as if someone had told him the Easter Bunny was a myth invented by a greeting card company.

"We'll get you another forensics kit," Meredith assured him. She called Gorman over and asked her to call into headquarters and send someone out with a kit from the Investigations Section. She watched as one of Tate's people scraped dirt samples from the tire tread of Carnes's car.

"How about we look at the contents of her purse, Mr. Tate?"

"Yes, ma'am." Tate was glad to have something else to do while they waited. He seemed stressed and nervous, and Meredith couldn't know if it was his usual state or just the pressure of today's events.

He collected the purse from the front seat, making sure that one of his fellow CID agents, a woman named Tolstakov, had photographed it in place first. Donning a fresh pair of latex gloves, Tate dumped the contents of the purse onto the trunk of the Pontiac.

They had searched the trunk earlier. The car had been unlocked, the keys in plain sight on the floorboards. The trunk contained a sweat suit, running shoes, a tennis racket, some muddy BDUs, and a multitude of dirty socks. All they could tell so far was that Lieutenant Carnes hadn't liked washing socks.

The purse contents didn't reveal much more helpful information. Keys, breath mints, lipstick, tissues, loose change, three Chap Sticks, two hair clips, and an elastic ponytail tie. The usual miscellaneous junk a woman thinks she might need and other stuff she doesn't know what else to do with.

"What's that?" Meredith pointed carefully to a small piece of stiff paper. Using outsized plastic tweezers he pulled from his jacket pocket, Tate picked it up and examined the square of manila cardboard. One side was ragged where it had been torn along the perforation.

"Looks like a pawn ticket," Tate said. "Mack's Loan Shop."

He held it up for her to examine.

"It's dated yesterday." She read the scribbled information in the blanks. Besides the date, the only data were Carnes's scribbled name and a ticket number. "See what she pawned."

"Yes, ma'am." Tate put the stub in a plastic envelope and wrote the information down in his notebook, then looked up at her. He checked to see if anyone else was within earshot. There wasn't.

"Colonel," Tate began. "I'd like you to know . . . I'm a little out of my depth here. The matériel theft I, maybe, can handle . . . but this homicide . . . It's my first and . . ."

Meredith noticed Underhill approaching them. Tate didn't see the CSO.

"You might be overworked, Mr. Tate," Meredith told him. "And that won't get any better—in fact, it might get worse—but I've been watching you. You're thorough and efficient. That's all you need to be a good investigator. We're just picking up bread crumbs in the forest right now. We get enough of them and we'll find the path that gets us out of the woods. You keep on doing the fine job you're doing. Collect all the bread crumbs. We'll find the path together."

Tate nodded and smiled, and began to inventory the purse contents. Meredith's "attaboy" seemed to have the desired effect, and he appeared to pull himself together.

Meredith walked away. Underhill intercepted her.

"Cars aren't all you know, huh, Colonel."

Mcredith continued on without comment, allowing herself a smile only when she was out of Underhill's sight. She had won a point there, maybe two.

While Tate continued his forensics work, Meredith borrowed a legal tablet from Sergeant Gorman and began her preliminary notes for her report to Levy. Ten minutes of investigation equals six hours of paperwork—that was an old equation once taught Meredith by a gray-haired CID investigator. Like any bureaucracy, the Army's first line of defense and offense was a bulwark of paper so high and so wide no enemy dared go against it. Unfortunately, cover-your-ass, C-Y-A, was every soldier's first and foremost command, and many fell victim to putting reports above their mission and often their people, too.

Luckily or not, for Meredith paperwork was an anathema, and she put it at the bottom of her list of priorities.

Underhill walked over to her, waited for her to look up from her writing.

"We've canvassed the area. It looks like Carnes's vehicle appeared during the night. It wasn't here last night when the batting cages closed—the cashier said he would have noticed. He has that Subaru for sale over there next to Carnes's Pontiac. He saw her car when he opened up this morning."

Meredith nodded, made a note, then looked back at him.

"Want to go check out Carnes's residence with me?" she asked.

"I prefer to leave the detective work to the investigators," he answered. Meredith wondered if that was a reprimand for her own investigative efforts or just a statement of personal preference.

"All right. I'll be in the office as soon as we get back from there," she told him.

"By the way, the Meddac confirmed the Carnes ID," he said. "The fingerprints match."

"Just covering all the bases."

"I don't mind that a bit," Underhill said as he walked to his car. "See you at the station."

Lieutenant Georgia Carnes had lived about three miles off the post in a small, high-end mobile-home court. There was a community center with a swimming pool, and the individual lots were large with well-kept lawns and those curving roads found in most housing developments, easy to get lost in. The address was made even more difficult to find because of the word "Hollow" attached to every street name. They took Ashe Hollow to Apple Hollow, made a left at New Hollow, a wrong turn on Deep Hollow, and finally found 4203 Sea Hollow.

Neither Gorman nor Meredith commented on the fact that the nearest sea was a thousand miles away.

The trailer was a double-wide with a carport large enough for two vehicles. The carport was empty. Gorman parked on one side. Tate, who had been following them closely, parked on the other. Another CID vehicle pulled in behind them.

The MP assigned to watch the residence was sitting on the front stoop, three preformed concrete steps with a thin railing. He put down his reading material, snapped to attention, and saluted her.

She returned the salute. "Anyone come or go?" she asked.

"No one, ma'am," he answered.

Meredith turned to Tate. "Did you call the roommate?"

"Yes, ma'am. She gave us the okay, said she didn't need to be here."

Just a formality, but a necessary one.

"Let's do it," she ordered.

Tate took out the keys he had retained from Carnes's purse and, after his third key selection, opened the door. He stepped aside, and Meredith led them in.

It was always an odd feeling entering another person's home when they weren't there, especially if you knew they weren't ever coming back.

Meredith heard a dog barking.

"Her roommate said Carnes's bedroom was on the left," Tate said.

The trailer was a lot bigger inside than it looked—a living room, kitchen, and dining room furnished cheaply but nicely laid out.

"A double-wide. I used to live in one of these," Tate offered.

"Take your people and search the whole place, top to bottom," Meredith ordered.

"Her roommate's things, too?"

"Top to bottom," she reiterated.

Tate went back outside and called his people and they went to work.

"Be neat about it, Mr. Tate," she added. "Put everything back nice and tidy."

"Always, ma'am."

As the investigators went about their work, Meredith walked

through the trailer trying to get an impression of the woman who had lived there.

The living room, being neutral territory for the roommates, bore no one's individual stamp. A *TV Guide, People, National Geographic, Vogue,* and several issues of *Outside* were on the coffee table. Someone was a hiker or fresh-air enthusiast.

The answering machine in Carnes's bedroom had two messages from a woman named Kate, one asking where she was, the next chiding her to call with a good excuse. Three more messages were from Ringstall's secretary, advising Carnes that the General was looking for her. Meredith recognized the voice.

"Look for a Kate in her address book," Meredith instructed Tate. "And take the tape for evidence."

The address book was next to a large brass bed on a nightstand. The bedroom was dominated by the bed, neatly made with what looked like an antique quilt. The clothes in the closet all appeared to be a woman's; there was no discernible trace of a man's presence in the bathroom. One of Tate's people was swabbing the tub drain for loose hairs and putting them in an envelope. The sink would be given the same treatment; the hairs would be checked to match Carnes's head and pubes, those that didn't match held separately.

Meredith herself pulled the bedcovers back, looking for hairs or stains.

"Take the sheets and pillowcases," she told the MP. "Bag 'em."

Who knows. So far there were no signs of a man's presence, but that didn't mean anything. There was a vibrator in the nightstand, two condoms, and a copy of *Reader's Digest.*

There was a bookshelf holding mostly fantasy books—dragons and knights and magical maiden genre—and a stack of CDs. A lot of Nina Simone, a favorite of Meredith's, too.

On the dresser were several framed photographs. An old black-

and-white of a man and a woman dressed formally, perhaps the wedding of Carnes's parents. The rest were of Carnes herself, Meredith supposed. A twentyish woman with her dog, with some friends, some children—perhaps nieces and nephews. She was a dark-eyed woman with a big white smile, a lot of teeth. Meredith had to pull herself away. She hated this.

The bedroom was getting crowded with the investigators sorting through the woman's possessions, and that was excuse enough for Meredith to leave and check out the roommate's bedroom.

The layout was identical to that of Carnes's room, but the decorating wasn't. Paintings and photographs of horses dominated the walls. Carnes had favored Maxfield Parrish prints. The roommate's bed sloshed with a water-filled mattress that was surprisingly warm to the touch, and the books were bodice-rippers with a few antique-looking Nancy Drews. Another, smaller TV—Carnes had none in her bedroom—and a VCR with a few tapes. *Snow White, Aladdin,* and one of those Tim Conway "Dorf on Golf" videos. Meredith hoped it had been a gag gift.

Meredith was learning nothing helpful. She walked back through the trailer and into the kitchen. Nothing remarkable. Someone had a predilection for sugared cereal, a dozen different brands. There was also a collection of salsas and hot sauces. No chips. Meredith mused about sugared-cereal people and salsa people and wondered if you could tell anything about them based on that preference.

The inside of the refrigerator looked strange. Everything— yogurt, low-fat milk, condiments, sodas, fruit juices, margarine, and vegetables—was duplicated, and the two sets of food divided by six inches of clear space. Yours and mine. Nothing extraordinary, just odd. Somebody filched somebody else's frozen Snickers and now the combatants had been separated.

A big dog—Meredith didn't know much about breeds but it looked like some kind of retriever to her—was jumping around the backyard, aware of the presence of people in the trailer. It had been barking excitedly since they arrived, and Meredith had found it irritating until now.

Now it just seemed sad.

She left orders for someone to feed the poor animal after they finished their search.

On the way back to the post Meredith was silent, and Gorman didn't disturb her.

The photographs of Carnes had made inroads into her objectivity. Georgia Carnes was now a person, and who had killed her was preeminent in Meredith's mind.

The who and why of murder. Meredith didn't come across that many homicide cases, but when she did they tended to haunt her for years. Killing in the line of duty she understood. She had done it, pulled the trigger herself, but murder—premeditated, calculated murder—was hard for her to understand.

When she had been stationed in Washington, D.C., at the Pentagon, she attended one of those cocktail parties that seem to crop up on a nightly basis in the capital. Meredith was decked out in her dress blues, when a pretty young socialite in a form-fitting Armani evening dress, as if it were *her* uniform, sidled up to Meredith and looked at the row of ribbons above her left pocket.

"What is that one for?" she asked, indicating one ribbon, then another, repeatedly until it became irritating.

When she pointed to the Silver Star, Meredith answered, "I got that for killing someone." The abrupt response was meant to shut the woman up.

Meredith as a young first lieutenant had been assigned to one of the major roadblocks in Grenada in '83. It was her first combat assignment, and though it wasn't a full-blown war, there was gunfire, and enough Purple Hearts were being handed out to keep you on your toes.

It was early in the morning when Meredith was checking the guard mount, going from station to station making sure her people were not only awake but alert. She had reached a roadblock and was making her presence felt to the sleepy MPs when a car approached, a baby-blue '54 Ford with rusted-out rocker panels, more rust around the headlight mounts, the shine of the finish oxidized by the sun to a powdery softness.

The Ford approached the fifty-five-gallon-drum barrier erected by the Americans. At about two hundred meters from the roadblock the driver stepped on the gas and accelerated instead of slowing. It took Meredith a moment to realize what was happening. She shouted to her people to take cover. They did, but Meredith, for whatever reason, stood stock-still and raised her M-16. "No one passes" was her order. This guy wasn't getting through.

She heard the big eight-cylinder roaring under the Ford hood. There was no muffler, and the noise was deafening as the car catapulted toward her.

She put the sights of her M-16 on the figure behind the wheel. He was backlit and it was hard to discern his features, but she had a clear silhouette.

Then Meredith lowered the weapon and tried to shoot out the tires. She had never shot anyone before. She didn't want to kill another human being. She shot out a front tire of the Ford.

The driver's-side tire blew with a very satisfying *pop* and the vehicle went into a skid, sparks flying as the wheel hub scraped pavement. The car hurtled through the fifty-five-gallon-drum barrier.

And hit Meredith.

She was knocked backward onto the ground and lost her grip on the M-16.

The Ford stopped. The driver jumped out with a shotgun, a double-barrel, his eyes wide with rage or drugs or both, screaming at the top of his lungs. He aimed the shotgun at one of Meredith's people and fired. The man, Private First Class Lockte, whose wife was recently pregnant, ducked.

Meredith rose to her knees behind the shooter. She was sworn to protect her people above all, and to fulfill her mission. She had just failed in both.

She emptied an entire clip of her nine-millimeter at the man's back. She didn't remember pulling it out of her holster or flicking off the safety, she just fired. One bullet hit him in the chest, probably by accident more than the accuracy of her aim. The man did a slow twist, propelled by the bullet striking him, or to see who the hell was shooting him—Meredith couldn't know. But he made eye contact with her, his expression puzzled, and Meredith saw the life in him drain away just before his knees gave out and he fell to the ground.

"You killed someone?" the Armani-clad young socialite repeated.

Meredith used to joke when she was stationed in D.C. that socialite should be spelled "social-light."

"I could never do that." And the other woman walked haughtily away, showing a visible panty line beneath the dress.

"I could never do that." Meredith had heard the words before and since, so she didn't bring up the topic or the incident anymore.

Anybody could kill. It was just a matter of circumstances. Self-defense, protecting someone else, stopping a madman. And from her own personal experience in law enforcement there was a list of other reasons—lust, greed, fear, and some so trivial as to be astonishing.

She once had to take into custody a thirty-seven-year-old Master Sergeant, the recipient of five Purple Hearts and a veteran of two tours in Vietnam, who got angry enough at two fifteen-year-olds who were tossing Junior Mints at the audience in a movie theater that he yanked out a Browning semiautomatic and pumped four rounds into the two boys, killing one and crippling the other.

Of course, what a grown man was doing walking around armed was a whole other story. Behind every murder, especially the seemingly trivial ones, there was a deeper history. The Master Sergeant had gotten addicted to PCP to ease the pain of the loss of his children in a boating accident. It was no excuse for his actions, but it was the reason.

That's what Meredith had to find.

The reason.

Not just the reason someone thought Georgia Carnes had to die, but why she should be killed in such a grotesque manner. If she was still alive when the fifty-caliber bullets hit her, someone had wanted her to die painfully. Someone had hated her. Hated her enough that a simple bullet in the head wouldn't have been sufficient.

Meredith remembered the face in the photographs.

She was going to catch her killer. She was going to find out why they killed Georgia Carnes and put them away.

That was Meredith's job, her mission.

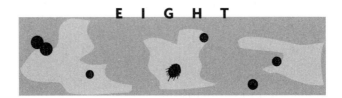

E I G H T

When Meredith returned to the MP station, there were two television news vans and a station wagon, with radio station call letters and "All News—All Day" painted on the door, parked in the lot. The news crews were waiting on the steps. They ignored Meredith as she walked toward the building until one of them noticed the crossed pistols on her uniform and recognized them as the Military Police insignia and began spitting questions. But it was too late—Meredith was already up the steps and through the doors.

Upstairs Mrs. Kappadonna informed Meredith that Mr. Under-hill and Mr. Tate were downstairs in the interrogation room with Carnes's roommate. Meredith made a call to the PIO, the Public Information Officer, and briefed him—with the emphasis on the word "brief"—then told him to clear the reporters from the MP station steps. The PIO, Mr. Stine, said he would prepare a release, coordinating with headquarters in D.C. and with Meredith, and asked if she would allow the reporters to use the MP Station parking lot. Meredith would have liked to ban the reporters from the post—pests is all they were to her, dangerous pests sometimes—but she knew the risk of bad publicity that action could entail.

She told Mr. Stine that they could use the parking lot and lit a fire under him for the press release to be prepared quickly. She hoped that would get the media out of her hair. The PIO thanked her for her cooperation and welcomed her to Fort Hazelton.

The interrogation room was in the basement of the MP station, a tiny little room with bare, pale-yellow cinder-block walls that had been painted so many times they were smooth and shiny.

Meredith and Underhill stood in front of the one-way window and watched Tate and Tolstakov talk with Warrant Officer Tocca, a rail-thin woman with huge, dark, almost black eyes. She had been waiting for hours, waiting for Tate to return from the matériel theft and then the lemon lot, so she was more than a little irritated despite Tate's best efforts to apologize. He had spent fifteen minutes so far trying to make amends, but to little avail.

"I didn't see much of her," Tocca was explaining as she eyed the tape recorder on the table in front of her. "Georgia was a General's Aide so, you know, she didn't have much free time. One of those 'high and tight,' you know what I mean?"

"High and tight" referred to the haircut worn by the Rangers. The sides and back of the hair were shaved down to the scalp, with a little saucer of hair a half-inch long sitting on top of the head. It was the preferred look of every gung-ho soldier. The males, at least.

"She didn't have the haircut," Tocca continued. "But she was all Army all the way, twenty-four-plus hours. Green robots. I'm not. I punch out—I'm out."

"Did she have any boyfriends?" Tate asked.

"Not that I know of. She didn't have time, like I said."

"Did she use drugs?"

"No. I don't think so." Tocca gave it a moment's thought. "She had a bottle of wine in the cupboard. Used to sip a glass when she had her period. She was afraid of drugs."

"Afraid? How?" Tate pressed.

Meredith turned to Underhill.

"He's good at this," she told him.

"He has potential," Underhill admitted.

"Only in that it might fuck up her career. That's all the girl thought about," Tocca explained. "Her career."

"Was she in financial trouble?" Tate asked. "She pawned a stereo system yesterday."

"She did that for some quick money. I don't think she was going to reclaim it. Her parents sent her a new stereo last Christmas. Yesterday the autotellers on-post were empty. The old stereo was still in the carport. . . ."

The interview went like that for a while. Warrant Officer Tocca didn't know anything about her roommate, didn't socialize with her—they hardly knew each other. Tate kept prodding and probing, but he couldn't drive a wedge into the woman's carefully laid wall of reticence.

But there was more, Meredith felt, so she knocked on the door and told Tate to let Tolstakov take over for a moment, thinking Tocca might open up to another woman. She explained her reasoning to Tate, and he agreed with her decision, at least verbally. Underhill was hard for her to read—as usual.

"So far," Meredith told Underhill and Tate as soon as Tate had joined them, "our Lieutenant Carnes has led an exemplary life. We need to dig deeper. No one lives an antiseptic life—no one."

She turned her attention back to the window. Tocca was becoming nervous, not relaxing into the interview as most people did eventually, even with Tolstakov's easy, low-key approach. The Warrant Officer was fidgety, pulling at a loose string on her blouse button until the button fell to the floor.

"I'm going to try something," Meredith told Underhill and Tate. She caught Underhill's momentarily unguarded look. He was not happy with her personal participation in the interrogation, what he may have considered her interference.

She went into the interview room anyway. Tocca looked at her, at the silver chevrons on Meredith's shoulder. Meredith told Tolstakov to take a break, sat down opposite Tocca and smiled, announced her presence to the tape recorder and gave the time. It was late, she suddenly realized, and Meredith had felt the impact of every second of the day.

But she willed herself to relax and offered Tocca a soda or coffee. Tocca declined and stiffened in her chair, preparing for the worst.

"Joan . . ." Meredith addressed Warrant Officer Tocca by her first name. "Did you notice that Mr. Tate didn't read you your Miranda Rights when he brought you in here? That is because you are not a suspect in this case. If you are a suspect, we have to read you your rights and you can ask for an attorney. At the moment we have a dead woman and we are trying to find out who killed her. You knew her, lived with her. We need your help. All right? Help me out here?" Meredith spoke so softly, Tocca had to lean across the table in order to hear her.

Meredith removed her jacket, getting the impressive ribbons and badges and rank out of sight.

"Now, how long were you two roomies?"

"Just over a year, fourteen or fifteen—no, sixteen—months." Tocca seemed to relax. She had answered this question before and

Meredith had heard her response already. "But I was looking for a new place, a place of my own," Tocca added.

"Why was that?"

Tocca shrugged noncommittally. "Different lifestyles."

"I know." Meredith smiled amiably. "She was a green robot, and you are . . ." She let the sentence dangle, waiting for Tocca to fill in the blank.

"Looser. Just looser." Tocca smiled back. "The Army is not the be-all and end-all of my life."

"What is?"

"I like the Army. It's a good job. But that's all it is—a job." Tocca shrugged. "I like to bicycle, hike, camp . . ."

"Why were you so mad at Georgia?" Meredith said it to provoke Tocca. The other woman was taken aback.

"I'm not mad at her . . . wasn't. We were . . ."

"What?"

"Nothing."

"Nothing, Joan?" Meredith stood up. "She was just killed. Brutally murdered. You probably heard how it happened. You have no feelings of sorrow? No remorse? No condolences for her family? Did you know her family?"

"I . . . I . . . met 'em once. They visited her. Nice folks."

Tocca's voice sounded choked and strained.

Meredith was silent. Most people hated silence and sooner or later tried to fill it in. It was a trick senior officers had used repeatedly on Meredith over the years.

Tocca fell into the trap.

"She was a good person, Georgia, helped me out when I was having trouble with my CO. I had a dog, too, a cocker spaniel—he had leukemia. He died and . . . Georgia . . . We used to watch old movies together. *Bambi* and shit . . ." Tears were starting to fall.

"So what were the problems?" Meredith asked.

"I wasn't mad at her." Tocca wiped her nose. "She was mad at me. Well, maybe I was a bit. . . ."

"Why?"

"Okay, okay, I don't care anymore, okay? This bullshit policy—" Tocca stopped herself.

Tocca was on the brink—Meredith knew it.

"What did you do to her?"

"I didn't do anything!" Tocca slammed a hand onto the table so hard the tape recorder jumped.

"What did she do?" Meredith kept her voice soft, even, non-judgmental.

"She . . . she . . . she didn't *do* anything. It was her attitude."

Tocca looked up, wanting Meredith to understand, willing her to understand.

"I never touched her. Never wanted to. She wasn't my type."

Meredith found herself holding her breath.

"I'm gay." Tocca said it flatly. "I think Georgia always knew—suspected it, at least. I never hid it. Didn't rub her face in it—I have to be . . . discreet, you know. 'Don't ask, don't tell.' What a bullshit policy." Tocca spit out the curse, calmed down.

"Georgia walked in on me and my girlfriend on the sofa . . . draw your own picture. She was supposed to be working late. She freaked out. Complete homophobic shit-storm. They say the ones who react like that have some latent . . . I don't know, maybe she was worried about her own self, her precious career, people might think she was queer. Like I said, she had a shit-fit. I threw one back. We weren't talking. It got petty. She . . . some of it was mine. I . . . liked her. It hurt, I guess. . . ." Tocca was getting teary-eyed again.

"Where were you from last night until this morning?"

Tocca looked at her, realizing the implications of the question.

"I'll say it again." Meredith smiled gently. "You are not a suspect." *Not yet,* Meredith amended to herself.

"I was at my girlfriend's house." Tocca had a hard look in her eye. "Fuck, I knew this was going to happen. Look, she's in a delicate situation. She works for the city, we *are* living in the Bible Belt, and she has a couple of kids. Her ex-husband is always giving her grief about custody. If he finds out she's gay, in this state . . ."

How long did Tocca think they could keep it a secret? Meredith thought, but she didn't voice the question. "We will be discreet," Meredith promised. "If you're telling the truth."

"I am." Tocca was calm now, as if the confession had freed her. Meredith had seen it happen time and time again.

"Do you know of anyone who might have wanted to kill Georgia?" Meredith asked.

"No." Tocca shook her head for emphasis. "She didn't have any enemies. She went out of her way to not make any enemies. Career enhancement, she called it. That's all she talked about, her career. She wanted to be a general."

Meredith asked a few more routine questions and Tocca answered them, even volunteered additional information. It was time to give the interview back to Tate, so she excused herself and left the room.

Facing Underhill, Tate, and Tolstakov, she asked, "Any thoughts?"

"Maybe she killed Carnes to hide her sexual proclivities."

"What a polite turn of phrase, Mr. Tate." Meredith smiled at him. "But, no . . . I don't think so. She doesn't care about her military career that much, and she gave up the information too easily."

"Her girlfriend might want to hide their relationship. If Carnes saw them . . ." Tolstakov ventured. "A woman would do a lot to keep her kids. Maybe Carnes was blackmailing the woman?"

"I doubt the prospect of blackmail. I don't know why . . . but we do need to talk to this woman. Get her name and talk to her before Tocca can warn her. Check out the alibi."

Tate nodded.

"Discreetly," Meredith added. "As we promised."

"Yes, ma'am," Tate answered with a serious look. "Do you want to be there?"

"Not unless you think you need me," Meredith told him. "Bring her in if she gives you any trouble, but otherwise try to keep it low-key. Not at her work.

"One other thing." Meredith took on a little more command presence to give weight to her words. "No hint of Tocca's 'proclivity' is to leave this investigation. Is that understood?" She looked at Tate.

"Yes, ma'am."

Tolstakov came under inspection. "Yes, ma'am. Not a word."

Meredith didn't look at Underhill, hoping the pass would serve as a compliment: *I trust you so much, I don't even have to ask you.*

"I have a report to write," she said, and walked away.

Underhill followed her, and on the stairs they almost ran into Lieutenant Vernor, being escorted by an MP.

Vernor smiled and nodded to Meredith. It was as noncommittal an expression as she had ever seen. She wondered if he practiced it in front of the mirror.

Meredith continued on up the stairs.

"Green robots." She wondered if that's what they called her. She heard Underhill's footsteps close behind her.

At the top of the stairs Meredith entered the squad room, held the door for Underhill, then turned and looked out the windows. It was dark outside.

"Darn," she exclaimed. "It's night already."

Mrs. Kappadonna came out of Meredith's office.

"Colonel, your appointment with Mr. Wojahn is on your desk.

General Levy called to tell you that he's waiting for your report. Do you want me to wait around to type it?"

"No," Meredith said. "I can type it myself. Thanks anyway. You go on home."

Meredith went into her office. On her formerly bare desk was a sandwich, a Styrofoam container of what looked like soup, a can of soda, a paper napkin, and a plastic spoon. Meredith was touched and grateful.

She went back to the reception area, where Mrs. Kappadonna was locking her files and desk.

"Are you responsible for the meal on my desk, Mrs. Kappadonna?" Meredith asked.

"Annika," the other woman suggested. "You've been gallivanting around so much I figured you missed lunch, and dinner didn't seem likely, so . . . You owe petty cash. 'Night."

"Good night, Annika."

Mrs. Kappadonna took her purse and left. Meredith went back to her office, popped the tab on the soda, took a bite of the sandwich, and turned to the computer keyboard.

It took Meredith almost two hours to write the report, what with occasional calls to Tate for his input, figuring out how to get the computer to print out, then reloading the printer with paper when it ran out.

While Meredith was working on her report, a copy of the PIO's press release was delivered to her. She read through it, making notes on her copy, and sent it back via the MP who had brought it over. He was the soldier she had seen earlier that day talking to the pretty civilian woman. Meredith asked him what had been going on during that incident.

He told her he had been lecturing the woman for cruising through a stop sign. Meredith asked if he had written her up.

"Couldn't, ma'am," he replied. "I have orders for Germany— leave in less than thirty days. I'm too short to be able to show up in court."

That was true. It usually took more than a month for a driving citation to get onto a judge's docket, and if the arresting officer couldn't be there to testify, the judge found for the defendant. The official policy was for anyone with "short time" to refrain from writing tickets.

Meredith, on another post, would have yanked the man from traffic duty, but Underhill and Kahla were probably shorthanded and had no choice. She let the young MP go and wished him well on his new assignment, then went back to her paperwork.

She finally finished and hand-carried the report over to headquarters herself. The press were gone; no one was waiting in the parking lot—the hour was past their broadcast window. Headquarters seemed empty of people. She could hear the energetic hum of a vacuum cleaner somewhere in the building, but she didn't see the appliance or the operator.

Lieutenant Vernor was back at his desk, the only other person she had seen in the building. Vernor looked up from working at his own computer.

"Tell the General I have his report." Meredith stood in front of Vernor's desk.

"He's left for the day," Vernor told her. "I'll put it in his in box. He'll see it first thing in the morning."

Vernor reached out a hand for the report. Meredith gave it to him without comment. She knew she had reason to be steamed, but she was too tired to say anything about it.

"We're all terribly upset about Lieutenant Carnes, ma'am," Vernor said. "I hope the investigation is proceeding well. I hope I was of some help."

Vernor spoke with all the emotion of a voicemail recording. Meredith looked down at him.

"Lieutenant, do you know the name of the robot on that TV show *Lost in Space?*"

Before he could answer, she turned and left. The last she saw, Vernor was actually thinking about the answer.

Meredith's car was still in the visitor space where she had parked it seemingly so long ago. The seats were damp from the moist evening air. She should have put the top up, but . . .

She backed out and was shifting into first gear when Underhill pulled alongside in his El Camino.

"Nice wheels." Underhill looked her car over from stem to stern.

"My father left it to me." Meredith volunteered the information. She was about to add that it was just four days ago, but she started to choke up and decided she still wasn't ready to really talk about it.

"Quite a car," Underhill continued. "Tate pinned down the timeline on Carnes. She and two friends were going to watch *West Wing* at twenty-two hundred hours. She never missed an episode. Left her place at twenty-thirty for an 'important meeting.' Never made it to *West Wing.*"

"Good work," Meredith acknowledged. "That must have been the voice on the answering machine. Did he get anything useful out of Vernor?"

"It was like talking to . . ."

"A green robot," Meredith finished for him. "Well, Mr. Underhill, what else could happen in Mayberry? Opie get caught selling dope to the boys down at Floyd's Barbershop? Good night."

"Good night." He drove away.

Meredith took her foot off the brake and pulled out of the parking lot. A few meters away, she had to stop as a car edged out onto the same street. She saw Vernor behind the wheel. The type of car he was driving surprised Meredith—it was a silver Saleen Mustang.

The Saleen cruised through the beam of her headlights, and she got a good look at the car. She thought it might be an S281, but no, it was the distinctive front spoiler, side skirts, and rear wing of an S351. A hundred and seven miles an hour in a quarter mile, designed and built by Steve Saleen in Irvine, California.

Vernor may be a robot, but he had great taste in automobiles. She followed the Saleen's taillights all the way to the main gate, where he went one way and Meredith went the other.

N I N E

Meredith checked into a Holiday Inn a few meters from the freeway on-ramp. The desk clerk gave her a room on the ground floor. She parked near the room, unloaded her suitcases from the car, and carried them in and started to unpack one. This was going to be her home for at least a few days.

She started the tub running, dropped in a capful of bubble bath, and finished unpacking the first bag while the water frothed. All she wanted to do right now was soak until her bones melted, then go to bed and sleep until retirement.

As she unpacked her toilet articles and arranged them on the bathroom vanity, her thoughts drifted to the vanity in Georgia Carnes's bathroom.

There was so little personal evidence of the woman who had lived there. Why was that? It didn't look lived-in, but rather only temporarily occupied.

Meredith thought of her last residence at Fort Sill, Oklahoma. When she had phoned back to Oklahoma to arrange shipping her things to Fort Hazelton just after Schwaner's call to her, she was surprised to realize how small the shipment was—even with her furniture, it wasn't anywhere near a full truckload. She had conducted a mental walk through the condo while she had been on the phone with the movers. Twenty years and that was all she had to show for it. A few souvenirs from her foreign assignments, but otherwise there wasn't a lot there to tell anyone much about Meredith Cleon. She had spent so little time in her condo because she was always on the job, and had such little downtime for vacation or recreation. None of those activities that accrue the mementos that defined a personality.

Meredith was a "green robot."

Maybe she needed a hobby. She laughed to herself at that thought.

Meredith had undressed down to her underwear, tested the water, and found it was just scalding enough. She was about to get naked and parboil herself when her beeper went off.

She cursed, searched for her briefcase, found the beeper, and read the number. The number was unfamiliar, but it would be. She dialed.

It was the MP station.

"Colonel Cleon here. I was beeped."

"Yes, ma'am," said the voice on the other end of the line. "There's been an incident. We called Mr. Underhill, and he said to page you, keep you informed."

"An incident? Where?"

"I can give you the address—Two-Six-Four Feder Lane."

Meredith scribbled down the address hastily. "I have a map. I'll find it. I'm on my way." Meredith paused long enough to ask, "What kind of incident are we talking about?"

"Hate crime, ma'am."

Meredith hung up and turned the bathwater off, sighing as she did so. The froth of bubbles and the waves of heat rising from the tub were so inviting.

She dressed hurriedly, suddenly aware of just how tired she was. The mere idea of putting her arm back through the sleeve of her shirt seemed too much of an effort.

Not wanting to take the time to unpack further and seeing that her Class A uniform was wrinkled beyond wearing, she decided on the jeans and T-shirt she had worn on the drive. Jeans and a T-shirt actually looked better when they were wrinkled, she rationalized. Besides, after all, she was off duty.

It didn't take Meredith long to find the address, but when she pulled onto the street she regretted her choice of jeans and T-shirt and wished she had broken out a fresh pair of BDUs after all.

Feder Lane was in the Officers' Residence Area, tree-lined streets fronting massive, old brick houses spaced far enough apart to give each one a large, green yard. From the size of the houses Meredith figured she was amid the highest echelon of Army officers. Big white Tara-style front porches bracketed by white columns.

It wasn't hard to find number Two-Six-Four. It was the house with two MP vehicles and a civilian car parked out front. Meredith parked and walked over to where Sergeant Kahla was supervising an MP with a camera who was taking photographs of the house.

Meredith looked to see what he was focusing on.

"JUDE—KILL THE JEWS" spray-painted in white across the front of the house and a crude swastika scrawled upon the door, a black obscenity that violated the pristine white paint.

Kahla looked at her. "You didn't have to roll on this, ma'am."

"It's my job," Meredith replied. "Any witnesses?"

"Just the Colonel," Kahla said, and Meredith felt her skin go cold. That's how she tired she was—she hadn't put the obvious clues together at once.

Turning in the direction Kahla was pointing, she saw Levy standing in the picture window between the drapes and the glass. Swallowing a curse, she walked up to the front of the house.

Levy came out on the porch and met her. He was in his pajamas and a robe, both with some designer name over the left pocket. Meredith tried to recognize the logo, but she was never good at keeping up with the latest clothing trends.

Levy's face was livid with a rage he could barely contain. He looked at Meredith's jeans and T-shirt, and his mouth pressed together so tightly his lips disappeared.

"I want you to get the scum who did this!" His voice strained to keep from shouting. "I want them caught! Caught immediately and punished! To the fullest extent!"

"I'll do the catching, sir." Meredith kept her voice level and spoke quietly. "The punishment is up to the judge advocate. Did you see who did this?"

"No. The cowards." Levy's hands kept flexing into fists. "I just heard 'Heil Hitler' and the screeching of tires as they drove away. The cowards!"

"You didn't see the car, sir?"

"I just said I only *heard* them. I want this . . . this filth cleaned off before first light. Get someone on it." He threw a fist in the direction of the graffiti without looking at it, refusing to acknowledge it with anything but that angry fist.

Meredith paused, trying to restrain the first impulsive remarks that came to her mind. The MPs were watching her. It wasn't their job to clean the paint off the Colonel's house. They had enough to do—more than enough after the day's events.

"That's not our job, sir," she stated calmly. "You'll have to call Engineering and Housing."

Levy's whole body trembled with anger. Meredith braced herself—but the storm didn't break. Finally the Colonel took a deep breath.

"Yes, yes, of course." Levy suddenly just deflated. "I . . . I . . . just don't want my daughters to see this. I never expected . . ."

He was upset, as emotionally vulnerable as Meredith had ever seen him. All at once Meredith could see him as a human being, a man with children he was trying to protect.

"One of my people could call, sir, but it might be more effective if you called them yourself. Bring some fire on them, sir, you're good at that."

Meredith smiled as she spoke to him. He smiled back. It was the first time Meredith had ever seen him smile when he wasn't deliberately causing someone else distress.

"That I am." He nodded. "Remember that, Cleon. I have an important couple of days ahead of me, and I don't want them spoiled by obscenities like this. Keep me updated."

"Yes, sir." Meredith took that as her dismissal and walked slowly back to the MPs.

"Find any skid marks from the vehicle?" she asked Kahla.

"None." He gestured at the pavement. "There's some dew on the asphalt, so the tires may not have left any rubber."

Meredith walked a short distance, looking cursorily at the surface of the street for any sign of skid marks. It was too dark to see clearly; they'd have to check again at first light.

"Then they wouldn't have screeched. Skidded, yes, but the Colonel said they 'screeched.'"

"Maybe he misspoke or misheard. He has a lot on his mind with the ceremony coming up."

"Colonel Levy has never mis . . . Ceremony?" Meredith stood and looked questioningly at Kahla.

"His star. Levy's being promoted to General. In a couple of days." Kahla was preoccupied watching the MP taking casts of footprints in the flower bed in front of the house. He tossed the information in Meredith's direction and failed to see her reaction.

It hit Meredith like a two-by-four.

Levy. A General. She tried to find a way out of the daze that bit of information put her into, in her usual way, by focusing on the immediate situation.

"Be sure we get some samples of the paint," she told Kahla. "And send someone down the road to search for any discarded spray cans. We could get lucky."

"We should conduct a door-to-door, ma'am," Kahla said, letting the rest of the statement hang. This was not a neighborhood where waking the residents at one in the morning would be welcome. The MPs would be doing their job, but high-ranking officers had a myriad of ways to make their displeasure felt.

"Save it for the morning," Meredith told him, letting him off the hook.

Meredith headed back to her Shelby, calling over her shoulder. "Feel free to page me if anything else comes up."

She got into her car and looked back at the house. Levy was standing in the picture window again. Their eyes met for a second, then Levy ducked back around the drapes and was gone.

"General . . . ?" She muttered the word, still not believing it, then drove away.

Checking the map as she drove, she found that the northwest

gate, the Hallbruin Gate, was closer than the way she came in so she turned off the main street.

The post was quiet, very few cars, the houses lit and glowing warmly from inside. The barracks and administration buildings were mostly dark. "General . . ."

When Meredith arrived at Hallbruin Gate it was closed, a black-and-white-striped barrier arm across the road, padlocked and chained. There was a sign mounted on the barrier announcing that this entrance was closed after 7:00 P.M., or 1900 hours, and would reopen at 0500. It also advised the reader to use the main gate for all other hours.

The advice didn't make Meredith any happier as she made a U-turn and headed back through the post. All she wanted was her hot bath and some sleep. Deep, oblivious sleep.

"General Levy . . ."

Why did that upset her? Envy? She usually wasn't the envious type. Levy *was* due. He had put in his time. Was it anger? She didn't like the man, or the officer he was, that was sure. But other officers she disliked were promoted and she just shrugged it off. No, it was the kind of officer that Levy was that irritated her and made the promotion unpalatable. He was a bully, always putting his career above the welfare of his people, aggressively ambitious at the expense of everything else—even his mission or his underlings.

Meredith recognized some of those characteristics in herself, the ambition at least, but she had never tried to get ahead by stepping on or over the bodies of the people she was sworn to protect.

She was so involved in her analysis of the situation that she almost rear-ended a car that was stopped in the road.

She slammed on the brakes!

It was an MP vehicle, and the driver's door was open.

The MP was on foot, running across the field to Meredith's right in pursuit of a small, dark figure who was going pell-mell for the tree line.

Meredith jumped out of the Mustang and instinctively ran after the MP to see if they needed help.

Once she reached the trees it was pitch black, and if it hadn't been for the flickering of the MP's flashlight, Meredith wouldn't have found the pair at all.

The MP and the fleeing person had reached the perimeter fence, twelve feet of chain link that delineated the limits of the Fort Hazelton property.

The MP was Sergeant Gorman, and she was pulling a teenage girl off the fence. The two of them fell to the ground and struggled for a moment. It wasn't that Gorman couldn't handle the kid—Meredith had seen the stocky woman take on a two-hundred-pound, PCP-propelled male—but it was evident that the Sergeant didn't want to hurt the teenager.

Meredith waited while Gorman finally gave in and applied a wristlock. That did the trick.

"All right! All right!" the girl whined. "You don't have to Rodney King me!"

The girl went limp. Meredith retrieved Gorman's flashlight and helped both of them to their feet.

The girl was fourteen or fifteen—it was harder for Meredith to tell these days. Her hair was dyed black with a couple of blue streaks, and a nose ring glittered at one nostril like silver snot. Black lipstick and nail polish, applied over bitten nails and now chipped, and a scuffed, worn, oversized black motorcycle jacket completed the girl's uniform.

Kids. They thought they were rebelling against the status quo and just created a new one. Meredith remembered her hippie days. What was the uniform then? Oh, geez—Meredith blanched at the image. Elephant bells, tie-dyed . . . If each generation of "rebels" were truly honest with themselves, they would salute each other. Or maybe they already did, thinking of how often teenagers gave each other the finger.

Gorman took her flashlight back, obviously surprised at Meredith's presence. "Thanks, Colonel."

"I was passing by. Thought you might need an assist. Wrong as usual."

Gorman marched the teen back through the woods and across the field to the two cars. The kid didn't make it easy for the Sergeant.

"Lemme go! Lemme go! I didn't do nothing. Go catch yourself a serial killer or something." The girl kept up a litany of protests all the way.

"This is it, Shelly," Gorman told the girl. "Out past curfew, resisting arrest, climbing the fence, whatever the charge is for that. . . ."

"Unauthorized Access and/or Egress of a Military Reservation," Meredith offered in the interest of accuracy.

"Thank you, ma'am," Gorman said as she put the teen into the backseat of her patrol car.

"What you gonna do?" Shelly spit it out. "Send me to fucking Leavenworth?"

"Maybe," Gorman responded, bending down and looking into the car. "We might just chain you to the front of the PX as an example to the others. You do know that the only one who really takes a hit on this is your father."

That remark made Shelly fall silent. Gorman turned to Meredith to explain.

"Her father is the Artillery Battle Simulation Chief, Chuck Daisen. That's Shelly."

"Do you have to gig him?" Suddenly Shelly was the contrite

child. "He's got enough problems right now . . . he's . . . I don't want to . . . Can't you just punish me? Beat me, throw me in the slammer?"

Gorman closed the back door on the girl.

"Wait here."

Gorman took Meredith aside.

"Colonel, if you weren't here I'd let her go," Gorman told Meredith. "Officer discretion and all that."

"Have you done that for her before?" Meredith asked.

"Three times." Gorman admitted it reluctantly.

"Being a little soft, aren't we? She needs to learn she can't do this. A girl her age, wandering around at night . . . This may be Mayberry, but there is . . . I don't have to tell you, Gorman."

"I know, ma'am." Gorman looked back at the girl's woeful face, visible through the car window. "Her mother died a month ago. Cancer."

Meredith felt her heart stop beating for a second. Her shock must not have registered on her face, because Gorman continued.

"It . . . it took a while. The father is . . . he's in some kind of depression and the kid, well . . ."

Meredith looked at Shelly, her sad, overmascaraed eyes; the attempt at looking tough was now just flimsy emotional armor. It was too painful for Meredith to watch, and she looked away, outside at the Mustang, her car now, but once . . .

Meredith's father had purchased the Shelby during her last year in junior high school. A frugal man, mean with every dime, it was a huge expenditure for Rudell Cleon, and Meredith heard him justify the cost to his cronies by bragging how much he would win at the drag races with what he called "the hottest wheels in Hamtramck."

Meredith could have been jealous of the car, the way her father talked about it. She was "a beaut," "prettier than two puppies"; she was "sexy" and always referred to as "she." Meredith's new "sister," or her wicked stepmother, the Shelby was the mistress that had replaced her mother. He did in fact seem to take all the emotion he had once invested in his wife and transfer it to the Shelby. He was seldom demonstratively affectionate, so when he was it became even more precious.

Meredith, since her mother's death, hadn't been the recipient of any of that affection. Her father was uncomfortable around her, saw enough of his beloved wife in her that it could bring him to tears. Being the kind of hillbilly stoic that he was, he stopped feeling that emotion, put it aside like he would a carburetor with a worn throttle shaft. And as she became older and began to show the signs of womanhood, he shied away from her even more. Her first period was more traumatic for him than for Meredith, prompting emergency calls to her aunts, long-distance calls, something that occurred so rarely in her house that it always had the ominous taint of death or crisis. Once he handed the phone to her as if it were a weapon and made her tearfully explain to her aunt Judi about the blood and everything. And while the mystery was explained to her, Rudell Cleon watched his daughter from as far across the room as he could get, staring at her as if she had just metamorphosed into some kind of fifties movie monster. And she had.

Her breasts were another problem. They had developed early, and the first noticeable swellings required another phone call and a visit to a downtown women's store, where she was fitted with her first brassiere. Her father had ordered the clerk to "set her up with what she needs" and waited outside.

And her breasts grew quickly, requiring repeated visits to the same store and the same kindly clerk. Brassieres were the only new articles of clothing Meredith ever owned; everything else was from the secondhand store. But she never had any joy in these purchases. Every time her father would drive downtown, glowering behind the wheel as if Meredith had done something wrong.

The boys at school were a problem, rude remarks and snickers, but she would see her father trying not to look at her chest. His quickly averted eyes if his gaze drifted below her face made her feel even worse. She hated her breasts, would wear her old bras, though too small, as long as possible, binding the parts of her body that caused her so much grief. For years Meredith had trouble shopping for underwear, knowing it was silly, but feeling deep down that her breasts represented some sin she had committed.

Her father cut her out of his life more and more, and then her very body became something that drove him further from her. She had no one in the world except him, and everything she did or became seemed to cut away the meager scraps of affection they did share.

So when the Shelby came into the garage and into her father's life, Meredith had every reason to be jealous of the car, every reason to despise the object that took from her the last bit of affection her father was capable of giving.

But she didn't.

She loved the car as much as he did.

The sleek curves, black paint as deep as dark water, the menacing profile of the front air intake, the deep throaty anthropomorphic rumble of the big engine. She even liked the smell of it: She would get home from school before him and sometimes go out into the garage just to sit in it. Once she had been sitting on the hood, chamois carefully laid out under her butt, and he had keyed the ignition. The sudden vibration and torque of the car made her yelp with joy.

She loved the Shelby and wanted desperately to be part of the car and her father's love affair with it. The routine was invariably the same: He would come home from work expecting his dinner to be ready, Meredith would do the cooking, then he would sit and watch the TV for a half hour, usually some game show he never participated in or seemed amused by, sipping a lone beer. Then he would retire to the garage and spend the rest of the night listening to the country music Meredith despised and tinker with the car.

Meredith lost count of how many times the Shelby had been taken apart bolt, washer, and nut; cleaned, examined, commented upon; then lubed and returned to functioning order. Hardly ever entered in the drag races, Rudell Cleon always found an excuse; the race was reportedly crooked, low-class, or something else equally undesirable. The few times he did race he won, but the trophies were stuck in a closet, uncherished, and he bitched about the wear and tear on the car until he never mentioned racing it anymore. Sometimes some of his cronies from work would come by with a six-pack and a compendium of lame and dirty jokes, and lend a hand. Rudell Cleon was their leader. He tolerated no relationship where he didn't have the upper hand, and though he wouldn't partake of the beer if he had already drunk his nightly ration, he would snort at the jokes and lecture on his amazing vehicle and the cesspool of the American political landscape, his observations made ludicrous by his aversion to television news and the newspapers—Jewish lies, according to him.

One of the men, Neil Hubin, hung around the garage more often than the others. He had a harelip and spoke little in the presence of the other men, but alone with Meredith's father he would jabber away in a stream-of-consciousness commentary on any topic that took his fancy, mostly a racist diatribe against everyone on the planet who wasn't white, male, and from Tennessee or Kentucky and he wasn't so sure about Kentucky.

Rudell Cleon would nod or snort derisively, a sound that would change the topic under discussion faster than some people changed channels on their TV.

Meredith didn't like Neil Hubin. The harelip caused her a lot of consternation. She didn't know where to look at his face so as not to appear to be staring at the deformity. She had trouble understanding what he said half the time, and when she did comprehend his words they so offended her that she had to grit her teeth so as not to reply.

But in spite of all that, she envied him.

She was jealous of him because he was allowed to help her father work on the car. Very few people were given the privilege. Rudell Cleon was particular about who touched the Mustang. Some had their privileges taken away for just stripping a bolt or losing a wing nut. Neil, a former mechanic, never failed her father and he knew his way around a toolbox. Rudell, his upper torso buried under the hood or hidden beneath the undercarriage, would call out for a tool and Neil, between sips of his beer or his winter schnapps, would slap it into her father's palm like a nurse assisting a surgeon, confirming the tool as he did so.

Meredith wanted that. She wanted that kind of contact with her father. She wanted him to need something from her and her to be able to provide it instantly. She didn't know why until years later. Maybe it was because she had failed him when her mother had died. His grief had been so deep, so profound that there was nothing Meredith could do to assuage the pain, nothing she could do to take her mother's place.

But as a teenager all she wanted to do was hand him the timing light, slap it into his grease-stained hand, and say, "Timing light."

But Neil Hubin got to do that. She hated Neil Hubin and felt bad about it, because Neil Hubin was already hated and made fun of over his harelip. Meredith knew he was aware of her animosity, and she wanted desperately to tell him that it wasn't because of his deformity. She wanted him to know that she wasn't the kind of person who made fun of people because they were different. But she kept silent and hated the man.

She was in the tenth grade and had been asked out on her first date—Homecoming. It wasn't a big date, the team quarterback or anyone like that, just a quiet boy in her Government class who didn't stare at her chest before he looked at her face, and she had asked her father for permission. He took a few days to answer, a dreadful few days of putting off the boy, Alex, sure he was going to ask someone else. But Alex was patient, and her father finally gave his assent after grilling her about the boy's family, ethnic background, and what kind of car he drove. She lied about the family and background, too embarrassed to ask Alex, giving her father the answers he wanted to hear. But the car she told the truth about, knowing her father would see it when Alex came to pick her up. And it was the car that got his approval, Meredith knew.

A 1954 Hudson Hornet, straight eight, two single-barrel carburetors, that Alex had put together himself.

Her father said yes, then Meredith fretted over her dress and Alex brought her a corsage. Her father shook the boy's hand and asked him when he'd be bringing Mere-Jo home. Alex said 10:30, and the look he gave Meredith told her she hadn't heard the last of "Mere-Jo."

Then her father walked them out to the street to take a look at the Hudson, a big, low-riding chunk of steel that looked like an overturned bathtub with a slit of a windshield. He and Alex discussed the merits of old cars, the hardiness of the old engines, and then Rudell Cleon looked through the narrow window at the interior—red leather.

And saw the knob on the steering wheel. In some circles it was called a Brody knob, used to facilitate fast turns. Other people called it a bootlegger's knob, a handle affixed to the steering wheel that made it possible for the driver to make turns with one hand.

"What's that there, boy?" her father demanded.

"Came with the car," Alex said.

"Don't lie to me, boy. C'mon, Mere-Jo." And he grabbed Meredith's arm and steered her back to the house, Alex following with his mouth open in surprise.

"What's wrong, Mr. Cleon?"

"Don't play dumb with me, boy. I know about what that there is. It's a necker's knob, so you can drive with one hand while the other one is free to molest my daughter. Get your butt out of here."

And after a few feeble protests, Alex left. Meredith was shoved into the house, ordered to take off the fancy dress, wash off the damned makeup, and left to cry through the night.

The next day she came home from a traumatic day of school, where she knew everyone was staring at her, aware of her shame, and Meredith put her books on the dining-room table and went out to the garage and took a screwdriver and cut three lines down the side of the Shelby, digging deep into the black paint until the silver of the metal was revealed. Then she went back to the house to prepare dinner, her father's favorite: Kraft Macaroni & Cheese with cut-up hot dogs.

Rudell Cleon and Meredith didn't speak for eight days. He never mentioned the damage, just sanded the side panels down to the bare metal, primed and painted it until you couldn't tell that it had ever been damaged.

Meredith hardly went into the garage after that, never sat behind the wheel of the Shelby again until a few days after being called back to Michigan and her father's deathbed. She had gone to the house to pick up her aunt Lorrayna and gone into the garage and lifted the tarpaulin car cover. She got behind the wheel, but could stay there only a few seconds while Aunt Lorrayna talked to her husband, who couldn't find anything without her help.

The car still had that smell, that feeling. She wondered whatever happened to Neil Hubin, but never asked her father.

That he had specifically left her the car meant something, Meredith was sure. An apology? A reprimand? Maybe he left it to the only person he knew would take proper care of the damned thing.

She didn't know.

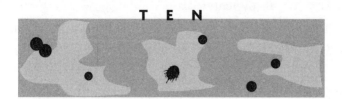

T E N

Meredith wasn't sure what transpired in Gorman's car between the MP and the girl, but by the time she had followed them to the Bowser Burger, Shelly was in a much more mellow mood. Maybe it was just the food. The kid ate french fries at an amazing rate, sucked down a milk shake like it was water, and then dug into Gorman's chicken sandwich.

Meredith remembered eating like that, in the days before she measured a Snickers bar by how many miles it would take her to run off the calories. Putting envy aside, she enjoyed watching the teenager scarf up the food without a hint of conscience.

"You know, Shelly," she told the girl. "My father died last week."

"Yeah?" The girl was surprised. She probably thought, with that teenage "I am the center of the universe" theology, that she was the only person whose parent had ever died.

"I lost my mother when I was eight," Meredith added.

"Sorry . . ." Shelly ventured.

"Cancer's an evil thing." Meredith fiddled with her iced tea, demolishing the lemon slice she had asked them to omit. "Slow and mean."

"Yeah . . ." Shelly put a lot of emotion, a brief history of pain, into that one word. "Do you . . . miss your dad?"

"My old man and I didn't get along," Meredith confessed after a moment. She could tell that Shelly would be able to detect a lie. "I was an only child, and a daughter at that. I think my father had no clue about what to do with me. He had depended on my mom for that. If I had been a son, maybe . . . But, we . . . we didn't get along. I think I joined the Army just to tick him off."

Shelly nodded as if she understood. Meredith looked at Gorman, who was watching the teen, then continued.

"Watching him die, I tried to think of the good times . . . there weren't that many. It was sad. He was a bitter, mean man and all he had was this hillbilly, redneck toughness—and the cancer took that away. It was ugly and sad, and he became what he never wanted to be—weak and pitiful. We didn't get along well, but . . . he was my dad."

Meredith caught herself, surprised at how much she had revealed.

"Did you and your mom get along?" Meredith asked Shelly, changing gears abruptly and on purpose.

"Yeah." Shelly nodded solemnly. "Most times. I pissed her off a lot."

"Well, I think I spent my whole life trying to tick off my old man. Whatever I am, all I've ever done was in order to . . . make him angry. Now he's gone, it's funny. I'm kind of at loose ends."

It was a few moments before anyone spoke. Meredith kept quiet, afraid she would spill more of herself.

Meredith, like her father, wasn't the type of person to open up to strangers, but she knew what Shelly was going through losing her mother, and she wanted the teenager to know that she wasn't alone, that others too had suffered the same loneliness, the same sense of abandonment, guilt, and overwhelming loss.

And Meredith *had* been alone, receiving no succor from her father; she had no one with whom she could share the pain, no shoulder on which to cry, no one at whom she could howl and rage. She was just alone in her room with a sweater that still smelled of her mother's Sunday perfume and a photograph of the two of them together on a pleasant summer day perched on the hood of the Ford Fairlane wearing matching dresses with big red poppies on a white field. Her mother had made the dresses. Meredith still had both of them in a box that traveled from post to post with her. She had found them in a pile of her mother's possessions that Rudell Cleon was burning in a fifty-five-gallon drum in the backyard.

Meredith had come home from school and seen the smoke and gone into the backyard and watched. When her father went into the garage to get some gasoline to hurry the fire along, Meredith rushed over to the pile of things and grabbed both dresses and hid them behind the propane tank and retrieved them later. She understood why he was destroying her mother's things: They were painful reminders that had to be removed from the house.

But she didn't understand why he had taken Meredith's own copy of the dress—at least she hadn't understood then. She did now. Meredith had reminded him too much of his beloved wife as it was; the dress would have made that memory cut too deeply.

Shelly finally spoke.

"My mom was proud of me, I think."

Meredith could see the girl summon the strength to talk about her mother. "I was on the basketball team. We were winning. I . . . I think she was proud of me."

"Cherish that." Meredith ventured to lay her own hand on top of Shelly's. The kid didn't pull away. "It's something you'll always have. And you still have your father."

"Yeah. He's cool. It's just . . ."

But Shelly shut up, not wanting to go any further. She looked around, seeking refuge, or another topic. She found one.

"At school we heard there was a murder." Her eyes lit up with excitement. "A real murder. On post. All gory and stuff. Is that for real? So cool . . ."

"Very real," Meredith said, her expression grim. "It wasn't pretty, and a young woman lost her life. Murder isn't cool, Shelly."

Great, Meredith chided herself, *"murder isn't cool."* Make up some bumper stickers and put them next to the DARE slogans on all post vehicles.

"Sorry," Shelly apologized, but the glint of excitement was still there. "But you're gonna catch the guy who did it, right?"

"Or woman," Meredith corrected. "Yes. We *will* catch them."

"So, you got any clues?" Shelly's eyes bored into Meredith's, totally absorbed as only a teenager can be.

"We always have clues," Meredith answered. "It's making sense of them that's the challenge."

"Did you do an autopsy?" Shelly continued, not waiting for the answer. "Any suspects? You gonna break the case pretty soon? The first seventy-two hours are the most critical in any investigation. After that the trail gets cold."

"You watch a lot of television, don't you, Shelly?" Meredith asked. The question went right past the girl.

"You need any help, I know this place like nobody," Shelly offered. "Me and my friends, we hear all the good dish." She leaned toward Meredith conspiratorially.

"There's a lieutenant at the Artillery S-2, he's Mormon and he's got six mothers. Six." She nodded, impressed at her inside information. "It has nothing to do with your case, I know, but that's the kind of stuff you hear if you keep your ear to the grindstone."

"Ground," Meredith corrected. "Six mothers . . . that's a major investment in Hallmark cards every May."

Shelly laughed. It was delightful—for a moment she was just another giggling teenager, innocence intact. Meredith laughed with her, and Gorman joined, the contagion spreading.

There was a chirping sound. Meredith checked her beeper. Nothing. Shelly checked hers, attached to the belt of her jacket.

"It's me," she announced. "My dad. We have a code." Shelly finished off the last dark little crumbs of fries. "Maybe I'll go home."

"There's no maybe to it," Gorman said, speaking for the first time since they ordered. "I'll take you."

"Front seat this time?" Shelly asked.

"Front seat," Gorman agreed.

They cleaned up after themselves and walked outside to their respective cars. Gorman unlocked her patrol car and let Shelly into the front seat, then walked over to Meredith.

"Thanks, Colonel. She's a good kid, just going over some rough terrain."

"We all do that, Gorman."

"That reminds me, ma'am." Sergeant Gorman fidgeted with her gunbelt. "I never thanked you for Panama. I . . . it was a rough time for me . . . and I . . . I could have gone a bunch of ways. But now . . . I owe what little career I have to you."

"Are you impugning the stature of the Military Police, Sergeant?" Meredith asked jokingly.

That brought a smile to Gorman's face.

"No, ma'am. I just . . . I'm going to WO school and . . . well, I wanted to thank you for putting me straight."

"You won't stay that way if you keep pulling these double shifts, Sergeant."

"No choice, Colonel. Some of the patrol officers have been assigned to the investigations. I *tried* to get in on the detective work, but . . ."

"I'll see what I can do." Meredith smiled at Gorman's not-too-veiled hint.

Gorman smiled back, then saluted and went back to her patrol car.

Meredith watched Gorman drive away, remembering the angry, immature kid she had known during the Panamanian incursion. Sergeant Gorman had been on the verge of being discharged.

A good MP, even exemplary, when she was on duty, Gorman seemed to fall apart off duty. She got inebriated, managed to get herself into altercations with civilians and some of her fellow enlisted personnel. There were suspicions of drug use, and after a final confrontation between an officer and Gorman in a club, Meredith had the young Corporal brought before her.

Instead of chewing Gorman out, Meredith took her for a ride around the POW camp.

"You know the difference between you and them, Gorman?" Meredith had pointed to the Panamanian faces inside the fence.

"No, ma'am. Yes, ma'am." Gorman was confused. "I don't follow you, ma'am."

"A cup of coffee."

"A cup of coffee, ma'am?"

"I had a cup of amazing coffee this morning. That means I'm in the mood to talk to you rather than just court-martial your butt."

Gorman had nothing to say in response to that.

"What is your problem, Gorman? You should know. I can't figure it out. Authority figures? Hate the Army? Drug addiction? Tell me, Gorman. Have you thought about it at all? Are you not concerned with what is going on here?"

"Yes, ma'am." Gorman sounded contrite. "But I just . . . get . . . It's hard, you know, being female, being black . . . you wouldn't know."

"Why wouldn't I?"

Gorman looked at her. "You're a Major."

"And how did I get here? I scratched a lottery ticket and it said, 'Congratulations, you're a Major'? I came up the hard way. I'm not black, but when I enlisted being female was enough to put me on the dirty end of the stick. I've fought hard for every bit of my career. But we're not talking about your duty hours. I know that's hard on you, but you seem to manage fine when you're on duty. It's off hours that are apparently the problem. What's going on there? Is that a black thing, a female thing?"

"No, ma'am. I just . . . It sounds silly when I say it."

"Say it. I've been in the service for thirteen years. I've heard it all."

"I get bored."

"Bored?"

"There's nothing to do. I get off duty, I go back to the barracks. I read, but I run out of books, especially down here, so I go looking for something to do. There's nothing to do. And I don't do drugs. I *don't* do no drugs, ma'am. But I drink a bit, I hang around with some folks. I don't know, they're interesting, things happen when I'm around them. Sometimes bad things, I don't know."

"Yes, you do. You hang out with a bad crowd, you get a bad rep. You learn that in high school. That's no excuse." Meredith tried to keep the lecturing tone out of her voice. "You're better than this, Gorman. What's with all of this off-duty aggressive behavior?"

"I don't—" Gorman caught herself. "I drink a little, somebody gets in my face, and I don't back off like I do when I'm on duty."

"Well, I don't know if that's a drinking problem or an attitude problem. See the abuse counselor. Or visit the psych and get a check on the attitude." Meredith paused a moment. "But you still haven't answered the question: Why are you doing all this, Corporal Gorman?"

"It's kind of dumb," Gorman replied. "But I still think I'm just . . . bored.

"Bored." Meredith almost laughed at Gorman's continuing assertion, but she held it back, knowing how counterproductive that response would be. Gorman was serious.

"Yes, ma'am." Gorman nodded. "I think. I got all this energy. I'm kinda hyper, and I got to do something. I volunteer for all of the extra duty I can get. It's the downtime that gets me."

"Well, I could work you to death," Meredith offered. "Put you on every scut assignment I can find until you pass out on your cot, but sooner or later you'll still have to deal with these other problems, Gorman. What do you do when you're on leave or when you get a pass?"

"I go home to Philly if I get the chance, visit my sisters. They have lots of kids. I like being Auntie—gives my sisters a chance to go out, get some free time, and I get to know my nieces and nephews. I like being Auntie." She smiled. "I don't get into any trouble back home. I don't drink hardly at all."

"Well, for the time being, we'll make you an auntie here. Check with the First Sergeant this afternoon." Meredith made it an order. "You're a good soldier, Gorman. I don't want to lose you."

Gorman was about to thank her, but Meredith stopped her before she could start.

"*But* you have to fix this. And I don't think 'bored' is really the problem. Fix this or I cut you loose."

Gorman nodded.

That afternoon the First Sergeant assigned Gorman to help out at the local orphanage. The specialist thrived there, picking up the language, making herself so invaluable that when the unit left to return to the States the children cried and sent letters to Meredith, begging her to let Gorman come back to them.

It was two months later, back at Fort Hood, that Gorman asked to see Meredith.

"I think I know what my problem is, ma'am." Gorman stood in front of Meredith's desk. Meredith took her on a walk-and-talk, and Gorman waited until they were outside.

"I've been speaking with the counselor like you told me, but I think I figured it out myself, no offense to Ms. Brett."

"Tell me, Gorman," Meredith urged. "I've been waiting."

"Well, ma'am, I think what it is, is that I see a lot of stuff all day that makes me mad. Waste, bad leaders, people stupider than me giving orders, bad orders. I'm not putting you on that list, ma'am, but I think it all builds up and then on my off time I just kind of explode."

Meredith couldn't help but laugh. She just burst out laughing from deep inside her chest. She laughed until it hurt.

When she could talk again she asked Gorman, "And how are you going to manage this . . . frustration, Specialist?"

"I'm going to focus it—by making the Army a better place to be. I'm going to work on getting promoted above the people who aren't qualified to give orders. I'm going to fix things. Right now I'm studying for my sergeant's stripes, thinking of going to Combat Leadership School, too. I'm going to fix the Army, ma'am."

Meredith almost laughed again, but turned and offered her hand to Gorman instead.

"Well, I'll help you, Gorman," Meredith finally replied. "Between the two of us, we'll fix the Army."

Meredith was transferred soon after that, but she kept track of Gorman through the Army grapevine and was pleased when she flourished. The Army didn't change much, but Gorman did. She made sergeant, received great marks on her reviews, and now she said she was on her way to Warrant Officer School.

One of Meredith's successes.

But the flush of pride had left Meredith by the time she returned to the Holiday Inn. She was so tired, she tripped over the threshold on her way into her room.

The water in the bathtub had cooled hours ago and the bubbles were now just a dirty-looking slime on the surface. She put a hand in and tested the water. Tepid.

Meredith opened the plug and let the water drain out. She gave up on the bath, just wanting the sanctuary of the bed. She lay down, kicking off her shoes, unbuttoning and unzipping her jeans but leaving them on—too tired to take them off.

And then she couldn't sleep.

The day's incredible events all came back to her.

Discovering Levy was her commanding officer. The horrible homicide—she'd never seen anything like it. The hate literature followed by a hate crime—she had to get on that one immediately. Immediately. Of course, the homicide couldn't wait either. Shelly, too much TV or not, was right—if a homicide wasn't solved in seventy-two hours, there was little chance it would ever be solved. And the matériel theft. Was there anything else she could do about any of it right now? Had she missed something?

Meredith lay there, her mind churning through possibilities, the few facts, the political and personal ramifications, the who, what, and why of it all. She kept at it until her mind was as exhausted as her body and she finally fell into a fitful sleep.

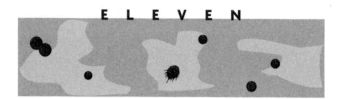

ELEVEN

Meredith felt better in the morning after she had showered and dressed in a fresh set of pressed BDUs. She felt more comfortable in the camouflaged Battle Dress Uniform than in the Class A's she had worn the previous day. The dress uniform was just that, too dressy. Wearing it gave her the same uncomfortable feeling she had in her prom dress. It was nice, a little thrilling to see the rows of bright ribbons, the shining yellow brass, the silver leaves of her rank, but she didn't feel like herself in the uniform.

She didn't feel that she was necessarily an imposter, but she was like someone playing dress-up. Maybe it was because she had wanted it for so long, had desired it so much, that the reality was still a little imposing—Lieutenant Colonel Meredith Cleon.

The BDUs were more like work clothes. The forest-green camouflage or the mottled "chocolate-chip" brown that was worn for desert warfare, pants tucked into her boots, the loose tunic or blouse, the beret with her silver rank pinned to the front, all suited her. She could get dirty in them and not feel guilty. That was probably the answer. Her uneasiness was more of a class thing. She was from blue-collar, working-class stock, not often comfortable in the elite officers' apparel. She wondered how long it would take her to get over that feeling of inadequacy. If she ever would.

Meredith drove onto the post just as the sun was coming up. There were already soldiers out jogging in the half-light, their breath visible in the cooler morning air. She wished she could be out there running with them. Her daily five miles were a vital part of her routine, but she knew she was too tired to get anything out of a workout today but more fatigue. She also knew she was going to need every bit of strength she had to get through the coming day.

Cruising to the MP station, she didn't see Underhill's El Camino or any of the other staff parking spaces occupied, so she continued driving past headquarters. Again empty parking spaces—except for Vernor's Saleen. A pretty machine. The green robot was at his duty station.

Meredith was still pondering the reason for her antagonism against the young Lieutenant when she found her way to the officers' residence area. Was she just displacing her dislike of Levy onto his Aide? Had Vernor actually done anything to spark her antipathy? She didn't want to be unfair to the young officer; he was obviously hardworking, dedicated, and just following the orders of his superior.

Two civilian maintenance workers were in the process of cleaning the graffiti off the Levy house when Meredith drove by. They had some kind of big, high-pressure steam blaster trailered behind their pickup, but were using only Levy's garden hose and a couple of scrub brushes to remove the obscene words.

Something about that bothered her. Meredith pulled over and parked and walked across the street to Levy's house and watched them work for a moment. The paint removal was going easily. The swastika on the door wasn't even a ghost of a memory. The brick walls were cleaning up just as completely.

Walking along the shoulder of the road, Meredith checked again for skid marks. There were none. She had wanted to look more closely last night, but she had been hesitant to double-check Kahla's judgment in front of his people. She paced the street for ten, then fifteen meters on either side of Levy's house. Not a mark. Exactly what you would expect in a fifteen-mile-per-hour residential zone, considering the rank of the people living here. No one was going to dare get a Colonel or a General mad at them by speeding.

But not a sign of getaway-car skid marks. Maybe she was making too much of Levy's description.

The side door of the residence opened. Two girls came out of the house, teenagers about Shelly's age. Dressed a little too preppily for Meredith's taste, they cast a glance at her as they walked over to a white Econoline van parked in the driveway and climbed inside. Their mother, equally preppy with a severe French twist, came out of the house behind them.

Feeling a little self-conscious as the girls watched her through the van window, Meredith went back to her car and drove away. She was behind the van as far as the next intersection, where it went right and she continued on to the MP station.

"A forty-five slug?" Meredith asked. "They're sure? And it didn't kill her."

She was looking at the autopsy report. Underhill, Tate, and Kahla were in her office. She had come back to the MP station to find Underhill's El Camino in his parking space, the man himself in his office, and a report of last night's patrol activities and the Carnes autopsy on her desk. The reports were clear, concise, and thorough. She had made a few calls, then had Mrs. Kappadonna round up the others for the meeting.

"The coroner says that she was probably alive when the first fifty-caliber round hit her," Tate reported. "There were a few what he called 'postmortem signatures.'"

"Alive . . . ," Kahla whispered. There was a quiet moment while everyone realized what that had meant for Georgia Carnes.

Tate continued reading from the autopsy report. "The forty-five-caliber wound occurred at least four hours prior to her death, maybe longer. Death was between approximately oh-nine hundred and ten hundred hours. Very little postmortem blood. She had nearly bled to death before the first fifty-caliber hit her. It's impossible to tell which round actually killed her—there were over one hundred and twenty separate, countable, fifty-caliber wounds."

"Jesus . . ." It was the first time Meredith had seen Underhill react emotionally. He quickly collected himself.

"Who uses a forty-five anymore?" Meredith asked.

"Nobody on post," Kahla said. "We're all on nine-mils."

The nine-millimeter Beretta had replaced the big, heavy old 1911A1 .45 side arm a few years before. The Beretta was the pistol commonly issued these days to Army personnel, except for some CID officers who carried a SIG-Sauer, which was also a nine-millimeter weapon.

"There are plenty of old surplus forty-fives at the gun stores and in private hands," Underhill noted.

"Well, let's get a ballistics on the slug," Meredith advised.

"It's on the way to the Fort Gillem CID forensics lab," Underhill replied. Fort Gillem, Georgia, located near Atlanta, was CID headquarters and the center for all Army forensic labs.

Meredith was listening for any attitude this morning from Underhill, but so far had heard none.

"We also have some trace fibers from Carnes's clothing—carpet fibers, I'd guess. That's on its way to Gillem and the FBI lab, too," Tate added.

"Anything come up on the background check?" she asked.

"Nothing." Tate checked his report. "She had no steady boyfriend. We're following up on the few dates she did have, in case there's a stalker somewhere. Looks like she was just a typical workaholic aide clone."

Tate looked up suddenly to see if he had offended anyone. Meredith made a mental note to advise him about culling his personal asides from his reports. She didn't mind, but there were those who were always looking for red capes to charge.

"We still need to interro—interview General Ringstall." Tate looked at Meredith.

"I'll set that up," Meredith responded. "I'll try to make it this afternoon. Now, on the matériel theft . . ." She looked at her report. "I see here that Knox has found weapons missing."

That information in her report had soured what had at first been a tasty cup of morning coffee. There was nothing worse than a weapons theft on a military installation—except maybe a homicide involving the headquarters staff. "Are they sure the theft originated on our end?" Meredith turned to Underhill.

"The container was sealed with what sounds like one of our bogus seals. The container was filled with sandbags for ballast, like ours. No need to add ballast if the contents were stolen on their end. They're sending us a sample of the bags and dirt for comparison, but we can assume the worst." Underhill put down his writing tablet. "Right now we have a bit of a jurisdiction dispute—but it'll be in our laps by the end of the day. They don't want this mess any more than we do."

"That's an argument I'd like to lose. How about the FBI? A weapons theft, even the homicide on a military reservation, falls under their purview."

"It does, but our local agent doesn't want any cases that aren't already solved." Underhill's lip curled in disgust. "Ruins his statistics. Same with the ATF. We can ask all we want, but I don't see us getting any assistance unless we all of a sudden get a big media splash." He looked at Meredith.

It was one way to pass the buck—leak the media enough information to cause a ruckus. But it wasn't Meredith's style to pass on her problems to anyone else. And riding the tiger of publicity had gotten more than one officer mauled.

"Then we're alone." Meredith sighed despite herself. "For a while until, or if, it becomes a D.C. political football, then they'll grab it and kick us out of the playground. How are you doing with the personnel interrogations?"

"Sergeant Kahla gave me some of his people." Tate smiled his thanks to Kahla. "And we're interrogating on the matériel theft as we speak. But the list of personnel who had access is a long one. Permission to use the lie detector, ma'am?"

"No need to ask, Mr. Tate," Meredith agreed. She didn't believe in the accuracy of the damned machines, but used as an interrogation threat they could be surprisingly effective.

"Better touch base with the Union and the Directorate of Personnel so we don't get into dutch with the civilians," she advised. "Any trouble, buzz me."

"I'll handle the Directorate," Underhill put in. "We've danced this dance before."

"I didn't mean to step on any toes," Meredith said to him, being cautious.

"None bruised—yet," he replied.

She took note of the word "yet."

"While we're at it, would you like to be there when we talk to General Ringstall, Mr. Underhill?"

"Not particularly," was the succinct reply.

"You've read Sergeant Kahla's report on last night's hate crime. Colonel Levy gave me this yesterday."

She handed Underhill the hate literature. He looked it over.

"This is a Xerox of one of the originals," he noted.

"Could you get me an original and a report on the case so far? All hate crimes on and off post in the last year," Meredith requested. "Levy's hot on this and after last night . . . but I, too, would consider this a priority investigation."

"Consider it done, ma'am," Underhill replied with more eagerness than she expected.

"Back to the Carnes homicide. Anything on the rope that tied her, the tire tracks, any other prints?"

Tate flipped through his notebook.

"Standard nylon parachute cord, olive drab, so that denotes a military connection . . . maybe. The stuff they sell in the local hardware stores is white. But the military surplus, camping suppliers, and survival stores carry it. We're checking for lot numbers on the cord, but that's a long shot. Humvee tracks, not enough distinguishing marks for us to set up a match profile. Hard to tell when the last Humvee went through there, but I haven't given up on it. A few civilian vehicles—we've got clear prints on four. Age of prints . . . hard to tell. No footprints worth logging."

"Was Carnes's vehicle among the four?" she asked.

"No."

Meredith sighed and stated the obvious for everyone.

"Not a lot to work with." She looked at Underhill. "Can I get Carnes's two-oh-one file? Maybe there's something in her personnel records."

Underhill nodded and made a note on his legal pad. Mrs. Kappadonna entered.

"Staff's ready," she announced.

"We'll be there in a second, Mrs. Kappadonna," she told the secretary. Meredith turned back to the others. "Let's see if we can find some kind of linkage between these three crimes—or any two of them, for that matter. The hate crime, the theft, and the homicide. It's a lot to happen in one day—too much. Maybe they have something in common. I'm not a believer in coincidence. Think on it."

She rose, and they came to their feet with her.

"Let's have this meeting and hope the hell we don't get a sniper on the roof by noon, or somebody digging a latrine doesn't find Jimmy Hoffa." Tate laughed; Underhill didn't.

They left her office and went into the squad room.

Meredith had a start of déjà vu. There they were, gathered around the table again—Fire Chief Lindell, Game Warden Bosch-Stuckey, and a couple of MPs Meredith didn't yet know. She took her seat and was introduced to the unfamiliar MPs, Daniels and Jerome, MP investigators transferred to help out Tate.

"Well, thank you all for coming," Meredith began. "We have a busy day ahead of us, so we'll get right down to it."

She caught herself and turned to Mrs. Kappadonna.

"Mrs. Kappadonna, hold all calls. Unless the President of the United States goes postal with an AK-47 in our Officers' Club, I don't want to hear about it." Meredith turned back to the others.

"Well, as you all know by now, we've got our collective behind in a Cuisinart, so let's just hit the high points this morning. I need to know only about crises right now. Everything else takes a backseat until we clear some of these high-profile incidents off the road. You people can help a lot by maintaining operations as usual and giving whatever assistance is asked of you. We have three, *three*, major cases in process, and any ideas or information you may have on any of them, please filter it through Mr. Underhill. He will provide you with status reports. Now, Traffic and Safety, Sergeant Kahla."

"Nothing that can't wait," he reported. She knew that already, but had asked him first to set the tone of what she wanted to hear from them all.

"Mr. Underhill?" she asked, knowing the answer to that one also.

"We have a joint Emergency Response Exercise next week. It's not a biggie, but it could drain personnel. It's a twenty-four-hour sequestered exercise."

"I hope by then we'll have cleared up one or two of these cases," Meredith said. "Anything else?"

"The promotion ceremony." Underhill looked at his notes. "Colonel Levy is getting bumped to General, day after tomorrow. That's mostly Traffic, but again, a draw on all personnel."

Sergeant Kahla reported. "We have it covered. You'll need to clear the overtime for our new cases."

"I'll get on it," she replied, making a note. That's right, Levy was going to be a General. Meredith had a feeling he would clear the overtime. "Ms. Bosch-Stuckey, glad to see you again. Can you tell me what's up with your department?"

Ms. Bosch-Stuckey straightened in her chair. "Squirrel hunting opens this weekend. That's a big thing around here. Drunks with guns. Everybody should keep a lookout for those idiots shining deer at night. And be careful approaching any of them. Every time you walk up to one, remember he's armed—and as I said before, most likely drunk. Oh, and I have a minor environmental violation out on

Lake Fenning." The Game Warden was also responsible for any environmental enforcement on the military reservation.

"In fifty words or less," Meredith cautioned her.

"Someone's dumping garbage into one of the feeder streams. Civilian garbage."

Meredith sighed. There was always one who didn't read the instructions on the box. Her impatience must have been apparent, because Bosch-Stuckey backpedaled.

"We're on it," she assured. "Sorry I brought it up."

"No, don't be." Meredith smoothed the woman's feathers. "As soon as we can free up some people, we'll help you on it. Chief Lindell?" She turned to the Fire Chief.

"We are dangerously in need of new fire hose."

That was it. No preamble, no hesitation. Meredith remembered yesterday's encounter with the Chief in the stairwell. The man was serious.

"New hose," Meredith repeated. "Dangerously?"

"Yes, ma'am. I've written up a report." He slid it across the table to her. "Two-and-a-half-inch, sixty-five-millimeter, woven-jacketed, rubber-lined, with couplings and adapters."

"I'll read it. And what do we need to do to procure your new hose?"

"We need an emergency expenditure allotment from the DRM."

"The DRM." Meredith winced a bit inside. "Mrs. Kappadonna?"

"Annika," Mrs. Kappadonna corrected. "Your new appointment is at eleven hundred hours."

"I will be there." She looked around the table. "I called the CID HQ this morning, and it doesn't look like we're going to get any help from them. They're overextended as it is—some major fraud investigation is about to pop. Five states. Also a negative on any FBI or ATF assistance."

She acknowledged Underhill, who had made those calls.

"We're on our own," Meredith continued. "I have every confidence in you and your people. Every confidence. From what I've seen so far this unit is a well-run operation, the personnel top-notch. All that will be tested now. Tested to the utmost. So let me call in my report to Colonel Levy and we'll move forward the best we can. Thank you, ladies and gentlemen. I hope to get to know all of you better as we work together. And if you have *any* problems at *any* time, my office door is always open. Carry on."

Meredith rose. The meeting was over.

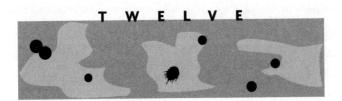

TWELVE

Meredith went into her office and read Chief Lindell's report while she drank a Dr Pepper. The thought of more coffee revived her sour stomach, and she didn't think it was the quality of the brew.

Then she began to plow through the various memos and documents that had accumulated on her desk. Underhill had provided her with a pretty thorough briefing on personnel and status. She had fifty law-enforcement people under her command, about twenty-five people short of what she was allowed. Still, even the full seventy-five would have been inadequate. For a civilian city the same size as Fort Hazelton, a police force of three to five hundred would be required. With the fifty enforcement personnel, twenty staff, and sixteen civilians, Meredith was spread way too thin.

With those eighty-six people she was responsible for the entire installation. Traffic and Accident Enforcement, Misdemeanor Investigations, Physical Security, Crime Prevention, Environmental Compliance, Game Warden responsibilities (state and federal), the Fire Department, Range Safety, a Hazardous Materials section, and an Emergency Medical Department (paramedics).

The CID was in the same boat. Tate and his staff of six were responsible for all on-post felony investigations and any case involving military personnel or ex–military personnel, with an off-post area of operation consisting of nineteen counties and three states.

She read her copy of the Serious Incident Report from Underhill's office. The Carnes homicide, matériel theft, and hate crime seemed so simple in the terse bureaucratic vernacular. So simple. No pain. No grief.

Meredith noticed she had a Crime Council meeting on the first Thursday of every month. Looking at her calendar, she saw that it was next week. That meeting was when the CID, MP investigators, the civilian police (local and state), and the local district attorneys and their military counterpart, the Judge Advocate, sat together to share information, plan strategy, and grease the wheels for cooperation, both investigative and political.

She was looking forward to the gathering, not just for the professional benefits. She could use all the help she could get in her undermanned position. She wished she had the time to get together with them all right now. The next item in her stack was a government credit card for her gas requirements. Mrs. Kappadonna was on the ball.

Then came Tate's CID Serious and Sensitive Report, a rehash of Underhill's without the misdemeanor incidents. Tate wrote a good report, a bit flowery with some two-dollar words, but clear and concise.

A memo, a personal note from a General at the Pentagon, was

next. She read through it and called Underhill and asked him to see her when he had a moment.

While she waited for Underhill, Meredith perused the updated press release from the PIO's office. With the input from Levy, Schwaner, and D.C., the announcement of Carnes's death and the investigation was so bland it was as if the murder was of no more importance or interest than a parking ticket. She knew that the paucity of information wouldn't satisfy the media vultures who hovered over every bloodletting, but that wasn't her problem—yet.

Underhill knocked on the open door, came in at her nod, and sat down.

"Any news from the matériel-transfer personnel interrogations?" she asked him.

"It's going on now." Underhill stated it flatly, not answering her question. "And Kahla has put his MI people doing the house-to-house down 'Brass Alley.'"

"Brass Alley" was the nickname for the officers' quarters area on every post.

Meredith nodded. She would stop by and observe part of the theft interrogations later. She lifted the memo to show it to Underhill.

"I have a note here from General Vause at the Pentagon, of all places, in regard to a certain Mrs. Kate Young, who is not satisfied with our response to a, and I quote, 'series of crimes that your staff has chosen to ignore,' end quote. Do you know anything about it? Like how this Mrs. Young got a line to General Vause?"

"Mrs. Young is the widow of the late Brigadier General Bond Young, former commandant of this post." Underhill took the memo from Meredith and read it. "It appears that she has maintained some of her old social contacts."

"And the crimes to which she refers?" Meredith asked.

"The last I knew, she reported that Janet Reno and Gorbachev had two hundred Cuban women secreted in the basement of the Pentagon, creating some kind of psychological bombs out of them so they could destroy the sanity of any country these women were released into—as prostitutes, of course."

"Of course." Meredith nodded.

"Mrs. Young also wants us to sue Fidel Castro for sprinkling white dust over her house, but we needn't worry about it affecting her, because she has lined her home with aluminum foil."

Meredith continued nodding. Underhill seemed to enjoy filling her in on the eccentric Mrs. Young.

"Lately her complaints have been about the jets taking off over her house. They set the trees in her backyard on fire. There isn't an airfield within fifty miles of her house. And the trees show no damage whatsoever. She has a theory—only a theory, she insists—that the burned leaves are replaced with fake plastic ones at night when she sleeps. The helicopters they're using to do that have woken her."

Meredith waited until he was done and took the memo back. "I'll write the General and tell him that a thorough investigation has been made and that perhaps someone from the family could check on Mrs. Young and make sure that she can take care of herself properly."

"Actually, she isn't that much of a problem," Underhill said. "A few of the investigators have grown fond of her, and they stop by from time to time and drop off some fresh fruit and vegetables. She suspects it has been tampered with, but they guarantee that it's been irradiated and she eats it and bakes them some very tasty cookies. I allow the personal visits as long as it doesn't interfere with their duties."

He waited for Meredith's reaction.

"I see nothing wrong with that policy," she said.

Underhill nodded and bestowed upon her a rare smile as he stood up to leave. "We'll see that you get your share of the cookies."

"I'd appreciate that," Meredith said, and went back to her paperwork.

Mrs. Kappadonna brought in Carnes's 201 file, and Meredith read through the dead woman's personal history for a while. The file contained just cold, periodic entries worded in military jargon, signposts on the road of her military career, the scenery left out. It was like driving a highway at night, just quick glimpses as the headlights briefly illuminated some landmark off in the darkness.

What Meredith was really doing was delaying her call to Colonel Levy. Not normally a procrastinator, she believed work that was put off somehow festered from neglect and became only more painful in the interim. But she knew Levy would give her grief no matter how complete her report, and she had more than enough problems on her desk as it was.

Finally, she called him and was rewarded with a barrage of questions she wasn't given time to answer and assaulted with a shopping list of directives. Then, without drawing a breath, Levy attacked her for bringing in Lieutenant Vernor for questioning and asked her how long she was going to disrupt the matériel transfers with her interrogations of the shipping personnel. She ignored the Vernor dagger and parried the last thrust.

"Sir, we must interview everyone involved in the loading and movement. Especially now that we have a weapons theft. It is imperative."

"Everyone? Everyone?" Levy asked. "Well, just do it with as little interruption of daily operations as possible. I have a post to run."

"Yes, sir. I realize that, sir." She took a beat, hoping he wouldn't fill the empty air. He didn't. "I need to talk to you as well, sir."

She could imagine his face growing red on the other end of the line. She thought she could feel the receiver heating up in her hand.

"Lieutenant Colonel Cleon, do you actually think that I have nothing better to do than sit and answer some inane questions that you already have the answers for? I'm a busy man! Busy! Don't you have better things to do? I *know* you have better things to do. What about that obscenity that occurred at my home last night?! What are you doing about that?!"

"We're working on it, sir." Meredith kept her voice calm. "We just have no clues yet, sir."

"No clues! No clues!" Levy exploded again. "I was there. *I* saw clues, for God's sake!"

"Well, yes, sir, there *are* clues." Meredith chided herself for misspeaking like that. She knew better, but Levy had rattled her. She settled her thoughts and tried hard not to sound patronizing. "I misspoke. What we have are no clues that add up to anything yet, sir. We're still working on it."

"Then why are we talking, Cleon?" Levy spat the question. "Call me when you have something to report."

And he hung up.

Meredith fought against the inclination to slam down her own receiver. Instead she laid it gently in the cradle and started to close Carnes's 201 file, still open on her desk. She couldn't concentrate on it right now.

But as the cover was closing, something caught her eye and she reopened the file.

She read, picked up the file, and left her office. Mrs. Kappadonna wasn't at her desk, but Underhill was in his office frowning over what looked like a patrol schedule.

Meredith walked in and sat down and waited for him to finish, looking around. There were framed photographs scattered all around the office, on every shelf and table, nook and cranny. They were all of the same two children, two girls, from baby pictures up to around the age of ten or eleven. Soccer uniforms, Little League, ballet, and rather hysterical dual Halloween costumes as tinfoiled teapot and cup. The children were cute, and in one photograph they were with their mother, one of the most beautiful women Meredith had ever seen. Tall, lithe, smart-looking, a woman with penetrating green eyes.

Underhill looked up from his work. He caught the focus of her gaze but didn't volunteer any family information. Closemouthed, Underhill obviously didn't bring the office home or vice versa. With most parents, you couldn't stop the flow of child anecdotes with a tank assault.

"Did you request our overtime? We're going to need a truck-load of it."

Meredith cursed herself for forgetting.

"No, sorry. I'll take care of it immediately." She chided herself mentally. She couldn't let Levy intimidate her to the point that she wasn't doing her job. She set the Carnes file in front of Underhill.

"Lieutenant Carnes was Jewish." She knew she didn't need to say more.

Underhill was obviously surprised, but she could see the wheels start turning instantly.

"Her maiden name was Schliel," Meredith said, and pointed to the pertinent line in the file. "She converted to Catholicism when she married in . . . 'ninety-two. Divorced in 'ninety-four, but she kept her ex-husband's name and the religious designation. I know it's slim, but with the hate crime . . ."

"I knew her maiden name, but it didn't register that it was Jewish. Slim or not, it's a connection." Underhill picked up the file and began reading. "And those racist bigots aren't necessarily the logical type. Though you'd expect some kind of red flag at the murder scene. Those people do like to brag."

"You're right there, but . . ." Meredith thought about the FBI-issued hate-crime profiles. It was time to check them out again. "At least we should check out her ex. Maybe he never accepted the divorce, you know."

"On it," Underhill said, this time with some enthusiasm.

"Any suggestions for my meeting with the DRM?" Meredith asked.

Underhill answered by opening his desk drawer to reveal his holstered Beretta. Meredith smiled. Maybe she was making some inroads past that brick wall Underhill had built around himself.

"No, thanks," she declined. "But that does remind me. Colonel Levy's on my case to qualify. Can you ask Mrs. Kappadonna to get my weapons issue set up and find a range for me to practice on? I need it—I'm not my best with the M-9."

"Perhaps for things like that you should tell her yourself." Underhill looked distant again. "I'm not a message center, Colonel."

Meredith had pressed too far. One step forward, two steps back. That he was in the right didn't help.

"You're right, Mr. Underhill," Meredith confessed. "Excuse me for stepping outside the boundaries of our working relationship. It won't happen again."

"Words to live by, Colonel." Underhill's voice was neutral. "Good luck with Wojahn. Here's your hate-crime file and your emergency funds request."

She glanced at the papers Underhill had handed her. He had put Chief Lindell's request in proper form for the DRM without Meredith asking. Now, that was definitely outside the parameters of his job description and she could have reprimanded him, but she held back the criticism. She decided to take it as a peace offering or as part of his usual working procedures.

She left Underhill's office frustrated. Most people she had worked with she could figure out pretty quickly, almost on a visceral level. A few she had to think about, plan an approach, but Underhill baffled her initial attempts.

Meredith went back to her office and read the funds proposal. When Mrs. Kappadonna returned she put in the range and weapon request, then went back to the stack of paperwork on her desk. Memos, letters, *Field Training Manual* updates, reams of the Army's first line of defense and offense—paperwork. It was amazing—her first official day and she was already receiving memos, the paper machine in full grind with her on the receiving end. She prioritized the pile: immediate read, can wait, and junk. Then she re-sorted the junk, just in case she had missed something that was of value but had been written up so badly its importance was obfuscated. She found one, an announcement for the local VFW concerning a 10K run in three weeks. The last sentence was a request for the route that would originate in Walhalla to go across the post. That meant road security and all sorts of red tape. She put it in a stack to discuss later with Underhill.

She then opened the *Indiana State Driver's Manual.* It was best to be up to date on local laws. It never looked good for the Provost Marshal to get a driving violation, and you never knew when some obscure little law could trip you up or even come in handy. In Alabama it was the law that if you had your windshield wipers going you were required to have your lights on—in the theory that if it was raining, a car with headlights on was more visible. Most people ignored it, but it was a good, legal excuse to pull over a suspicious car. More than one drug or drunk-driving bust owed itself to an officer's knowledge of that one traffic law.

Soon it was time for her to scoot across the street to her appointment with the DRM. Meredith grabbed a stack of reading in case she had to wait, and advising Mrs. Kappadonna of her destination, she left the office.

Meredith was out of the MP station and down the steps when the door slammed behind her and Tate came running after her.

"Colonel! Colonel!" he called. "We've got the main personnel from the Knox outload downstairs for interrogation. I was wondering if you wanted to be present."

"No, thank you, Mr. Tate," she responded. "Only if you find some gold. And be careful. Conserve your energy—this . . . these might be long cases. Did you get any sleep last night?"

"As much as you, ma'am."

"Even so, you don't see me doing any running. Pace yourself, Mr. Tate. We need you alert."

"Yes, ma'am."

"And thanks for the invitation. Oh, and check with Mr. Underhill. He has something on the Carnes case."

"Will do, ma'am."

Tate turned and started to run back inside, but stopped himself and walked the rest of the way. Meredith smiled. The energy and enthusiasm of youth. She remembered that feeling.

As she continued toward the office building she thought about Georgia Carnes tied to that target, alive. She wondered if the woman had been conscious, if she had known what was coming.

And who would commit such a sadistic act upon another human being? In her career Meredith had seen more than her share of killings, but they were usually spur-of-the-moment so-called crimes of passion, spurred on and unleashed by drugs or liquor after years of pressure, abuse, or perceived abuse. Sometimes it was solely the passion or rage that had accumulated until it reached the breaking point of blood and death. She could almost understand that kind of killing; at least she saw a cause, a motive.

But she had never seen a death of such brutal torture as the

Carnes murder. And she had no concept of the kind of person who would go to the lengths to which Carnes's murderer had gone to make sure someone suffered that much before they died.

The situation more than depressed her—it took her to a dark place Meredith had to visit too often in her profession. She shoved those thoughts aside; they were doing her no good right now.

If anything, Wojahn's secretary's hair had gotten bigger overnight. It looked like brittle cotton candy today. Meredith had announced herself, checking the clock on the wall to make sure that she was indeed ten minutes early.

"You'll have to wait a minute," the secretary declared. "Mr. Wojahn is busy."

"Of course," Meredith replied amiably, and went over to the chairs next to the water cooler and took out her files and began to read. The hate-crime file was at the top of the stack. She paged through the chronological listings of incidents, minor altercations where the word "nigger" or "spic" had been shouted. Some racist graffiti had been sprayed here and there. Probably teenagers pushing the envelope of hooliganism. A civilian barber in Walhalla refused to cut African-American hair—his shop was put off-limits at the recommendation of the former PM. Meredith would need more information on that one.

But there had been nothing extreme until the copied pamphlets and single sheets of paper had appeared a month ago. They had been stapled to telephone poles and pinned to bulletin boards around the post. No one had observed anyone doing the posting—or no one had come forward to admit it.

Meredith examined the original material; three pieces had been saved in the file. The paper was crinkly and slick and had a faint chemical smell. She located the most recent copy that Levy had given her—rough Xerox-style paper. She wore a puzzled expression.

There was a beep.

Meredith looked up. It was Levy's office fax machine spewing out a sheet of paper. She rose and walked over to the machine just as Wojahn's secretary retrieved the transmission.

"Excuse me, ma'am." Meredith tried out a smile on the secretary. "But could I see that fax paper?"

Meredith's smile seemed to scare the woman. "I . . . I don't think . . ." The secretary actually seemed startled and confused by the request. "I'd have to ask Mr. Wojahn."

"Not the document," Meredith corrected. "Just the paper."

That further confused the woman. Which helped Meredith, because the secretary handed over the sheet of paper without further comment.

A total breach of DRM security here, Meredith mused, the fax was an invitation to an office retirement party for someone in another department. A pie party. BYO Pie.

"I can see why you'd want to clear this with your boss." Meredith's sarcasm was wasted on the perpetually oblivious secretary.

Meredith examined the paper. It was plain copy paper. Not shiny, but the rougher, thicker, standard copy paper.

There was a rude buzzing sound and the secretary went into Wojahn's office, probably to report Meredith's unstylish, close-cropped, undyed hair or her mysterious interest in fax paper. Coming back out almost immediately, the secretary told Meredith, "Mr. Wojahn will see you now."

Meredith handed the faxed invitation back to the secretary and went into Wojahn's office.

Wojahn gestured curtly for Meredith to take a seat, much as a

Roman emperor probably commanded the games to begin. *How many Christians do we have today? You know how sluggish the lions can get when they overfeed.*

Wojahn leaned on his desk and made a steeple of his hands and peered over them at Meredith. He clearly didn't like what he saw. Had he ever? Meredith decided to feign repentance.

"Mr. Wojahn." She smiled at him amiably. "I'm so sorry for yesterday, but you probably heard what called me away."

"You found a dead soldier," Wojahn answered. "Would she have been any more alive if you had waited five minutes?"

Whoa! Meredith felt the full blast of the man's hostility. So much for repentance and amiability. She handed the funding request across the desk, deciding to put everything on a purely professional basis and see how that played.

"I have here a request for emergency funding for—"

Wojahn snatched the material from her hand and pointedly did not look at it. He put it into his in basket.

"I'd really like you to look at it." Meredith let her eyes go as dead as his.

"I will," he said. "In its proper time."

This was a test, Meredith told herself, just a test.

"Now, sir?" she asked, then belatedly added, "Please. While I'm here to discuss it."

"No."

That was it. Plain and simple. No.

All consideration pushed aside, all discussion moot.

Meredith was getting steamed.

"I did use the word 'emergency,'" she said.

"Colonel," Wojahn said in a patronizing tone as if to a child. "Every request that comes into this office has a goddamn 'emergency' or 'highest priority' tag on it. 'Of supreme importance' is my favorite. You're going to have to do better than that. I control the fiscal needs of a small city. Impress me."

Meredith took a breath. "Look, Otto." Maybe a more personal approach would help. "We got off on the wrong foot, and it was my fault entirely. . . ."

Perhaps an apology would warm his soul.

"That's for certain, Colonel," Wojahn agreed. "Are you going to beg now?"

Wojahn leaned back in his chair, clearly relishing the thought.

Meredith visualized Underhill's offer of the Beretta and regretted not taking him up on it.

When Meredith entered the service in '76 the Army was just beginning to privatize, transforming itself from an Army where every job was performed by only military personnel. Every soldier dreaded KP, kitchen police duty, and all clerical and support services were once filled with GIs. But with the New Army, the all-volunteer Army, the military focused on a highly trained specialized soldier, preparing for a more sophisticated war scenario and a liberalization of the idea of the soldier's job. Gone were the days of Beetle Bailey peeling potatoes. Better-educated, more motivated career professionals were desired, even required, and not only would these new soldiers not tolerate the scut work of the old Army, but it would have been a waste of their time and training.

That was when civilians came into the picture. They took over the culinary positions, the clerical support, and even assimilated some of what were once sacrosanct areas like the Military Police. Underhill's position, for instance, enabled Meredith or any other Provost Marshal to be available for any combat situation overseas without abandoning the stateside mission.

The Army was smaller and leaner, but in many ways more effective.

Of course, there was friction between the "green-suiters," what the civilians called their military counterparts, and the white shirts. It was inevitable. The goals of a career soldier and a civilian government job holder were many and varied. There was an old joke, tiresome but true, among the soldier contingent: "How is a civilian worker like a Russian rocket? You can never fire it."

Government jobs attracted a certain sort of person, Meredith was sure, and that sort was sure to butt heads with a gung-ho soldier. Government service was also an easy alternative for many people who couldn't cut it in the Army. Many early military retirees or even soldiers who had been weeded out of the Army at eight, twelve, or even fifteen years found refuge in a similar position still working for Uncle Sam but not having to wear the uniform or salute. The trouble was that some of these people grabbed an attitude with their discharge.

And of course, some were just autocratic little fools who enjoyed making everyone around them miserable and would have done the same if they were working in a shoe store in Ohio.

Meredith didn't know where Otto Wojahn fit in, but she had to find out how to handle the difficult little man. Her mission and her people depended on it. She decided to start asking around, inquire of other officers if they had been successful in dealing with the DRM. Everybody has a human side, a good side—Meredith believed it was just harder to find it on some. But if you can't find the good in a person, find a vulnerable spot and jab it with a pointed stick.

T H I R T E E N

Meredith had been under hostile fire in Somalia, Panama, Desert Storm, and Afghanistan. Before that she had been through the hellish rigors of Ranger training, and during Jump School she had a parachute collapse on her third jump and she had to cut loose her main chute and use her reserve. She had been battle-tested.

But Otto Wojahn had beaten her.

She hated to lose and was still replaying and analyzing the encounter, trying to think of another tack she could have taken, when she stepped out of the building.

Chief Lindell was standing next to his car, the traditional fire-engine-red sedan, apparently waiting for her. He straightened up when he saw Meredith and walked over to intercept her.

"Colonel?" He looked hopeful. "You met with Mr. Wojahn?"

"Yes, Chief." Meredith nodded. "And I don't have any good news for you. I tried my best, but . . ."

"I understand, Colonel." Lindell's shoulders sagged with disappointment. "It's nothing new. I was just hoping . . . with a new PM . . . It is a dire situation, Colonel."

"I read your report, Chief, and I agree with you. I haven't given up. As soon as I can focus on it, I will try something else."

The Chief nodded glumly and got into his car, muttering his thanks. Meredith walked toward the MP station.

She had let one of her people down. And on her first official day, when she should have come through for them and prove that she was there to provide for their needs. Oh, no, she wasn't through with Otto Wojahn, not by a long shot.

Still mulling over how she might deal with the unpleasant DRM as she entered the MP station, Meredith was so preoccupied that she almost ran into Sergeant Gorman coming down the stairs.

Gorman was excited about something; her eyes were animated with enthusiasm.

"Colonel! Colonel! I was looking for you!" she exclaimed.

"You're not still on duty, are you, Sergeant Gorman?" Meredith asked with concern.

"No, ma'am. I'm on my own time. Already had some Z's. Colonel, I'd like your permission to pursue an angle on the Carnes homicide—if it's okay with you."

Gorman was as eager as a puppy with a pull toy. Meredith couldn't help smiling. Had she had that kind of enthusiasm once?

"As long as it doesn't interfere with your assigned duties, I have no problem with it," Meredith cautioned, and added, "Coordinate with Mr. Tate, though, he's the case officer."

"Thank you, ma'am!" Gorman charged down the stairs to CID. Meredith continued up with little of the same energy.

When she got to her floor, Meredith made a point of stopping by Sergeant Kahla's office first. She passed on Gorman's request to work with the MP investigation team. Making it clear that Meredith wasn't trying to usurp Kahla's authority, she put in a good word for the female sergeant.

When she entered Underhill's office next, he was on the phone with someone who sounded like a representative of the civilian employees union.

"If you want, George, I'll take the lie-detector test first, show all your people that it doesn't make them sterile, if that's what they're worried about."

Underhill paused for a response from the other end. He noticed Meredith and held up a finger for her to wait. She continued the mute interchange by nodding her head, mouthing the words "no problem," and taking a seat.

"George, George," Underhill chided. "We are not going to be asking any damned questions about possible drug use or their personal habits during their off-duty time. We have a weapons theft. We can deal with it internally here on the post, or you can leg-wrestle with the FBI and ATF. And I might add if you are so worried about this whole drug issue, then maybe it's time we started a series of urinalysis spot checks for everybody working in sensitive areas."

Underhill waited and listened again, smiled.

"Fine, George. You want a union representative present during the tests, we can accommodate that, within reason. But it may never come to that. The machine is just a last resort if we think someone is withholding information." There was another pause, a shorter one this time.

"That's great, George, just so we are on the same wavelength regarding this. See you on the picket line." After a beat. "That's a joke, George."

Underhill hung up and looked at Meredith.

"It's his job to holler 'wolf' and it's mine to say 'ssshhh.' How'd it go with the DRM?"

Meredith took a moment and tried to think of a good slant to put on her conversation with Wojahn.

"I'd rather take the hair off my legs with a cheese grater than go into that office again," she finally confessed. "I don't think I did us, or the Chief, one bit of good."

She slid the hate-crime file across his desk. "But . . ."

"Take a look at this hate literature." She drew his attention to one of the sheets of copied paper. "Notice on the originals that the paper is that thermal fax paper. Most of the places I've been on post have the newer, plain-paper faxes and copiers. Do you think there are many of the old thermal type still around?"

Underhill took the paper between two fingers, feeling the finish, confirming her observation.

"I wouldn't be surprised if, on this post," he said, "someone was still using a slide rule and an abacus. Easy enough to find out, though. So you think this originated on post?"

"Not necessarily," Meredith replied. "But if there are no thermal faxes or copiers on the post, we *can* state that the literature did not originate here. That's a step. And it would make some people in the higher echelons very happy."

"I get you." Underhill nodded. "Oh, Carnes's husband is out of the service, remarried, in Utah . . . Provo. He has an alibi—sounds legit. I have the local police confirming it. They're not in any hurry, but I don't think there's anything there. He seemed authentically shocked when I gave him the news."

"Okay." Meredith took it well. Carnes's ex-husband had been a long shot anyway, and she wasn't the gambling type.

"I need to set up the Ringstall interrogation. Whoops, interview." She got up to leave. Underhill stopped her with a look.

"Are we going to interrogate, whoops, interview Colonel Levy concerning the matériel theft?"

"We should," Meredith confirmed with a mental sigh.

"We should," Underhill agreed.

"I'll set that up, too," Meredith told him as she left the office thinking how much fun it would be trying to interrogate Levy.

She found a whole new stack of paperwork on her desk and sat down and prepared to tackle it. One chose the Military Police as a specialty for a variety of reasons, usually having something to do with some lame TV cop show or detective movie. Car chases, exciting detective work, gunfights, and wisecracks. Like Shelly's perception of Meredith's job as Provost Marshal, it was a far cry from the reality. In Georgia, Meredith had once roomed with a second lieutenant who was on the Olympic swimming team, Lisa Byers. Meredith would tune in to every televised swimming event in which Lisa was participating and watch the spectacular few minutes as the other woman butterfly-stroked her way across the length of the pool.

But then, on one of her days off, Meredith once watched Lisa practice. Six hours in the pool, lap after lap, three hours in the gym, repetition after repetition with free weights, then back to the pool for more laps. Meredith asked her how many training laps it took her to get good enough to compete, and Byers replied, "Thousands upon thousands." Lisa made the race look easy, the butterfly stroke so graceful, but few watching the competition saw the years it took to get there. If you wanted the prize, you did the laps. You didn't complain about them; they were part of the gig.

So for every time Meredith encountered a part of her job that no one saw, the unglamorous routine, the mind-numbing paperwork, mentally draining office politics, frustrating personnel problems, she thought of Lisa Byers and told herself, "It's just one more training lap." If she wanted the office, she got the paperwork that went with the desk.

Before she plunged in she called Levy's office without hesitation this time—no putting it off, facing the beast. He kept her on hold for ten minutes. She didn't get peeved; she used the time to read the memo that was at the top of the stack.

When he came on the line she again asked for the appointment to interview him, using the matériel theft, which was directly under his command, as leverage. "Sir, I need to know as much about the transfer as possible for the investigation."

"I'll send you over the files," he answered.

Great, she thought, more paperwork.

"That will be of great help, sir," Meredith replied with as much enthusiasm as she could muster. "But I will need to follow it up with a face-to-face."

"Yes, yes, yes," he said irritably. "Talk to Vernor. He has my schedule."

She let that suggestion slide; she would have to follow proper procedure. When Vernor stalled, as she suspected he would, Meredith could call Levy directly again.

"While I have you on the horn, sir, there are a few other minor things." Meredith looked at her notes. "I've transferred some of our MP investigators to the theft case, stepping outside our protocols. Plus, I have an overtime request, due to our present caseload and the upcoming ceremony. It will be on your desk by the end of the day. I would appreciate a quick response if possible, sir."

"I'll look for it," he said, not committing himself. "Is that all?"

"No, sir." Meredith poised herself on the edge of the cliff . . .

then dove. There were rocks jutting up from the surf below. "I called CID headquarters to request assistance. They declined. A call from your office, sir, might get us some help."

"Are you saying you can't do the job, Cleon?" Levy asked.

"No, sir. I'm saying we could use some assistance and the expertise that the CID could provide."

"Declined." Levy spit out the word. "If you can't do the job the Army requires of you, Lieutenant Colonel, step aside and we will find someone who can." He hung up.

And nothing would make you happier, Meredith thought, and she went back to the paperwork. It was almost pleasant after talking to Colonel Levy.

Ringstall was one of those men who had both the head and the hair made for a crew cut. The hair stood straight up stiffly, and the top had been cut with surgical precision. The color was salt and pepper now, but he had an unlined face and the look of a jock, an impression further reinforced by the photographs of his son, a relief pitcher for the Anaheim Angels, that were hanging on the wall.

The only bright moment of the interrogation was when Tate recognized the son's uniform and Ringstall ran off some meaningless— at least to Meredith—baseball statistics and the prospects for the next season. Meredith wasn't a baseball fan; that had been her father's passion and, thus, something in which she refused to develop an interest.

Through most of the ensuing questioning Ringstall had been quietly morose though responsive, still seeming deeply affected by Carnes's murder.

"I've lost people before," he said at one point. "In combat. I even lost two soldiers on an exercise in Puerto Rico once. A terrible accident. But this . . ."

Meredith thought he was going to cry. The officer in her felt sympathy and respect for another officer who cared about his people to that degree. The suspicious PM in her wondered if there had been something personal going on between the General and his Aide. She let Tate do most of the actual questioning so she could better watch Ringstall's reactions.

"Lieutenant Carnes gave no clue as to her being in a bad relationship?" Tate asked.

"She had none that I knew of, good or bad," the General answered. "She was dedicated to her work . . . our work. She was a professional soldier in the best sense of the term."

"We know that, General," Meredith finally interrupted after many similar responses from Ringstall. "Everything we've learned so far demonstrates that Lieutenant Carnes was an exemplary soldier. But . . . we need to get behind that and find out what in her personal life might have caused someone to want her dead—if anything."

"Maybe it wasn't her personal life," Ringstall suggested. "Maybe it was her work."

"What do you mean by that, General?" Meredith asked, intrigued.

"There are a lot of people out there, Americans, who think *we're* the enemy," he explained. "Those militia groups, terrorist groups, domestic or otherwise, extremists—just crazies."

"Sir." Tate took over again. "Have you or your office, specifically Lieutenant Carnes, come in contact with any of these groups?"

"No" was Ringstall's only reply. And he seemed genuinely disappointed that they were no closer to finding a reason for Carnes's murder.

So were Meredith and Tate.

"When did you last see Lieutenant Carnes?" Meredith asked Ringstall.

"At the end of the day, the day before yesterday," he answered, visibly annoyed at the short span of time. "We worked late, as usual, until nineteen hundred or so."

"Did she seem upset or tense about anything?" Tate asked.

"No." Ringstall shook his head. "Nothing like that."

Tate was about to ask a follow-up question when Meredith laid a hand on his arm to stop him. Something about Ringstall's expression said to her that he wasn't finished answering. They waited.

"Well . . ." Ringstall thought for a moment. "Now that I think about it . . . she could have been a bit . . . preoccupied."

"Any idea what that preoccupation might have been about?" Meredith asked.

"None. Sorry . . . sorry." He looked down at his lap. "I had to write to her parents this morning. I tried to last night, but . . ." He didn't need to finish.

Meredith took over the next phase of the questioning to protect Tate from any repercussions. "Sir, what were you doing that night?"

"My alibi?" He smiled sardonically. "I was home."

"Are you married, sir?"

"Divorced. Recently divorced." He didn't seem to be adjusted to it yet.

"May I ask the reason?" Meredith said.

"Must you?"

"Yes, sir."

"We grew apart. We . . . changed. People do. Sometimes not in the same way."

"Do you have . . ." Meredith thought for a moment. "Another relationship?"

"No." It was a firm, almost angry answer.

"I'm sorry, sir, but we have to pursue every avenue," Meredith offered.

"I understand. Proceed."

"I have to ask, sir. . . . Was there any relationship between you and Lieutenant Carnes outside your normal professional duties?"

"No. *None*." Ringstall started looking like a General again, eyeing Meredith with laser intensity.

"I think that's about all, then," she finished.

"Good." Ringstall then subjected Meredith and Tate to a good fifteen-minute harangue, urging and commanding them to catch Georgia Carnes's killer. She listened patiently, figuring tit for tat.

When Meredith and Tate left Ringstall's office, there was a new Aide in evidence at Carnes's former desk. He was a white male lieutenant who looked like a recruitment poster, a Caucasian counterpart to Colonel Levy's Aide Vernor, who was working at his computer.

Meredith gave the new Aide a glance. He was self-conscious under her gaze and shifted restlessly in the chair. She felt sorry for him and the position he had found himself in—suddenly a chance to prove himself, to get an edge up on the competition, and the General's office didn't really want him, they wanted Carnes alive again. In fact, he would be a daily reminder of her sudden death and loss.

Then Meredith thought of her own position. Whenever she appeared it was to bring bad news or to remind people that the world was full of darkness and evil. Her very presence bespoke crime, theft, murder, assault, everything people didn't want in their lives.

Meredith thought about all the rooms she had left, someone crying in the background, victim or perpetrator, someone bemoaning their fate. It was part of the job, and you coped with it or got out. Some people in her profession built up a facade of cynicism, some dealt in black humor, sick jokes—a few got mean, alcoholic, or clinically depressed.

And some got hard. Meredith fought the part of her that wanted to build a tough shell around herself. She thought that her empathy with the victim, or even the criminal, was a powerful tool in her work. She didn't want to lose that ability to put herself in their place.

So she paid the price.

Her job was like the cleaning crew who washed the graffiti off Levy's house. Yes, she prided herself in her preventive programs, but she was fully aware of how little impact they had on crime. What she did mostly was clean up the bloody mess, wiping everything clean so work as usual could continue. And the solvent that worked best, the soap that took the bloody hand prints of the victim off the wall, was justice.

That was what kept her going. Justice. She didn't mete it out; she just made sure it was possible.

Justice.

Meredith stepped over to Vernor's desk. He looked up at her from his computer screen.

"Lieutenant, we need to speak to you and the Colonel regarding this matériel theft investigation," she told him.

"I'm at your disposal, Colonel Cleon." Vernor gave her one of his dead smiles. His mouth turned up at the corners, but his eyes didn't register the apparent emotion. "I can't speak for Colonel Levy, of course, and he is very busy with the promotion ceremony and all. . . ."

"Coordinate it with Mr. Tate's secretary," Meredith advised. "And please emphasize to the Colonel that time is of the essence. I need to speak to him concerning the homicide and the theft."

"Yes, ma'am, I will."

"Oh, I noticed the other night that we have something in common, Lieutenant Vernor," Meredith began. She'd see if there was any blood pumping in his veins.

"What's that, Colonel?" he asked.

"Mustangs. That's a nice Saleen you have."

Vernor took a beat, didn't become at all more sociable, but seemed to close down even more.

"It's transportation" was all he said.

No blood, just oil in the robot lube system. Most men loved to talk cars. Cars, sports, and women. Meredith didn't follow sports much, and women was out of her purview because of her gender, and sexual preference. But cars—she could hold her own on the subject of cars.

Meredith left with Tate.

"Might as well be talking to an answering machine," she muttered on their way out. Tate laughed.

Outside it was sunny and clear. Meredith and Tate both blinked in the light and donned their sunglasses as they walked away from the headquarters building.

"One dry hole after another, Mr. Tate," she said to him as they headed toward the MP station. "Do you think Carnes's murder is part of a these hate crimes?"

"No offense, Colonel," Tate began. "But the fact that Carnes was Jewish was buried deep in the files. I don't know how some hate group would know it."

"Maybe someone found out in casual conversation," Meredith mused.

"Maybe." Tate nodded agreeably. "But there's also no signature of a hate crime at the murder scene. Those people usually like to brag, advertise. It was a . . . demonstrative way to kill someone."

"It was that," she conceded.

"But there were no swastikas, no burning cross . . . ," he continued.

Underhill was walking toward them. He was smiling.

"Colonel." Underhill nodded to Meredith, then Tate. "We have three thermal fax machines on post. I thought you and Mr. Tate might want to check them out."

Underhill handed Meredith a short list. She looked at it, not reading it, but considering the opportunity it presented. An opportunity outside the investigation.

"How about we do this together, Mr. Underhill?" she suggested. "We haven't had our traditional tour of the post yet. That kind of got forgotten in the melee of yesterday. Can we do that now and see these people along the way?"

The Community Safety Officer usually gave the new Provost Marshal a tour of the post, an informal get-to-know-the-facility-and-each-other during an orientation drive around the military reservation.

Meredith thought Underhill looked a bit suspicious at her suggestion, but he nodded. She hoped she was just mistaking simple caution for suspicion.

"Fine." Underhill tried to sound enthusiastic. "A tour it is."

He started walking toward his El Camino. Tate followed after Underhill, but Meredith stopped him.

"Mr. Tate, we'll report back to you. Can you proceed with the theft inquiry while we're gone?"

"On it, ma'am." Tate peeled off toward the MP station.

Underhill opened the passenger door for Meredith. It was a little gesture, but Meredith wondered if it was chivalry or just convenience—these old cars didn't have automatic door locks. She hoped as she got in that it wasn't chivalry. The last thing she needed was Underhill thinking of her as a woman first.

The interior of the El Camino was as immaculate as the exterior.

Underhill drove with both hands on the wheel even at the slow speeds required on the post, the sign of a trained driver or a cautious man.

"What we have left on Fort Hazelton are an Artillery Battalion, the Chemical Warfare School—very top secret, high security—and the EOD Training Battalion," he informed her.

"Just Explosive and Ordnance Disposal Training?" Meredith asked. "No field units?"

They drove past the grandstand that had been erected the day before. It was now being decorated with red, white, and blue bunting. Three 105-millimeter artillery pieces were being set up on a hill next to the parade field.

"EOD has a bomb squad that deals with military munition calls," Underhill explained. "Jurisdiction is over a three-state area. Indiana, Illinois, and part of Michigan."

"What kind of missions can they have out here in the Corn Belt?" she asked him.

"Weird stuff," Underhill began. "Some third-grader brings a live grenade to show-and-tell. Daddy brought it back from his National Guard exercise. Somebody finds an antitank mine in a soybean field—I swear to God. Elves, I guess."

"Well-armed elves." Meredith interjected with a smile.

"Two years ago," Underhill continued, "they got called out when some old woman—her husband had died, and she was cleaning out the garage for a yard sale—found a two-hundred-pound aerial bomb so old it's sweating nitroglycerine. Tricky one, that. Here we go . . . the first of our suspicious fax machines."

Underhill pulled into the parking area of the Motor Pool—also called the Equipment Concentration Site, the Consolidated Equipment Pool, or whatever other label the Army was using this year. Since Meredith had been in the service, the unit working in the area of chemical or nuclear warfare had been called the Atomic Biological Chemical Division, the Nuclear Biological Chemical Division, and a half-dozen other synonymic variations. She imagined there must be a special section of the Pentagon that was devoted to changing nomenclature, probably paid by the change and the number of words used.

This would always be the Motor Pool to her. And the one here at Fort Hazelton was huge, twenty acres of oil-stained dirt with corrugated tin-roofed sheds for maintenance. In the midst of all this bare dirt were a wooden administrative building and a dozen Humvees, trucks, and semis. They were lost in the huge expanse of available space.

Meredith felt a transient longing for the days when it would have been crowded with vehicles and men making them ready.

"You do the talking, Mr. Underhill," Meredith said. "If you don't mind."

He nodded, a hint of suspicion in his eyes again.

Sergeant Ramos was a small man with a spectacular mustache, a big black smudge of hair under his nose so thick that it was impossible to see skin through it.

Ramos showed them the fax machine, a battered old Sharp, the once beige plastic cover now stained from thousands of greasy fingers. He spoke with one of those laconic Texas accents.

"Take the blamed thing—I don't want it." Ramos glared at the fax machine as he spoke. "Been bitching for a new one, but we're too low on the food chain, I guess. Don't work half the time."

"Have you ever seen this?" Underhill showed Ramos one of the handbills from the hate-crime file.

Ramos's face twisted in an expression of disgust. Meredith watched his reaction closely.

"No, I haven't." He handed it back to Underhill like he didn't want to touch it any longer than he had to.

Underhill asked a few more questions about who else had access to the fax, whether it was locked up at night, and so on. Ramos seemed to be openly cooperative and answered each question without much hesitation.

Meredith asked him to copy a piece of paper on the fax machine, which he did without question or protest, and she and Underhill left.

Once in the car, Meredith compared the copy Ramos had just made for her with one of the original pages of hate literature. She looked closely but could find no matching anomalies or scratches and imperfections.

"A bad copy," she told Underhill as he pulled away from the Motor Pool and continued driving. "But not our bad copy. Carry on with the tour, Mr. Underhill."

"We have a large influx of Reserve and Guard units who train here every summer. That sets us up for the usual weekend warrior problems. They're like conventioneers with automatic weapons."

He cruised through a series of barracks and fields that were empty but well-maintained.

"How'd you wind up here, Mr. Underhill?" Meredith interrupted to finally ask the question that was one of the reasons she had asked him to accompany her—to try to get to know him.

"Oh, I don't know," he finally answered.

Meredith should have known he wouldn't make it easy for her.

"When did you join up?" She had seen a plaque on his office wall from a unit of the 173d Airborne Brigade in Vietnam that cited the accomplishments of Specialist Fourth Class Marcus Underhill.

"Out of high school. Went to Vietnam in 'sixty-seven, grew up in the service. I was a rowdy kid from Milwaukee. Decided to stay. Put in my twenty."

"Why not go for the thirty?" she asked.

"Oh, I knew I wasn't going to make Sergeant Major. I was a First Sergeant, but the next step up . . . ? Not with my record, my early years. Like I said, I grew up in the service, but I grew up the hard way. Nothing significant, but it's a different Army now. You need a spotless record for advancement, and, you know, one blemish and it's goodbye career. My jacket looked like it belonged to the Elephant Man."

Meredith couldn't believe it: Underhill had made a joke. This was working out fine.

"Plus," Underhill continued, "all the overseas duty. Germany was hell on my family—the exchange rate almost put us on welfare. Then Guam—we don't even have to talk about duty on Guam. So I cashed out and took the civilian route. My wife's family is from Indianapolis—the girls get to go to one school for more than a year. It worked out fine for everyone.

"Fax number two." That announcement ended the conversation as Underhill pulled into the parking lot of the Fort Hazelton Museum.

The museum was the old Officers' Club, a beautiful eighty-year-old single-level brick structure with highlights of ornate tile work.

Inside, though, the displays were stuffy, dry exhibits with faded lettering. Some of the uniforms were dusty, while others could be seen to be falling apart at the seams. A large diorama of the fort as it looked at the turn of the century, complete with little horses and soldiers, was covered with peeling paint, and a couple of the plaster buildings were cracked and broken. It looked a bit like the post did now.

Mrs. Oakley, an old woman whose dowager's hump curled her six inches shorter than her already meager five-foot height, received them. Meredith made a mental note to take her calcium supplement. But the woman was chirpy and full of energy despite the disability, and she seemed glad to have their company. There were no visitors to the museum that Meredith could see.

Mrs. Oakley led Meredith and Underhill into the office and showed them the fax machine. It was as clean as it was the day it was purchased.

"It's a fine machine." The old woman looked up at them with little birdlike glances. "Makes copies, too. Of course, we don't require much here at the museum. We exist on donations, you know."

There was a large Plexiglas case a few feet away with a sign inside it soliciting the donations to which Mrs. Oakley referred. There wasn't more than twenty dollars in change inside.

Meredith reached into her briefcase and rummaged around until she located a five. She dropped it inside, and Mrs. Oakley beamed.

Underhill handed the old woman a copy of the hate literature. "Have you seen this before, Mrs. Oakley?" he asked.

She read the sheet of paper and looked at them.

"I have a theory, you know," she said. "That the kind of men who create and distribute obscenities like this—and you *know* it's some men—are endowed with particularly small penises. Don't you agree?"

Meredith and Underhill were still laughing as they drove out of the museum parking lot. Meredith looked at the copy Mrs. Oakley had made for her on the museum fax machine. There were the usual odd smudges and scratches from the glass, but none of it matched the original of the hate literature.

Underhill pointed out a rather new structure as they approached and passed it. A big, solid, single-story structure surrounded by a large parking lot.

"That's the Club," he said. "The surrounding counties are blue, so on Sunday this is the only place you can buy alcohol for forty miles around. Sundays we earn our pay. A few drug busts, a lot of DUIs, a few fights. It's a pain in the ass."

Meredith knew what he was talking about. She didn't drink, never had. In high school she didn't have many friends, and none who experimented with drinking, and in the service she felt vulnerable enough as a woman and didn't want to weaken her position by risking getting drunk with the men, her peers or superiors.

But she knew a lot of soldiers thought they needed the release a few beers or drinks gave them. And on post that was the Club, formerly segregated by rank, officers or NCOs, now unified into one facility and still trouble. The Club was always the focus of a multitude of arrests. She tried not to hold it against the establishment.

Fax machine number three was in the office of the Ammo Dump Supervisor. A Quonset hut occupied a space at the edge of the huge dirt-mounded bunkers where all explosives that were allotted to Fort Hazelton were stored.

Long, wormlike berms twenty feet high, a hundred feet long, row upon row of them holding artillery rounds, small-arms ammunition, plastic explosive, mines, grenades, handheld rockets, and other assorted munitions. The theory was that the mounds of dirt would contain any explosion and the distance between the berms would check a chain reaction. Meredith had never seen the theory tested. She hoped she never would.

Double fences, razor wire, and large exclamatory signs warned everyone entering the compound: DANGER, NO SMOKING, and EXPLOSIVES.

Underhill parked and they stepped out of his El Camino. The oxidized tin-roofed Quonset hut served as the main office for the facility.

Inside there were a half-dozen desks, most of them empty and long unused. Only one person was present, a civilian, a skinny white guy with a bit of an Elvis twirl in his reddish-gray hair and just a hint of sideburns. As he looked up, she could see he had a smattering of freckles surrounding gray eyes.

"Help you?" he asked as he rose from behind the desk. An unseen radio played some talk show in the back of the building.

"Director of Public Safety," Underhill introduced himself, and stuck out his hand to shake. The civilian squinted at Underhill's hand, then shook it. It was just a slight pause, but Meredith caught it as she watched him.

"Dean Piedmont." He gave Meredith a glance, then dismissed her and looked back to Underhill. For once being ignored was fine with her.

"You have a fax machine?" Underhill asked.

"What of it?" Piedmont's tone was argumentative. "Over there." He jerked a thumb in the direction of a utility table. "That a crime?"

Piedmont's last remark caused Underhill to give him a second look.

Underhill handed Piedmont the hate literature. Meredith watched the skinny man's every move, every expression. He noticed her scrutiny, and it seemed to bother him. Piedmont gave her a sullen look, then skimmed the hate literature. His face went flat, his expression deliberately neutral.

"Never seen it," was all he said, just as flatly.

"Are you sure?" Underhill prodded.

Piedmont looked Underhill directly in the eyes.

"I'm sure."

"Do you mind if we talk to the rest of your people?" Underhill took the material back from Piedmont.

"No problem," Piedmont tossed off. "I'll call them."

Piedmont went back to his desk and picked up the phone. Meredith walked over to the fax machine and called across to Piedmont.

"Mind if I use this a second?" she asked.

Piedmont shrugged.

Meredith took a blank sheet of paper from a stack on the typing table near the machine, inserted it into the feeder tray, and pushed Copy. She was sure she knew what would come out the other end.

The three other Ammo Dump employees had as little to say as Piedmont. When Underhill finished questioning them, he met Meredith outside the Quonset hut.

Meredith showed Underhill the fax copy.

"Look at the scratches and anomalies on this copy, Mr. Underhill." She pointed them out. "They match our hate literature. It's the same machine. I think we have justification for a search of this facility—immediately. And I hate to say it, but an audit of all munitions under this man's supervision. The Ammo Dump, for God's sake."

"Are you sure it's Piedmont?" Underhill asked. He was being cautious, and Meredith understood. The search and audit would be a big drain on an already overextended pool of manpower.

"He looked at you . . ." Meredith tried to think of a tactful way to explain it. "The way my father looked at black men."

Underhill's eyes narrowed as he looked at her.

"My father was a racist," she explained, not wanting to say more.

"And you?" Underhill asked her without preamble.

"No, not at all." She knew she had to choose her words carefully, not wanting to get any deeper than necessary in the subject matter of bigotry.

"So what you've been doing to me came from some other place entirely." He spoke softly.

"I'm not sure I understand you, Mr. Underhill," Meredith said, though she was pretty sure she did understand him.

"You used me as a stalking horse," he told her. "To see how the suspects would react to the big black cop."

"Yes, I did," Meredith confessed. "I admit it. And it worked."

"I'm not complaining about the tactic." He looked straight into her eyes as he spoke. "What I mind is you not telling me. Didn't you give a speech yesterday about us being partners, working together, and a bunch of horseshit like that?"

Meredith paused before answering. "Mr. Underhill, I am sorry. I apologize. I got carried away with my own cleverness. I am sorry."

"Sorry don't cut it, Colonel."

"Then I don't know what else to say to you, Mr. Underhill. I'm trying here. I'll make mistakes. I'm doing what I can."

"I suppose so." He nodded slowly. "But all I know is that a man wouldn't have been sneaky like that. It was duplicitous. A man wouldn't have done that," he repeated.

Underhill went over to his El Camino and got on the radio. Meredith watched him.

So that was it. "A man wouldn't . . ." She was in some real trouble with Underhill. It was nothing she couldn't fix with time. But more important, she now knew where his antipathy toward her, slight as it appeared to be, was coming from. "A man . . ."

It was over a pair of jeans, not even real Levi's but a pair of faded Wranglers that Phyllis, her only friend, had given her in one of those closet-cleaning expeditions where you toss out last year's clothes and anything else that fashion deems no longer wearable. Phyllis was a victim of fashion, a quite willing one; she loved to shop. Meredith hadn't succumbed to the habit; much like drugs, she couldn't afford the first taste and was spared the addiction. People gave out drugs sometimes, boys handing out freebies to get laid or at least a smile and a cuddle and the right to lie about getting laid. But current fashion wasn't so easily passed out. Once in a while, Phyllis would loan Meredith something more au courant than her father's conservative taste would allow, but size was a problem since Meredith was much larger on top, Phyllis larger on the bottom.

In sorting through old clothes, Phyllis found a pair of last summer's jeans and said, "These might fit you."

Meredith was seventeen and this was the first pair of jeans she had ever worn, the first slacks of any kind. Her father insisted she wear skirts, of a conservative length. It was the seventies, and jeans, tie-dye, halter tops, and no bra was the look—even in high school. The brassiere was Meredith's requirement, even if her father had a stroke and allowed her to dispose of it—her breasts caused her enough embarrassment as it was. But she wanted to wear jeans, pants, even bell-bottoms like everyone else at school, on TV, and in the magazines.

The Wranglers fit, the denim worn pale in all the right places as if she had owned them for ages. Meredith took the jeans home, washed them carefully in cold water so they wouldn't shrink, and the next morning put them on. Her father took off for work before she left for school.

It was a great day. No one at school noticed the jeans, no one commented on them, and she felt she belonged somehow, that she was like everyone else. Such a desperate teenage yearning that was, for one day, fulfilled.

When she came home, she changed immediately and put the jeans under her sweaters in a drawer.

And so it went for a month or so. Every once in a while she would pull out the jeans and go to school and pretend to be like everyone else, with a father who talked to you and a mother to tell secrets or admit fears to and a life just like on *Father Knows Best* and all that.

Then one day, the fifth time she had worn the jeans to school, she came home and saw the Fairlane in the driveway. The production line had shut down from lack of parts, a strike in Pennsylvania. Meredith thought she might just slip past him like she had everyone at school, no comment, maybe it wouldn't be bad, he would just accept the jeans and give her money to buy another pair or two.

She summoned all her resolve and entered the house, heading straight to her bedroom to change. He was sitting in the living room paging through the *Reader's Digest*. The door between the living room and the hall that led to her bedroom was the same width as every other doorway in the United States.

Thirty inches. Her area of exposure was the time it would take to cross thirty inches. Two paces, a second or two at the most. He was buried in his magazine. A few seconds.

"Girl, come back here!"

She stopped in her tracks, turned, and stood in the doorway that had betrayed her.

"What you got on?" His face had taken on a flat look, the eyes narrowed. That expression scared her more than anything.

"Jeans. Phyllis gave 'em to me." She didn't want him to think she had doubled her sin by purchasing the forbidden clothing.

"We don't take no charity. You know that."

"Yes, Daddy." She felt a flash of relief. It wasn't the pants; it was how she got them.

"Take 'em off."

She stood there, not sure she had heard him correctly. Hoping she hadn't heard him correctly.

"Daddy . . . ?"

"Take 'em off, I said. Don't make me say it again."

She set down her books, terrified. It had been two or three years since he had last strapped her, beat her with his belt. It always started with the horrifying instruction "Lift your skirt." She was seventeen now; he wouldn't dare.

She reached for the top button of the jeans, her fingers trembling. "Daddy . . ."

"Women don't wear no pants. I told you that before. A certain type of woman wears pants—sluts and slatterns. Women wanting to be men, wanting to sex up with other women. Low-class people. Your momma never wore no pants. She was a lady."

Meredith hated it when her mother was brought up as an example to live by. She couldn't be her mother, never would be. It wasn't fair.

She unzipped the jeans slowly. A tear surprised her by falling and splashing against the back of her hand. She didn't know she was crying. Then her panties were revealed, plain cotton panties with little tulips on them, faded from too many washings, the elastic barely doing its job.

And she was ashamed. She had never been naked in front of her father, not that she could remember, though there was a photograph of a naked two-year-old Meredith in the bathtub with her mother that he must have taken. But not in her memory, ever, not since her first period, not since she had grown breasts, not since her body had become an object of male attention.

She paused with the zipper undone.

"Take them off!" The anger in his voice was like acid. He was standing now, his face red with rage.

She slid the jeans down her legs, crying all the way, sniffing back the snot that threatened to drip from her nose, humiliated to the very core of her soul. Stepping out of the jeans, she almost lost her balance. He didn't reach forward to help her.

"You know better than this. You doing it to get me riled? This what your friends put you up to? Toss 'em here."

She held the jeans out, not daring to throw them. Flinging the jeans to her father was suddenly a violent act that she couldn't perform, fearing the movement might be too inciting. Whom it would incite, her or her father, she wasn't sure.

He yanked them away from her. "Get some decent clothes on! Now!"

And she ran to her room holding the waistband of her panties, knowing she would die if they fell.

Meredith flung herself on her bed sobbing, wailing into the mattress so he couldn't hear her. After a while she rose and put on a skirt, the yellow polyester double-knit one, the one she hated the most. And she saw him through her bedroom window cutting the jeans up with her mother's pinking shears and burning them in the fifty-five-gallon drum where he had burned her mother's clothes. The smoke was black, the flames orange.

On her first two-day pass during Basic Training, with her first meager paycheck, Meredith went downtown to the JCPenney and bought two pairs of jeans. Wrangler.

The first few times she went home to Michigan on leave she wore jeans around the house, jeans and a T-shirt, another of her father's pet peeves. And he said nothing about it. Not a word. That was worse than an argument. She felt no triumph or closure. He had won again.

That one incident focused many of Meredith's attitudes about what was expected of her and what she would do in her life. It was reflected most obviously in her rejection of the skirt part of her dress uniform. That was supposed to be optional in the New Army, but on some posts where the Commanding General was still blithely living in the glorious age of hoop skirts and crinolines, the uniform skirt was not only expected, it was required. Meredith had beaten her head bloody against that particular wall.

Besides the mere symbolism of the pants issue for Meredith, the event focused forever her battle over what women could do and what men thought women could accomplish or how they should behave. And it forever defined her enemy, the men who made those inane rules or acted upon them.

Underhill had put himself on the other side of the battlements. She felt bad. She had been getting to like him and wanted him as an ally. Now he was in the ranks of all the rest of *them*. One long rank filled with macho, posturing fools and just plain "old-fashioned" males. Levy led that parade. She didn't want or need another enemy. She hoped it wouldn't come to that with Underhill.

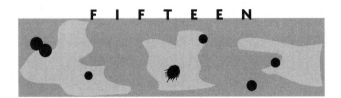

FIFTEEN

It took all afternoon to get enough CID and MP personnel out to the Ammo Dump to search the Quonset hut and storage buildings. Meredith had someone bring her out a sandwich and a soda. It was one of those Subway artery-cloggers, but she figured she needed the protein and was surprised by how fast it went down.

Two hours later, nothing in connection with the hate crime besides the fax machine had been found in the administration buildings and office. Piedmont sat at his desk, watching Meredith and the MPs with a smirk on his pallid face. The MPs were now double-searching, trading places with each other so no one covered the same area they had searched before.

The munitions inventory was being supervised by Underhill himself. That would take all day at least. He and Meredith hadn't shared more than six direct sentences since their confrontation—and that was perfunctory, immediate business and nothing else.

Tate walked over to Meredith.

"Nothing yet besides the fax machine," he said. "Do you think there is anything else here, ma'am?"

"I doubt it. But we might get lucky," Meredith told him. "We'd be foolish not to proceed as if there might be something. Sometimes the suspect helps you out by being stupid."

Tate nodded and started walking back to the CID agents.

"Mr. Tate," Meredith called him back. "Do you think the match of the fax-machine paper is enough to obtain a search warrant for Mr. Piedmont's private residence? You know the Judge Advocate better than I."

"I don't know." He thought about it. "It's slim . . . but everybody is sensitive to these hate crimes today. The JA may be flexible. Maybe if we didn't single out Piedmont, but included all of the Ammo Dump employees . . . But that's stretching it, too. Want me to give it a try?"

"Let's see what we get here first," she said, and let him get back to work.

Meredith looked over at Piedmont. The man looked too familiar to her. Not in features or coloring, but in attitude. She knew his type too well.

To keep herself busy, Meredith glanced over Tate's notes on the interviews of the matériel-transfer personnel. Nothing of consequence had come of the whole process. Twenty-two people, but all they uncovered were a few possible potheads and a man who might be pilfering office supplies.

Meredith pulled her tablet out of her briefcase and wrote a note to review the gate spot-check schedule. The random checks might need to be stepped up for a while, as soon as they had the manpower to spare from the three major cases in progress.

Meredith noticed Tate standing by himself and approached him. "Mr. Tate," she said, and got his attention. "Did you have a chance to confirm Warrant Officer Tocca's alibi?"

"Her girlfriend." Tate nodded. "Yes, ma'am, just haven't had a chance to write it up yet. I was coming back from town when this popped."

"Can you give me a verbal for now?"

Tate pulled out his notebook and glanced through the pages. "Nice lady. Looking at her, you'd never think she was a . . ." Tate stopped short, blushing. Meredith treasured him for that. "I met her at lunch with her daughters, a little restaurant in town. They try to go out once a week. The kids and their mom take turns picking where they eat. I advised her we could speak out of the children's presence, but she refused. Said she hid nothing from her kids.

"I asked if she had a relationship with WO Tocca. She confirmed this. I asked what they were doing the night before last. She stated that they had a pajama party for her girls and some of their neighborhood and school 'chums.' Her word, not mine. The children confirmed this. They were there late, cleaning up. Tocca spent the night."

"Did you believe her?"

"Yes, ma'am, most definitely."

"Did you inquire about her attitude and relationship with Georgia Carnes?" Meredith asked.

"I did, ma'am." Tate checked his notes. "She said she barely knew Lieutenant Carnes, and except for the night she and WO Tocca were caught in flagrante delicto she had little contact with her. She bore no grudge against Carnes and seemed very upset by her death. The children also."

"In flagrante delicto," Meredith echoed. "Your words, not hers?"

"Yes, ma'am." Tate nodded shyly.

"In your opinion, was she telling the truth?" Meredith asked. "About Lieutenant Carnes?"

"In my opinion, ma'am, I saw or heard nothing to make me suspicious of this woman."

"That's good enough for me," Meredith said. "Thank you, Mr. Tate, you may return to your search."

Tate walked away, almost visibly strutting from her ego-stroking. Meredith wondered if he was correct in his assessment of Tocca's girlfriend. Well, she could always interview the woman herself if necessary.

Meredith hated micromanaging. She would rather let people do their jobs and trust their results. There were only two circumstances that justified her stepping in. One, when the people were known incompetents, and, two, when she had no idea of the level of competence of the people involved and the mission was important.

She was still learning about the people under her command, and the gravity of the situation was becoming more significant by the hour.

By dark nothing had come of the search of the Ammo Dump and the unfinished munitions inventory was put off until the next day, the ammunition bays sealed, and an MP guard put on the whole site. Meredith's mood was not its sunniest when she returned to her office in the MP station.

Mrs. Kappadonna was just leaving for the day and there were several little pink message slips on Meredith's desk, three of them from Colonel Levy demanding updates. Underhill's door was closed.

Meredith typed up a report for Levy and made her fourth call of the day to his office. Her other calls had been shunted off on the secretary, Kay, who told her that Colonel Levy was busy and would get back to her. But this call was answered by Lieutenant Vernor, who informed Meredith that Levy was gone for the day, but he, Vernor, would wait at the office if she wanted to deliver her report. She had done all she could at that point, so Meredith took the report over to headquarters and gave it to Vernor.

When she returned to the parking lot of the MP station, Underhill's El Camino was gone.

Deciding to eat something before her stomach rebelled any more loudly, and too tired to search out a different restaurant, Meredith drove to the Bowser Burger and ordered her salad with the chicken breast, still feeling guilty about her noon fat intake.

She was picking the croutons and cheese off the salad when Shelly Daisen came in and flopped down on the chair opposite her.

"Hey, Colonel!" she exclaimed with an energy that made Meredith feel even more tired. "Saw your car outside. Hey, do I have to call you Colonel? I ain't no green-suiter."

"No." Meredith smiled. "I'm Meredith, Mere to my friends. You could call me Ms. Cleon. . . ."

Shelly ignored the little joke.

"Cool. So, Mere, any clues on the case?"

"Which one?"

"The murder."

"No. No clues. Unless you have one for me."

"I don't know." Shelly played it coy. She was going to break a lot of young male hearts. "Maybe. What's it worth to you?"

"Worth?"

"Isn't there a reward or something?"

"I could buy you dinner."

"Not enough." Shelly shook her head. "I need money, cash."

"What for? A tattoo?"

"Got one. Wanna see? No, I wanna buy my dad a PC. Can I have some of your Mountain Dew?"

Meredith pushed the cup across the table to Shelly, who gulped down some of the neon-green liquid.

"A personal computer for your father?" Meredith asked.

"Yeah, he's . . ." Shelly thought for a moment. "I think he's lonely, and you can, like, talk to people on the Internet, and I thought, you know . . . I think he's lonely."

"Yes, I suppose he is," Meredith acknowledged. "What happened to your nose ring?"

Though looking much as she had the previous night, Shelly's nose ring was no longer in evidence.

"You never see a detective with a nose ring, do you?"

"A detective, huh?" Meredith smiled. "You could be the first."

"Nope. The perps wouldn't treat me with respect. Under-cover, maybe."

"The 'perps'?"

There was a sudden beeping, and both Meredith and Shelly checked their pagers. It was Shelly's.

"Perpetrators," she said, reading the beeper. "Gotta go. I'm on the case, Mere. You don't want these?"

She grabbed a fistful of the salad croutons and dashed out of the Bowser Burger. Meredith watched her go with a smile and a little longing for the times when life was so simple that a handful of dried bread cubes was a cool thing.

A familiar car pulled into the parking lot outside the window. Meredith was trying to place the vehicle when Mrs. Kappadonna stepped out of it. That was where Meredith had seen the blue Oldsmobile before—in the parking lot of the MP station.

The woman, wearing sweatpants and a baggy sweatshirt, entered the restaurant and went up to the counter and ordered a cup of ice cream, then noticed Meredith and walked over.

"Evening, Colonel. Just dropped my boys off at the batting cages. . . . I'm sneaking dessert." She looked at Meredith's salad. "Is that your dinner?" Mrs. Kappadonna *tsked* and went back to the counter to get her ice cream.

When she returned to the table, Meredith gestured for her to sit.

"Join me, please. If I don't run every morning, I have to watch what I eat. I haven't had time for any exercise."

"How was your second day on the job?" Mrs. Kappadonna asked.

"Terrible," Meredith admitted. "We didn't get anywhere with the homicide or the theft. Maybe we're close to a solution to the hate crime, but I'm not too hopeful yet. And then there's . . ." She stopped and looked at the woman sitting opposite her scooping up ice cream in a rather dainty manner.

"Annika," Meredith began. "Can I ask you something? Tell me it's none of my business if you want, but . . . is Mr. Underhill a . . . Does he have a problem with women officers?"

"Oh, you just noticed?" Mrs. Kappadonna smiled so quickly she drooled ice cream down her chin, but she mopped it up with her napkin and continued. "Not just women officers. He thinks every woman should be barefoot, pregnant, and chained to the stove. He's not mean about it, but . . . you know."

"I know too well," Meredith confirmed. "Maybe he's right."

"What did you say?" Mrs. Kappadonna exclaimed in surprise. "Did I hear that right? Hey, I thought you were a real piss-cutter, a fire-bringer, the Brass Lady, the Iron Maiden."

"Is that what they call me?" Meredith asked. "You know, my father died recently and . . . on his deathbed . . . What an odd phrase. But once he turned to me and said, 'Don't let the Cleon bloodline die out. You're the last, Meredith. Have some kids.' And I nodded, said I would. A lie for a dying man. But now . . . All my life I fought him. On everything. But now, when I was driving down here I was think-ing—maybe I missed something."

"Colonel." Mrs. Kappadonna set down her empty ice-cream cup with a hollow plop. "You haven't missed a thing. I think that every woman who gets the urge to have a baby—and we all get it—should be required to rent a two-year-old with an earache for a week. Get rid of that notion lickety-split. I'd loan you my two, but that would go down as 'cruel and unusual.' I gotta go back before the boys brain each other."

Mrs. Kappadonna rose and looked down at Meredith.

"And don't you pay Mr. Underhill no nevermind," she continued. "He's a good egg with a prime misunderstanding of how the universe works, that's all. We'll set him straight. You go on home and get some beauty sleep. See you in the morning."

Mrs. Kappadonna dropped her cup into the trash and left. Meredith watched her go with a sudden rush of fondness. Well, maybe she'd made at least one friend. Mrs. Kappadonna got into her Oldsmobile and drove away.

Meredith took another look at her unappetizing salad, got up, and walked over to the counter.

"A hot-fudge sundae, please."

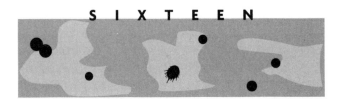

S I X T E E N

When Beth Gorman was thirteen she was sent to a summer camp where they taught the kids to ride horses. One day she walked too close to the rear end of one of those neurotic beasts and it flicked back a steel-shod hoof and kicked her in the chest.

That's what raced through her head as she was flung back by the impact of the bullet. The flash of the gun blinded her momentarily.

As a child she had been called roly-poly by her brothers because every time she was knocked onto her butt she would bounce right back to her feet. That unique response became the source of a game they would play with her—knocking her down to see her pop back up again and again. The game went on until the boys got bored or until their mother caught them at it.

Her mind in shock, if not yet her body, Gorman reverted to that childhood behavior and bounced to her feet, stunning her armed assailant. Staggering in a circle, confused and disoriented, Gorman clutched a hand to the bullet hole in her gut and wandered into the street.

Thankfully, Walhalla at 2:35 in the morning was deserted. No traffic, so she was in no danger of being hit by a car. But by that same token, there was no one around to help her.

Beth Gorman shuffled farther out into the street, barely able to stay on her feet, slowly becoming aware of where she was and what had happened to her. She looked back, saw the figure with the gun. Suddenly that wasn't one of her brothers, it wasn't a game anymore, and she was afraid. She looked around for her mother, but she didn't see her anywhere and she began to cry. The cry was only a whimper, because any stronger movement caused the pain to flare where the horse had kicked her, where the blood was leaking between her fingers.

There, up ahead, she could see it: across the street was sanctuary. A McDonald's, open twenty-four hours a day, a safe place. Happy Meals. She remembered Saturdays with her mother: a cheeseburger, fries, a Coke, and a toy. She had a whole collection of the toys on the windowsill in her bedroom.

There were people inside, and she could see someone behind the counter. It looked so warm inside the Mickey D's, and she was suddenly so cold.

Gorman opened her mouth to call out to the girl behind the counter, but nothing came from her throat. She tried and tried to call out, but all she got for her efforts was an overwhelming impulse to vomit.

Then she tripped and fell. The pain exploded with a small nova that contained only Gorman. She curled into a ball, crying and gasping for breath, and saw the person with the gun coming across the street toward her.

Clambering to her feet, she saw what had tripped her. The curb. It took her three tries to get her foot up and onto the eight inches of higher concrete.

She heard the footsteps behind her and tried to run. And fell again, in agony as the pain paralyzed her for several seconds. Flailing about, she tried to get to her feet again and couldn't. Her legs weren't working right.

Gorman began to crawl. There was blood everywhere. On her hands, on the ground, down her denim shirt, onto her pants.

Creeping, one hand in front of the other, one knee after the other dragging across the ground, she looked up. The golden glow of the restaurant looked like it was miles away. Sanctuary was so far. The footsteps behind her were closer.

Then she saw it! A safe place! A cave, a tunnel to freedom like when her mother used to drape a blanket over the kitchen table. She crawled to safety and got inside.

It was dark. Not scary dark, but safe dark. There was an orange glow through the blanket—the bunkie, she used to call it when she was little.

She kept crawling, but somehow the tunnel started sloping upward and the floor turned slick and she was sliding backward. She slipped on her own blood and fell out of the cave back to where the monsters were, where the bears could eat you, and she tried to crawl faster, faster. But now she was crying she was so scared and snot was dripping from her nose and tears from her eyes and then there was a shadow over her and another . . .

BAM!

Inside the McDonald's, Barbie Holmes woke up, lifted her head from the counter, and wiped the drool from the side of her mouth. She looked around with sleepy eyes.

What was that?

She looked at Adam behind the grill; he had looked up from his geology textbook with a surprised expression on his face. They both listened, looking at each other. Nothing. No more noise. Both looked out the window. Nothing moved. Barbie sighed and put her head back down on the counter, pillowing her face on her forearm. Adam went back to glaciation.

Outside, Beth Gorman was dying.

And she knew it. With sudden clarity, she knew where she was and what was happening. She knew she was dying and she knew who had killed her and she knew she had fucked up. Fucked up real bad and she needed to fix things, needed to somehow make things right, but she was fading, her strength was gone, her feet and legs were no longer working. Only her upper body felt anything, and that was pain, although that, too, was fading and that was how she knew she was dying.

Gorman knew all that—and she knew one other thing.

She knew who had killed Carnes, and it was her job to report that information.

But how?

She tried to focus, tried to find the strength, tried . . .

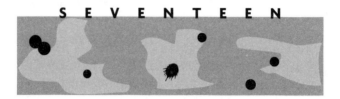

SEVENTEEN

BAM! BAM! BAM!

Meredith squinted down the sights of her nine-millimeter and tried to put a few holes in the targets that had been located fifty meters away down the pistol range.

BAM! BAM! BAM!

The Range NCO walked over to Meredith's side and looked down the range at the targets.

"Pitiful." He shook his head. "Just pitiful."

His name was Staff Sergeant Trevor, and Meredith wanted to please him so much. He had been so patient, so kind as she had fired round after round at the sky, the dirt, even adjacent targets, but nothing near what she was supposed to be aiming at—the targets facing her at the other end of the firing range.

He was the Pre-Marksmanship Instruction NCO whom Mrs. Kappadonna had arranged for her.

"I'm really good with a rifle," she told him.

"Well," Trevor drawled in his Georgia accent. "Maybe you should get a holster made for it."

It was such a nice day. The sun had been coming up when Meredith went to get her weapons issue, the nine-millimeter, and took it out to the range. The procedure and schedule for both activities had been laid out in nice neat memos from Mrs. Kappadonna. Now the sun was starting to warm her back and a slight wind rustled the trees surrounding the pistol range.

It was such a nice day for Meredith to be sucking so bad.

"Try it again," Sergeant Trevor urged patiently. "Pause, focus, aim. Take a breath, let half of it out, *squeeze* the trigger—don't jerk it. Let's try it again."

Meredith inserted a new magazine, took a deep breath, and chambered a round. Maybe if she just threw the bullets at the target.

Meredith could still smell the cordite on her fatigues as she entered the conference room in the headquarters building. It was filling up fast. She saw a nameplate on the long table with her name and title on it: "Colonel M. Cleon—Provost Marshal."

On every other post she had been pleased to see her nameplate on the table for a Generals' staff meeting. But today there was no pleasure, just irritation at the waste of her time.

She didn't want to be here. There were three major cases that needed her attention, but Meredith and Underhill were going to spend the next two hours, at least, listening to the various department heads recite their reports covering what had happened in their respective units during the past week and was already in written form in the meeting agenda.

Usually Meredith looked forward to her first Generals' staff meeting at a new post, if for no other reason than to see whom she was going to be working around during her tour of duty at that assignment. Put a face to a name and title, do some glad-handing to pave the way for future encounters.

But, again—not today.

Underhill entered. His tie this morning was a particularly gruesome mélange of colors on a beige background. She had seen the pattern before—gangrene.

It was a long room, with a long table surrounded by two dozen chairs. More chairs lined the walls, with nameplates above each chair.

Vernor had a chair against the wall, Ringstall's new Aide next to him. Underhill's position was farther down the same wall.

Meredith sat, the Chaplain on her right, Captain Elleston. Elleston had the longest eyelashes she had ever seen on a man, she noticed as he introduced himself.

Levy and Ringstall entered and sat down, Levy laughing and making small talk, Ringstall more subdued. Meredith wondered if this was Ringstall's usual demeanor or if he was still suffering from the loss of Carnes.

Ringstall was one of the reasons Meredith had not slept well. The other cases were percolating through her subconscious, but Ringstall was at the forefront of her thoughts. Why had he and his wife divorced? Two people work closely together, both burdened with the same concerns, the same problems. Sometimes if the two people involved are male and female, the relationship spills over from professional to personal. Dangerous waters.

It had happened before. Meredith had witnessed it between

some of her peers, had nearly been a participant herself. Sometimes the situation went bad. She had witnessed that, too, in her role as a police officer.

She wanted to know more about General Ringstall, but she didn't know how to proceed—safely. He was a general, and the Army had walls of tradition that protected the higher echelons from personal invasions. Meredith had never considered a general a suspect in a crime before, and she had to be careful.

Ringstall noticed her staring at him and returned her look with his own, fiercer gaze. Generals were good at that. She looked away for something else to focus on.

Not knowing anyone and for some reason not in the mood to go around introducing herself, Meredith glanced through the agenda for the meeting. There was a copy in front of every chair at the table and on the seats of the chairs along the wall.

"Ladies and gentlemen," the Sergeant Major announced, "the Commanding General."

Everyone stood.

Schwaner entered the room, nodded to everyone, and took his seat at the head of the table.

"At ease."

Everyone sat, and Schwaner waited for the shifting of chairs and shuffling of papers to subside.

"We have quite an agenda before us today," Schwaner began. "But I want to begin with one item, an important item. In this day and age, a unique event."

He looked around the table and let his eyes rest on Levy.

"We're going to make us a new general tomorrow."

Levy beamed. Schwaner turned back to the rest of the room.

"We all know what the screening process is like. Something like this doesn't happen every day."

Levy preened a little, tried to be humble for a second, failed, and preened some more.

"Congratulations are in order, but we'll save them for the reception. Now, the operative term for the ceremony tomorrow will be 'flawless.' We only get to do this once, so let's do it right. Any foreseeable complications, Commander?"

Schwaner addressed Ringstall, who cleared his throat before he spoke.

"We've got it all well in hand, sir, except for the weather over which I have no control."

"We'll leave that to the Chaplain," Schwaner joked. "That's his area of responsibility."

Chaplain Elleston laughed politely with everyone else.

Ringstall continued, looking through a stack of papers on the table in front of him.

"In case the Chaplain isn't as well-connected as he claims to be, we're prepared to move into Crowder Auditorium for inclement-weather ceremonies. The sequence is as follows—at zero-nine-hundred-fifty, soldiers will be in formation at parade rest on Quiller Field. At zero-nine-fifty-five . . ."

The conference-room door opened slowly and an MP, Corporal Wolfe, literally tiptoed into the room and slipped Underhill a note, then left. Underhill read it, his face betraying nothing, then he leaned over and passed it to Meredith. She read it and smiled.

Ringstall went on with his promotion ceremony schedule. Then Schwaner went around the room getting the various departments to report verbally.

The Director of Engineering and Housing broke down his efforts at fighting the "epidemic" of potholes.

The Meddac Deputy Commander asked about ear-protection

provisions for affected individuals during the eleven-gun salute for
Levy's ceremony.

The new regulations regarding trick-or-treating on military re-
servations were explained by the Director of Community Activities,
and the Sergeant Major groused about the grass on post residence
yards "getting high as Kansas wheat" and recommended that the
various commanders get their people busy with the lawn mowers.

And so they went around the table until it was Meredith's turn.
But before telling Meredith to proceed with her report, General
Schwaner turned to the others.

"I want you all to welcome a new member to our little community, Lieutenant Colonel Meredith Cleon, our new Provost
Marshal."

There was a smattering of applause that Meredith acknowledged
with a smile.

"And Colonel Cleon has had a hell of a first day," Schwaner declared. "The floor is yours, Colonel."

"Yes, well." Meredith glanced at her notes. "We have the homicide of Lieutenant Georgia Carnes, assailant unknown. The inquiry
is proceeding. We have the theft of various matériel that was in the
process of being shipped to Fort Knox. That inquiry is also proceeding. And we have a hate crime, the investigation originating with
some handbills that were posted around the facility and traced to
what may be a source at the Ammo Dump."

Everyone at the facility had been interviewed, and Piedmont had
volunteered for a lie-detector test. Piedmont was the primary suspect, their only suspect, and the man whom Meredith had ordered
pressure be put upon. He had been relieved of his duties until the investigation was completed, and an MP was stationed at his house
with the cooperation of the local police to make sure Piedmont

didn't cut and run. Meredith reminded herself that she still hadn't introduced herself to the local law-enforcement authorities.

She picked up the note that Underhill had received from the MP.

"An inventory of the Ammo Dump revealed a shortage of twenty-eight pounds of C-4 plastic explosive. That's enough to do a lot of damage and enough to justify a search warrant for the suspect's private residence."

She looked around and registered the impact of that fact on the various faces around the room.

"That information is not to leave this room, if you please," she cautioned.

"The suspect is civilian?" Schwaner asked.

"Yes," Meredith replied, knowing the next question.

"All proper procedures are being followed?" the General queried.

"Precisely, sir," Meredith was happy to answer.

"Any link established between the homicide, the theft, and the hate crimes?"

This was another reason Meredith liked General Schwaner—they thought along the same lines.

"Not yet," she told him. "Nothing substantial, but it's not out of the realm of possibility. We're keeping an open mind."

"Keep us updated," he advised, just as a formality.

"Yes, sir." Meredith took a breath and tried not to look at Colonel Levy. "One other thing . . . I have a critical shortage in our Fire Department, a shortage of fire hose, that we need to address immediately."

Peripherally Meredith could see Levy react with a start. She couldn't see Otto Wojahn, sitting to her far left, as she remained focused on General Schwaner.

"Has a request been submitted to the DRM?" Schwaner asked her.

"Yes, sir," Meredith replied.

"Status, Mr. Wojahn?"

Now Meredith turned and looked over at Wojahn. His face was deep red, and he didn't look at Meredith.

"It is under advisement, General," Wojahn replied. Meredith could see his teeth were clenched, his jaw muscles flexing.

"Make that serious advisement," Schwaner recommended.

In the brief silence there was a beep.

All of a sudden forty people were fumbling in their pockets, in their purses and briefcases, or checking the beepers on their belts. *I should get out of the Army and go into the pager business,* Meredith thought as she checked her own beeper.

To her surprise, it *was* her beeper going off.

"Mine," she announced.

Meredith looked at Underhill, who motioned for her to leave and pantomimed curtly that he would stay.

"Sir, may I be excused?" Meredith asked the General.

"You have more than your share of higher priorities. Go," Schwaner directed. Meredith got her things together quickly and got up from the table.

"Mr. Underhill, can you update us on the traffic control for the ceremony?"

"I can, sir."

Meredith handed Underhill her copy of the traffic-control proposal as she left the conference room.

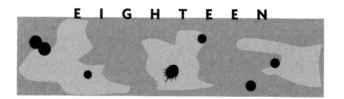

EIGHTEEN

Meredith found Tate waiting for her in his own car in front of the headquarters building. It was a ten-year-old Volvo, and it didn't seem to her that it fit his personality. She climbed inside.

"What's up?" she said, hoping there had been a break in one of the cases. But one glance at his face and she knew whatever news he had brought her couldn't be good.

"We have another homicide, ma'am," he said. "In town."

"Another?" Meredith was stunned, but recovered and put herself mentally into her working mode. "What do we know so far?"

"Not much. Kahla got the call. Soldier down at . . . Fourth and Rodman. Gunshot. Dead. I was still out at the Ammo Dump when I got the call, and I had them beep you."

Meredith had a thousand more questions, but she knew Tate

could have few, if any, answers for her at this point. She would have
to wait until they reached the murder scene. As he pulled out of the
parking lot and drove toward the main gate, she looked around the
inside of the Volvo. She had no fondness for these Swedish boxes.
There was a menagerie of stuffed animals decorating the back window ledge.

"Nice car," she offered politely.

"My wife's. Her parents gave it to us when they bought themselves a new Buick. My pickup is being used to haul the hay for the
school rodeo."

"You don't use the government vehicles?"

"Too much paperwork. Did you ever have an accident with a
government car? There's a new level of bureaucratic, red-tape hell
for you."

Meredith knew what he was talking about, and she also preferred
driving her own personal vehicle. It used to be a six-year-old Jeep
Wagoneer, but she now had her father's Shelby and the old 4×4 had
been given to Aunt Lorrayna, who had enough grandkids to fill it.

They drove off of Fort Hazelton proper and were quickly inside
the city limits of Walhalla. Then they were traveling through the
area surrounding the college. Lots of students carrying books, loaded
backpacks, walking toward the campus. A shopping area geared
toward the student population, with record shops, a couple of fast-
food restaurants, bookstores, and a head shop.

Military posts and the towns adjacent to them endured a strange
love-hate relationship. The civilians grew to resent the hordes of
rowdy party-'til-you-puke soldiers who invaded their peaceful village
every night. The dependence the local economy had on the post created its own kind of pique. Even though a good many of the town
population were retired service people who used the base hospitals
and PX with the attendant discount, the last thing they wanted was

a soldier dating their daughter—or son these days—or a military family moving next door.

As for the military personnel, no one likes to be a pariah, and those running the post were always trying to accommodate a civilian mind-set that seemed in constant conflict with the military mission. There were clashes, large and small, every second of every day. All this while both the town and the post needed each other. Without the other, neither would exist.

Part of Meredith's duties as Provost Marshal was to be the mediator between these antagonistic parties. It was not her favorite component of the job.

Local police cars, an ambulance, and spectators held behind black and yellow plastic crime-scene tape told Meredith and Tate they had reached the murder scene. The street was blocked off, and traffic was being rerouted by an officer at the intersection.

Tate flashed his badge for the traffic officer, and they were waved through the barricade. He parked, and they got out and ducked under the crime-scene tape as they walked toward the McDonald's.

Tate spotted a man in plainclothes and walked over to him. "Hall, what do we have here?" he asked.

"Hey, Tate. Sorry, one of yours. Dead. Homicide," Hall answered, writing in his notebook. "Heard you had another one day before yesterday. What's going on with the Army—some war I haven't heard about?"

"Got an ID?" Tate seemed uncomfortable with the other man's badinage. Meredith wondered if his discomfort was caused by her presence.

"Yeah, we should require civilians to wear dog tags, make identification easier for us." Hall flipped back a page in his notebook, looking for the name. "Uh, Gorman, Beth. Know her?"

"Oh, fuck . . ." Meredith surprised herself with the exclamation.

"Sorry," she said, embarrassed at the outburst of profanity. She felt her throat tighten, bile rise from her stomach, and a deep, penetrating sadness made her suddenly very, very tired.

"We got it pegged for sometime between zero two hundred, that's Army talk, and three A.M., civilian time." Hall checked his notes, looking over his notebook at Meredith. "They found her an hour ago."

Hall led them over to the kiddie playground, which was swarming with police and technicians. He pointed to the play tubes, a maze of brightly colored plastic piping that was large enough for children to crawl through.

"Some kid crawled up inside part of it, came screaming back to her mother, blood all over the poor thing. Freaked both of them out."

Hall nodded toward a woman who was sitting at one of the picnic tables in front of the McDonald's. The woman, being interviewed by a police woman, held a little girl in her lap, dark stains on her playsuit. The child was twirling the officer's hat.

Meredith looked at Tate.

"Sergeant Gorman came to me yesterday, said she had an angle on the Carnes homicide. She asked for my permission to pursue it. I told her to clear it with you. Did she?"

"No, ma'am," Tate said. "I had a message from her, a couple of them, but we never connected. I was pretty busy yesterday."

He sounded as though he felt guilty.

"I know. Believe me, I know." Meredith remembered her last encounter with Gorman, her excited face beaming in the dim stairwell.

Hall motioned them closer to the play tubes. Gorman's body was being extracted from a bright orange tube that had been disconnected from the maze. Meredith braced herself for what was to come.

"Oh, Beth . . ." Meredith looked at the young woman's dead body. There was blood everywhere. A puddle in the tube, all over her clothing—her denim shirt over a yellow T-shirt were both stiff with dried blood. There was a bullet hole in her back—an entrance wound that Meredith could see when the technicians turned the body over—and another in her abdomen.

Gorman's eyes and mouth were open, as if she was crying out for someone. Someone who wasn't there. Meredith felt a rush of guilt overcome her. She wanted to turn away, but she kept her eyes on the body, not wanting some man to think she couldn't stomach her job.

"We had to take the thing apart to get her out," Hall explained needlessly. "Two bullet wounds, one through the tube here. Big round."

"Could it be a forty-five?" Tate asked. Though also shocked by the sight, Tate was taking notes. Good man. And he had known Sergeant Gorman, too. She thought ahead to the day when he would take the sight of another dead body in stride. In some ways she hoped it would never come.

"Forty-five-caliber? Could be," Hall agreed. "There's blood in the street. Looks like she might have been shot the first time in the parking lot over there, bled her way across the street, crawled up into the tube. . . . God knows why . . ."

"You take a forty-five round, you might not be thinking that clearly," Meredith told him, more reprimand apparent in her voice than she intended. "Any witnesses?"

Hall looked at Tate, mutely questioning—*Who is this?*

"Oh, Detective Jeff Hall, this is Colonel Cleon, our new Provost Marshal."

Hall nodded to her, looking at her in a new light. She nodded back silently.

"No eyewitnesses. But look at this."

Hall walked a few steps away from the body to where part of the disassembled tubes had been laid. He bent down and pointed inside one section. Meredith and Tate knelt down and looked.

Inside the tube, written on the curved wall, scrawled in blood, were two figures—

"A Star of David and a cross, looks like to me," Tate observed. "A clue . . . ? Gorman was trying . . ."

"Do you have photos of this?" Meredith asked.

"We will," Hall assured her. "Sheriff's seen it," he added for no reason.

Meredith was about to take Hall to task for not having taken photographs of the drawings inside the tube already, but she quickly reminded herself that this wasn't her jurisdiction. The civilian authorities had their own procedures, their own protocols to follow.

"Is the sheriff here?" she asked. "I'd like to meet him."

"I'll do it," Tate told Hall. Hall nodded and went back to work.

Tate looked around for the sheriff. "I see him," he said, and led Meredith across the street to the parking lot where Hall thought Gorman had first been shot. It, too, was marked off with the yellow crime-scene tape.

As they walked across the street Meredith looked at the pavement and could see blotches of rust-red stains that had been circled with chalk. Gorman had lost a lot of blood just making her way across the street.

Meredith felt another wave of guilt wash over her. Why didn't I deny her request? Why didn't Gorman wait until she had gotten clearance from Tate? Why . . . ?

Meredith stopped herself, knowing the futility of such reproachment.

Tate ducked under the crime-scene tape and held it for Meredith. She followed him as he walked over to a cluster of uniformed officers. One of the khaki-clad men had his back to them. There was something familiar about the head, she thought.

"Sheriff," Tate said as he touched the man's shoulder. "I'd like to introduce Colonel Cleon, our new Provost Marshal. Colonel Cleon, Sheriff Earl Ryder."

Sheriff Ryder turned to greet them. Meredith gasped in surprise. Ryder's mouth flopped open.

Meredith recovered first, sort of.

"Holy Hannah . . . ," she said, then stopped.

"Forgotten my name already, Mere?" Ryder responded.

"Hello, Earl." She could finally string a couple more words together. "Long time."

"Way long," Ryder confirmed. "You've done well for yourself . . . Lieutenant Colonel. Though I figured you'd be General by now."

"Any brass left by the shooter?" Meredith purposely put things on a professional footing—for her own composure as much as anything else. He looked good, had kept his hair.

"None. Must have picked it up," Ryder reported. "Sorry, policed it up."

That was unfortunate; the shell casing would have helped them identify the weapon that had been used. Later, if the murder weapon was ever found, the hammer and ejection marks on the casing could assist in obtaining a conviction.

"What do you make of the religious signs?" he asked.

"I don't know—yet," she replied, looking him in his clear blue eyes.

"I might have a couple of earwitnesses."

"Earwitnesses?" Meredith asked.

"The kids who worked the graveyard shift last night when your soldier was shot. One of my officers spoke to them on the phone this morning. They both heard something at about two-thirty. 'Graveyard shift' takes on a whole new meaning for them now, I bet," he mused. Ryder had always been the poetic type. Read a lot of Carl Sandburg, Robert Frost, sometimes out loud to her.

"How are you doing, Mere?" he asked. "Happy?"

"Not right now." Meredith tried not to look at Ryder. His eyes were too distracting, her memory of him reading poetry in bed too strong. "I just lost one of my people."

"One of yours?" He frowned. "She was an MP?"

"Yes, we served at Hood together, and in Panama," Meredith said. "I knew her."

"Sorry." It was only one word, but he meant it. "Do you think this is linked with your other homicide?"

He would have received a report. Whenever possible, the on-post and off-post law-enforcement agencies shared information out of courtesy and necessity, as so many investigations crossed into each other's territory and jurisdiction. Underhill would have been keeping him up to date.

"Could be." She nodded, more comfortable as long as they were on neutral ground. "Ballistics will tell. I'll get you the specs on the Carnes bullet. I'll send you a copy of the whole file."

"And I'll get you a report on this as soon as I get my hands on it." His expression was serious and professional. "As far as I'm concerned, losing an MP is like losing a fellow cop. We'll all give special attention to this, Meredith, my whole organization. One of yours is one of ours."

"Thanks, Earl" was all she could say. His commitment meant a lot to her.

"Nice to see you again," he said. "We gotta catch up later under more convivial circumstances."

"We will," she told him.

There was an uncomfortable moment for both of them. Ryder broke away first, nodding to her and going over to confer with one of his technicians. Meredith watched him work. He had kept in good shape, too. Trim, maybe a little too thin. She wondered how she looked to him. Then he gestured as he spoke to the technician, and she noticed it, a glint in the sunlight.

The gold band around his finger. Married.

That's right. She had heard that somewhere, sometime in the last ten years or so.

"So we have a working relationship with the local sheriff." Tate smiled. "Better'n the old PM. He and the sheriff fought like pit bulls over a baby. You two seem to get along fine."

"We should," Meredith said. "We were almost engaged once."

They had met at Officers' Candidate School, thrown together in what seemed more like an endurance test than anything else. There was no relationship between them to speak of, no more than that of two people among a hundred all tossed off a raft and forced to swim to shore against the tide. But then, like the survivors of any potential catastrophe, they developed a bond that no one else could share.

She had admired Earl Ryder first for his sense of humor, a kind of ironic commentary on the world as it went by him, hiding his own ambition and sensitivity. Most people saw him as a wiseass. That was only because they didn't understand his jokes. Meredith did.

She also admired the way he carried himself. Most men in Basic Training and OCS were almost constantly trying to prove how macho they could be, how tough they were. Ryder never bragged, never strutted; he just accomplished the task in front of him, mental or physical, with as little angst and dramatics as possible. He just did it, cracked a joke, and moved on. Meredith found that to be an estimable quality and even tried to emulate him.

After OCS Meredith reported to Fort McClellan, Alabama, for

her specialty training, Military Police, and discovered Ryder in the ranks at orientation. They were thrown together again, but in smaller classes, and they started spending time with each other when they were able to find any off duty.

That was where it began. The love of her life. So far, she kept correcting herself, hopefully, sometimes with a hint of desperation. The love of her life—so far.

And she had walked away from it.

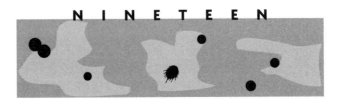

N I N E T E E N

Meredith was able to forget her responsibility for Sergeant Gorman's death while she investigated the crime scene, but on the ride back to Hazelton the other woman was foremost in her thoughts. The car was very quiet, as Tate followed her lead and refrained from talking.

The walk up the stairs to her office seemed especially difficult. By now the news of Gorman's death had reached the MP station. The mood was somber at the booking desk downstairs, and even darker upstairs in the squad room. On a small post like Fort Hazelton, everyone knew each other. They were close, a team, and the loss of one person had a profound impact on the rest. Meredith now had additional work cut out for her—to find a way to get their morale back on track.

And there was only one sure way—to find Gorman's killer.

Meredith went into Underhill's office and took a seat, not hiding how she felt. He laid down his pen and looked at her.

"You heard about Sergeant Gorman?" she asked.

He nodded silently. They were both quiet for a moment.

"I heard," he finally said. "I also heard about her hot-dogging it." He let that statement hang in the air between them.

"Where did you hear that?" Meredith asked.

"She told another MP that you had given her permission to play detective on the Carnes case." He didn't bother to hide the accusation in his tone.

"That's not exactly how it went." Meredith wasn't going to make excuses for herself, but she didn't elaborate. "Did she tell that MP anything about what she had in mind?"

"No."

Damn. Meredith changed the subject.

"Where are we on the alibi checks for the headquarters staff and personnel?" She had asked for a check on their whereabouts when Carnes had gone missing and through the time of her death.

"Everybody at HQ came up rosy. Well, not rosy, but everyone's pretty much alibied until midnight, when most claim to have been asleep in their beds. Carnes could have been shot after midnight, but other than that they're in the clear." He replied. "Secretaries, Ringstall . . ."

"What about Colonel Levy?" she asked.

"Levy checks." He looked at his notes. "He and Lieutenant Vernor were working 'til midnight. Like I said, we can't track anyone past midnight. Why Levy?"

She pulled a Polaroid from her pocket and handed it to Underhill. It was a shot of Gorman's dying scrawl.

"This is what Gorman drew before she died," she explained. "In her own blood. A Jewish star. Levy is Jewish, he's going to be a general—hence the star? Tell me if you think I'm stretching too far."

"I don't know. 'Going to be' is pushing it." He looked at the photograph again. "And what does the cross mean?"

"I don't know." She sighed in defeat. "Anything going on here I should know about?"

"Nothing significant." He looked at the desk report. "We have a missing-persons report, Shelly Daisen, fourteen." Meredith started at the name. Underhill noticed as he continued. "She went truant from school. Ran out about an hour ago. One of her teachers saw her leave. She's been a little wild lately, from all reports. Her father's worried. Could be a runaway."

Underhill handed Meredith the report. There was a Xerox of a photograph attached. Shelly looked a lot more clean-cut here, her hair longer, and she was smiling through braces.

"I know this kid, I've seen her twice. Once with Sergeant Gorman."

That piqued Underhill's interest.

"When?"

"Last night. The Bowser Burger. About twenty-one hundred." Underhill made a note.

"It was just the girl last night. No Gorman. Keep me updated." She handed the report back to him. "What else?"

Underhill had one hand on a piece of paper possessively, she noticed. But he handed it to her.

Meredith glanced at it, then read it more thoroughly with something akin to joy. Not a lot of joy, but the first and only good feeling she had experienced all day.

It was a search warrant from the Judge Advocate and the local DA. For the personal residence of one Dean James Piedmont.

"Want to help me bust a racist?" Meredith asked Underhill. "I figure since I used you to bird-dog him, you'll want to see us bag the bird."

"I think the animal I referred to was a 'stalking horse.'" Underhill replied. "And, yes, I would. In fact, I'm looking forward to this."

Underhill rose and grabbed his jacket, paused as he thought for a second, then grabbed his pistol from the drawer and clipped it to his belt.

Meredith offered to drive. Underhill accepted, a bit reluctantly she thought.

"Nice wheels," he said, looking admiringly around the custom leather interior.

As she pulled out of the parking lot, Underhill looked at her. "You know, Colonel, Sergeant Gorman could be a warning."

"A warning?" she echoed. "Directed at whom?"

"You, ma'am."

Meredith was taken aback by the suggestion.

"You think the killer was trying to communicate with me?"

"Not exactly. No. I was thinking you might want to be a little more cautious."

"Cautious? In what way?"

"Sergeant Gorman was looking into areas outside the boundaries of her mission."

"Supposedly under the supervision of Mr. Tate. That's no excuse on my part, just fact. Are you implying that I am stepping outside *my* mission, Mr. Underhill?"

"All I'm saying, ma'am, is that some soldiers, trying to prove themselves . . ."

". . . as good or better than men sometimes overdo it," she finished the thought for him. She wished she hadn't offered to drive so she could look at him more directly.

"I'm not trying to prove that I have balls, Mr. Underhill, I'm trying to follow the directives of my senior officers. And yes, Sergeant Gorman went out of bounds. I encouraged her, so part of her death is my own fault. I'll try to live with that.

"But, Mr. Underhill, women wouldn't have to step out of bounds in order to prove themselves better than men if they got a fair shake in the first place."

She couldn't take it anymore, and she pulled over to the shoulder of the road and turned to face him.

"I'm not going to lecture you on women in uniform, Mr. Underhill. I'm sure you've heard it a thousand times and it hasn't sunk in yet, so why bother?

"I *am* an officer, your Provost Marshal. So far I have been impressed by your work habits and your people. I try very hard not to let the fact that you are a sexist old fuddy-duddy get in the way of our work. Can you attempt to not let the fact that I'm a female get in the way of your work performance?

"Thank you."

She put the car in gear and drove on. Underhill didn't say anything in response. She didn't want him to. Meredith felt self-conscious enough about her outburst.

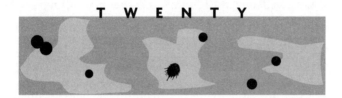

TWENTY

Sheriff Earl Ryder joined Meredith and Underhill at the Piedmont residence. Piedmont met them all at the door and insisted on reading both search warrants, the local DA's and the Judge Advocate's, before he let them inside. Meredith doubted that he understood what he read—the legalese was beyond even her comprehension—but Piedmont was making his little statement; he wasn't going to make it easy for them.

Piedmont's wife, a slightly overweight, mousy woman with dark hair and a pronounced overbite, went out onto the porch and sat on the glider, her arms crossed, a pinched expression on her face. She didn't say anything, but her opinion was evident. Later, when the school bus pulled up at the corner and dropped off the two Piedmont children, a boy and girl, about eight and ten respectively, Mrs.

Piedmont—Meredith wasn't told the woman's first name—gathered her kids together and kept them on the porch with her, protecting them from the big bad enemy who had invaded their home.

Tate had a half-dozen MPs and CID agents searching the house. Piedmont sat on the living-room sofa, chain smoking, but otherwise betraying nothing about his feelings concerning the search.

Meredith, seeing that Underhill and Tate had things well in hand, checked occasionally on Piedmont in the living room. As the afternoon wore on, she went through the house making sure no one was abusing the directive—issued by her—to search thoroughly but not destroy or damage anything. Everything was to be put back exactly the way they found it.

For legal protection, Tate videotaped each room prior to its being searched. The house was a one-story ranch, and if it had a unifying decorative theme it was brown. Variations of brown were everywhere. The furniture, carpet, wallpaper, kitchen appliances, all brown, and not all of them pleasant shades, with an occasional highlight of glaring orange. The living room displayed eight paintings of clowns that were particularly frightening.

Meredith returned to the living room to check on Piedmont and perched on the arm of the chair opposite him.

"What kind of name is Cleon?" he asked, lighting yet another cigarette.

"American," she replied.

"You're gonna pay for this," he whispered as he leaned forward and knocked his cigarette ash into the orange ceramic ashtray on the coffee table. "Letting a nigger in my house, letting niggers touch my things."

He couldn't have shocked her more than if her father's ghost had appeared at his side.

She leaned toward him and whispered back.

"That's nothing, Mr. Piedmont. I've got a Jew in the kitchen spitting in your food."

He sat back as if she had slapped him.

"Keep smoking, Mr. Piedmont," she advised. "*That's* a slow, painful death."

Her beeper went off. She looked at it. Only five numbers: 7-7-3-4-5. Meredith watched and waited for the other two numbers. They didn't come. A mistake. She cleared the beeper. The beeper went off again: 9-1-1. Nothing else. Meredith wondered what was going on, and she was about to go out to her car and call Mrs. Kappadonna, Annika, she reminded herself, when Tate and Earl Ryder approached her.

"Nothing," Tate said.

"Sugar!" Meredith cursed. Ryder couldn't resist a grin at her version of profanity.

Piedmont was also grinning, superior, smug, and not about the same thing.

Meredith rose from the arm of the chair and walked through the house again, trying to calm down, to think of something they had missed. In the rec room two MPs were putting videotapes back on the shelves and straightening the furniture. They had checked the contents of the tapes on the VCR, hoping for a Klan meeting in a decoy John Wayne movie box. No such luck.

Through the kitchen door she could see Underhill searching the garage. Maybe there was some hope out there amid all those boxes of Christmas decorations. She heard Underhill admonish a CID agent.

"Put it all back just like you found it. You heard the PM."

Walking through the bedrooms—one for the parents, two for the kids—and a sewing room, she thought about her confrontation with Underhill in the car. She wondered whether she had gotten into his face a little too much.

No, this was not the time to think about that. Focus on the job in front of you. The search. Nothing had been found. Was Piedmont innocent after all? Hardly.

She found herself in the rec room again, the heads of dead, mostly small animals staring back at her from the walls. A deer, a stuffed raccoon, a bobcat, and, of all things, a rabbit with some antlers glued to its fuzzy skull.

Frustrated, she was about to leave when she noticed a chair out of place. She put it right, setting the legs into the matching indentations in the carpet. She wanted Piedmont to have no legitimate reason to complain.

But then she noticed something else. A fan pattern on the carpet where the nap had been rubbed the wrong way—and more than once. The area was against a wall in front of the small built-in bookcase.

Piedmont, accompanied by Tate, came into the rec room. She looked at him, then looked pointedly at the pattern on the carpet. He ignored her, seemingly on purpose.

Underhill entered.

"We came up with nothing in the garage," Underhill told her, looking at Piedmont. "That's it."

But Piedmont didn't seem relieved by Underhill's news. In fact, he was working hard not to show any emotion.

Meredith walked over to the bookshelf, knocked against the wall, pressed her hands against it. She began removing the books.

"We already checked the books, ma'am," Tate told her. "Even checked inside, flipped through the pages of each one."

With some of the books out of the way, Meredith began gently pushing, then pulling on the bookshelf.

Everyone was watching her.

The shelves were adjustable, two rows of quarter-inch holes along the inside walls of the cabinet, the shelves resting on metal pegs inserted into the holes. Under the second shelf from the top on the right side there was an extra peg two notches below the one holding up the shelf.

She pulled on it. The peg didn't pull out.

She pushed it. The peg went in easily.

There was a click.

With amazing ease, Meredith swung the whole built-in book-shelf out of the wall.

Everyone displayed various expressions of amazement. Except for Piedmont. His jaw was set, muscles flexing, his eyes narrowed. He was not a happy man.

Meredith looked into the dark opening. There was a light switch a foot or so inside the opening on the right. She flicked it on.

It was a small room, a narrow T, four feet across, maybe six feet long, ending in a wider section about eight by six. A Nazi flag hung on one wall over a small table on which was perched a personal computer with a flat-screen monitor. German daggers and an assortment of weapons—pistols, submachine guns—hung on another wall. There were bookshelves, a file cabinet, and a very familiar handbill on the bulletin board. Meredith had thermal fax copies of the same handbill in the hate-crime file in her car.

Piedmont was going to wish he had purchased his own copier.

Meredith turned and faced the others.

"Mr. Underhill, Mr. Tate . . . Either we've found Hitler's long-lost playroom or Mr. Piedmont is in big trouble. Call the others."

Underhill left, calling for the MPs and CID agents. Meredith looked at the neo-Nazi, who stared back defiantly. She spoke to Tate, but never took her eyes off Piedmont.

"Cuff him."

Piedmont had amassed quite a collection, and it took a while for everything to be photographed, inventoried, and carted outside. One of the unit 4 × 4's was called in to carry everything else, the trunks of the sedans had been filled, and Underhill had sent an MP into town for a dozen banker's storage boxes.

Meredith discussed quietly with Ryder whether they had to arrest Mrs. Piedmont. There were circumstantial grounds, but Meredith was against it as it didn't apply to her case on the post. Besides, the children would have to be put in official care until their mother could make bail. Ryder was for making the additional arrest, afraid Mrs. Piedmont might destroy evidence they hadn't found yet, or alert other members of the hate group, who would then be able to destroy evidence linking them to her husband.

"The news will get out without her help, Earl," Meredith said. "And just because Piedmont has a whacked view of the world doesn't mean his kids or his wife follow the same party line."

"I guess not," Ryder conceded. "Let me talk to her."

And he went and did just that. Ryder had always been a fair man. It was nice to see he hadn't lost that quality.

Meredith had Tate supervise the weapons inventory personally. "Any full auto?" she asked.

"Two semis converted, but no military issue yet."

The MPs and deputies were searching all over the house and garage again, knocking and tapping on the walls, checking for more secret rooms. Underhill had called an architect friend of his in to help check the overall dimensions inside and out. No more hiding places had yet been found.

"Do you have the stolen weapons inventory from our Fort Knox theft?" she asked Tate as he walked by.

"Checking it, ma'am."

Underhill came out of the secret room carrying two plastic packets of what looked like narrow blocks of window putty. C-4. Plastic explosive. Military issue.

"Busted." Underhill grinned. "Found it stuck in the rafters."

"Double busted," she told him. "Tate found some converted semiautos."

One of Ryder's deputies carried the computer monitor and hard drive out to his patrol car. Meredith ran out and intercepted him. Ryder hurried over to them. "I'd like to take this," he said.

"This isn't a rummage sale, Earl," she told him. "It's a federal crime now."

She held up the original hate-literature handbill that was most likely generated on the selfsame computer and was now in a plastic sleeve—tagged as evidence.

Ryder took umbrage at her tone.

"I know, Mere," he said. "I'm not trying to get into a pissing contest with you. I know better. Do your people have a computer expert on post?"

Meredith looked at Tate, then Underhill. They had come out of the house as soon as they had gotten wind of the confrontation. That pleased her. Both men shook their heads in response to Ryder's question.

"Well, I do," Ryder said with satisfaction.

"All right, it's yours, Earl, but with the proviso that anytime I want it back I get it. No argument, no excuses." She would have sent the PC and files to Fort Gillem, but it could take weeks to get the results from them.

"Deal," he said, and the deputy stowed the equipment in his patrol car.

There was a beep. Everyone checked their pagers. It was Meredith's.

"This thing is starting to spook me." She read the number. This time the number was a full seven digits and one she recognized: the MP station's. "Has one ever brought good news?"

She went over to her car and called in on her mobile phone. It wasn't good news.

It was the bad news that she had been expecting ever since the Generals' staff meeting.

Meredith braced herself in front of Colonel Levy's desk.

"What the hell were you doing this morning, Lieutenant Colonel?" he growled.

"I'm not clear about the question, sir." She was, but she wasn't going to make it any easier for him. He was about to ream her, and she wasn't going to bend over voluntarily.

"That bullshit about fire hose! Fire hose?!" He looked like he was about to burst a vein. Probably the one that was pulsing on his left temple. "I told you we do *not* bring up anything in front of the General that we have not already taken care of or at least discussed. You have *not* discussed fire hose shortfalls with me."

"With all due respect, sir," Meredith replied evenly, "that is because I haven't been able to talk with you, Colonel. I have called repeatedly and requested an interview with you, and I have had no response."

That took Levy down a couple of notches.

"I thought it was over this Carnes thing."

"That, too, sir. Is there any reason you do not want to talk to me about Lieutenant Carnes, sir?"

"Am I a suspect?" he asked bluntly.

"No. But the first seventy-two hours of any homicide investigation are critical." Meredith felt odd quoting Shelly. *Where was the girl? What had happened to her?*

"I know nothing of Carnes that would help you."

"Pardon me, sir, but it's not your job to decide that—it's mine. You worked across the hall from the victim. We are interviewing *everyone* in this section to see if they might have *any* information that could help us."

"I don't," he said flatly.

"Well, we don't know even that until we speak to you, sir."

"And what's this speaking to my family to confirm my whereabouts?"

Suddenly Meredith's beeper went off. Irritated, she glanced at the pager readout: 7-7-3-4-5. Darned thing. She turned back to Levy and tried to calm herself, reaching one hand down to shut the beeper off.

"Procedure, sir." She stated it simply. "We confirmed the alibis for everyone in this section. When we have no obvious suspects, we check acquaintances of the victim. You fall into that category, sir."

Levy looked at his hands for a second, splayed out on the desktop, then at her.

"This is all about you and me, isn't it, Cleon." He said it, for once, softly.

Meredith was suddenly even more on guard. She knew Levy was at his most dangerous when he got quiet.

"Meaning what, sir?"

"Some kind of vendetta. You're trying to screw up my star."

"I can hardly do that, sir. And I resent the implication you are making, sir."

"Vengeance," he sneered. "That's what this is all about. You are perilously close to a line you shouldn't cross, Cleon. You do and your career is dust. Dust."

Meredith took a breath before she spoke again.

"Does this mean I am refused an interview concerning the Carnes homicide, sir?"

"No." Levy sat back in his chair. "Have my secretary set it up. As soon as possible. I want this out of the way. We'll see where you're really going, Cleon. Dismissed."

Meredith saluted and left the office, proud of the control she had been able to maintain. But still frightened, as scared as anyone who had just taken their first step into a minefield.

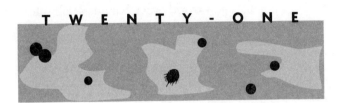

TWENTY-ONE

Piedmont was behind the one-way glass, fidgeting, reaching for his cigarettes, pulling one out, fiddling with it, putting it back in the pack.

He had bitched about the no-smoking rule to Tate right off the bat, but hadn't lit up. Meredith wondered why. The man had nothing to lose with the evidence and charges already in place against him. Smoking in a nonsmoking area would be small change.

Meredith watched as Piedmont spit out his vitriol.

"There's a war coming, a race war, and you're in the wrong Army. You're the right color, but that's the wrong uniform. There's only one race fit to govern the United States of America—the white race. Ain't no nigger, chink, or spic fit to rule no white man. You're working for the wrong people, boy. Wise up. This here government isn't run by white folk no more. The Jews, the 'Illuminati,' are using them niggers and other mud races as pawns to do their dirty work. Read the 'Protocols of the Elders of Zion' if you don't believe me.

"There's gonna be a new world order. Satanists will rule supreme, and every white Christian American is gonna be a sacrifice at their blasphemous altar . . ."

Underhill entered the observation room. "The inventory of the Piedmont residence is done," he said. He listened to Piedmont spew his rhetoric for a few seconds.

"The demonic forces are poised for a bloody overthrow of this here America. Your right to bear arms is in big trouble—that there's the first sign. We'll be slaves. A cashless society, a cashless society— check out Revelations—installed by the shadow government. You heard about the slave auctions in Las Vegas, corporate jets, Arabs in turbans buying our white children for sacrifices, sex slaves. You know what a blond, blue-eyed ten-year-old sells for? Fifty grand. Boy or girl, don't make no difference to them."

"Any of our stolen matériel?" Meredith asked. She was hoping that even if some of the stolen weapons weren't found there would be at least a typewriter or a calculator that appeared on their inventories.

"Nothing." Underhill shook his head. "I've put out an alert to the local and state pawnshops and police agencies."

"Good." Meredith thought for a moment, wondering if this was the right time to try and rebuild her relationship with Underhill. "Do you see any other link between this guy and our theft? Or with either of the homicides?"

"Not on the surface," Underhill said. "There's always a possibility, though. We've got the C-4 from his place. And we have one Jewish victim, one black."

"But what about Gorman's clue? What does that mean?" she asked.

"The Star of David was not painted on Levy's house, but the word 'Jude' was. Piedmont or one of his buddies could have done that. In fact, they are our most likely suspects right now. And as for the cross, a burning cross is a big symbol with the KKK."

"Maybe we should check the Piedmont sheets," Meredith joked. "See if they have eyeholes."

Underhill smiled. Something Piedmont was saying in the interrogation room caught her attention.

"What was that?" She leaned toward the one-way glass.

". . . the General will lead us to a new nation." Piedmont was droning on. "A white nation—"

Tate had caught the remark, too.

"The General?" Tate interrupted Piedmont. "This is a General in the Armed Forces of the United States?"

"We have our own army," Piedmont bragged. "Yours is but a corrupt tool of the government that has betrayed its people, the Constitution, and the Bill of Rights. The Bill of Rights says . . ."

Piedmont's ranting continued.

Tate tried to get him back to "the General," but Piedmont knew he had made a mistake and he wasn't going to reveal any more about his leader.

"That's all I need," Meredith moaned. "Another General on my case."

Meredith listened to as much of Piedmont's diatribe as she could take, but before long it was like a damaged CD. The same noise over and over, it became so irritating she went upstairs to her office.

She sorted through the stack of memos and mail that had accumulated, prioritizing them and making a phone list. The completed interviews of the transfer personnel were sitting in the center of her desk, a stack three inches high, imposing. Tate had said nothing more had come of it all, a few minor infractions, office supplies and petty theft, but Meredith thought she ought to read it once thoroughly just in case something had been missed. There was also a potted plant on her desk, a small begonia with a card: "Welcome, from Annika." That made her smile, and the gesture caused more emotion than she expected. She almost felt like crying, but resisted the impulse and wrote it off to being too tired. She needed some caffeine and maybe some sugar. She debated between coffee and Dr Pepper.

Her beeper went off. She had turned it back on after leaving Levy's office, and it was now resting on the top of her desk. She glanced at the readout: 7-7-3-4-5. She almost picked up the beeper and threw it across the room. Then, just for the hell of it, she dialed the number. Nothing. Dead air. Then the pager sounded again: 4-1-1. She shook her head and cleared the beeper.

She scanned the phone list she had prepared and made her first call. Meredith identified herself and asked for Sheriff Ryder. He came on the line quickly.

"Mere, anything from your little hatemonger?"

"No," she answered, cheered up by the sound of his voice. He still seemed buoyed by enthusiasm for his work even after all these years.

"Did you get the list of stolen equipment Mr. Underhill sent over?"

"Someone just laid it on my desk. Lot of stuff there. You could open your own office-supply store and outfit your own private army."

"It's worse. I just received a notice that Knox found six more empty Conex containers. We'll send you over an updated list," she reported.

"It's an afterthought, but there's one particular local pawnshop I'd like you to check out. It's just a hunch. Mack's. Do you know it?"

"I know it. Hell, I know Mack personally. He's a real piece of work. I'll get on it."

"I appreciate it." She checked off the first item on her list and went on to the next. "Also, I have a missing persons, Shelly Daisen, fourteen-year-old white female. Could you put the word out on her? I've faxed you the sheet."

"Certainly," he said. "Is this a personal request?"

She never could get anything past him.

"I know the kid. I'm a little worried," she admitted. "How's it going with your computer expert and Piedmont's PC?"

"Nothing yet" was all he said about that, then paused. "Why don't you come over to the house tonight for dinner and I'll introduce you."

"Dinner . . . ?" She didn't know if she was ready to meet his wife yet. But this was work—at least work was the excuse for her answer. "I guess so. . . . Are you sure it's no bother?"

"Bother? It's just another plate. C'mon," he urged.

"Okay," Meredith agreed. It sure beat Bowser Burger. "When and where?"

"I'll fax you directions. Seven?"

"See you then." She hung up, not sure what she had just committed herself to. Mrs. Kappadonna stepped into her office.

"Colonel, the CG would like a word with you in his office as fast as your little wings can take you. My words, not his."

"You don't get wings until you're a full-bird colonel. I'm on my way," she said, rising and grabbing her beeper. "By the way, thanks for the plant, Annika. And could you fax the Daisen missing-persons report to Sheriff Ryder?"

Meredith followed Mrs. Kappadonna out of the office and into the reception area.

"I keep getting this message on my beeper: 7-7-3-4-5, sometimes followed by 9-1-1 or 4-1-1. Am I missing something here?" she asked the secretary.

"I have no idea, Colonel."

"Could you get me another beeper when you have time?" Meredith asked. "Maybe it's malfunctioning."

"I'll see what I can do, ma'am."

Meredith was on her way.

As she descended the stairs, Meredith's mind once again darted back to her last encounter with Beth Gorman. The woman was almost a physical presence in the stairwell.

Meredith stopped suddenly midway down the stairs. The letter. She would have to write to Gorman's parents. It was her duty, an obligation. She had written a few condolence letters in her career, but never for someone she had known as well as Gorman. Those letters had been difficult enough; this one would be nearly impossible.

What could she say? Should she keep it short and formal, with as little detail as possible? Or should she dig deeply into herself and tell the parents exactly how their daughter died, doing her duty and more, and how much personal information? How Meredith felt, how culpable Meredith was in their daughter's death?

There was surely a guide somewhere in the files, a manual the Army had cooked up for this very eventuality, but Meredith was loath to look for it. If she couldn't do this properly on her own, she had no right to wear the uniform. Meredith had a momentary flash of empathy for Ringstall—writing to Georgia Carnes's parents.

She put thoughts of the task aside for a while. She had other things to occupy her mind, like who had killed Gorman. That was her true obligation to Gorman's family—finding the killer.

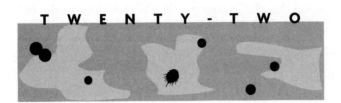

TWENTY-TWO

As she walked over to Schwaner's office Meredith wondered what the General might want, but her mind was so full of questions about the various cases that she couldn't focus on second-guessing him. The Commanding Officer was just one of her many concerns.

BOOM! BOOM! BOOM!

Meredith was startled out of her contemplation by the explosions. On the parade field the 105-millimeter cannons were firing for some reason. Then she remembered: practice rounds for the ceremonial salute at Levy's promotion tomorrow.

Car alarms were going off all over the post like a flock of mechanical birds, all sorts of chirps, beeps, and honking horns, set off by the concussion of the shots.

She could imagine the MP station switchboard lighting up like a

Christmas tree. Another minor problem that would steal their time and manpower.

Meredith entered the headquarters building, glad she hadn't put an alarm on the Shelby, happy she wasn't adding to the cacophony and confusion.

She announced herself to General Schwaner's secretary and was ushered into his office instantly.

General Schwaner's office was larger than Levy's, as was proper for the Post Commander. The glory wall was bigger, with more swords, guns, a few foreign military helmets and hats, and more photographs, all mementos of a long, illustrious career in the Army.

There was a second door in Schwaner's office, slightly ajar at the moment, revealing a glimpse of a sink. A private bathroom. *RHIP—Rank Has Its Privileges,* Meredith mused.

Schwaner motioned for her to sit. She knew him well enough to wait for him to direct the conversation.

"Meredith, I don't need to outline the sensitive nature of your position as Provost Marshal," he began. "Your investigations often take you into areas that require tact and . . . You know where I'm going."

"Is it Colonel Levy or the civilians?" she asked.

"This isn't the time to name names or add fire to what shouldn't be burning in the first place. What I'm saying is, tread lightly, Meredith. I know you can do it. I have confidence that you will use discretion in an already volatile environment, but still, I emphasize, still perform your mission."

"Yes, sir," Meredith replied. "I'll do my best."

"We expect your best, Meredith." He smiled. "You've gotten us used to it."

She thought that was the end of the interview and she began to rise, but he held up a hand to stop her.

"But since you brought up Colonel Levy," he continued. "Is there something between you two?"

Meredith cursed herself silently. Would she never learn to keep her mouth shut? The first rule of the higher echelons: Don't give away ammunition.

General Schwaner pressed her. "I checked the records and saw that you and Colonel Levy served together at Bragg. Is there something I should know?"

The question was, How much did he already know?

"It's . . . history, sir."

"I'm a student of history," he went on amiably.

Meredith had seen more than one officer fall into Schwaner's trap of amiability.

"I'll make it easier," he continued. "Does it have something to do with the charges you brought against him?"

Damn.

Schwaner leaned across the desk. "It will not leave this office," he promised.

Fine, but the whole incident was never to have left another office so many years ago. It clearly had then. Could she really trust Schwaner? Did she have a choice?

"The charges were dropped," she finally told him. He must have already known this, but maybe it was enough to satisfy him. "I requested a transfer and received it."

"Mere . . . Colonel."

Meredith knew from the change in the way he addressed her that she wasn't going to get away with anything. "This is an order. I hate saying that. If I have to say it, I've already lost command respect. Don't embarrass me further, Meredith."

It was amazing—the man had made her feel guilty. She gave up.

"I was a First Lieutenant, Levy was a Captain, my Commanding

Officer," she began. "He kept . . . finding ways to get me alone and then he would proceed to . . . sexually harass me, sir. I tried all other avenues, but finally brought charges. It was my word against his. . . . There was a satisfactory resolution. I hold no grudge."

That was about as clean and objective a description that she could give, especially since it was describing the worst year of her military career. A year of unwanted "accidental" fondling, innuendo, escalating to outright vulgar propositions and comments about her body by a man who, at the time, could have ruined her military aspirations at any second. She had tolerated the abuse as long as she could, trying tactfully to avoid him and defuse the situation, then risked everything by reporting the incidents. She didn't know if the old-boy network would help her, punish her, or even listen to her complaint in spite of the clear regulations against Levy's behavior.

The issue had been settled with Meredith's transfer out. Levy hadn't been punished; Meredith knew nothing negative was noted on his record. At the time she had just been glad to get out of the nightmare, happy to keep her rank. Only later was she bitter about the Army's solution, wondering how many more women Levy would beleaguer with his attentions, how many would quit because men like him wouldn't be penalized, much less disciplined as they deserved.

But it was over, put behind her. Or so she had thought.

"You hold no grudge . . . ," Schwaner repeated.

"Yes, sir, that is most definite, sir." Meredith tried to sound convincing.

"I'm sure." Schwaner nodded. "Does Colonel Levy?"

That was a good question. Meredith paused a moment to frame her answer.

"I can't speak for the Colonel," she replied carefully.

"But you bear him no antagonism, you have no ax to grind."

"None, sir. Absolutely none."

"Keep it that way. Dismissed."

She rose to leave and saluted. He returned it.

"And thank you for your candor, Meredith."

Meredith turned to leave, then stopped and looked at Schwaner. "Permission to ask a few questions, sir?"

Schwaner was surprised at her request, but agreeable. "Proceed."

"Has Colonel Levy been the target of sexual harassment charges since the incident at Bragg, sir?"

"Is this for your personal benefit or part of your homicide inquiry, Colonel?"

"My homicide inquiry, sir." She didn't begrudge him his suspicion.

"Then . . . Yes, nothing official, but unsubstantiated rumors have been circulating. I caution you that they are nothing but rumors and should be treated accordingly."

"Yes, sir. Any recent . . . rumors?"

"No, not since he has been under my command."

Meredith wondered if that was a self-serving statement.

"How about General Ringstall?"

"Ringstall?" Schwaner looked surprised at the idea, then his surprise dissipated. "Oh, I see. No. Nothing there."

"His divorce. Do you know the reason?"

"His wife—she was his second wife, you know—demonstrated a dislike of Army life and the role of a General's wife."

"I see," Meredith said. "Sir, do you know of any specific incidents of conflict between Colonel Levy or General Ringstall and Lieutenant Carnes, sexual or otherwise?"

"I do not."

"Thank you, sir, for *your* candor."

"I've never been interrogated before, Colonel. Is this what's it like?"

"No, sir, I withheld the use of the rubber hose out of deference to your rank."

"I appreciate that." He laughed. "Oh, one other thing. I've been getting a lot of pressure from various quarters on this weapons theft. Some people put more significance to it than the homicides. I tell you this not to transfer the pressure to you and your people, but to make you aware of what may be in our future."

"Yes, sir." Meredith knew what was coming. "Thank you, sir."

She excused herself and was dismissed.

Outside General Schwaner's office Meredith glanced at her watch, noticed that her interview with Levy was only minutes away. She remained at the headquarters building, but went outside and paced back and forth in front of the old building to kill time. She heard the flag rope clatter against the pole, felt the warm breeze and the sun on her face. The General's questions had touched upon a tender scar in Meredith's psyche.

Was she over it? Did she bear no antagonism toward Levy? She was working hard not to carry any old animosity toward the man into her position here. But new animosity was something else—it went beyond rubbing her the wrong way; he seemed to be deliberately trying to make her job, if not her life, difficult. Whatever buttons he pushed, they were all the right ones to anger Meredith.

If she held any antipathy, old or new, toward Colonel Levy, she had to get rid of it now. She needed a clear head, total objectivity, to be able to do her job properly.

BOOM! BOOM! BOOM!

The 105-millimeter cannons went off again. Again she was startled, and once more the car alarms filled the air. This time Meredith could hear dogs barking in the distance, contributing to the noise.

She saw Tate walking toward her from the MP station, joining her for the Levy interrogation. He looked so young. And worried.

"Are you ready?" she asked.

"Yes, ma'am. I'm just a bit . . . a little trepidatious," he answered, and adjusted his tie.

"Trepidatious . . . good word, Mr. Tate. That's a good word. But why? Levy is only a Colonel. Heck, we interviewed a General not too long ago."

"Yes, ma'am, but . . . well, Colonel Levy is a horse of a whole different color."

"Yes, he is." She smiled at him. "But don't be intimidated. You are simply interviewing another witness. The witness is a Colonel, and is about to be made a General, but for you he has no rank. He is a source of information concerning an investigation. You may be more polite to him because of his rank, the same way you might be to a cranky old lady, but otherwise you just ask the questions and see if he's lying to you."

She ushered Tate inside, hoping she could follow her own advice.

Colonel Levy kept Meredith and Tate waiting for fifteen minutes past their appointed time, then had Lieutenant Vernor show them into the office. Rather than taking the third chair that faced Levy's desk and the Colonel, Vernor carried the chair behind Levy's desk and set it next to him. Levy and Vernor together faced Meredith and Tate.

What is this, team tennis? Meredith wondered.

She nodded to Tate, and he set his microcassette recorder on the desk and turned it on.

"Do you mind, sir?" she asked Levy.

"No, not a bit." Levy nodded to Vernor, who put his own tape recorder on the desk and turned it on.

Fifteen all. Meredith tried to maintain a neutral front, and she waited for Tate to pose his first question.

Tate opened his notebook, got his pen ready, opened his mouth. And was interrupted by Levy before he could start.

"Now, my question to you, Lieutenant Colonel," Levy said as he glared at Meredith, "is why are you still bothering us when you have these people in hand?"

"These people, sir?" she responded.

"This hate group." He spit out the words. "They obviously killed Carnes and your MP. And they seem to be behind the transfer theft, too."

"We have no links between the three crimes, sir."

"The message your dead MP left, the missing C-4 . . ."

"The C-4 was within our suspect's own purview. There is no link between that theft and the missing transfer cargo. As for the murders, we are still in the midst of our inquiry, sir, and begging the Colonel's pardon, we're here to *ask* the questions, not answer them."

Meredith and Levy stared at each other. Finally, he leaned back.

"Ask away," he said. It sounded like a dare. Meredith braced herself and turned to Tate. He was very pale.

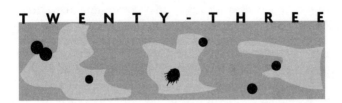

TWENTY-THREE

Meredith and Tate both got the beep on their pagers at the same time. Meredith used Levy's secretary's phone to call in to Mrs. Kappadonna, who gave her the news.

They left the Levy interview early, though it was clear they weren't getting anywhere as it was. Questioning Colonel Levy was like removing a recalcitrant sliver from your hand—each probe caused more pain and difficulty and just drove the splinter deeper. They had been getting nothing but grief from the senior officer; his answers were short and perfunctory and gave them no new information about Carnes or even Levy's own perception of the dead Lieutenant. It was as if he had never met her, let alone worked in the same area.

As for the transfer theft, he stated that he had gotten no closer than processing the paperwork that crossed his desk. Meredith didn't believe either of them. Levy was a micromanager who knew everything and everyone around him. Whether he was lying out of contrariness or because he really had something to cover up, she couldn't tell. He also reiterated the concern from higher-on-higher about the weapons theft. Unlike General Schwaner, Levy had no qualms about putting the pressure directly on Meredith.

Tate drove, since he knew the way, and Meredith read through her mostly useless notes. Once off the post they cruised just over the speed limit to the business route into Walhalla, then around the town and past the bars, fast-food joints, and strip malls.

There were four Walhalla County police cruisers and two MP vehicles pulled off the shoulder of the road just beyond an intersection. Tate pulled alongside the lead car, where Earl Ryder sat behind the wheel. Meredith rolled down her window.

"You invite me to a party, I invite you to one," he said cheerily to her.

"Lead the way," she told him.

He pulled onto the road, and Tate entered the caravan.

It was a textbook raid.

The seven cars converged on a simple cinder-block building and circled around it. There was a cheap sign above a simple doorway with a steel security gate, now unlocked and open. The officers and MPs jumped out of their vehicles and entered Mack's Pawnshop from the front and back simultaneously, weapons at the ready.

Meredith didn't rush in, and neither did Ryder. They let their troops do the job. They smiled at each other, sharing the moment. It brought back some great memories for Meredith: she and Ryder in OCS, in MP training, teamwork so close, so deep that it was hard to ever completely erase.

They entered the pawnshop together.

"That's Cas MacAtee." Ryder pointed out the fat man in bib overalls who was being read his rights. Long salt-and-pepper hair fell greasily to the middle of his back, with a beard to match, tattoos—faded and blurred. Mean-looking if he hadn't been barely five feet tall.

"I want my lawyer," MacAtee kept saying.

Ryder walked over to the pawnshop owner, with Meredith following.

"Mack, you're in deep kimchee." Ryder watched as MacAtee was handcuffed. "Stolen goods—stolen *government* goods. Federal time . . ."

"I want my lawyer," was all the pawnshop owner would say. A pro. Meredith knew he wouldn't talk unless a deal could be made, with a lawyer present to work out the details.

Meredith went into the back room, the storage area where typewriters and computer equipment were being checked for serial numbers. MPs and deputies were calling out numbers and checking them against their lists of stolen goods.

Ryder followed.

"Good call, Mere." He slapped her on the back. It felt good to her. Whether it was because Ryder was doing her the honor or because so little had gone well since she first got to Fort Hazelton, she didn't know.

"I had one of my undercover people come in, a new one. Mack knows all the rest, and she pegged one of your stolen IBMs right off the bat. There were none visible on the floor, so she conned her way into using the toilet, did some snooping, found it in a box. Looks like they were getting ready to ship them out, or maybe destroy the stolen goods. How'd you know?"

Her beeper went off. She checked the readout: 7-7-3-4-5. Meredith smacked the pager a few times, trying to jostle it back into working order. Ryder laughed.

"Can't take the pressure, don't wear one," he advised jokingly.

"Carnes had a pawn ticket in her possession dated the day before she died." Meredith ignored the dig. "From here."

"So there's a connection between your cargo theft and your first homicide?"

"Apparently, but what kind of connection it is, I have no idea." She watched as Cas MacAtee was put into the back of a squad car. "You said you know this guy? Is he capable of murder?"

"We're all capable, Mere, that's the first thing this job teaches you, but . . . I don't know. Mack, he's more of a middleman."

Her beeper went off again. She was about to smack it like the irritating bug it was, but stopped short. The number was her office number. Digging her mobile phone out of her briefcase, she dialed. Mrs. Kappadonna answered and told her Underhill wanted to speak to her. While Meredith waited for Underhill to get on the line, she looked at Ryder.

"I'd like one of my people to be in on MacAtee's interrogation—not that I expect we'll get much out of him."

Ryder nodded, then Underhill was on the line. Meredith listened, and the news made her smile for a brief moment. She looked around for Tate.

"Mr. Tate! You're racking up the mileage today!"

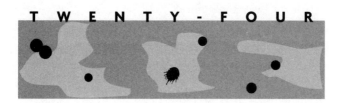

TWENTY-FOUR

By the time Meredith and Tate arrived at the Piedmont residence, two MPs and two of Ryder's deputies were already there watching Corporal Wolfe move the snowmobile trailer away from its parking space next to the garage. For some reason the snowmobile itself sat a few yards away, covered with a plastic sheet.

The other three men raked aside the pile of leaves under the parking spot and began to dig into the loose dirt. Underhill walked over to meet Meredith and Tate. Ryder was close behind them. The four of them walked over to the garage and watched the digging.

"An anonymous call, huh?" Meredith confirmed with Underhill.

"Didn't call through the front desk, probably knew we tape all incoming calls. Came in on my private line. Distorted, like he was talking through Saran Wrap or something."

"A male voice, though?" She looked at him, and he nodded. "At least we have that."

"Maybe," Ryder put in. "Have you ever heard what those male hormones do to a woman's voice?"

Meredith was about to pursue that statement out of simple curiosity when one of the MPs yelled. He had hit something. Everyone moved closer and looked.

Under the dirt in a shallow depression was a long plastic-wrapped bundle. The MP pulled it free and opened it.

Guns. Three M-16s and an M-60. Tate pulled out his inventory of the stolen matériel and weapons and started checking serial numbers.

"Dollars to doughnuts," Underhill said. "They check."

No one took the bet.

"Darned convenient," was all Meredith could say. The others looked at her.

Meredith had Tate stop at the Holiday Inn so she could pick up a change of clothes for later, then they went back to the post. Meredith went to her office and found a memo from Otto Wojahn denying her request for funds to purchase the fire hose Chief Lindell needed. She sat and fumed for a moment, trying to think of another tactic she could try on the little tyrant. Nothing came to mind, so she started working on her report to Levy. She hoped that putting the day's events on paper would help her sort them out, possibly help her see a connection among the three crimes, but the process merely deepened her confusion.

All right, she thought to herself, so Georgia Carnes goes into the pawnshop, recognizes a typewriter or an old computer she had used on the post. That was a long shot right there. And MacAtee sees her recognize the item. Even more unlikely. Or she confronts him about the item—"Where did this come from," she asks innocently—and MacAtee decides she has to die.

Then MacAtee and/or his confederates, possibly Piedmont, who was also involved with the matériel thefts, either as instigator, participant, or receiver of stolen weapons, shoots Carnes. And because they have a particular animosity toward Carnes or just toward women in general, they set her up to die in an unusually cruel fashion.

Then Sergeant Gorman stumbles across a piece of information about Carnes's death or the matériel theft that requires her death also—simpler this time, two bullets.

But what was the connection between MacAtee and Piedmont? How did either of those two lure two women—one of them a suspicious Military Police Officer—away to be murdered?

And how about the very convenient timing of the anonymous call tipping them off as to the whereabouts of the buried weapons? Meredith had solved many a minor case with a disgruntled relative or compatriot selling out a suspect with a simple phone call, but this was too easy and out of the blue.

She decided to make no suppositions to Levy, just set down the facts so far in all three cases.

Meredith finished typing the report and had the Desk Sergeant send it over to Levy's office with a patrol MP. She couldn't risk doing the errand herself and accidentally meeting Levy. Facing him one more time today was too much for Meredith.

She went into the bathroom and washed her face, wanting a shower but knowing this would have to do. She changed out of her BDUs and into her usual casual attire of jeans and a polo shirt, but added a navy blue blazer to make it look a little more formal. She looked into the mirror, only to see a very tired woman. *Buck up, girl, you're going to have dinner with the love of your life and his wife.*

Coming out of the bathroom, she found Underhill waiting in the hall. She smiled at him. "You didn't have to wait around, Mr. Underhill."

"I had to get the Traffic Safety assignments out for the ceremony tomorrow." He handed her a copy.

"Oh, that's right." She glanced at the top sheet of paper. "These other things keep piling up, and I tend to forget we have our daily operations to maintain. Thanks for keeping it off my back, Mr. Underhill."

"It's part of the job. And it works. Those were a couple of good calls today, the hidden room at Piedmont's, the pawnshop. Good calls."

She smiled. Maybe she was getting somewhere.

"Here, you might want this back." Underhill went over to his office. She followed him, and he handed her a folder. Meredith read the tab. Carnes's 201 file.

"Mr. Underhill," she began, "you stated the other day that Georgia Carnes was a friend of the family—a friend of your wife, in particular."

"I did say that." He wasn't going to volunteer anything. Maybe he had learned that tactic during his Army career. Reveal no more than required.

"What could you tell me about her?" Meredith asked.

"My wife took Georgia under her wing more than I," Underhill started. "She met Georgia, recognized the type."

"The type?" Meredith pursued.

"All Army all the time. I fell into that category once. Jackie, my wife, thinks it isn't healthy, not having a life outside work. That it leads to a certain . . . 'a barren soul,' she calls it. She's a religious woman. So she tried to get Georgia, Lieutenant Carnes, involved in other things, activities outside her job."

"Was she successful?" Meredith asked.

"Not really. Jackie hadn't give up, though."

"Have you discussed the case with your wife?"

"Well, I'm more or less forbidden from bringing my work home with me, part of Jackie's philosophy that I heartily agree with, but it has come up." He nodded to himself.

"And I'm sure if she came up with anything that would be helpful, you would pass it along."

"I would, of course." Underhill didn't appear offended by the statement, which was more of a question. "Mrs. . . . Jackie and I both are eager for the apprehension of Georgia's killer."

"Thank you for the information, Mr. Underhill."

"I should have discussed it with you earlier," he said.

"By the way, any feedback yet on that paint analysis from the graffiti at Colonel Levy's house?" Meredith asked him, changing the subject on purpose.

"Yes, ma'am. Nothing special. Tempera. Water-based paint found in most hobby and toy stores. Unless you want us to follow up by checking all the stores, I . . . What's wrong?"

Meredith had been looking absently through her copy of the traffic report and came to the final page.

"The distribution list." She pointed it out for him. "What's this asterisk?"

Underhill looked. Behind the names of General Schwaner, Colonel Levy, and General Ringstall was an asterisk.

"That means that a copy also goes to that officer's Aide."

"Aide, aide . . ." Meredith walked back into the squad room and over to the assignment board. She picked up a marker.

"What if Sergeant Gorman, instead of making a cross, was starting to draw this . . . ?"

Meredith made a cross with two lines.

"What if what she wanted to draw was . . . ?" And Meredith added two diagonal lines, drawing an asterisk.

"And she died before she could finish it." Meredith looked at Underhill. "A Jewish star, Levy, and an asterisk, Vernor."

Underhill's expression was doubtful, Meredith could see that. Then, as it usually happens, the other shoe fell for Meredith. She remembered trying to talk car talk with Vernor about his spiffy Saleen Mustang.

"Pull Lieutenant Vernor in for questioning," she ordered.

"Do you think that's smart, ma'am? Considering the heat you're getting and the ceremony tomorrow."

So Underhill had heard about her problems with Levy, too.

"Just for questioning. I'll take the heat," she said. "I have only one question for Lieutenant Vernor. How does a thirty-two-thousand-a-year lieutenant afford a sixty-thousand-dollar Mustang? Cars. I notice them." She looked at her watch.

"Let me know what he says," she told him as she left. "I'll be at Sheriff Ryder's for dinner."

She took Carnes's 201 file to her office and tossed it on her desk. The folder flopped open, and Meredith caught a glimpse of Carnes's photograph before she walked out the door.

Meredith stopped downstairs to notify Tate about the Vernor APB and the basis for her suspicion of him. She asked Tate what he thought of her reasoning.

"Well, ma'am," Tate said. His tie was gone, his shirt sleeves rolled up, and he looked very tired. "I have a tentative theory myself."

"And that would be?" she prompted.

"Could we have one of those serial killers?" he offered. "We have some basic similarities between the two homicides: female members of the military, the same weapon was used. . . ."

"True." Meredith thought for a moment, trying to recall her readings of the FBI serial killer profiles. "But the actual number of serial killers is so low."

Contrary to the media coverage, serial killers were quite few in number; they just got all the lurid publicity. The likelihood of a serial killer operating at Fort Hazelton was slim, but Meredith didn't want to discount any possibility right now.

"Why don't you—tomorrow is soon enough—put a call in to the FBI and give them the case files, see if they can give us a profile of the perpetrator," she suggested. "It'll take a while to get a response, but who knows?"

"Will do, ma'am," Tate responded enthusiastically.

"*Tomorrow*," she cautioned. "Get home as soon as you can and get some rest."

"Yes, ma'am."

Meredith left Tate typing up his reports, stopped to ask the Desk Sergeant if Shelly Daisen had turned up—she hadn't.

Meredith walked outside. It was nice to breathe fresh air. She took a deep gulp of it, then climbed into her car.

Meredith had second thoughts about Vernor as she left the post and drove to the Ryder home. It did seem to be a leap of logic, the connection between the Star of David and the cross/asterisk, but she had learned a long time ago to go with her gut instinct and she knew deep in her soul that there was something wrong with Vernor.

Or maybe her problem with the Aide was just a spillover of feelings from her ongoing conflict with his boss. Maybe, but her question for the Lieutenant was a legitimate one. Maybe he had rich parents, maybe he had won the lottery. She would wait for his answer.

What was really bothering Meredith was the quick glimpse of Carnes's photograph she had gotten before she left her office. For a brief second Meredith had seen herself. A young, eager lieutenant looking forward to a life in the Army, hoping to be a General someday, someone had said.

Coupled with that and Jackie Underhill's comment about "a barren soul," Meredith was again reconsidering her life, her career, and her future. None of it was making her happy right now. She tried to put it all aside and concentrate on her driving.

Using the directions Ryder had faxed to her earlier that day, the Ryder residence was easy to find, speaking well for his OCS map training.

It was a pleasant-looking house, dark brown with a green roof and green trim, a large yard with an arbor connected to the front fence. There were three cars in the driveway: Ryder's sheriff car, a ten-year-old Buick Special, and a white Econoline van with a magnetic sign on the door advertising a local real-estate company.

The sky had been darkening when she drove off the post, and it was fully night by the time she arrived. She parked in front of the house and called the MP station from her car. The Desk Sergeant told her that Underhill was still there and connected her.

"Cleon here. What's up with Vernor?"

"He's not at home, not in his office either."

"Then, Mr. Underhill, I suggest we put an informal APB out on Lieutenant Vernor."

"He could have just gone to a movie."

"I agree. That's why I said informal. But, Mr. Underhill," she warned him, "if we don't find him by morning I'm going to recommend we go to the Judge Advocate and seek a warrant to search his residence."

"I hope it doesn't come to that," Underhill said. She could hear the doubt in his voice.

"Go home, Mr. Underhill," she recommended. "It's been a busy day. Good night."

She punched out the connection.

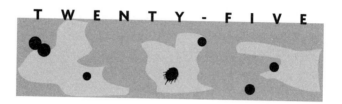

TWENTY-FIVE

It was a strange feeling on so many levels that it took a while for Meredith to get comfortable with Earl Ryder and his family. Sitting at the dining-room table conversing with them about everything but work—whether she liked beets or Johnny Depp, did she have to shave her legs if she wore fatigue pants all the time, and so on. Trivial, often pleasant conversation with the two adults and the children. But overall it was an odd feeling for Meredith.

The other strange sensation for her was watching Ryder in his domestic environment. Meredith was an outsider—and she felt it.

Not that Ryder's wife, Charlotte, didn't do her best to make Meredith feel at home. From the moment she had answered the door and introduced Meredith to their four daughters—Carly, Michelle, Gerry, and Leslie, fifteen and down, a year apart—Charlotte had been open and welcoming. Meredith tried to imagine the household during the first four or five years of their marriage, toddlers and babies seemingly everywhere.

The girls kept up a barrage of questions all through dinner, most of which, besides the usual preteen trivia about which actor or singer was a hunk or not, centered on Meredith's years with their father. They seemed to have been pretty well briefed by someone.

"Your father and I went to OCS together," she explained to the youngest, the Johnny Depp fan. "And then we went west to the MP school in Alabama."

Ryder picked up the chronology. "Then we didn't see each other for a couple of years. We met again at Bragg in North Carolina. Meredith was a First Lieutenant already."

"You weren't that far behind," she reminded him.

"Then she made Captain *way* before I had a chance." He sounded a bit peevish.

Meredith couldn't tell if he was teasing or not. Quite often he hid his real feelings by pretending they were a joke. Or he used to.

"It's taken Earl quite a while to admit that women are just flat-out superior at all times." Charlotte smiled as she said it.

Charlotte was a pretty woman, blond and brown-eyed, a few normal pounds over her cheerleading days, but athletic-looking, smart, and obviously the disciplinarian in the house. She was a real-estate agent who didn't seem to need to talk about her work. Meredith had felt self-conscious around the woman at first, but Charlotte had treated her as part of the family.

"You were engaged then, right?" Gerry, the quiet one, asked.

"Almost," Meredith answered. "I was at Benning, Earl was at Gordon, both in Georgia. We had this shuttle romance between the two places. Are you sure you want to hear all this?" The last was directed at Charlotte.

"I've heard it all before." Charlotte waved away the question. "That's all he talked about for the first two years we were together. I was contemplating a tongue-ectomy at one point."

"Well, I married *you*, dear," Ryder reminded her. "And Meredith married the Army."

Meredith thought she detected a bitter tone in his voice and wondered what he might be acrimonious about after all these years.

"And you went on to make all these beautiful children," Meredith replied, and turned again to Charlotte. "When we were together he said he wanted only one of each. He was adamant about it."

"One *perfect* boy, one *perfect* girl," he said. "We're still trying."

The girls all groaned at hearing the old joke. They finished their dessert, strawberry shortcake made with fresh shortcakes, hot from the oven. And the meal preceding dessert was the best Meredith had eaten in a long time. Fresh salad, baked potatoes, corn, and a rib roast. It was a far cry from the Bowser Burger fare.

"All right, kids, we're done," Charlotte announced. "You can clear the table."

"Leslie is excused from cleanup tonight," Ryder said. "She has work to do for me."

Leslie, of course, caught flak from her sisters. Charlotte took Meredith's arm and led her into the living room. She leaned closer and whispered in her ear.

"Don't pay Earl no mind. Great loves cause great wounds. Mine was Zack Woodruff."

Meredith smiled, grateful for the confidence from the other woman. Ryder was close on their heels. Leslie ran on into what appeared to be his home office.

"And don't think I haven't heard enough about ol' stud boy Zack," he said.

"Earl doesn't let go of things easily," Charlotte shot back. This banter seemed to be part of their relationship—punch, counter-punch—a part they seemed to enjoy. Meredith was a bit envious when she saw them exchange a warm look.

"That's what made him a good cop," Meredith observed.

"You haven't seen tenacious 'til you've seen Mere sink her teeth into something." He took Meredith's other arm and ushered her into his office.

The house looked as if it could have been professionally deco-rated, but it didn't have that cold, sterile *House Beautiful* look. It was tasteful, but comfortable, a place for people to live, not a setting for designer furniture. Meredith liked the house, and thus, Charlotte. Ryder's office was done in masculine Arts and Crafts furniture with real-wood file cabinets.

The Piedmont PC and hard drive were perched on the desk. Leslie had it up and running.

"Okay, Les girl, show your stuff," Ryder urged.

"Holy Hannah," Meredith exclaimed, looking at the twelve-year-old. "This is your computer expert?"

After she had seen the dinner table set for only one guest, she had assumed that they would be meeting with Ryder's "expert" after dinner.

Leslie gave Meredith a look of irritation. Ryder put a proud hand on his daughter's shoulder.

"Best in the state," he said. "Les busted an illegal computer bet-ting operation for me just last year."

"Child's play," Leslie said, and giggled at her joke, then turned to the glowing screen. "Right now I've gotten access to all of his files. . . ." She read through the data on the screen. "Not a lot here. . . . His taxes—he's in trouble there, his checkbook is never balanced. . . ."

"Les thinks we can access his Web site, all the other Nazis he talked to, maybe his so-called general—" Ryder began, but Leslie interrupted him.

"The software on a lot of the Web sites, you dial it up, log on, it tracks your phone number, address, and stuff like that. So if you get on one talking about cars, Chrysler can start sending you junk mail. That data is stored and sometimes encrypted. I'm sure they tracked to get a mailing list—I just have to see if I can access it."

Meredith was impressed as the girl's fingers clicked rapidly over the keys.

Someone's pager beeped.

"Sugar!" Meredith cursed, and checked her beeper. Ryder checked his. It was neither of them.

"It's mine," Leslie said, and checked her readout. "That's Rachel. I'm 537, 'Les' upside down. She wants to talk on the Net."

Leslie looked up at Meredith. "Why do you cuss so funny?"

"Well, Leslie, I used to use all those words I'm sure your mother tells you not to say, but it was like I was just trying to be more macho than the men I was competing against. I decided there was no way I could outmale them, so I wasn't going to play their game."

"Meredith plays her own game," Ryder interjected. "Her rules. That's how she always wins."

"Not always," Meredith said. "Not always."

It was a school night and the Ryder girls all did their homework together, so Meredith said her goodbyes to them. It was a "school night" for her, too. Charlotte and Ryder walked her to the door.

"You know," Charlotte said as she gave Meredith her briefcase. "The citizens of Walhalla are really concerned about Fort Hazelton closing down. A lot of people here depend on the military for their livelihood. Just recently, during Operation Enduring Freedom, some of the stores had fifteen and twenty percent drops in their revenues. That's life or death for some merchants."

"I know," Meredith empathized. "But there's not much I can do about it."

"A few of us are organizing a task force to mobilize our elected officials, state and federal. Would you be interested in helping us?"

"I don't know. . . . I'm not usually a political person." Meredith felt uncomfortable. "But I'd be glad to consult with you anytime."

"It would be appreciated." Charlotte didn't seem to take the rejection personally. "Where are you living, Meredith? On-post?"

"No room," Meredith admitted with a sigh. "I'm on the waiting list. Meanwhile, I live at the Holiday Inn. I haven't had time to look for a place in town."

"Do you want me to check out a few things for you?" Charlotte asked. Meredith was about to reject the offer out of politeness, not wanting to bother the other woman, especially after declining to help with the task force, but, well, she had little choice right now.

"That would be a blessing," she returned gratefully. "I don't need much, just a—"

"Don't tell me, don't tell me," Charlotte stopped her. "I like to play matchmaker. Let me find the perfect place for you."

Meredith nodded her assent. Charlotte took one of her hands in both of her own.

"And it was great to meet you in the flesh after all these years." Charlotte spoke with what appeared to be sincerity.

They concluded their good nights and Ryder walked Meredith out to the Shelby. They stopped next to the car.

"You look happy, Earl."

"I am." He looked back at the warmly lit house. The bickering girls could be faintly heard. It was a pleasant sound. "It could have been yours, Mere."

The statement shocked her, actually hurt, too. "Don't be mean, Earl."

"That was mean? I guess it was. I'm sorry," he said. "You made your choice. I wasn't part of it. I was hurt, that's all. For a long time. It still hurts."

"You know how it is, Earl." She looked into his eyes, those very blue eyes. "You get to a crossroads in your life. You make a decision, and you don't know if you're right or wrong until years later. I made a decision—for my career."

"And were you right or wrong?" he asked.

She had known the question would be coming—she had set him up to ask it—but she still was somehow caught by surprise.

"You came out okay in the deal, Earl." Meredith looked back at the house and all it represented. "More than okay, as far as I can see."

"We're talking about you, Mere," he retorted.

"No, we're not," she said, and gave him a quick, polite peck on the cheek. She climbed into her car and leaned on the open window.

Earl smiled—a bit woefully, in Meredith's judgment—and she drove away. She took a look in the rearview mirror, one last glance at the perfect home, then concentrated on the road ahead of her.

Meredith and Ryder had arranged to take a seven-day leave together in Charleston, South Carolina. They rented a house on the ocean for the last week of September after all of the tourists had left and the beach had been almost totally theirs.

Meredith had been dreading the trip for weeks.

She knew Ryder had planned something.

And she wasn't ready for it, not at all. Well, she was ready, she just didn't want to face the decision right then.

He was going to ask her to marry him.

Marriage wasn't in her plans; it never had been. She knew women in the Army who had married and carried on successful careers. But she wanted an exceptional career; merely successful was not enough.

She felt marriage would hamper her, take time away from her job. She knew Ryder would be okay with the demands of her career, but she also knew she would feel obligated to spend more time with him.

And then there was the question of children. Ryder wanted kids, that was clear, and Meredith had enjoyed their sporadic idle speculation about having children, but did she really want to put her career on hold for that maternal wish? She had debated with herself and had decided on her career yet again.

But she hadn't told Ryder.

He was just too dreamy-eyed and full of optimism about the whole idea of marriage and family. She didn't want to be the one to kill that part of him.

She loved him. She didn't want to hurt him, and it was inevitable that she would do so.

He set the scene so beautifully: a home-cooked meal, a gentle, popping fire in the fireplace, Dinah Washington on the stereo, the two of them cuddled beneath a quilt.

She stopped him before he popped the proverbial question. "Earl, I know what you're about to say, and I want to stop you before you even start. I love you. I do. But right now marriage is out of the question. It will be for a few years. And children . . . even further away. So if that's what all this is leading up to . . . please don't."

He pulled away from her.

"What makes you think I was going to ask?" He stood up and looked at her with a smile. But then his face twisted out of the grin and tears filled his eyes. He rushed from the room.

Meredith watched him walk along the beach for an hour. She had found a little velvet box under the quilt, but didn't dare open it. She knew what was inside. When she looked back out to the beach, he had walked from her sight and into the dunes.

Ryder came back about dawn. He packed his suitcase and left. She tried to talk to him, but he told her he couldn't talk right then.

They never did.

Meredith mailed the jeweler's box to him, never having opened it. She kept track of him through the grapevine until his discharge.

And every once in a while, when things were going badly for her professionally, she would think back to that night in the beach house and wonder where her life would be if she had not stopped Ryder, if she had said "yes."

Like tonight.

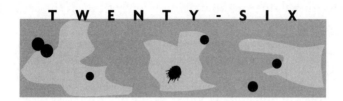

TWENTY-SIX

Meredith was in a blue funk as she drove back to the Holiday Inn. Driving usually cleared her head—she could use the time to sort things out, think things through—but not tonight. Too much was happening: on the job, in the background, emotionally . . . Maybe tonight she could make time for that long, hot bath.

She pulled into the motel parking lot and swore to herself when she discovered that all the parking spaces in front of her room were filled. Meredith had to pull all the way to the end of the lot before she could park the Shelby.

Taking her gun bag out of the trunk, she trudged toward her room, grousing to herself about the kind of people who couldn't read the numbers on the assigned parking spaces and then wondering why she was bitching about having to walk forty feet when she was also mentally complaining that she didn't have time for her morning run. Well, she never claimed she was consistent, she thought as she unlocked her door and entered.

Meredith didn't see the car cruise slowly through the parking lot behind her.

Closing the curtains, Meredith took a look around the room and realized how sick she was of the place already. She had spent much longer times in other hotel rooms—while on temporary duty and attending different training schools—but for some reason she didn't want to spend any more time here. She wanted a place of her own. An apartment, maybe even a house—a home, like . . . Meredith cut that thought short.

The room depressed her, that's all. She was cranky and she needed a hot bath, plus a good night's sleep.

Putting the gun bag on the table, she unclipped her beeper and began to undress. She walked over to the pile of suitcases she had shoved in one corner. She had to get out a pair of BDUs for tomorrow, see if they needed ironing. It was the last thing she wanted to deal with right now.

Meredith decided to start running a tub first. She dumped in a dollop of bubble bath and turned on the hot water, then went back to the suitcases.

Her beeper went off as she was bent over one of the bags. Rising, she stepped over to the table and checked the readout: 7-7-3-4-5. She had to get a replacement pager from Annika tomorrow. She thought briefly of throwing this one into the tub, but she merely cleared the readout and went back to looking for her BDUs.

She got on her hands and knees and rummaged through her folded clothes.

That action saved her life.

She was in the process of pulling out clean underwear when she had a nondestructive thought about her beeper.

She sat back on her heels and looked toward the beeper on the table. . . .

And the first bullet exploded the mirror above the bathroom vanity. The glass shattered and burst into a myriad of silver fragments. She hadn't even heard the gunshot.

But she heard the second shot, then the third.

Turning to the door, she saw the wood suddenly spit splinters into the room, saw the big plate-glass window cascade a waterfall of glass onto the floor, the drapes leap into the air as bullets ripped through the fabric.

The air was filled with noise, the stuttering booming of a full-automatic machine gun. If she had been standing, she would have been cut in half. As it was, bullets flew by within inches of her head and she instinctively hit the floor.

Low-crawling across the room, Meredith made it to the table where she had left her gun bag. She reached up toward the bag, but a red tracer round that blew plaster dust across the room changed her mind. She quickly withdrew her hand, grabbed the leg of the table, and yanked, toppling the table and tossing the gun bag onto the floor.

She grabbed the bag, fumbled with the zipper, tore out the weapon and loaded it.

The room was being demolished before her eyes. Bedding exploded. Plaster, wood, and glass flew through the air.

Meredith crawled to the window, chambering a round as she moved, preparing to fire back.

The machine-gun fire was a deafening roar, an awesome, thundering din.

Then it stopped.

It was quiet. She heard a car door slam, then tires squeal on pavement.

Quickly looking outside, Meredith didn't even see taillights.

Then the night became noisy again. Car alarms pierced through the roaring sound in her ears, a woman was screaming, people shouting, doors slamming.

But no more gunfire.

Meredith flicked the safety back on her pistol. Her hands were trembling.

A half hour later, a Styrofoam cup of coffee in her hands, she was still shaking. Even with both hands on the cup, she couldn't stop the liquid from jiggling. She was sitting on the hood of her car, watching the circus that had developed around her. Usually she was the outsider stepping under the crime-scene tape and into the collection of police vehicles, ambulances, and the like. This time she was the focus of it all, and it was disconcerting to be the victim instead of the investigator.

The night was filled with the flashing of blue and red lights. She had a headache and was thinking seriously of asking someone to turn the lights off.

Tate walked over to Meredith. In his T-shirt and old letter jacket he looked like a high school jock cruising for girls. She had called the MP station from the motel desk and reported the incident to the Desk Sergeant. She put down the coffee cup and clasped her hands together to try and stop the shaking.

Tate held out his hand toward her. A copper-jacketed slug lay in his outstretched palm, both the slug and his hand covered with chalk dust.

"Dug it out of the wall," he said. "Looks like seven-point-six-two, NATO rounds, I think. A fella going to the ice machine saw a vehicle pull up, and someone stepped out of the car, started blasting away."

"Description?" Meredith asked, pulling a tiny sliver of glass out of her palm with unsteady fingers.

"Average guy sighting." Tate dropped the slug into an evidence envelope and consulted his notes. "Too dark to see anything. Same with the vehicle. The witness smelled like a Jack Daniel's aging barrel. The shooter could have been Elvis in a pink Caddy and this guy wouldn't be able to describe him."

Ryder walked across the parking lot toward them. He looked Meredith up and down. He was the one who had gotten her the cup of coffee. She was wearing his jacket around her shoulders. It smelled of him, a comfort to her right now.

"No one else was hurt," he reported. "But I think there're a lot of people changing their pajamas before they go back to bed. The people in the room behind you are particularly shook up. They were dead asleep. Rounds started coming through their wall. The husband kicked his wife out of bed, hit the deck himself. They're damned lucky to be alive. You, too, Mere." He picked up her coffee and took a sip, looking at her over the rim of the cup.

"Meredith, a bit of advice . . . I'd carry that nine-mil everywhere I go for the next few days."

"The way I shoot?" Meredith tried to smile. "You really think it would help?"

"Wear it anyway," he advised. "Scares away the amateurs."

"I don't think we're dealing with amateurs here, Earl," she replied. "This was full-automatic fire, an M-60 machine gun."

"What's going on here, Mere?" Ryder was serious. "Are you too close to these Nazis?"

"I don't know," she answered. "I have a million-dollar matériel and weapons theft, two murders, and some loonies who hate anyone who isn't a white Anglo-Saxon male."

She shoved herself off the hood of the car, but her knees suddenly gave way and she nearly fell. Ryder caught her. They were close—looked at each other. A little spark from long ago burned brightly for just a second.

Meredith pulled away unsteadily.

"You okay?" Ryder's voice was a bit husky.

"Adrenaline depletion," she mumbled, and pushed him away firmly when he approached her again. Underhill walked over to Meredith.

"Why do you do this, Mere?" Ryder was suddenly angry. "The bureaucracy, the politics, the Mickey Mouse fighting for everything . . . ? I'm glad I got out. I owe you that. But why do *you* stay?" he demanded. She didn't even have to think about it before she answered.

"It's what I do, Earl."

Ryder nodded, but clearly it made little sense to him. He turned and walked away. She wanted to go after him, make him understand.

Underhill held his hand out to her. In it was her beeper.

"I was hoping it might have taken a bullet," she said laconically.

"No such luck." He grinned at her. There was concern in those eyes. She reached for the pager.

It went off as soon as she touched it.

"Sugar!" she cursed. Grabbing the darned thing, she reared back her arm to fling it across the parking lot.

Then she remembered the thought that flicked across her mind just before the machine gun went off. She looked at the pager.

The readout bore the same numbers as before: 7-7-3-4-5. Meredith turned the beeper upside down.

S-H-E-L-L. She said it to herself. "Shell."

Then it beeped again, and 3-3-5 printed out.

S-E-E. S-E-E S-H-E-L-L.

"See Shell," she muttered. Meredith turned to Underhill and Tate. They were looking at her with more than curiosity. *They probably think I've fallen apart, she thought.*

"Like 'She sells . . . on the seashore,'" Tate offered. Meredith couldn't help but laugh.

"Mr. Underhill," she began. "Get Shelly Daisen's father on the horn, and get her beeper number. Please?"

The call to Chuck Daisen was quick. The man must have been waiting next to the phone for word of his daughter, because he answered on the first ring. He gave Underhill the number. Meredith dialed Shelly's beeper, input the number to her own mobile phone, and they waited.

Everyone gathered around Meredith's car and watched her mobile phone, perched on the hood as if it might do something important of its own accord. Ryder brought more coffee for everyone—Meredith, Tate, Underhill, and himself.

"Are you sure you want to do this now, Mere?" Ryder asked. "You might want to go and get some shut-eye."

"No, I think this kid's been trying to call me all day," she answered. "By the way, your daughter Leslie gave me the clue."

"She's the smart one in the family," Ryder agreed. "Her and her mother and her sister Gerry—and Michelle, of course, and I can't forget Carly. Actually, when you think about it, the only slow one in the Ryder clan is me."

They all got a polite chuckle out of that.

A nervous woman in a red windbreaker chose that moment to walk over to Meredith.

"Miss Cleon, I'm Caroline Inman, the manager here," she introduced herself. "We've, uh, gotten you another room for the night, but, uh, we have to . . . request that you go somewhere else for, uh, the rest of your stay. We, uh, can't afford to . . . endanger the rest of our guests. . . . We don't even know if our insurance covers this."

Meredith could only look at her in surprise.

"You're kicking me out?"

"We don't . . . What I mean . . . uh . . . This is very difficult . . ." the woman stammered.

All of a sudden, Underhill was between the motel manager and Meredith.

"Ma'am, did I hear correctly?" He towered over the woman, who clutched her hands together in front of her as if she were about to pray. "Are you discharging a guest of this establishment because someone shot at her, because she was the *victim* of a crime? Do you realize how this will look in the paper, on television—that if a woman is attacked while staying in this motel you boot her out?"

He stepped even closer to the manager, an inch away from the poor woman's face.

"And furthermore, do you realize how much business the Army does with your company? How much business the *government* does with your company? That our base does with this very motel? Why, I think we had our last reunion here. I would think very hard, *very,* very hard, about telling my boss, my friend, that you are withdrawing your much-publicized hospitality from her. If I were you, I'd go back to the office and find a key to one of those fancy suites you have on the top floor."

The woman opened her mouth a couple of times to speak, but no words came out. She chose instead to turn and run back to the motel office.

Meredith almost felt sorry for her, but she didn't have the time. Her mobile phone was ringing.

She snatched it up.

"Shelly?"

The answer on the other end was very small.

"Yes . . ." If anyone could have analyzed the amount of fear in that one little word . . .

"Where are you?" Meredith asked urgently.

"I can't tell you," Shelly said in that same small voice.

"Well, is there a place we can meet?"

"Yes . . . The place we ate the first time we met, the Bowser Burger. Alone." There was some force and insistence in that last word.

"You can trust my people," Meredith countered, confused.

"Alone. Just you. Nobody else." The little-girl voice was pleading, on the verge of tears.

"Okay, okay. Alone. You and me. No one else."

"Promise?"

"Promise. Fifteen minutes?"

"Fifteen minutes."

And Shelly hung up. Meredith punched out the connection and looked at the others.

"She sounds scared. Real scared," she told them. "I'll go meet her. Can you all stand by?"

"Be careful," Ryder warned.

"What else can I be afraid of tonight?" she tried to joke. "Unless the kid is driving an Abrams tank with a ninety-millimeter cannon pointed at my chest, I'll feel safe."

"We'll stay close," Underhill said, and handed her a walkie-talkie.

"In case there's a tank missing," Tate completed.

They all smiled. Meredith sensed her heart swell with pride. She felt suddenly like she was part of a team, that they were all behind her. She pulled herself out of it. This was not the time to get emotional.

"Not too close," she ordered. "Completely out of sight." She turned to Ryder. "You can go home."

"No," he said. "We'll stay available until you're done for the night. As usual, things happen when you're around."

Meredith opened her car door. The hotel manager came running across the parking lot and thrust a room key into Meredith's hand.

"Your room for tonight," the woman said. "And the rest of your stay . . . as long as you want. At the same rate as your . . . previous room."

And she skittered away. Meredith looked at the key. A suite on the top floor. Underhill leaned into the driver's window.

"You have your side arm?" he asked.

"In my briefcase," she acknowledged. She laid her hand on his. "Thanks." She showed him the key.

"Well, Colonel, it's like a family," he said. "We can bicker all we want with each other, but some outsider starts to pick on one of our own and we present a united front. Don't we?"

"We do." She smiled. He smiled back.

She started the car.

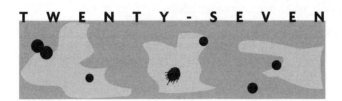

TWENTY-SEVEN

On the way to Fort Hazelton, Meredith called in on the walkie-talkie and told Underhill to get on the radio and tell the regular patrols to keep a good distance away from the Bowser Burger so as not to scare off Shelly.

When Meredith drove into the restaurant parking lot there was no sign of Underhill or any of the MPs. And no sign of Shelly Daisen, either.

She took a seat near the front window so the girl could see her easily if she was watching from somewhere nearby. It was another five minutes before a dirty, tired, and very suspicious Shelly made her appearance, slinking out of the men's room.

The girl looked around fearfully and sat opposite Meredith, then launched immediately into an angry tirade.

"Where have you been?! I've been beeping you all day! Where were you?! I called and called, and every time I went to a phone . . . It was scary. And you didn't answer! You didn't answer!"

Shelly was very angry, but also very near tears.

"I'm sorry, Shelly, but I didn't know the code."

"And you call yourself a detective," the teenager shot back scornfully.

"I don't," Meredith confessed. "I'm the PM. The detectives work for me. Why didn't you just call me?"

"You're never in your office."

"Oh." Shelly was partly right. Meredith had been in and out of the office all day. "I've been busy. You could have called my mobile phone."

"They wouldn't give me the number. Said to leave a message or my name."

"And you couldn't do that?" Meredith asked.

"No, he might find out." Shelly looked around, suddenly more paranoid. "Can we go get a booth?"

"Certainly." They got up, and Meredith led her toward the back of the restaurant and put her into a booth.

Meredith went quickly back to the counter and ordered some food for the girl. Shelly sat facing the front of the restaurant, slouching low in the booth so no one could see her from outside.

In a few minutes, Shelly was sucking up a milk shake and chomping into a cheeseburger and fries like she had been a member of the Donner Party.

"Now," Meredith began calmly. "Who are you afraid of, Shelly—and why?"

"The guy that killed Sergeant Gorman. She was my friend. He killed her. He'll kill me, too."

"Who, Shelly?"

"Lieutenant Vernor."

"Colonel Levy's Aide?"

"Yes."

"Why would he want to kill you?"

"'Cause I can blow his alibi." She was working on the fries, the cheeseburger having been almost inhaled.

"I told Sergeant Gorman, and now she's dead. She said she was going to check on it. Then she was dead. He killed her. He'll kill me."

"You saw Lieutenant Vernor the night Georgia Carnes was killed?"

"The next morning, after I met you, I saw Sergeant Gorman when I was walking to school. She was finishing her shift and we was talking and everything, about the murder and stuff, and I told her I was thinking about, you know, getting to be a detective, and she said wow, like, so was she. Maybe she didn't say 'wow,' but she said she was going to be a CID detective and we was talking some more and she said that they didn't have no leads 'cause everybody had alibis and everything. And later, at school, I thought about that and I remembered seeing Lieutenant Vernor that night and I called her at home—I know where she lives 'cause I seen her in her yard once— and asked her if Vernor had an alibi, and she said yes, that he was with Colonel Levy from seven to midnight."

Meredith made a mental note that she had better remind everyone in her unit that the details of any case were not to be discussed with anyone outside the investigation, especially an enthusiastic fourteen-year-old.

"Where did you see Lieutenant Vernor?"

"Out by the old K-9 barracks. They've been abandoned, and some of us kids go out there to smoke dope. Not crack or nothing, just grass. And I won't tell you the other kids' names, they're not . . . relevant to the investigation."

"Did these other kids see Lieutenant Vernor, too?"

"No. I went outside to . . . pee. The boys go and pee in the corner, but if the girls do it the boys see your butt and get all weird. So I went outside, and I saw Vernor and another guy, looked like Yosemite Sam, the cartoon character."

Yosemite Sam. Cas MacAtee, the pawnbroker.

"What were they doing, Shelly?"

"Loading sandbags into a van."

"Sandbags . . ." Meredith felt the tumblers clicking into place.

"Yeah, there's sandbags all over the place out there—part of the old stockade, I think."

Meredith let her finish the fries before speaking again.

"Shelly, I'm going to call your father and tell him you're okay. Then I know a place where you'll be safe tonight. One more kid there won't be noticed. And you'll need to tell your story to Mr. Tate."

Shelly looked at her, deciding whether she could trust her or not.

"I won't let anything happen to you, Shelly," Meredith assured her. "I promise."

"Is my father going to get in trouble because I was out smoking pot or ran away or anything?"

"No, not at all," Meredith assured her.

"Amnesty or something like that?" Shelly offered.

"Something like that. We're all just glad you're alive and safe."
Those were the wrong words. Shelly's mood instantly darkened, and her eyes teared up.

"It's my fault Sergeant Gorman's dead, isn't it?" she asked. "After I saw you last night, I called her and told her about Vernor and she said she was going to confirm his alibi. She went and saw him, and he killed her, huh?"

"It's not your fault, Shelly." Meredith took one of the girl's hands in her own. *No, it's mine,* she felt like adding. "Now let's put you someplace safe."

"Okay."

Meredith picked up the walkie-talkie and called Underhill, and there were three MP cars in the Bowser Burger parking lot in less than thirty seconds. She didn't know where the cars had been hidden, but she felt a little more comfortable and, yes, even safer that they arrived so quickly.

Meredith also called Ryder, and he showed up not two minutes later. It felt good to know that there were so many people out there who were concerned about her safety.

Shelly was upset by all the official activity at first, but she soon settled in comfortably with being the center of attention. Tate took her statement in the presence of her father, whom Underhill had waiting in a vehicle.

Meredith had watched the teenager run into her father's arms when he entered the restaurant. The two of them held each other, tears in both their eyes. They squeezed and kissed and apologized and accused, then hugged and cried.

The scene between father and daughter touched a deep, painful part of Meredith.

Separating Shelly and her father and getting them to settle down was difficult, but taking the statement was easier. When that was over they hit a snag, as Meredith tried to convince the girl to get into Ryder's car and stay with his family for a while. Shelly didn't want to go; she didn't know Ryder as anyone but a cop—a local cop at that, her nemesis and the enemy of all of her friends. Chuck Daisen didn't understand why his daughter couldn't go home with him.

Meredith talked to both of them at some length, outlining the danger to Shelly as long as Vernor wasn't in custody. Shelly then wanted to spend the night with Meredith, who wasn't about to tell the girl or her father about the attack on her at the Holiday Inn. Being with Meredith would be the least safe place for Shelly.

Finally Ryder asked Meredith's permission to speak with the Daisens, and he took them aside. Meredith left them in his hands and conferred with Underhill and Tate.

"Anything at Vernor's residence?" she asked.

The girl's statement had been enough to generate a search warrant for Vernor's residence, and Meredith had sent a team over quickly.

"He was vapor," Tate said. "No car, no bankbooks. There was a police band tuned to our channels. I think when we sent out the first call to bring him in for questioning, he heard it and went rabbit."

"You think he's in a hole somewhere nearby?" Meredith asked. "Or is he on his way to Canada or the nearest airport?"

"If you ask me," Underhill broke in. "I think he hung around long enough to pump five hundred rounds from an M-60 at you." He nodded toward Meredith.

"Why would he hang around to do that?" Tate wondered.

"I don't know," Meredith admitted. "We were closing in—why waste the time coming after me? Get a full-blown APB out on Vernor, with photos to the FBI, airports, all agencies."

"Yes, ma'am." Underhill looked outside at Earl Ryder and the Daisens. Ryder and Chuck Daisen were shaking hands. Shelly climbed into the front seat of Ryder's cruiser.

Meredith shook her head in rueful appreciation. He hadn't lost any of his charm or powers of persuasion. Underhill got her attention by touching her arm lightly. It was surprisingly intimate contact.

"Colonel," he said softly, "do you want to brace Colonel Levy with the news about his Aide tonight? I'll do it if you want."

Meredith thought about it. She was tired and she knew it, so she took the moment to consider her next move. She had to proceed more than carefully with Levy.

"No, I'll tell him." It wouldn't do for an underling to deliver the bad news—from Levy's point of view, or from Meredith's for that matter. "But not tonight. I'm tired, you're tired, and what good can we do tonight?"

She wanted to be at her best when she had to confront Levy with this kind of information.

"Tough call, Colonel," Underhill added.

"What's that, Mr. Underhill?"

"Do you ruin the man's day before or after he gets his star?"

In the excitement Meredith had forgotten about Levy's promotion to general, the ceremony tomorrow. She needed to get some sleep. She headed outside to say goodbye to Shelly.

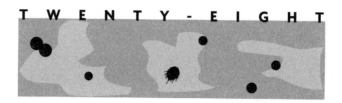

TWENTY-EIGHT

Meredith's new room at the Holiday Inn was a lot nicer: two beds, a living-room area, and a comparatively spacious and well-appointed bathroom. Her clothes and toilet articles had been moved for her—the things that hadn't been destroyed—everything hung up or arranged neatly on the vanity, the suitcases lined up inside the closet, she discovered. In the morning she would have to thank Caroline Inman. Then Meredith locked the door with both the deadbolt and the chain.

Starting a bath, but skipping the bubbles this time, she stripped, dropping her clothes onto the floor. She caught her reflection in the full-length mirror mounted on the bathroom door. She had cuts on her knees, forearms, and palms from crawling across the broken glass, and a couple of large bruises, the source of which she couldn't remember.

The cuts stung when she lowered herself into the hot water, but the heat soaked into her bones and she felt all the kinks in her muscles start to melt away. Leaning back and closing her eyes, she emptied her mind and tried to become a puddle of flesh with a few bones floating in the middle of it all.

Her gun was on the floor within reach.

Piedmont and his hate group seemed to be implicated in the transfer theft—some of the stolen weapons had been found buried in the racist's yard.

That meant Vernor, whom Shelly had seen with Cas MacAtee, was somehow linked with Piedmont, too. How did a racist like Piedmont and a black Army officer, Vernor, ever get together? Did their mutual greed somehow overcome all that prejudice? Or had Vernor planted the guns to divert suspicion and cement the case against Piedmont? Maybe they *were* separate cases.

It was hard for her to concentrate on the cases. Images of Earl Ryder kept creeping in at the edges of her consciousness. Him holding her close, his face inches from Meredith's, his eyes looking deep into hers, his lips so near . . .

She yanked herself back to the case.

Georgia Carnes must have seen something at the pawnshop when she had taken in her old stereo. Something that Vernor learned about and was afraid she would pass on to Ringstall. Maybe it was inconsequential as far as Carnes was concerned, maybe it was Vernor himself at the pawnshop, but his excuse for being there wouldn't hold up under prolonged examination.

So he killed her.

Then Sergeant Gorman had started digging into Vernor's alibi and she had to die, too.

But why did Levy provide an alibi for Vernor? Was he protecting his Aide? That wasn't like Levy. Meredith knew the man, it was purely C-Y-A for Colonel Levy. Cover *Your* Ass, and to hell with anyone else. Maybe Vernor had something on Levy and could blackmail the Colonel—excuse me . . . General. She was going to have to get used to Levy's new rank.

One time Meredith and Ryder had gone to Myrtle Beach on a weekend pass. They had lain on the sand necking and kissing. No sex, but as close as anybody could get to it, touching, caressing lazily for hours through the day and into the night. The tide came in and licked at their feet, the water as warm as a bath, adding to the sensuality. . . .

There were all those other puzzling questions.

Who was Piedmont's general?

What was bothering Meredith about that graffiti spray-painted on Levy's house? She had to put her finger on it.

Who shot at her? Vernor? And why, if he was on the run?

Maybe he just didn't like her. There were enough people around who felt the same way.

Meredith wondered why she wasn't happier. She had all three major crimes virtually solved. There were plenty of loose ends, but there were always loose ends, even after you closed the books on a case.

The water was cooling. Her nipples had puckered from soaking so long, and she covered her breasts with her hands to warm them. And wished they were Ryder's hands. . . .

Meredith quickly climbed out of the tub, dried herself with more vigor than required, put on panties and an old Ranger T-shirt, and climbed into bed.

She set her gun on the night table, argued with herself about putting more clothes on, just in case, then discarded the idea as silly. And she was too tired to get up again.

But she couldn't sleep.

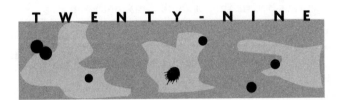

TWENTY-NINE

The sun was just beginning to lighten the night sky as Meredith drove onto the post. It was that peculiar predawn time, and when she reached the Senior Officers' Residential Area she stepped out of her car and craned her head skyward to admire it.

It was a nice moment, peaceful, quiet. Not even the birds were awake yet. It was the first respite she had enjoyed in days, she suddenly realized. There was a chill in the air, not a frost, but close to that, and some of the leaves had started to turn color—gold and hints of red and orange in the trees.

A red and white Chevrolet Caprice sedan pulled up and Fire Chief Lindell stepped out. Even at this hour of the morning he was in his uniform. He walked over to her.

"Sorry about the early hour, Chief," she apologized. "But I have a hell of a day ahead of me."

"You have a couple of bad ones behind you," he replied with genuine sympathy. She might get to like this morose man.

"Tell me about it." She smiled at him.

"Well, you certainly don't have to bother with me right now, ma'am."

"No, no." Meredith shook her head. "I'd like to start today out by making just one thing work. Did you bring it?"

"Yes, ma'am."

"Hook it up there and run it over to that house." She pointed to a large brick house a short distance down the street from the curbside fire hydrant.

"That house?" Chief Lindell looked at the house, at her. *Mr. Tate would call his look "trepidatious,"* Meredith thought.

"That house," she confirmed.

Chief Lindell nodded and went back to his sedan, opened the trunk, and got to work.

Meredith felt that surge of satisfaction when a soldier took an order they weren't sure about, but carried it out because they had confidence in their officer. They trusted you.

The Chief was working on the hydrant when the MP vehicle rolled up and two officers helped a sleepy-eyed Otto Wojahn out of the back and escorted him over to Meredith.

Wojahn wasn't too sleepy to get into Meredith's face.

"Your people said this was an emergency," he said, his voice heavy with disdain. "It had better be a crisis of major proportions, Lieutenant Colonel."

"Judge for yourself." Meredith didn't back down. "Walk with me, Mr. Wojahn."

Meredith led Wojahn over to the fire hydrant, where Chief Lindell had hooked up a fire hose, then along the length of the uncurled hose to where it ended in a shiny brass coupling. Lindell stood there waiting, watching.

"Fire hose," Wojahn noted. "You are begging for trouble, Lieutenant Colonel."

"No, you are, Mr. Wojahn," Meredith replied evenly. "Do you see that house?"

She pointed to the grand, redbrick house.

"Yes," Wojahn said impatiently. "Commanding General Schwaner's house."

"See how far away it is from here? What would you say, a hundred meters, give or take?"

Otto wasn't interested or impressed.

Meredith went on. "If that house caught fire—and remember how old the wiring is in these residences, how dry that old wood framing might be—and the Chief here responded with his fire trucks . . . He would hook up that hose there and he would not be able to reach the flames. "It's too far away.

"And he couldn't get any closer, because this is the extent of the fire hose he has for these old hydrants. Now, he asked for the old hydrants to be replaced in the past, but the cost was prohibitive and his request was denied by you and your department. I'd say that was reasonable.

"But if the hydrants aren't replaced, then we need enough fire hose to enable the Fire Department to perform its mission.

"As it is, to be succinct, Mr. Wojahn, the General's house, among others, could burn down because *you* will not give us the funds for new fire hose. Human lives could be lost because you won't allot the funds."

Otto Wojahn opened his mouth to protest or make excuses, but Meredith didn't care and didn't let him talk. She got into *his* face and continued.

"To be cynical, Mr. Wojahn, lawsuits and possible criminal negligence charges could ensue because your department will not see to providing the minimum equipment needed for the safety of this post.

"And I, for one, would be most willing to testify at your trial."

Wojahn took a moment, pursing his mouth, testing the sourness of the words he had to say.

"Your point is made," Wojahn said tersely. "May I go now?"

"No," Meredith said flatly. "I *will* have the approved funding on my desk by noon today *or* I will repeat this demonstration for General Schwaner himself."

Wojahn nodded, taking the orders in, looking at the General's residence. "You'll have it by noon."

"Thank you, Mr. Wojahn." Meredith softened her voice and her stance. "And I apologize for any problems we may have had during the past few days. I hope our dealings will be much more amicable in the future."

It was just enough stroking to placate Wojahn and help him save face. He even smiled. His teeth were yellow.

"And at a better hour. May I go now?" he asked.

Meredith nodded to him and turned to the two MPs. "Take Mr. Wojahn wherever he wants to go," she told them. "I'm going to the pistol range to practice. Tell Mr. Underhill I'll be in a little late, but he can page me for an emergency."

The MPs saluted and walked Wojahn back to their patrol vehicle and drove away.

Chief Lindell was rolling up his fire hose in that neat, flat manner typical of all firemen. "Thank you, Colonel," he said. "Thank you so very much."

"It was my pleasure entirely, Chief." And it was. "It's part of my job." She smiled, deeply satisfied.

That satisfaction was still warming Meredith's soul as she parked at the pistol range. It was empty, no Range Officer or NCO at this hour. They wouldn't be on duty for a couple of hours. It was against regulations for her to be on the range alone, but she needed the practice and her day was not going to allow her any other time. She wanted to qualify tomorrow, get Levy off her case.

Meredith had brought her own targets, a half-dozen filched from the range NCO in expectation of this eventuality, and she pinned them up and walked back to the firing line.

She took her pistol out of the bag and loaded her magazines with the box of nine-millimeter rounds, inserted one magazine, chambered a round, and took her stance. She fired.

She was awful.

Sometimes she missed the target entirely.

But she persisted, following the Range Officer's directions of the previous day, and something started to happen.

Concentrating on her shooting, trying to steady her breathing and focus on the sights and the targets, raising the pistol and aiming, taking a breath and letting half of it out, squeezing the trigger gently—being surprised by the muzzle blast and the feeling of the weapon jumping in her hand. The process seemed to calm her, give her some kind of Zenlike peace, and her mind began to wander.

The focus was there, the target—the nine-mil in her hand—but she felt herself step away from it all, almost an out-of-body experience.

Once she had been standing in the back of a five-ton truck parked below a ridge that was lined with eight-inch artillery pieces and one of them, without warning, fired a practice round. The concussion blew her off the truck; the giant sound wave that surged from the muzzle threw her body, with one instant jolt of pain, down and out of the truck.

Lying there in the dirt, more unconscious than conscious, she had suddenly found herself floating above her own body—looking down at Meredith Cleon. She was stretched out on the ground, stunned from the impact. For that brief second or two, things had become clear to her. Things she had been struggling with for months, some for years. Big things, like her career, her love life, little things like her cursing, the color of her lipstick. In that brief instant Meredith made a whole slew of decisions and changed her life. Just as quickly she was back in her body, muscles sore, head splitting with a headache that would last a week, bleeding from one ear with some permanent hearing loss in the higher registers.

But she had felt better than she had ever felt in her life.

Meredith had never experienced that fugue state again. She had wanted to, been eager for it a few times when she was lost in confusion or desperation. At one point she wondered if people who did drugs found that state, but she was too afraid to experiment with chemical mind-altering, too knowledgeable about the effects and consequences to try.

All at once on this bright, clear morning on the pistol range she touched on it again, albeit briefly, almost tangentially, but it was long enough so that many pieces of the puzzle of the last few days and her life fell into place. Not all of them, but it was enough to give her a feeling of great satisfaction.

Her shooting itself was as lousy as ever. But she didn't care.

Meredith would have continued shooting, but it was getting time to get back to the MP station. She had reports to write, a painful letter to compose, and she wasn't going to put any of it off. She unloaded her pistol, saw that it was past due for a cleaning; gunpowder residue was starting to cake in the chamber. She should have cleaned it yesterday or last night and chided herself for violating the first rule of a soldier. Maintain your weapon as if your life depends on it— it does.

Taking a walk out to the range, she collected the targets, gazing at them ruefully. Holes all over the place except in the black circle that scored.

Stevie Wonder shoots better, she thought to herself, then went back to the firing line to police up her brass. She was bent over collecting the empty shell casings and dumping them into her gun bag, still musing about her moment of revelation, when she heard the noise.

She straightened up to look.

It was a car coming down the road, revving rather fast, faster than necessary. The range NCO early? The head-on outline of the car looked familiar.

A Mustang.

The car jumped the ditch between the road and the range. It was coming down the firing line.

Aimed directly at Meredith.

And it wasn't slowing down. The engine, a straining whine, sounded angry and malevolent.

Meredith ran.

The roar of the motor got louder and louder. She glanced back. She recognized the car now, a silver Saleen Mustang.

It was Vernor, his face grim behind the windshield, expression intent on his target—Meredith. The car was gaining.

Meredith ran harder, faster.

She realized she had her gun bag in one hand, had picked it up instinctively, she guessed. She would have discarded it now, but wanted nothing to slow or interrupt the mad pumping of her arms.

The Urban Tactics Range was ahead of her—the maze of concrete walls, doorways, windows, and alleyways created to help soldiers practice house-to-house searches. Cold, ugly cement block pocked and scarred by bullet holes—it suddenly looked like a safe haven.

Meredith sprinted toward it.

The car was closer, louder—she thought she could feel the warmth of its engine on the backs of her legs.

There was a wall ahead with a window, just a square hole four feet off the ground. Meredith ran for it.

But she was trying to outrun a car, a Saleen Mustang, zero to sixty in four point nine seconds, a quarter mile in thirteen point four seconds.

She was going to lose.

There were a few loud crunches behind her as the Mustang bottomed out on the berms.

Meredith wanted to look back, but she was afraid that would slow her down, afraid the car was too close, just plain afraid.

The wall was mere meters away. The window was too small.

She thought she jumped too early, was going to fall at the base of the wall, become crushed between the car and the concrete. But she sailed through the window with room to spare.

She banged her elbow painfully on something, but she was suddenly on the other side of the wall. She heard the car skid behind her as Vernor slammed on the brakes.

The wall exploded. The car hit it and the wall burst on Meredith's side, with cement blocks and mortar flying.

She heard the car door opening over the noise of the engine cooling, the shattered radiator hissing out fluids. She rose to her feet.

BAM!

A bullet chipped the wall near her head. She ran.

BAM!

A bullet chased her. She heard it slice the air past her head.

Ducking behind another wall, she opened her gun bag, yanked out her nine-millimeter, pocketed the remaining loaded magazines, jammed one into the handle, yanked back the slide.

Locked and loaded!

She looked around the corner to fire.

Vernor was coming through the window after her.

BAM! BAM! BAM!

Her shots went wild, digging into the wall three to five feet away from him. But they distracted Vernor long enough for Meredith to run.

Vernor fired back. He was good. The bullets ripped the concrete only inches from her head. A chip of concrete shrapnel flew and slashed her cheek, but she hardly felt it.

Meredith ducked behind a wall and fired again, not seeing if the bullets hit. Vernor told her how well she did.

"Damn, Colonel, you can't shoot for shit," he hollered, taunting her.

"You think killing me will save your butt?" she hollered back.

"No. But it might slow things down long enough so I can get my money and get out of the country."

She popped out and fired. He shot back. The bullets were close; one creased the sleeve of her BDU.

"You know I fired Expert with the nine-mil, Colonel?" Vernor called.

"Soldier of the Month, I bet."

"And of the year."

"What went wrong?"

"Who said anything went wrong?"

Meredith wasn't going to lecture the man about good conduct right now. She was just vamping as she reconnoitered the area trying to find a way out. But this was one vast concrete maze. And she wasn't familiar with the layout. The Soldier of the Year might be very familiar with the place.

"Why did Lieutenant Carnes have to die?" she asked.

"She saw me at the pawnshop, unloading," he answered. "It wasn't my decision. I want you to know that."

"Cas MacAtee made that decision?"

She turned, fired, and ran. Vernor fired back. The bullets were still close; she swore she saw a ricochet fly past her face.

The slide of Meredith's pistol was in the open position. She was empty. Reaching into her pocket, she grabbed a magazine and reloaded.

She had one clip left. She thought she had pocketed more, but obviously she had lost some in the chase.

"Why reload, Colonel?" Vernor called, hearing the metallic slam of the slide. "Give it up."

She turned to fire.

Vernor ducked behind a narrow wall just a little wider than his body, enough to conceal him from her.

Meredith looked around—she was in more trouble. The maze reached a dead end here. She was boxed in—only one direction out, and Vernor was waiting there.

"You know, Colonel, you never had a chance." Vernor spoke almost conversationally. Maybe he knew she had no way out. "You don't have one now, and you haven't had one since the day you set foot on post."

Meredith was starting to get angry. She tried to focus it. She was in a gun battle where she was totally outmatched. Well, maybe not . . .

Meredith turned and emptied a magazine at the wall, chanting to herself mentally. *Take a breath, let half of it out, squeeze the trigger, don't jerk.*

Then she ducked behind her cover. Vernor fired back.

She could hear the click and clatter of Vernor reloading as she chanced a look at the results of her shooting. Fifteen rounds, some of them scattered, but there was a fist-sized hole halfway through the cement block wall about chest high. Nice shot group; the range NCO would be proud of her.

Vernor fired. Meredith ducked, reloaded.

It was her last clip. She readied herself.

"Lieutenant Vernor!" she shouted. "You are under arrest for the theft of government property and for murder!"

"Murder?" Vernor laughed. "Not yet."

And Meredith turned to fire. Focused. Proper stance. Trigger control.

And she emptied her last clip at the hole in the block wall.

Cement flew and turned to dust.

Then silence. Her weapon was empty.

Vernor stepped out from behind the wall. He raised his weapon. Meredith looked at the hole she had created. She could see daylight through it.

Vernor aimed his pistol at Meredith. His teeth were clenched.

Meredith faced him directly, an easy target.

Vernor fell to the ground, onto his face. There was a huge, bloody hole in his back. A hole about the same size as the one in the block wall.

Meredith walked over to Vernor and kicked the pistol out of his hand. She needn't have bothered.

He was dead.

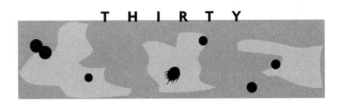

T H I R T Y

The medic was driving Meredith crazy, wanting to cut off the sleeve of her fatigue shirt to get to the graze on her arm, then putting a huge bandage on her cheek, one that Meredith ripped off and had him replace with a regular-size Band-Aid.

She figured the young medic had never treated a real combat casualty, someone who had just killed another soldier. The poor kid kept glancing over at Vernor's body, which was being examined, photographed, and searched by Tate and his forensics crew.

Earl Ryder arrived and launched immediately into an attack on Underhill that Meredith couldn't help overhearing.

"You let her go out alone?" he demanded. "After last night? What the hell's going on here?!"

"Aren't you a little out of your jurisdiction, Sheriff Ryder?" Un-

derhill responded calmly. That question took some of the steam out
of Ryder. Underhill continued. "The Colonel is the Provost Marshal—we take orders from her, not the other way around. I tried to
protect her, but she overruled me."

That was all too true. Meredith had left her hotel room this
morning to find a pair of MPs, one outside her room on a folding
chair, another in an unmarked vehicle in the parking lot. She had ordered them back to Fort Hazelton and had given them a message for
them to relay to Underhill: "Thank you, but there are more important uses for the limited number of personnel we have available."

Ryder accepted the probable truth of Underhill's words and
walked over to Meredith, dropping his game face for a touch of
his charm.

"We have to stop meeting this way, Mere," Ryder joked. "I have
a present for you from Leslie, and Shelly, who seems to be quite the
computer whiz herself." He handed Meredith a slip of paper.

"The General of the Guardians of Babylon," he announced.

She read the paper. Ryder watched the medics bag and cart Vernor's body away.

"Hell of a way to qualify with the nine-mil," he said.

"And I don't think Colonel . . . General Levy is going to be
pleased about this," Underhill added. His tie today looked like the
mess you saw when you stepped on a particularly ugly bug.

Meredith knew that a death brought out a strange sort of black
humor; she had even fallen into the banter herself a few times in the
past. Today she didn't. *She* had killed a man.

"How did he know I was going to be here?" she asked of no one
in particular.

Underhill answered. "There's a police band in his car. He probably heard the MPs call Dispatch this morning to tell me that you
were going to the range."

Meredith nodded. The late Lieutenant Vernor had been a thorough man.

"Any luck with MacAtee?" Meredith asked Ryder.

The DA and the Judge Advocate had been negotiating with MacAtee's lawyers—the pawnshop owner had two lawyers on retainer.

"Not a peep. He's either being paid big-time not to talk or he's scared, or both."

Meredith sighed. She wanted some hard answers.

"Mr. Tate!" She called. When Tate finished and joined them, she addressed them all. "What say, gentlemen, we go arrest us a General?"

Grover Eberton was 280-plus pounds in white pants, white shirt, and a white paper hat. Black may be slimming, but it would have made no difference on the five-five frame of this man. He had a little face in a big head, black eyes that were too close together, a petulant little mouth. Like two tiny raisins and half of a cherry in the middle of a big white cookie. A cookie with three chins.

Above the almost voluptuous lips was a narrow black streak of a mustache that, along with his temperament, had earned him the sobriquet "Little Hitler." Nobody on the kitchen staff knew how appropriate the nickname was.

Grover Eberton was the assistant head cook at the main post Mess Hall. Fifty-two years old, civilian, long divorced, and the main contact of the Guardians of Babylon through Piedmont's Web site.

When the first MP entered the kitchen, Eberton was in the process of chewing out poor Charlie Sillet, the dishwasher, for hanging the colander where the chinois was usually hung. The fact that

Eberton had mishung the colander himself didn't seem to make a difference to the fat tyrant.

But seeing Corporal Daniels with his MP armband, helmet, and pistol belt step through the doorway stopped Eberton's harangue short. He shoved the colander into the dishwasher's hands and edged toward the loading dock door. Another MP, Sergeant Jerome, appeared on the loading dock accompanied by a tall black man in a white shirt and rather handsome tie. Their eyes met, and Eberton became truly frightened.

The fat man broke out in an instantaneous sweat and, as casually as he could manage, ambled toward the dining room. There a formidable-looking woman stood, an MP at one side, a young man in an ill-fitting suit and wispy mustache at her other arm. The Band-Aid on her face and the disheveled state of her BDUs did nothing to lessen her inherent power.

Eberton backed up, looked behind him. The MPs and the tall black man were walking toward him.

"Don't let them kill me!" he screamed to everyone and no one in a rather feminine voice that was too small for such a big man. "Don't let them hurt me! Who has a video camera?! Someone record this!"

Eberton didn't run. He probably couldn't without asking for a heart attack, and he succumbed meekly to the MP who handcuffed him.

THIRTY-ONE

Over the radio Meredith had ordered Grover Eberton's employment file and his military record faxed to her office while they were on their way to the Mess Hall to pick him up.

The so-called General sat in the interrogation room at the MP station and sweated and fidgeted. Meredith, Underhill, and Tate sat on the opposite side of the table and read through his files. Eberton's eyes were focused on the tape recorder in front of him as if the lazily rolling tape had hypnotized him. He had not asked for a lawyer.

Eberton had spent six years in the Army during the late sixties and early seventies, but never served overseas. How he had avoided going to Vietnam or Germany—through blind luck or clever planning—Meredith didn't know. After that he had been discharged for repeatedly failing the physical and receiving low performance ratings. He had then taken a civilian position with the military, first in the Quartermaster Service and then as a culinary worker.

"So you're a General?" Meredith began. "Self-appointed, I assume. Because your military record shows you attained no higher rank than Staff Sergeant before you were discharged."

"I don't know what I'm doing here," Eberton protested. "I have broken no laws."

"We have stolen weapons that we found buried in Mr. Piedmont's yard. We have this material being disseminated by your people." She slid one of the handbills across the table toward him. "Do you know what a hate crime is, Mr. Eberton? We have direct linkage between you and Mr. Piedmont. And as we speak, a search warrant for your residence has been issued and we are about to act on it. What do you think we will find, sir?"

"Nothing your agents haven't found in previous clandestine searches. I know—I have ways of knowing. And those weapons were planted at Piedmont's by the CIA," Eberton replied haughtily. "Which is just another arm of the Jewish conspiracy." He pushed the handbill away with the tip of a pudgy finger.

"Do you realize, sir, that just distributing this on a military reservation is a violation of federal law?" She held it up and showed it to him again.

"I recognize no laws except the Bill of Rights."

"Well, whether you recognize them or not," Meredith continued, "you violate them . . . you go to Leavenworth."

"I'm not saying another word." His lips pursed in a pout.

"You don't have to." Meredith stood and leaned across the table toward him.

"I know your kind, Eberton, know them too well. You're a loser, and you can't face the fact that your whole life is a big failure. So you blame it on someone else. Your life is crap, but it surely can't be your fault. It must be some kind of conspiracy by the government, the Jews, the blacks, women . . . You're the scared fat boy on the playground who everyone picks on. You hate your job, you hate your life. So you make yourself a General and gather a bunch of other losers around you and you all play soldier—sneaking around in the dark putting up this *filth*!"

She slapped the handbill onto the table so hard that Eberton jumped in his seat.

"You'll like Leavenworth, Mr. Eberton," she continued. "You get to wear a uniform there, too."

"You can't send me there," he whined. "I'm not a well man. I have an irregular heartbeat. I have breathing problems. You can't do that to me."

From that point on there was a steady recitation of the names of every member of his organization, everyone who had ever expressed an interest in joining, everyone who had ever laughed at one of his racist jokes.

Meredith left the rest of the interrogation to Tate. She was sick of Grover Eberton.

Meredith went upstairs to type her report on Lieutenant Vernor's apparent crimes—and the circumstances of his death. She kept it short and added an addendum concerning the apprehension of Eberton. Printing out a copy, she slipped out of the MP station and walked across the post toward the headquarters building. It was very quiet and peaceful as she walked, no one else around. It was as if Fort Hazelton was finally abandoned, deserted.

They were all at the parade field.

A ceremony is one of the things the military does best. The parade field was a sight to behold, and Meredith walked closer and paused to watch. Soldiers in neat formation, polished boots, dress uniforms, the brass instruments played by the band catching the sun and bouncing it back tenfold, the civilian spectators adding splashes of color. There was a slight breeze to ruffle the flags, the Stars and Stripes, the various unit colors.

And in the center, the focus of everyone, the reason for them all being there.

Colonel J. Peter Levy.

General Schwaner and Mrs. Levy pinned the stars to Levy's uniform, then stepped back. His daughters handed him the leather General's belt, and he snapped it around his waist with the ornate brass buckle.

Everyone but Levy resumed their seats, and the band played "Ruffles and Flourishes" while the new General looked around the parade field. He was proud, full of the pageantry himself, the achievement of his lifelong ambition sparkling on his collar points.

Then his eyes met Meredith's.

Their eyes locked for a moment.

He didn't flinch.

She did.

Then he pulled his attention back to the ceremony.

Meredith felt bad, guilty somehow for having even suspected Levy could be responsible for the deaths of the two women. It clearly proved that she hadn't disposed of her history with him as easily as she had thought. So what if Levy was an autocrat? So were a good many of her superiors, and she didn't attribute anything more sinister to them than being just more obstacles to her career and profession. But Levy, because of his personal transgression against her when she was a very vulnerable lieutenant, had become the focus of her suspicion, her anger.

That was unjust. And that was what offended Meredith the most about her behavior. She believed in justice and she had become unjust.

Meredith walked on to headquarters, wondering if an apology to Levy was needed. She decided against it—he wasn't aware of her personal suspicions and she had not, thank God, acted on them. Making the new General aware of them would only give the despot, and he was still that, a club with which he could beat her into submission.

Inside the headquarters building it was totally deserted, not a soul in sight, everyone at the ceremony. She walked down the echoing empty halls and laid her report on the secretary's desk outside Levy's office. She looked over at Vernor's desk, reminding herself to have it secured and searched.

Levy's office door was open. Meredith looked inside, curious. Her eyes landed on the glory wall. Staring at the display for a moment, she was struck by the arrogance of the higher ranks. Leaving their offices open like this, vulnerable to theft, thinking no one would dare violate their domain.

Then again—Meredith brought herself back—maybe her antipathy toward Levy was again coloring her perspective. Now she was condemning all senior officers without proof. She walked across the reception area to Ringstall's office. His door was closed. She tried the knob. It opened.

Shaking her head, Meredith glanced inside and took in his glory wall, deciding to write up a memo on building security. She closed the door and headed back down the hall, walking toward the main entrance. Then she stopped and, for the sake of her spontaneous research project and just because she was curious, she walked over to General Schwaner's office. The door was open.

Meredith walked inside, feeling like she was trespassing, and stood in the center of the room and surveyed *this* glory wall. All the various glory walls had a lot in common. The de rigueur combat photograph with the subject in dusty fatigues posed in front of a destroyed enemy tank or bunker, looking macho and tough. Photographs with the various movers and shakers, Powell and Schwarz-kopf among others, ceremonial swords, presentation weapons, enemy rifles, engraved nickel-plated pistols in glass cases.

She stared at the centerpiece of Schwaner's display—a 1911A Colt .45 semiautomatic pistol. A big, ugly, mean gun that was designed not just to kill another soldier, but to knock him down so he wouldn't get up again. The gun wasn't that accurate beyond fifteen feet, but within that range it was as effective as a howitzer. Meredith had to qualify with the .45 when she first entered the service, before the nine-millimeter became the standard. She had "boloed" with it, also. This one had been prettied up with nickel-plating and gold etching, engraved ivory grips, but it was still an unwieldy block of steel, a crude machine that had one function—to kill.

Suddenly Meredith was struck with a thought and she left Schwaner's office, hurried down the hall, and looked into Ringstall's office, then Levy's. She pulled out her mobile phone and dialed.

"Just the basics," Tate repeated to Meredith, looking more terrified by the moment.

Obviously uncomfortable in General Schwaner's office, Meredith had taken him and Underhill out into the empty hall. Their voices seemed unnaturally loud.

"Don't we need some kind of warrants, clearances, or something?" Tate was still uncertain.

"You have my orders," Meredith said firmly.

To the man's credit, he left to organize his forensics team without further word.

Meredith looked at Underhill.

"You do know, Colonel," Underhill began. "That you are not only jeopardizing your own career, but that of everyone in your department."

Meaning his own, or to give him more credit, those of his people, including Tate.

"Yes." That was all Meredith said in return. That was all she could say.

"You're not doing this just because you and Levy have this . . . thing?" Underhill asked.

Meredith again wondered how much he knew about her history with Levy. The Army *was* such a small family.

"I'm trying hard not to," Meredith admitted.

"I don't know if I want you to be right or wrong," Underhill said.

"Me neither," Meredith confessed.

"I'll be with Mr. Tate. This is not a case where we can afford a mistake," Underhill said, and left her alone.

There was a boom. The windows rattled. Then another boom sounded as the eleven-gun salute thundered across the post. Meredith started making phone calls.

Meredith had told her father that she was making the rounds of the employment agencies, trying to get a better job than the one she had at the pizza joint. He was suspicious, probably thinking that she was going off to Ann Arbor to apply for college against his commandment that no daughter of his was going to be no overeducated, bra-burning hippie bitch. They had argued for two years about her educational aspirations and he had won.

Meredith took the bus to Detroit and reported to the Army Induction Center. She spent the day standing in line being prodded and probed, gave urine and blood samples and took psychological and intelligence tests. She passed them all. Then went home. She had given Phyllis's phone number to the recruiter. A week later he called her back. She went down to his cheap office next to the Marine, Navy, and Air Force recruitment stations. Master Sergeant McKormick had shaken her hand just like she was a man and told her she was in the Army.

Meredith went back home and stood in her room, realizing she was leaving all of this, leaving him behind. She had eight days before she reported to Detroit, and from there to Fort Knox for Basic Training. A long, slow eight days. She sold her car, a '62 Chrysler, a big old rusted land yacht she loved. Her father hated Chrysler products, considered the car a betrayal and wouldn't let her park it in the driveway. She didn't have anyone she could leave it with; Phyllis was going to Western University in Kalamazoo come fall and had her own car. So Meredith sold it to a kid at the restaurant. She was surprised at the tears she shed as he drove it away. After all, it was just an old junker.

She packed using the list of allowed clothing and personal effects that the recruiter gave her. All of it fit into one little gym bag. She took the photograph of her mother out of the bulky frame, cut two pieces of cardboard to press it between, and put that into a plastic sandwich bag to protect it.

The seventh day came.

Meredith waited for him to come home from work. She had not started dinner. For the first time since her mother's death, she didn't have to think about what he would eat for supper—or whether he would like what she had prepared. It was a breath of freedom, and she savored it.

When he came home and sat down in front of the TV, she put on her jacket, picked up her bag, and walked into the living room. She stood between him and the TV, turned it off—a major offense—and watched her father's face.

"I've joined the Army," she announced. "You can fix your own supper."

She had rehearsed a long speech full of accusations and rebuke, run through it over and over in her head, edited and rewritten until it was perfect.

But "I've joined the Army. Fix your own supper," once said, seemed to say it all.

It was the first time she had ever seen her father surprised. For a moment she thought he had stopped breathing, his body was so still, his mouth half open, his eyes staring straight ahead. Maybe he had.

Finally his mouth began to work, tiny movements without sound. Meredith decided she had best leave before he did regain the power of speech and she walked toward the front door.

She left the house and walked down the sidewalk, the screen door slamming behind her. Halfway down the block she heard the door open and his footsteps come down the walkway, not too many, just enough steps to take him to the same sidewalk.

"Mere-Jo!" She heard it, but she didn't turn. She couldn't tell if it was a shout of anger or alarm. She replayed it in her head over the years, endowing the cry with whatever emotion satisfied her at the time.

She wasn't Mere-Jo again and wouldn't be for a long time. She was Meredith. Lieutenant, then Captain, Major, and finally Colonel Meredith Cleon. The next time she heard the dreaded, hated "Mere-Jo" was when she came home six years after she enlisted, a Captain, wearing her decorations proudly. He had been in a car accident, totaled his Torino, and broken both hips. Aunt Judi was taking care of him.

Meredith wore her dress greens—with the pants, not the skirt.

She walked into the house. He seemed smaller, but that could have been the wheelchair. He looked her up and down.

"So, Mere-Jo. You got a man's job, you gotta dress like one, too?"

"Don't ever call me that again."

She spent a little over two hours in the living room, making sure he wasn't going to die, as she had been led to believe by Aunt Lorrayna's frantic call. He lapsed and called her Mere-Jo a couple of times during their brusque attempts at conversation. She couldn't tell if it was on purpose or not. She just stared at him, not believing this was where she had come from. She made sure that he was aware that she had gotten her college degree while in the Army, that she was working on her master's in criminology.

None of it seemed to faze him. He just sat in the wheelchair chain-smoking, eyes flitting back and forth between her and the TV. Meredith finally rose from the old chair, *his* chair, which she had taken on purpose. She said goodbye to Aunt Judi, went out and swept the snow from her windshield, and drove away.

She had been prepared to stay for a few days if necessary, but on the drive back to the airport through drifting snow she wondered why she had bothered to come back at all. To demonstrate how well she had done—to a man who had disdain for her ambition?

What did she want from him? An apology? A sign that she had defeated him. Surrender? What?

She found no answer then. And through the years until his death, and now even after it, she struggled with the question of her relationship with her father. The quandary of her life, no matter the degree of success in her career.

Then in that single relevatory moment on the firing range it had all become clear. She had based her life on rebellion; every move and decision she had made had been in reaction to some man. Mostly her father and his idea of what her life should be, but also any other man who had tried to put Meredith in a place she didn't want to be. Over and over she had been confronted with some man who pushed her the wrong way, put her in a category she didn't want to be in. She had bounced from one obstructing macho fool, one denigrating male to the next like a steel ball in a pinball machine, never choosing her own path, just bouncing from man to insulting man. And her father was the plunger that launched her into the game.

There on the firing range in that Zenlike moment she had refused to do that anymore. She was going to act for herself. Do what *she* wanted to do, not to prove anything to her father or anyone else.

Whatever she did, whatever she pursued, it would now be because it was what Meredith wanted.

The reception following Levy's promotion ceremony was a splendid affair, the civilian women and men in full dress, ball gowns, and even a few tuxedos. The Army attendees were in their dress blues, medals and brass gleaming, even a few West Point swords worn for display.

Meredith was totally out of place in her torn, dirty, bloody BDUs, and she tried to be as nondescript as possible by hugging the wall as she made her way around the room. She drew a few stares, but not enough to cause a commotion.

She found her way to General Schwaner, got his attention, and whispered her report in his ear. He betrayed no emotion, giving Meredith no clue as to whether she was in trouble or not, or if she was just digging herself a deeper hole.

Schwaner didn't even exhibit any surprise or disapproval of the state of her uniform or the appropriateness. That really worried her as she made her way toward Levy, who was surrounded by people congratulating him. He was wallowing in their praise. Meredith caught the eye of a private and sent him to Levy with a message. Levy did not take the message well, but he disengaged himself from the group and walked over to her.

The stars on Levy's uniform were very shiny, the ghosts of the spread-winged eagles still embossed into the material underneath. Meredith felt her eyes linger on the stars too long, and she jerked them to Levy's face.

The noise level in the room was such that she had to speak directly into his ear. She was glad of that. After she was done speaking, she didn't hang around for his response. She didn't want to have a confrontation there, on his territory. She wanted him on a battlefield she chose.

She chose his office.

Yes, in one respect that was his home ground. But she had done her reconnaissance, *she* had prepared the field.

Levy entered ready to do battle, at full charge, face pale with rage, that vein prominent in his forehead, his voice barely a whisper.

"You pulled me away from my reception." He didn't ask, but demanded. "You are determined to ruin the best day of my life. This personal vendetta has taken you beyond the bonds of your authority, Cleon."

"If you say so, sir." She wasn't going to rise to the bait, and that seemed to frustrate him. He looked at her torn, dirty BDUs.

"You couldn't even dress for the ceremony," he sneered.

"I didn't have time to change into my class A's, sir. My BDUs and I have been in a firefight."

That took him by surprise.

"A firefight?"

"Your Aide, Lieutenant Vernor, attacked me. Twice, actually. Last night with an M-60, which we found in his car, and earlier this morning with his side arm."

"That's why he wasn't at the ceremony?" Levy was watching her carefully, tense. "He's under arrest?"

"Dead," Meredith replied curtly.

"Dead . . ." Levy seemed to relax. "I don't believe it."

"Yes, you do, sir," Meredith said calmly. "You sent him."

There was a clear moment of silence. Then Levy spoke.

"Do you realize what you just said, Cleon?" Levy took a moment to walk around and sit down behind his desk, laid his hands out flat on the polished top, holding on to it for security.

"Yes, sir." Meredith spoke as confidently as she could. "Most definitely, sir."

"You accused me of a crime." Levy sounded as if he couldn't believe his ears.

"It's worse than that, sir." Meredith didn't take her eyes off him, just stood there with her arms folded.

"You are in deep water here, Cleon. Very deep and dangerous water."

"You killed Lieutenant Carnes and Sergeant Gorman." Her voice was level.

Levy seemed stunned, but recovered quickly.

"I hope you have evidence."

Was there a slight tremor in his voice? Meredith made sure there was none in her own.

"You and Lieutenant Vernor were involved in a conspiracy to steal government property—office equipment and weapons—and fence it through a pawnshop owned by a certain Cas MacAtee. Lieutenant Carnes saw Vernor and MacAtee in the midst of a transaction. She called you, not knowing you were part of the conspiracy, to report what she saw.

"And you killed her. Or rather shot her and set her up in that grotesque manner to die."

Levy just sat behind his desk watching Meredith silently, but she could almost see the wheels turning in his head.

"Then, to distract me and put suspicion on the hate group, you painted graffiti on your own house and called it in as a hate crime."

"Outrageous!" Levy almost spit.

"The paint was water-soluble tempera. The same type of paint your daughters use in school. I checked. What kind of self-respecting hatemonger paints his message in something that can be removed with a water hose? You shouldn't have been so considerate of your own home.

"You also planted, or had Lieutenant Vernor plant, some of the stolen weapons in Piedmont's yard to put suspicion of the matériel theft on his hate group, too. And you kept pressure on me to make the hate group the fall guy.

"Then," she continued, "Sergeant Gorman found a way to invalidate Vernor's alibi for the time of Lieutenant Carnes's murder, or more specifically, *your* alibi. I thought for a while you were covering for your Aide and I couldn't figure out why you were doing it. But Vernor was covering for you. Gorman must have also suspected Vernor, but only Vernor, and she called you to question his alibi.

"You killed her, too."

Levy started shaking his head, whether exhibiting denial or bemusement, Meredith couldn't tell.

"What makes you think Lieutenant Vernor didn't kill them to cover his own part in the theft? He could have been working alone," Levy proposed.

"It was something he said before I . . . killed him," Meredith replied. "He said that he hadn't committed murder . . . yet. And he attacked me with his nine-mil. Carnes and Gorman were shot with a forty-five-caliber—the same forty-five-caliber."

She looked at the presentation .45 mounted on Levy's glory wall.

"That?" Levy followed the direction of her gaze. "You think I used that?"

"A simple ballistics test will tell us," Meredith said.

He looked at her, and she stared back.

Then he smiled.

"Do your damnedest, Cleon." He stood up. "I'll see you at your Court-Martial. You have my permission to do whatever you need to do with that piece. Just don't damage it. I'm not even sure it is a working weapon, but it has certain sentimental value."

"Actually, I don't need your permission." Meredith picked up the phone and dialed. "This is a government reservation, and you work for the government. I have the authority to search as I see fit."

Levy walked over to the glory wall and stood in front of the case that held the gun. Meredith spoke into the phone.

"Mr. Tate, I want you to bring your ballistic kit over to head-quarters and test the forty-five-caliber automatic in Col—General Levy's office."

Levy walked over to his desk. Meredith watched his every move carefully as she listened to the receiver.

"Yes, we have his permission, if that eases your mind a bit. 'Do your damnedest,' I think were the words." Levy opened a drawer. That's where Underhill keeps his gun, Meredith thought. She frowned into the phone. "All right, Ringstall's and all the others, too. C-Y-A."

She hung up.

Levy had frozen with his hand in the drawer. Then he stood up suddenly, something in his hand.

He placed it on his desk.

A nameplate. *General* J. Peter Levy.

Picking up his old nameplate, he dropped it into the same drawer and kneed it shut with a bang. Meredith wondered how long the nameplate had been in the drawer. Levy's expression was grim as he looked at her.

"While you make a ruin of your career, I'm going back to my reception." Levy headed toward the door, but paused and turned.

"And tomorrow, Cleon, if I were you I would write up your resignation. Take the easy way out." And he left.

Meredith listened as his footsteps echoed down the hall. She heard a door open and close.

She waited there for a moment.

Had she failed? She had gambled everything on her incredible supposition. She called it logic, but it was only supposition—theory with a fact or two as the foundation, but still theory. Meredith walked out of Levy's office and down the hall, past Ringstall's office, down to the exit, but then past it to General Schwaner's office.

And she opened the door.

Levy was behind Schwaner's desk, taking the General's pearl-handled presentation .45 out of the case he had removed from the wall.

He looked up at Meredith, so much like a child caught with his hand caught in the cookie jar that she started to laugh.

Levy pointed the pistol at her.

Her laugh faded quickly.

"So you used the General's pistol," Meredith said. "He won't be happy."

Levy thumbed back the hammer.

"He won't be the only one."

"Tell me this, sir. Why?"

"Because I don't like you, Cleon. Never have." Levy was actually smiling.

"No, sir. The theft." Meredith clarified. "Why jeopardize your career, your star? Did you need the money?"

"It was my . . . retirement," he said simply. "I thought I had been passed over for General. Some bad scuttlebutt from my so-called friends at the Pentagon. I was . . . angry. I've spent my whole life serving my country. All I ever wanted, all I ever worked for was my star, a command of my own. And I thought they had taken it away from me. I've fought . . . and bled . . . and sacrificed . . . and . . . So I made up my own retirement plan. The government wasn't doing anything with that . . . matériel. Just boxing it up and storing it away until it rusted and was useless to anyone."

"Excuses," Meredith said. "Flimsy, petty, pitiful excuses. How did you feel about your 'retirement' when your star came in? Ashamed, I hope. Or is that too much to ask?"

"It would have been fine if you hadn't showed up," he said with malice in his voice.

"You killed two people." Meredith matched the malice with scorn.

"People die. Soldiers die." Levy shrugged. "It's in the job description."

"Sorry, but that doesn't cover this particular situation, sir." Meredith looked at him, at the gun he had pointed at her chest. "You betrayed your country, your oath, the Army, and most important, the people under your command. You *serve* them, not the other way around. Your job is to protect them, keep them out of harm's way. You did the opposite. You killed your own people.

"And as for Carnes . . . That was . . . cruel. Sadistic."

"She reminded me of you. Besides, I offered to . . . share with her. I offered her a unique opportunity and she . . . she . . . laughed at me. No one laughs at me. She had to suffer. I'd like you to suffer, too, but we have no time."

Levy raised the gun and pointed it at her head.

Meredith stared him in the eye, refusing to look at the gun. That damned smile of his, that self-satisfied, superior grin.

"This is quite a day for me. I get my star . . . and you, Cleon."

He pulled the trigger.

Click.

A simple click.

The anticlimactic sound stunned Levy more than the boom of the muzzle blast would have.

"We removed the firing pin, sir," she told him, "when we conducted the ballistics test an hour ago. We found your fingerprints on the clip, by the way. And confirmed that this is the same weapon that was used on Carnes and Gorman."

She keyed her walkie-talkie.

"We also dug some dirt from the tires on your wife's van. It is remarkably similar to the soil at the range where Lieutenant Carnes died. We've sent it and fibers from the van carpet for forensics testing. We have great hopes for a match, sir."

"If you had all of this, then why didn't you arrest me?" He looked stunned, suddenly a weak little man.

"That was for my benefit." General Schwaner stepped out of his private bathroom and into the office. "I told her I needed more. Now it looks like I'll have to testify at your Court-Martial, Pete."

"You're under arrest, sir." Meredith took the gun from Levy's slack hands. The man was looking at the floor, thoroughly defeated. The office door opened, and Tate entered with Underhill and two MPs.

"Take him away," Schwaner said with disgust.

THIRTY-TWO

Meredith met Charlotte Ryder the next morning at 1347 Jackson Avenue. It was a splendid old Victorian with hardwood floors, in need only of paint and a little TLC. Charlotte took Meredith from room to room, honestly pointing out the strong and weak points as they went. She needn't have bothered. For Meredith the house was love at first sight. Charlotte was indeed a matchmaker.

Shelly Daisen, cleaned up quite a bit with dark red nail polish instead of black, a windbreaker in place of the leather, tagged behind Charlotte.

"The owners are going through a messy divorce, so I can get it for you as a lease with an option to buy," Charlotte told Meredith.

"Hardwood floors, built-ins, sprinkler system, low-flow toilets," Shelly added, reading off the spec sheet.

"What's this?" Meredith asked the girl. "Are you into real estate, Shelly?"

"Detective work is too dangerous," Shelly replied.

"Tell me about it." Meredith laughed and turned to Charlotte. "I'll take it. As a lease with the option."

The three of them went outside to where Ryder was waiting for Shelly.

"C'mon, Shelly," he called. "Your father's waiting."

Shelly ran to the car. They got in as Meredith walked over to the driver's side.

"Did Char do great?" he asked her with boyish enthusiasm. "Doesn't she do great?"

"You both do great things, Earl."

He drove away with Shelly in the shotgun seat.

Meredith pulled into the MP station lot and parked in the Provost Marshal space. She sat there looking at the sign and the station for a moment.

She finally climbed out of the Shelby, grabbing the stack of real-estate documents Charlotte had given her.

"Colonel!"

She turned. It was General Schwaner in jogging sweats. She saluted, and he returned it.

"I wanted to tell you . . . ," he began, searching for the words. That was unlike him. "There would be some who would think that censuring a high-ranking officer would result in some kind of repercussion."

Meredith had been wondering how Schwaner was going to respond to the arrest of his Garrison Commander. Levy's actions were going to leave a black mark on everyone he had touched. And she had seen before that the arresting officer could often become more smudged than anyone else.

"I do my job, sir," Meredith said. "The rest is out of my hands."

"But it's not out of mine," he returned. "And . . . well, your career is in no jeopardy. Just the opposite, in fact."

"Thank you, sir."

"I just wanted you to know."

And he jogged away. Meredith felt bad for him. He was in a difficult position. The Levy scandal might have a negative impact on his own career. She hoped not. He was one of the finest leaders under whom she had ever served. She had no idea what, but maybe there was something she could do to help him.

Meredith entered the MP station preoccupied with those thoughts, so she didn't notice that the first floor seemed to be abandoned. Climbing the stairs to her floor, she didn't see anyone there either.

That was because everyone—the entire MP, Fire, and Game Warden forces—was assembled upstairs in the squad room. It was packed with people—her people.

As Meredith entered, Sergeant Kahla yelled out, "TEN-HUT!" And everyone, including Underhill and Tate, snapped to attention.

"HOO-YAH!" they all cried out at once.

Meredith returned their salute, fighting back the tears.

"Carry on," she said.

She was home.